Praise for

THE MINUSCULE
MYRA MALONE

"Audrey Burges has written a surefire hit—lively, stylish, and full of heart. *The Minuscule Mansion of Myra Malone* is decorated with gorgeous wordsmithery and magical trimmings, and I loved every minute spent inside."
—Sarah Addison Allen, *New York Times* bestselling author of
Other Birds

"*The Minuscule Mansion of Myra Malone* is that rare novel: a generous, big-hearted reprieve from our ever-more-troubling reality; a modern fairy tale about how we carry the burdens that choose us, and the magic of finding shelter—and love—when both seem meant for other people. Audrey Burges is a storyteller of warmth, wit, and stunning originality."
—Katie Gutierrez, bestselling author of *More Than You'll Ever Know*

"*The Minuscule Mansion of Myra Malone* is a refreshing and unique entry into the genre of mystical realism. Quirky and scarred yet very authentic characters populate this richly told tale of friendship, family, and timeless love. Perfect for fans of Sarah Addison Allen and for all book lovers searching for a fantastic read." —*New York Times* bestselling author Karen White

"There's nothing small about the worlds Burges makes.... Readers of *The Lost Apothecary* will devour *The Minuscule Mansion of Myra Malone*. Love, loss, and loneliness: this book explores it all, with Burges's characteristic humor and care. This book is a winner."
—Rachel Mans McKenny, award-winning author of *The Butterfly Effect*

"*The Minuscule Mansion of Myra Malone* is a poignant, beautiful debut filled with magic, fate, and redemption. This story captured my imagination and I just had to keep reading to see how it would end. I enjoyed every page."

 —Rachel Linden, bestselling author of *The Magic of Lemon Drop Pie*

"This well-written novel with heartwarming characters is perfect for fans of magical realism by the likes of Sarah Addison Allen and Isabel Allende." —*Library Journal*

"Fans of romances with a magical bent will adore this story of a blogger with a mysterious dollhouse that has rooms that appear and disappear overnight—and its connection with a handsome stranger." —*Real Simple*

"This creative, engaging debut weaves together an unusual family legacy, a romance between two lonely souls, and a touch of magic in the form of a tiny mansion that seems to know what's best for everyone." —*Booklist*

"Burges creates a magical, unique world, and her characters are incredibly lovable. . . . Perfect for readers who long to escape into a world of magic and romance." —*Kirkus Reviews*

"*The Minuscule Mansion of Myra Malone* charmingly combines threads of magic, whimsy, romance, grief, and loss in a debut novel of great feeling. . . . This captivating novel of miniature furniture and big themes braids strong friendships, romance, family ties, and the importance of stepping outside of one's comfort zone." —*Shelf Awareness*

BERKLEY TITLES BY AUDREY BURGES

The Minuscule Mansion of Myra Malone
A House Like an Accordion

A
HOUSE
Like an
ACCORDION

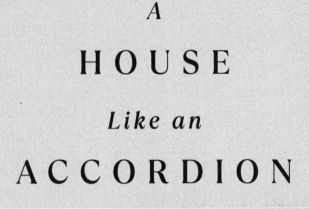

AUDREY BURGES

ACE
NEW YORK

ACE
Published by Berkley
An imprint of Penguin Random House LLC
penguinrandomhouse.com

Copyright © 2024 by Audrey Burges
Readers Guide copyright © 2024 by Audrey Burges
Penguin Random House supports copyright. Copyright fuels creativity, encourages
diverse voices, promotes free speech, and creates a vibrant culture. Thank you for buying
an authorized edition of this book and for complying with copyright laws by not
reproducing, scanning, or distributing any part of it in any form without permission.
You are supporting writers and allowing Penguin Random House to continue
to publish books for every reader.

ACE is a registered trademark and the ACE colophon is a trademark of
Penguin Random House LLC.

Library of Congress Cataloging-in-Publication Data

Names: Burges, Audrey, author.
Title: A house like an accordion / Audrey Burges.
Description: First edition. | New York: Ace, 2024.
Identifiers: LCCN 2023036904 (print) | LCCN 2023036905 (ebook) |
ISBN 9780593546499 (trade paperback) | ISBN 9780593546505 (ebook)
Subjects: LCGFT: Magic realist fiction. | Novels.
Classification: LCC PS3602.U74198 H68 2024 (print) |
LCC PS3602.U74198 (ebook) | DDC 813/.6—dc23/eng/20230825
LC record available at https://lccn.loc.gov/2023036904
LC ebook record available at https://lccn.loc.gov/2023036905

First Edition: May 2024

Printed in the United States of America
1st Printing

Title page art: Disappearing house © Sasun Bughdaryan / Shutterstock
Book design by Alison Cnockaert

For Andy, Payson, and Jamie

A
HOUSE
Like an
ACCORDION

1

The House on the Waves
AUGUST 2016

I WAS BRUSHING my teeth when my hand disappeared.

I was thirty-nine and naked, holding myself in a one-legged star pose on the marble floor of my bathroom, looking for balance. My focal point was in the mirror—my pink toothbrush, which was, I suddenly realized, suspended in midair, as if dangling from a length of wire hung from the bathroom's vaulted ceiling. I could feel it buzzing in the hand I couldn't see.

I thought it must be a trick of the light. Our house was full of windows, glass and sun bouncing reflections of the ocean into every living space, as cold as the Pacific sprawled beneath us. But no: I put down the toothbrush, held my hand in front of me, and gazed right through it to my face in the mirror, with its high cheekbones and widow's peak like my mother's. I grasped at my translucent fingers with my right hand and felt them, still solid, but nearly invisible. There was a softness to the skin I couldn't see, as if I could pierce it with the slightest pressure.

I heard the house begin to wake around me. Ellory was rolling her mat out on her floor, ready to force herself through the yoga workout she'd declared last spring she would do every single day because her routines—senior-year AP classes, driving too fast down our winding road along the beach, sniping at her younger sister—were "stressing her out." A summer's worth of classes at the community college nearby hadn't ended her determination. Mindy, fifteen and complaining already about the pace of high school, not yet a week underway, was hitting her snooze alarm for the third time. And Max was bumping into the same corner of the platform bed with the same bruised shin on his staggering path to the kitchen, where the coffee I'd made was waiting.

Max would leave me alone in the bathroom until I was finished, but our mornings had the expected ebb and flow of the mundane, and my disappearing limb was a disruption. I planted myself on the floor, a stump in the current, and flexed my fingers. I couldn't wear my rings at night. The encircling metal felt too constricting and claustrophobic as I tried and failed to sleep. They glinted on the ring keeper on the bathroom counter, and I tiptoed over to retrieve them, closing my eyes to slide them over the knuckle of my left ring finger. The stones— antique emeralds, handed down through Max's family—were sharp and caught on everything. This time, they caught a beam of sun from the skylight, casting greenish rainbows around the room and on the memory of my freckled hand. I willed it to reappear.

I jumped at the knock on the door. "Keryth?" Max's voice was tentative, still wounded from our fight the night before. "You in there?"

"Where else would I be?" I snapped. I evened out my breathing and started again. "I'll be out in a minute."

"Can I get you anything? You want some coffee?"

A peace offering. *I don't want coffee, I want you to leave me alone. All of you, for maybe five minutes, just leave me alone.* I was being unfair, and I knew I was being unfair, which only made the voice inside me more vicious. The fight had been over the doctor—Max's words, glancing lightly like a stone thrown across water, wondering if it might be worth getting some blood work done. Because surely there must be some explanation for these mood swings, some levels and numbers and precise indicia that could be calibrated, the way Max calibrated everything.

I looked at the vein on my forearm, snaking from the crook of my elbow and fading into nothingness. I thought of the unfriendly nurse who always complained about my treacherous blood, the way it hid from her needle, refusing to yield itself up for tests. *Your veins are practically invisible!*

The laugh that barked out of me was involuntary.

"I'll get myself some coffee in a minute." I took the rings off my finger and slipped them back over the porcelain hand on the counter, which was cold and unyielding, but tangible. My robe, oversized and ratty, terry cloth stained with the spit-up of babies long since grown up, was hanging from the hook on the door. I put it on and tied it, sliding my hands—present and missing—into the wide pockets, hoping I looked normal as I loped, slouch shouldered, to my closet. Beneath the shelves of purses I didn't carry and shoes I didn't wear, I had a dovetailed drawer filled with gloves the California weather never called for. Kid leather, mostly, in every color, with tiny covered buttons down the sides. Elegant, finger-lengthening gloves like I used to see in ads for expensive cars and perfume, back when such things seemed wildly out of reach.

I selected a Kelly-green pair and shoved my hand and my non-hand into them, breathing a sigh of relief at symmetry restored. I let my robe fall to the floor and dressed the rest of my body, which was still corporeal, for all that Max said I would fade away if I didn't eat. My long-sleeved shirts were mostly flannel, and August blazed over my head, but I was starved for other options. I put a white tank top underneath a green plaid shirt I left unbuttoned, flapping over jeans I needed to replace with a smaller pair, but hadn't yet. Finally garbed but feeling garbled, I strode out of the closet and bedroom and walked, as casually as I could, into the kitchen.

"Are you cold, Mom?" Mindy, long legs folded underneath her on the window seat next to the kitchen table, cocked her head to one side. "The AC is on too high, Dad."

"It's set to seventy-eight." Max turned from the coffeepot and furrowed his brow at my outfit. "Harold," he called to the ceiling, "run a diagnostic on the HVAC, okay?"

"Well, sure, happy to. But I gotta say, kiddo, look who's worried about the thermostat now." The voice that rang out overhead was reedy and puckish, exactly as my father-in-law would have been, if he were alive. Or so I guessed. I'd never met him—only the artificial version of him that Max had spent his life perfecting.

"Yes, Harold, thanks." Max barely looked up from his coffee.

"Have you thought about putting on a sweater?"

"That's enough, Harold," Max and I said in unison.

Ellory ran into the room in her customary rush, heading toward the coffeepot to retrieve the only substance I could convince her to put into her body before leaving for school each morning. "Mom? Are you feeling okay? Why are you wearing gloves?"

I shrugged and delivered the lie I'd already thought of. "I sliced my hands up pretty good gardening yesterday. These'll help the ointment work."

Max shook his head. "It was the blackberries, wasn't it?"

"No." I felt a rush of defensiveness creep into my voice. Max hated the blackberry canes I'd planted in our yard—he considered them weeds and disliked their thorny encroachment on his otherwise manicured garden, not that he manicured it himself. "It was the roses."

Max nodded. "The ones with thorns smell the best, but it's hard not to like the thornless ones better."

"I was just pruning them back and giving them some fish guts, ungrateful bastards."

"Nature, red in tooth and claw." Max stepped toward me and stopped, his eyes seeking permission, and I nodded. He kissed the top of my head. "What have you got going on today?"

Trying to figure out where the hell my hand went. "Some research, maybe."

"What kind?"

Hand restoration. Hand-disappeared-what-do-I-do. Marty McFly Syndrome, you know, when his parents never got together and he started to disappear—

Oh my God.

Two thoughts of equal volume, equal urgency, careened through my head at the same time.

One: my father must be alive. The thought filled me with a peculiar mix of relief and fury, remembering the look on his face as he stepped out of my life and into oblivion as I screamed on the banks of a long-abandoned pond. *How many years?* I pretended not to know. Nearly a quarter century now, and as vivid as the first moment.

Two: wherever he was, however he was drawing breath, Papa must also have been drawing *me*. Somewhere, somehow, he was sketching the bones and tendons of my hand as he remembered it. Just the left hand—the one I used to brace the page I drew upon as Papa peered over my head, staring down at my drawings.

He was drawing from life. The way he always taught me not to. And if he didn't stop, I would be as trapped as the Steller's jay I still carried with me in the sketchbook I always kept by my side.

2

The Thorn House
AUGUST 1985

THE FIRST TIME Papa got me a sketchbook of my own, I carried it around for days, its pages blank, its cover as pristine as I could manage to keep it. It wasn't pink or sparkly. Its black matte cover showed me it was real—a real sketchbook, for a real artist. It meant Papa believed in me, and shining under the light of his faith, any lines I sketched could only possibly be a disappointment. I clutched my blank sketchbook while I flipped through Papa's, filled with cupolas and arched windows and low adobe structures, incomplete fragments of stone and wood occasionally interspersed with whole buildings. Some were recognizable, and some we had yet to find. All of them came from the real world, and anything Papa drew from reality bore real consequences. But I didn't understand that then.

I was afraid to draw in my own book, but the images inside Papa's looked stark and lonely, and I longed to give them company. He found me crouched over a page with a red pen, my imagined cardinal already half-sketched atop the graphite needles of a spruce tree he'd drawn, and he bellowed at me with a thundering voice I'd never heard him use before. I dropped the red pen as if it were made of lava. I've never used a red pen since.

He knew I was frightened, and he dropped to his knees beside me, gathering me into his arms. "Keryth. I'm so sorry I scared you. But you didn't know what you were doing."

I sniffed—louder than I meant to—and ordered my tears to stay where they were, burning behind my lashes. "I know I don't know what I'm doing. I can't draw. Not like you. I'm sorry I ruined your picture, Papa."

"Is that what you think?" He smoothed my mousy-brown curls back from my face and looked into my eyes. "Keryth, is that why you haven't used your book?"

"I'm going to ruin it. I'll only draw something stupid."

"You're not going to ruin it. And nothing is stupid when you're creating something new. That's how we learn. I got the book for you because you said you wanted to draw together. I was going to show you some things."

"But I drew in your book, and now you're angry."

"I'm not angry." Papa sat cross-legged on the floor and pulled me into his lap. "It's just that the lines in that book have a price, or at least they do when I draw them. I don't know yet if it'll be the same for you. That's why I wanted to try it together first."

I looked at my scribbled cardinal, interrupted mid-beak. "Your tree was empty. Everything in your book is empty."

"As empty as I can make it, yes. And I still mess up sometimes. Have you ever seen a cardinal in person?"

I shook my head. "Only in Gran's Audubon book."

"Good. That's good."

"Why is that good?"

Papa stood up and reached for my hands, pulling me to my feet. "Follow me, and I'll show you."

We walked through the creaking screen door of our small cabin, and the hiss of the hinge slammed it shut behind us. I followed Papa to the blackberry bushes that ringed the house.

The fruit was so ripe that the canes drooped under the weight, surrounded by frustrated bumblebees. No animals foraged the berries, and birds would only swoop down close to investigate and then soar upward again, as if encountering invisible netting that blocked their beaks.

The berries were only for us.

Papa pointed out a determined Steller's jay, the tufted crest on his head cocked to one side as he puffed out his chest on a ponderosa branch high above the blackberry canes. "He's planning his next route of attack," Papa said.

"Why can't he get the berries?" I watched the jay make another V-shaped dive, another perplexed perch on the branch. "Why can't any of the animals?"

"Because we're the only animals I made them for. Now watch." Papa flipped open my blank sketchbook and grasped the pencil he always kept at the ready behind his ear. I watched the line grow behind his hand, curving into a sketched approximation of the jay more rapidly than I could follow, right down to the tilt of his head. I looked up to the ponderosa branch to compare the likeness, but the jay was gone.

I took back my sketchbook and peered at the shaded feathers, the intricate detail capturing even the minute fronds around the jay's eye. And then I looked at the eye, and my heart stopped.

"Papa." I felt my breath quicken, and I couldn't pull my eyes away from the jay's. "Papa. He's trapped."

"Yes, he is." Papa's voice carried a wistful finality as he tucked the pencil back behind his ear.

I kept gazing at the bird on the page. His wings, his tufted head, his curled feet around the branch were all silent and still, but the curve of the page looked like a caught breath, and I could feel his silenced heart trapped in his hollow bones beneath his feathers, all captured in a two-dimensional cage.

"Let him go, Papa! Please let him go!" The tears I'd held back earlier spilled over my eyelashes and burned my cheeks. "He's scared! Let him go!"

Papa knelt again and grasped my shoulders. "I don't know how. I never have."

I was eight, and I was confounded by any reality where my father was unable to do something. Anything. I was named for a princess—an imaginary one, an old family story about a royal girl's adventures in a kingdom full of saints and angels. But a princess nonetheless. And to my mind, that made my father a king. He was Papa, and his powers had no limits.

"He's all alone," I whispered, looking at the bird.

"Never draw from life if you can help it, Keryth. Every line has a cost."

I touched the shaded feathers around the jay's still eye, and his expression changed. I didn't know birds had facial expressions, but there was a relaxing in the tension of the lines—more of a sense of breathing and movement than had been there before. Something like trust. I looked at Papa with confusion. "If you knew he'd be trapped, why did you do it? And why in my book?"

"So you would always remember the most important thing I ever taught you."

"You could have just told me not to draw living things. I would have listened."

"You wouldn't have believed it, and the rule is bigger than that: It's not just living things. You can't draw anything from the real world. Or I can't, at least, not without capturing it completely, just like this bird. But that isn't the lesson."

"What is?"

Papa took the book from me and clapped its covers closed, snapping the bird inside, before he handed it back. "Don't grow up to be like me."

TECH GIANT ACQUIRES ETERNAI FOR UNDISCLOSED AMOUNT (from *The Technic Magazine*, February 2012 issue): Micronia Systems, Inc., has announced its recent acquisition of EternAI, a start-up that has been courted with great interest by a number of prominent investors since its announced launch of a suite of artificial intelligence technologies that reportedly represents an astonishing leap forward toward new frontiers. The company's proof-of-concept presentation at last year's TechPop conference excited attendees with tantalizing interactions with Harold, a program based on the deceased father of one of the company's founders, Maximilian Miller, who will continue to develop the product. EternAI is reportedly in talks to further enhance the technology, which is still in its infancy but is reportedly evolving fast through largely passive processes, the specifics and secrets of which the company guards closely. Mr. Miller is not known to be a fixture in the Silicon Valley social scene, but given the rumors about how much money EternAI fetched, he and his wife, Keryth Miller, have landed comfortably among some of their ritzier neighbors. Plus, Mr. Miller's new seat on the Micronia board of directors may necessitate a few more appearances on the cocktail party circuit. The Millers are also the parents of two children, which does tend to limit social occasions. Mrs. Miller is reportedly planning to establish a new charitable foundation with some proceeds of the sale, leading to hopes for a new series of galas that this reporter can attend with appropriate press credentials.

3

The House on the Waves

AUGUST 2016

MAX WAS STILL staring at me, expectant, as I tried to keep the panic from my face.

"Are you okay?" he asked. "I was just wondering what you were researching. You look like I accused you of hiding a body. Is it something to do with Harold?"

"Right here, kiddo. Hiding bodies is still a little beyond my algorithm, but keep on reaching for those stars—"

"It's not about Harold. Turn off listening, Harold." I waited for the three-tone chime that confirmed that my electronic father-in-law wasn't going to crack dad jokes while I was trying to figure out how much I could say. Could I just pull off my glove, lay it all out, show my husband and children the part of me that was missing? Maybe telling Harold was a better idea. Maybe a dad joke was the way to go after all—*Where does Mom keep her armies? Not in her sleevies . . .*

"Keryth?" Max's voice was a gentle nudge, but I recognized the alarm on his face. It was the expression that always preceded a suggestion to return to the doctor.

"I'm fine. I'm just—gathering my thoughts. I was researching some real estate." I tried to sound nonchalant. I grew up tangled in family secrets I'd spent my whole life trying to forget, but it seemed I hadn't lost the knack for coming up with explanations on the fly to deflect someone's interest from the mystery at hand. I learned it from watching Papa. I remembered the intense expression of concentration he wore when he sketched his structures and figures, trying hard not to draw inspiration from anything real. Why would he be breaking that rule now? And how could I find him?

"I've been thinking of tracking down some places where I used to live," I said.

"What for?" Max asked.

"I think—maybe—I think I want to buy them."

I had a single link between the woman I was and the lost girl I'd been—my sketchbook and its drawings, minutely etched details of the life I'd built for myself since I lost my first family at sixteen. I'd added moments and impressions in every place I'd ever been, every house I'd passed through—and those could form a path back. To find my father, I could trace the bread crumbs he'd left behind when I was growing up.

The only remnants of my father, of my family, were the houses he'd created for us out of graphite and paper, drawing them into existence between the pages of his sketchbook. Assuming they still existed, in some form, wherever we'd been, in the craggy deserts and abandoned forests where we had to find them in order to move in, hidden away from the world. Because he pulled the details of the structures from places he'd been, I thought I could use them to find where he was now.

Mindy, bent over her phone in a C that stood for "closed off," the DO NOT ENTER sign of fifteen, pulled herself straight and looked at me. "Are we going to move?"

"No. These aren't places we would live." Not that our current place felt particularly livable, either. The house around us was a

temple of glass and high ceilings, the kind of place that architects and designers conceive when someone tells them money is
no object, practicality be damned. The girls' bedrooms jutted
out over the beach like observation cells in a zoo, and I'd hissed
at Max that if we'd spent the money for something so ridiculous, we could also spend the money to enclose it. Our daughters each picked the color and fabric for their custom-fitted
draperies. Ellory's was teal and Mindy's was hot pink, and when
they were inside at night, their lit bedrooms hung like glowing
lanterns above the sand.

Max's face was pensive. "Investments, then? You've always
made the places you grew up sound pretty isolated—not the
kinds of places you could rent out, although I guess if we fixed
them up as get-away-from-it-all retreats, hired some managers,
that kind of thing—"

"Not everything has to have an angle, Max. Not everything
has to be a Harold—"

"Hey-o, folks. What can I do for you now? Did I hear something about investments? Because I gotta say, this is the conversation I've been waiting on ones and zeros to have with you!
After all, a penny saved—"

"HAROLD!" the four of us shouted together, a brief moment
of family unity.

"Dad," Mindy said, an eye roll in a single word. "You have
got to adjust his settings. He doesn't know when to stop."

"That's the most real thing about him," Max said. "Dad was
like that. But he's still learning. The more he listens, the better
he'll get."

"You aren't listening." Ellory sipped her coffee, casting her
eyes over the top of her mug. "What makes you think he'll
learn to?"

"Are all three of you against me today?" Max's face was

nearly expressionless, but I heard his frustration beneath the surface, his annoyance that we weren't all as invested in his experiments as he was.

I threw him a lifeline by changing the subject. "I know it sounds like a strange idea. I'm not thinking about finding these places and making them . . . I don't know. Earn. They don't need to earn anything. They don't need to be productive or serve as some kind of master class on ROI or whatever it is you're thinking, Max, I see it in your eyes. I just need to see them and figure the rest out as I go."

"That's . . . kind of a big ask, Keryth."

"I don't make many. It's not like I asked you for a pony." My sarcasm was more biting than I meant it to be. Max's eyes darted over to our daughters and back to me, the same superior tone he didn't have to put into words—*Not in front of the kids.*

"Oooh, Dad, can *I* have a pony?" Mindy asked.

"It's just an *expression*, Mindy, geez," Ellory said, rolling her eyes at her little sister. "You're acting like a kid."

"A good buddy of mine used to bet on the ponies every Saturday when he told his wife he was going to confession," Harold volunteered, his voice booming above us. "It wasn't the best investment strategy, but he had a few lucky guesses—"

"Go to sleep, Harold!" the four of us shouted.

Max took a deep breath. "Keryth, I guess you could sit down with Anthony, if you wanted. If you're going to set out on this project, you'll need a budget, and you can figure that out with him and not with me." His words carried an undercurrent of ownership, but beneath that was another unspoken message. Any meeting with our attorney—really, our company's attorney— was necessary because the company, and the money, belonged to both of us. Not just legally, but morally. The buyout and the stocks and the portfolios and the runaway success of our creations were attributable to our joint efforts, and Max would be the first to admit it. He didn't consult me much anymore—though we both had luxurious offices at our company's head-quarters, he was the only one who headed there anymore. When asked, he told everyone that I was busy with "whatever it was I did all day." When I was being charitable, I'd say he meant it as a brush-off: it was no one else's business. When I was an-gry, I'd say he found my work on our foundation to be as incon-sequential as I felt.

Max had never flipped all the way through my sketchbook, and I'd never really let him. He wouldn't know how to make sense of the small cross-hatchings of accomplishment squeezed into the corners of the pages, like every other solution I'd reck-lessly doodled into being against Papa's warnings. Max wouldn't know what he was looking at if he found them. He'd only ever seen the Steller's jay when the book, its cracked spine mended beyond all recognition, fell open in front of him once. He'd tried several times to convince me to let him frame the sketch of the bird. *It seems so unfair to keep something so lovely cooped up in a book.*

You have no idea how right you are, I could have told him, but didn't.

I sighed. "If you think this is meeting-with-Anthony level, fine, I'll give him a call today. But I'm not sure yet what the budget would be—I have a lot I need to find, and that'll take some looking."

"Mom, don't you know where you used to live?" Mindy was still listening and pretending not to.

"Not exactly. I remember the later places, when I was a little older than you. But the ones before that I mostly remember from landmarks or features, like the blackberry canes in one place, or the stained glass window in my grandmother's house."

Ellory took a sip of her coffee and sat next to her younger sister, momentarily still—an odd event in the mornings. I'd drawn her attention without meaning to. "Mom, you never talk about your childhood. Not even when we ask. We don't know anything about our family on your side. It's weird."

I bristled. "It's not weird. Not everyone knows their families. Sometimes they're not around anymore. Sometimes it's too painful. Not everyone grows up the way you've grown up, with everything—"

Max put his hand on my waist, a gesture meant as a gentle *you're upsetting the kids*, and I spun away from him and glared.

Ellory and Mindy watched us carefully, then exchanged a knowing look, the unspoken language of sisters. Ellory looked back at me and tried another tack. "I'm sorry, Mom. Is it like that first place we lived when I was little? I only remember blurry colors."

"Something like that. I remember feelings more than I remember where I had them. My memories kind of . . . fold in on each other, somehow. It's difficult for me to fan them out into a clear line." I saw my daughters' faces, matched like porcelain dinner plates and nearly as translucent, their mouths set. "We moved around a lot. My family . . . they're all gone. I've told you that before. There are lots of memories, and they're not all painful. Gran and my father were both really gifted artists. Mama . . . she was beautiful, and a blur. She was a really fast runner. And she was gone a lot when I was growing up."

Mindy shrugged. "We can relate to that."

"No, you can't," I said, with defensiveness creeping underneath my words. I traveled for work. They knew that—I'd explained it their whole lives. The fact that I couldn't quite recall where I'd gone, or why, and that my own travels collapsed into a series of blackouts that had become increasingly impossible to predict, had made those explanations more tenuous. And no one picks up on artifice more than a teenager.

How could I explain to my daughters, both of whom had only ever lived in one or two places and with most everything they ever could have wanted, what it means to grow up running? How to explain the fact that my homes rarely stayed in a place, but were defined only by the people who sheltered there, for however long shelter was possible? If I could find words to describe what it felt like to set out in the middle of the night, not sure when or where we would stop again, but knowing it would be somewhere unexpected and isolated, I might understand the experience better myself. There was a strict dividing wall in the timeline of my life—everything before sixteen, and everything after.

My disappearing hand threatened to dismantle that wall.

Ellory set her jaw, donning the same determined face she used to wear when she was trying to figure something out on her own, anyone else's plans be damned. "You can't blame us for wanting to know more. I used to watch my friends go to family reunions and big holiday dinners, and I had to tell them I didn't even know if I had any aunts or uncles."

"You had an uncle," I murmured. "He's dead. He drowned."

The silence in the room felt as solid as a pane of glass. Ellory and Mindy stared at me. The coffeepot hissed.

Max crossed to the coffee maker, switching it off with a click that seemed to restart reality. "Okay. Girls, we've talked before about the fact that there are things your mom doesn't like to talk about, and we don't push the things that hurt. Time to get out the door for school."

I restrained myself from rolling my eyes at language he had memorized from our counseling sessions. He looked at me as if I were a next item of business, another line on the checklist.

"Now—about these houses. Has it occurred to you that people may already be living in these places?" Max asked.

It hadn't, of course. The places I lived lost all meaning outside the context of my family living there, and the thought of other people in those spaces made me think of someone wearing an ill-fitting suit—unflattering, uncomfortable, not meant for them. I could conceive of the structures as abandoned, crumbling, even entirely collapsed, but not occupied—by anything other than ghosts, at least.

"If anyone's there, we'll pay them to move."

Max shook his head. "This is not a We project. This is a You project." He brushed his hands together as if physically ridding himself of my idea. "Work it out with Anthony."

I could feel waves of exhaustion pooling around me, but Max's words swirled them into a current of rage. Of course it was a Me project. Anything that mattered to me was a Me project now, teamwork long since thrown over for profit, or such were the words I would hurl at Max if we were in a therapy session and not in our kitchen, watched by our daughters' hawk eyes.

And he, in turn, would hurl back at me that I had shut him out, that the division between Me and Him, the near elimination of We was my choice, not his. The fact that he was right only made my anger worse. My mother always said that people blame others most for the things that are their own fault.

At some point, in my worry over the disappearing hours and days that preceded my disappearing hand, I'd stopped engaging. I'd skipped out of the well-worn groove we'd carved into the record of our lives together, and Max was still playing the same tune without me, bewildered, wondering when I'd join back in.

"I don't know how long this will take. I may be gone for a while." *Or forever, if my father starts sketching more than my hand.* "I can't just have someone else find these places and buy them sight unseen. I need to go inside, if they're empty. Especially if they're empty. I need to retrace where we went."

Mindy jumped off the bench. "Can I come? I could bring my camera."

"No. You have school." Max's answer was absolute, despite the fact that he'd recently threatened to withdraw both kids from their fine arts–based private school program. Mindy was taking a photography class, the teacher of which had a penchant for empty spaces. She had recently taken the whole class to an abandoned mall, helping them crawl under a fence with a broken padlock in broad daylight, snapping pictures of the skylight-lit retail temple with its graffiti and encroaching weeds until a squad car responded and ordered them out, notifying the school but not charging anyone.

I would have said no, too, of course, but the fact that Max said it first made me angry, and the fact that he was right made me even angrier. The script inside my head was chiseled in stone, and I couldn't seem to carve out new words to speak to him. And the truth was that I didn't know how long I'd be gone because I could never predict when I'd go, or where. The danger I posed to my family came not just from the mistakes I might make while trying to nudge reality to my will in ink and paper, but also from the fact that I was forced, lately, to do it, because I couldn't account for my own time. The blackouts were getting worse, and my periods of absence harder to predict and explain.

"The HVAC's running smooth as a top, kiddo," Harold chirped overhead. "If you're feeling cold, why not pop on a sweater?"

"Yes, Harold, thank you," Max and I said together.

"I'll call Anthony today," I said as breezily as I could. And then I retrieved my slim laptop from the kitchen bar with my empty glove, retreating to the narrow desk in my bedroom to begin to explore my own history, at once a more precarious and more loving place than my present. I would start with the structure I suspected might be nearest—a dilapidated beachfront motel where we'd squatted for less than a season.

As I clicked and swiped and jotted notes, I tried and failed to swallow my certainty that, if I didn't find my father, the hot California summer beating against my glass house would be the last season I passed.

TOWN COUNCIL MEMBERS CONFRONTED BY RESIDENTS OVER DISAPPEARING EYESORE (from *The Tatum City Bee*, Tatum City, Utah, May 11, 2016): Council members were confused when local residents appeared at the regular town council meeting to protest the sudden appearance and—as the meeting continued—evident disappearance of an expansive structure on the edge of Sprite Canyon, a protected wilderness area where construction is not allowed. The structure, described by one resident as "a church that got in a bar fight and vomited a bunch of other buildings onto itself," reportedly appeared sometime last week, when local business owner and equestrian Dan Burnett discovered it while leading a trail ride. "It weren't even there the week before," said Burnett, adding, "We all got mad as hell about that Walmart over in Barkley County two years back, and now we got this sprawled-out disaster teetering on the edge of a cliff, and who here's responsible? Who's reviewing permits around here?" Bewildered council members asked for more information about the reported structure, having not approved any construction at Sprite Canyon and protesting, correctly, that they have no authority to do so. Ultimately, council member Sally Eckert excused herself from the meeting and returned twenty minutes later, having driven to the reported location and seen "nothing—not a cactus out of place" before accusing Mr. Burnett of leading trail rides while intoxicated, as "only a drunk guide would forget you can't swing a dead cat around here without hitting another damn canyon."

The angered residents broke out in argument over whether to seek out the offensive structure elsewhere. They later reconvened at the Denny's on First Street to discuss legal action, the exact nature of which is, as yet, undecided.

4

University of California, Berkeley
NOVEMBER 1995

I FELL IN love with Max because he brought his father back from the dead.

I'd just been accused of trying to do the same thing, as it happened, by a therapist at the university's counseling center, where I'd begrudgingly gone for weekly sessions as a "strongly recommended" coping mechanism since coming to college more than a year earlier. I was a newly emerged foster care success story, the subject of others' self-congratulatory tales about what can be accomplished when the state provides "the right support."

No one could tell me what to do anymore, but that didn't mean they wouldn't try. I'd spent a lifetime learning the importance of keeping a low profile, and after a few years spent beating my own head against the brick wall of fighting that rule, I decided to duck down into compliance with the outside world's expectations. I checked in regularly with my adviser. She sent me to the university's counseling center with a note that I half expected her to pin to the front of my jacket. I didn't tell her that I had limitless experiences with counselors and therapists. Any number of foster parents had taken me to sessions, trying to get me to face the reality of my brother's death and my lack of responsibility for it. *He's not dead*, I would say, over and over, at every possible volume, in every language I could think of. *He's not dead.*

Every session meandered, but always wended its way toward one of several well-established reassurances. They all boiled down to the same central messages, delivered as if read by a greeting card recipient reciting italicized letters with a flourish. *Of course he's not dead. The people we love are always with us, even when they're gone.* And, inevitably: *It wasn't your fault.*

Tell a story enough times and have enough people with enough advanced education explain to you, over and over, that your story isn't true—and you begin to wonder whether they might be right, and whether you could possibly be wrong. Whether every story you've ever been told, and every story you've ever told yourself, is wrong. And then you stop wondering and accept what they tell you, because it's the only way to survive. Neil drowned in the pond behind our house while he was trying to escape people who were only trying to help him. To help us. Our parents abandoned us, and I'd done the best I could to keep us both safe, and I had failed. In the end, I had to accept that everyone I loved was gone.

And then I met someone who refused to accept anything of the sort.

After I stomped out of one particularly unhelpful session of dredging up memories best left behind, I stalked down the sidewalk to the student union to get myself a blistering cup of coffee and a muffin, and sat down at a table with a sheet of paper and a pen, looking around for something mindless—something wholly without significance—to sketch. I settled on a red silk gerbera daisy in a mason jar at the table near me, which was occupied by a young man my age. On the table, he fiddled with the buttons of a tiny handheld recorder and a battered spiral notebook, dog-eared and ragged. Beneath the table, an enormous computer balanced in an old-fashioned red metal wagon.

Click. "Well, hello there. Pleased as punch to meet you." The voice that emerged from the recorder held more resonance, more gravitas, than a tiny speaker should be able to allow. The young man hit another button, and the voice stopped. He scribbled furiously on the pad, then rewound the recording with a whir.

Click. "Well, hello there. Pleased as punch to meet you." Scribble scribble scribble. The young man seemed oblivious to the other people passing in and out of the café, and indeed, they seemed mostly oblivious to him, too. Eccentric people were unremarkable here. Still, he must have felt my gaze on him, and looked up to meet my eyes. He didn't smile. He just shrugged and pointed at the recorder.

"My dad," he said.

"He has a nice voice," I said.

"He's dead." He delivered this information without a trace of sentimentality, as matter-of-fact as an announcement that it was raining, or the sun was hot.

"I'm sorry." My voice was tentative, the words an offering.

"Thank you." He frowned, the first expression I'd seen on his face. "I know that's what I'm supposed to say, but it still seems odd to me, like someone gave me a gift. Social rules never make much sense to me. But, at any rate. Thank you, I guess."

I smiled. "Social rules never made much sense to me, either." I found myself searching for a way to continue the conversation instead of ending it. He had already turned his attention back to his recorder. *Click.* "Well, hello there. Pleased as punch to meet you." This young man couldn't seem less pleased to meet anyone, but I thought it might be worth a try anyway. "I'm Keryth."

He didn't look up. "Max."

"Hi, Max." The ball was bouncing around on my side of the court again, and I tried another volley back to him. I sat down in the chair across from the round table and pointed at the recorder. "Could I—could I ask what you're doing?"

"Sure, but you won't believe it. No one ever does."

"You might be surprised what I believe."

Max shot a look my way, one eyebrow raised, skeptical. "That sounds like an opening for some kind of evangelical speech, and I'm not interested, thanks. I've had more than my share of well-meaning come-to-Jesus types try to bring me into the fold. Cancer wards are full of them, and I spent years watching my dad die, so I listened to plenty of speeches. Thanks anyway."

"No—I mean I've seen things." I paused. "Now I'm just making myself sound even weirder. Let me start again. I'm alone here. I'm on scholarship, I'm a fine arts major, and I don't—I don't see the world the way everyone else does."

At this, he looked up at me again. "I think most art students would say that, right?"

It was my turn to shrug. "Maybe. Probably. But none of them are sitting here, asking you what you're doing with a recording of your dead father and a computer that looks like it could power a mission to Mars."

He smiled. "NASA wishes they had this technology. Soon, everyone will wish they had this technology. And they will, when it's ready. And when the price is right."

"What is it?"

"Artificial intelligence. But I don't like the word 'artificial,' because I'm making something real. A person. I'm training a machine to learn who my father was, so the machine can be my father."

"So it can be—"

Max shook his head. "Not, like, literally be my father. I'm not trying to create a robot dad or anything like that. But I'm trying to create something that understands, on a very deep level, who my father was, how he talked, and what he meant in this world. And then it can apply that understanding to let him continue to exist, in a way, and interact with the world. I'm trying to create someone I could sit down and have a conversation with, and believe that I've talked with my father as much as I did when I sat with him in a hospital room. Only this one won't die. Ever."

"So you're starting with his voice."

"Not just his voice. I recorded him. All of him. His routines, his stories. Hundreds and hundreds of tapes over the last four years of his life. We talked about every possible thing—our family, history, philosophy. Love. Advice. Scandals and myths. Anything that came to his mind. We didn't treat anything as irrelevant. Everything is relevant when you're creating."

The weight of his words thudded against my chest. *Everything is relevant when you're creating.* I thought of my father and my stick-drawn cardinal, my small-child conviction that my lack of artistic skill would make my work unworthy, stupid, not worth starting. *Nothing is stupid when you're creating something new.*

"If everything is relevant, how do you know where to start?" I asked.

"You must have forgotten your *Alice in Wonderland*," Max said. "We begin at the beginning, and go on till we come to the end. Only we won't stop. There isn't an end."

"Interesting," I said. "Would you mind having some company through the looking glass?"

Max's face was pensive. "I don't know that there's much worth joining yet. I can't even get a professor to sign on for my research or support my thesis. Everything's a matter of extremes—what I'm trying to do is either too impossible, or too risky. Everyone thinks I can't do it, or that I shouldn't."

"What would your dad think?"

Max smiled for the first time. "Dad thought anything was worth trying once. Even dying. And especially coming back from the dead."

"I'm an orphan." The words flew out of my mouth uninvited. "I don't know why I said that. But it's true."

"I guess it's my turn to say I'm sorry, then, according to those rules we talked about."

"And it's my turn to say thank you." I took a deep breath. "I lost my family a long time ago. If someone told me I could sit down and have a conversation with them—any of them—I'd want to know more. I wouldn't say it was impossible. I would want to know how."

"That's going to be very need-to-know information. Founders only."

"Who are the founders?"

"Right now, there's only one. Me." Max squinted in my direction. "But I might be taking applications."

I reached across the table for his spiral notebook and pulled my pen from its usual perch behind my ear. *My name is Keryth Anne Hartley,* I wrote in the notebook before sliding it back to him.

He read my words and grinned. "Welcome aboard, Keryth. Are you named after an elf?"

I shook my head. "A princess. An old family story."

"Sounds like we may have several of those in common." I saw a series of calculations pass across his face. "I'm remembering those social rules again. Would you like to discuss our stories over dinner? I'm an awful cook. But I order a good pizza."

"I like pizza. And . . . yes, I'd like that." I smiled. The life I had drawn for myself was solitary. I lived alone, I ate alone, I created alone. Other than my classes and my mandatory therapy, I didn't pass time with any other human being. It wasn't exactly by design, but the years I'd spent in foster care after losing my family had taught me it's better not to count on anything ever being the same from day to day, or on anyone being present in your life for long. I couldn't rely on anyone other than myself.

But I could eat a pizza. There was no commitment in that. No reliance.

Max hit the rewind button on his recorder again. *Click.* "Well, hello there. Pleased as punch to meet you," his father's voice said again.

"He would have liked you," Max said. "And you'll like him, too, I think. Just as soon as he's back online."

His voice was absolute, but gentle—a warm blanket wrapped around steel. Its heft and dimension filled the empty place I tried to ignore, where the jagged lines of my missing family tore through me like a hole through paper. *He's not dead*, the voice allowed. *He's just offline.*

To a girl who'd lost everything and everyone she'd ever loved, a man who could reduce the complexities of grief to a binary prospect—gone; back—held a powerful appeal.

"Do you like mushrooms?" I asked.

Max shrugged. "Whatever you'd like." That smile again—as

fleeting and angular as a bird swooping for a berry. "Everything after you said yes is pretty irrelevant to me."

As I looked at his face, I thought of my father again, and the pencil sharpness of his artist's gaze whenever he entered a room. I craved that sense of focus. I didn't know, not back then, what that intensity was trying to prevent.

5

•••••••

The Thorn House
OCTOBER 1985

MY MOTHER WAS missing. I opened my eyes on a crisp autumn morning, awakened less by any signal than by the absence of them. No smell of breakfast or coffee, no gentle sounds as my mother set about her morning routines at a volume intended to let the rest of us sleep. She had still been around enough for us to have an established route through our day, with her as our North Star. But lately her occasional disappearances had become more frequent. In my waning moments of consciousness the night before, when I couldn't be sure if I was asleep or awake, I'd heard her voice mingling with my father's, alto and bass forming a melody with no lyrics I could readily discern, but weaving into a minor key. There was tension simmering between them, but I was too young to have a name for it.

I slid out of my bed, settling the afghan Gran made over the depression my body had left in the mattress, and tiptoed into my parents' room. Papa was still asleep beneath a larger version of my own blanket, so motionless that I might have wondered whether he was breathing if I hadn't known—from countless campsites and motel floors and other places where we'd slept close together—that this was simply how he rested, so completely that he seemed to leave the world entirely for a while. I knew better than to try to wake him. He operated on some internal clock that could not be advanced before its time. I couldn't ask him yet if he knew that Mama was gone.

I stepped softly back into the room I shared with Neil, who always slept as if he swayed in a hammock instead of a bed—hands tucked behind his head, a gentle smile spread on his face. I hoped he would stay asleep as long as possible so I wouldn't have to see the hunger in his eyes that grew whenever our mother was distant.

The kitchen was cold. Our cabin had an old woodstove that Mama used for cooking, which was one reason for her early rising—the day couldn't start until the fire did. I sat in my favorite rush-seat chair next to the small kitchen table and wondered what to do. I didn't know how to cook. Papa did, but he was still asleep, and I was hungry.

Papa often drew at the kitchen table, settling himself in my mother's orbit as she hovered through chores. His sketchbook was open in front of his chair, the current page depicting a stone wall coated in ivy, a diminishing stub of pencil resting in the center binding, its back cover cushioned by stacks of papers and letters and clippings he always kept carefully tucked in the book's gusseted rear pocket. The book itself never ran out of room, and expanded in much the same way as the pocket—when his ideas were too big, he could tap the page's corner and the page would grow to encompass them. There was always another sheet, another hidden section to be folded out that, when finished, collapsed back into the book.

I knew he would be upset if I touched it again, let alone if I resumed my efforts to add my own work to his book. But I was cold, and I felt alone, and I grasped the pencil anyway.

The last time he caught me had been the moment I tried to

draw the cardinal, and I don't know what possessed me to try something different instead of electing never to try anything again. But the silence in the kitchen, and the cold, made me sad. With primitive lines and curves, I began to draw a warmer place.

The woodstove was a friendly, bulbous shape that didn't challenge my skill, and neither did the idea of flames, curving invitingly behind the square glass in the door. A curlicue above the kettle showed the steam for coffee. I was so absorbed in adding detail that the whistle from the stovetop made me jump to my feet in terror, sure that I'd been caught by Papa, or that Mama had returned, or that I was going to be in trouble.

But no one else was in the room, and the room itself was exactly as I'd left it before I was absorbed into my drawing. Except that it was warmer now. The light was glowing in the stove's window, and steam rose from the kettle in a welcoming cloud. The cast-iron skillet beside the kettle was filled with crispy strips of bacon next to perfectly circular fried eggs.

In Papa's book, my sketch was more of an impression than a drawing. It was a memory imbued by the feelings of happiness I'd recalled while adding details—rudimentary, untrained details—to the page. Papa's drawings were nearly photorealistic, flawless perspective and shading revealing a picture that often seemed more real than what it depicted.

I didn't have that skill. I only had emotions, and those coursed through me while I drew, imbuing my lines with a different kind of power than Papa's. I didn't understand, and I didn't know if Papa would, either. I was afraid to let him see. But I didn't want to erase what I'd drawn, or the comforting scene that now surrounded me. I would have to let him help me interpret what I saw. As I waited for him to wake up, I looked around the kitchen, and a small sound brought my attention back to the table where I sat, where I noticed I wasn't alone. A man and a woman—fuzzed against the bright light around us, but still visible—were standing over me and the book, pointing desperately at it, and then at me. Their mouths opened and closed as they talked to each other with words I couldn't hear, although they seemed desperate for me to understand them. I saw the spirits in our houses infrequently and, shamefaced, often ignored them—I couldn't understand them, couldn't give them whatever they seemed to want from me, and it made me sad. I shook my head at them and covered my eyes with my hands, willing them to disappear.

I don't know how long I sat there, hoping for things to feel more normal, wondering if my bewilderment might summon Mama back from wherever she'd gone. Instead, I heard Papa's heavy footfalls on the floorboards, staggering into the kitchen and grasping toward his chipped mug on the counter, scratching his belly while he glanced around for the percolator. As he looked behind him, he saw me sitting at the table. I was alone again.

"You're up early." He smiled, and I knew he didn't know yet. "Where's the coffee?"

"I didn't know how to make it."

"Why would you make it?"

"Because Mama's not here."

I watched the rise and fall of Papa's chest, the deepening folds in his forehead. "Since just now? Are you saying she got things started and then just—left?"

"She didn't leave anything. Everything was dark this morning. I woke up because it was quiet."

Papa was half listening, reaching his hand into the skillet and retrieving a strip of bacon with his bare fingers, breaking off one crisp end with his teeth. "At least she made breakfast."

I shook my head. "She was gone sometime before I woke up. She didn't make it. I did."

"She taught you how to start the stove?"

I set my mouth in a line. "No."

"I haven't had my coffee yet, Keryth, so I need you to speak plainly."

I felt frustrated, wondering how he couldn't understand. "The book, Papa."

"What book?"

I tilted my chin toward the sketchbook because Gran always taught me it was rude to point. "Your book. I'm sorry. I know I'm not supposed to draw in it, but it was cold and dark, and I was hungry. When I fixed it, I got scared. And then you came in. That's all I know."

Papa moved to the table and peered at my drawing on the page, furrowing his brow as he looked at the details and then glanced around the room, then at me. "Show me what you did," he said.

I was afraid. He didn't seem angry, and he wasn't prone to rages, but his reaction when he'd caught me drawing the cardinal still echoed in my head. "I don't think I can do it again."

"Try it anyway."

I approached the book slowly, as if it were more like a wild animal than a sheaf of paper. "What do you want me to draw?"

Papa smiled. "How about a cup of coffee?"

I looked at the cup in his hand and screwed up my face in concentration before beginning. As I traced the first line with the pencil, I thought of the heavy ceramic of the cup and the stains deep inside it, too dark to yield to the harshest scrubbing. I thought of the smell of the coffee and the way it warmed the cup and my father's hands as he held it. I thought of the way Mama smiled when she poured it for him, and the white porcelain cow in the refrigerator where she kept the cream, because it made us laugh.

I looked up to find my father still holding an empty cup. Nothing in the room had changed. Everything was static, and I felt tears prickle behind my lashes, sure that I'd disappointed him, but he put his hand over my hand and nodded. "Let's try something," he said. "I'm going to walk outside and pick some blackberries, way out in the hard-to-reach brambles, and while I do that, I want you to try again."

"But what if it doesn't work?"

Papa shrugged. "It may not. It probably won't. But I know how to make coffee. It's not a big deal. No pressure at all." He opened the kitchen door and walked to the far boundaries of the brambles that ringed our house, looking over his shoulder every few steps. He gave me a thumbs-up before ducking under branches and moving out of sight.

The farther he roamed, the more I could feel the air in the room around me lighten, taking on the character and possibility I'd felt before he'd awoken and come in to join me in the kitchen. I picked up the pencil once more and closed my eyes, thinking again about his cup, its weight, the smell of coffee curling in a steamy ring on cold mornings. My memory of the smell was shortly joined by its reality, and when I looked up from my sketch, I saw a twin of my father's favorite mug on the table in front of me, thick ceramic with a chipped glaze of sky blue, filled to the brim with the strong, black coffee he drank.

I felt a thrill of power, followed almost immediately by terror. This wasn't like my father's art. I hadn't captured what existed on the page. I'd drawn out something new. As quickly as I hopped up from the chair to run to the door, I froze in place, remembering his warning to me.

Don't grow up to be like me.

Was this being like him? What if he was mad? What if he was scared, like I was, or if he didn't know what to do?

What if—and I couldn't think that this was possible, not for a grown-up, not for Papa, but still—what if he was jealous?

"Keryth!" Papa's voice bellowed across the meadow. "Any luck?"

I glanced again at the mug I'd drawn into being. Before I could think concretely, I grabbed its warm handle, real and tangible as a stone, and dumped the steaming coffee into the sink, running the faucet with cold water, rinsing the smell away. I raced to my room and dived under my bed, pushing the mug as far underneath as I could reach, and shoving a stuffed elephant in front of it for good measure. I ran back into the kitchen.

"Keryth! Can you hear me? What's the verdict?"

I opened the door. "It didn't work!"

Papa's head popped up from behind the blackberries, and he slowly picked his way back toward me. "It didn't? Did you do the same things as last time?"

It was my turn to shrug. "I'm still not sure what I did. But whatever it was, I can't do it again. It isn't working."

Papa tilted his head, as if thinking about asking more questions, but he didn't. "Well, then. I guess it's time I show you how to make a pot of coffee the old-fashioned way. Until Mama gets back."

"When will Mama get back?"

"As soon as I can figure out how to help her stay."

"Can I help her stay?"

Papa put his arm around me. "You already do, honey. But there are bigger forces at work, and I still haven't figured out how to make them work for us."

I looked again at my sketch in the book, the friendly round stove, the flames behind glass. I thought of the look on Papa's face—curious, but guarded—and the mug shoved underneath my bed like a shameful secret. The skill didn't make sense to me, and I couldn't even feel the concentration in my fingers, the buzzing in my limbs, I'd felt when I was drawing before he entered the room. Maybe I imagined it. Maybe it was better if it wasn't real.

LOCAL COUPLE MISSING AFTER GETAWAY TO DISAPPEARED CABIN (from *The Heatherton Times-Ledger*, Heatherton, Virginia, July 12, 1985): According to neighbors, Mr. and Mrs. Frank Nelson were looking forward to a quick weekend trip to the cabin they bought recently near the Graves Mountain Reserve. But instead of spending a few days hiking and picking wild blackberries, they disappeared. Unverified reports indicate that the cabin itself is also missing. When the Nelsons did not return for work this past Monday, authorities dispatched to the site of the cabin found only a blank patch of ground. "It's been here for decades," said the sheriff, scratching his head. "The Nelsons only bought it recently. And they bought it from a priest, so you know he didn't make off with the place, not that it was small enough to steal! None of the trees are burnt or anything, so it wasn't a fire. It's just gone." Reached for comment, former owner Brady Smithson confirmed that he had built the cabin as a prayer retreat in the 1960s. Curiously, he had done so after a crisis of faith, when a portion of his home church had disappeared in a similarly unexplained phenomenon. "I can't understand it," said Smithson. "I had the place blessed, and I even had a guardian angel hanging over the mantel. It's like some kind of unlucky star or ill wind is sweeping my life's work away." Smithson noted he did not know the Nelsons personally, but they "seemed like a nice couple who just wanted to get away" and had paid over asking price for the cabin. Anyone with information is urged to contact the Heatherton Police Department.

6

● ● ● ● ●

The Sand House
AUGUST 2016

ANTHONY PERCIVAL GRAVES unfolded himself from a car so minute, so European and flawless, that it looked as if Grace Kelly in a headscarf, instead of an attorney in a tailored gray suit, should be behind the wheel. Anthony literally embodied the word *tony*, and probably with a capital *T*—except that no one would ever dare to nickname or abbreviate someone so solemn. If a pinstripe came to life and began negotiating complex mergers and acquisitions, it would have been named Anthony Percival Graves. Only it wouldn't have, because there could be only one. And he was standing in front of me, one eyebrow raised at the dilapidated motel stretching toward the waves behind me.

"An unusual meeting spot, if I may say so, Mrs. Miller."

"I wish to God you'd just call me Keryth, Anthony."

He nodded. "That is, alas, a wish that propriety will not permit me to grant."

Anthony had been our general counsel since we established the Steller Fund—had helped us create the foundation himself, in fact, after warning me that "Stellar Fund," with an *a* to indicate excellence, would make more sense to the average person.

Most people, Anthony surmised, would not be as familiar as I was with ornithology, Georg Steller, or his eponymous blue-black crested corvid. When I'd replied that I didn't care, Anthony gave me an almost imperceptible smile.

Anthony's scrupulous formality was the precise reason Max had hired him. He wanted a lawyer who looked like a lawyer, someone who had come from money and decided to help others make more of it, and not "some nine-to-five Silicon Valley dude-bro fresh from the beach." Mission accomplished. Interviews with several dudebros had left Max tossing up his hands and declaring a waste of the day, but when Anthony strode in with his Hermès briefcase and polished signet ring, looking like someone who not only knew what a cravat was but who had, most likely, worn one on at least a few occasions, Max was sold before Anthony even began to speak. With an accent that was decidedly European, if difficult to place.

"Did Max tell you anything about why I wanted to meet with you?" I knew the answer before I asked the question, but I wasn't sure where else to begin.

"Mr. Miller only stated that you wished to discuss some financial matters bearing on an independent venture, and my secretary informed me you wanted to meet in this . . . place." Anthony gestured toward the low-slung strip of rusting metal doors and warped shutters staring onto a sand-buried walkway that led to the sea. In its heyday, the Pop Inn Oasis hadn't been luxurious, and now it was nearly a ruin, vandalized by a generation of squatters.

We had been squatters, once.

"I'm going to be buying some property." I took a deep breath. "Properties, actually. Several of them. I'm not sure how many yet. But this was the nearest one I remembered."

"In your nightmares, I presume."

"Something like that." I walked toward the motel and trusted Anthony would follow me, and he did, his polished oxfords scraping along the sandy concrete. "Listen. Max and I grew up in different worlds. He may not have told you much about it, and that's because I haven't told him much about it, to be honest. And these days he mostly talks to Harold or whoever else he's working on, anyway."

"Ms. Miller, I feel I must interject. Remember that I represent your businesses jointly. There is nothing you can tell me that I may keep confidential from Mr. Miller. And if there is some conflict between you—"

"There isn't a conflict between us." That wasn't entirely true, and Anthony's face made clear he knew it. I restarted. "You don't need to sound as if you're reading from a law textbook, Anthony. Or a script from some legal drama. There isn't drama, and there's no conflict here. Max knows I want to buy several properties, and he knows I grew up in them. He also knows they're in odd places and may be difficult to locate. And he knows my upbringing was . . . a little unusual. Transient."

Anthony nodded. "This kind of establishment would seem consistent with that characterization."

Sometimes it was difficult to tell if Anthony was a buttoned-up lawyer or a robot. He didn't seem entirely real, in some ways. But he was the gatekeeper between where I was now and where I needed to be. "We were only here for a few months. We were only most places for a few months."

"Might I ask what brought you to this one?"

I tried to remember. The sequence of places we'd lived and places we'd stayed was difficult to retrace, and memories of my life before I turned fifteen became hazier every year, as incomplete as I was now becoming. The motel was early—a beach vacation, Papa said, but one that extended for some period of months before we were uprooted again. Neil was around the age he'd been in the Thorn House—maybe we'd gone after that? I may have been eight or nine years old. I remembered a seagull stealing an ice cream sandwich right from my hand, and never forgiving the ocean for the slight. I still glared at it sometimes from our glass house, wondering what else it might plan to snatch away.

"A change of scene," I ventured. "We were the only family. The location catered to vacationers, but the clientele was not on vacation. Neither were we, I don't think. But it was the only place I remember that already existed—I mean, a place my father didn't create."

"Your father was a builder?"

"Something like that." He was exhausted, I remembered. He would draw the curtains and lie flat on the bed for hours in the still daytime, while Mama took Neil and me to frolic in the waves. *Papa is sad*, I told Mama. *Papa is worried*, she told me back.

Worried about us?

Worried about everything.

"As your father wasn't behind its construction, I feel I can be candid, Mrs. Miller. The structure is in terrible condition. It has been abandoned for some time, and was not well maintained prior to its abandonment. The swimming pool—or what remains of it—may well pose environmental hazards. While I am loath to invest the funds for a full inspection, I believe it may be structurally unsound."

I nodded. "That all sounds about right."

"I would not recommend entering any of the rooms."

I shook my head. Papa hadn't drawn the place, but I didn't know what he'd done while we were here, so I had no idea if I'd find anyone inside. "I wasn't planning on it."

"Have I dissuaded you from purchasing it?"

"You have not."

"What would you have me do?"

"Find the owner and buy it."

"The owner is likely the government, Mrs. Miller. It's almost certainly been seized for unpaid taxes, and may well be condemned."

"Then pay the taxes, call the assessors, do what needs to be done. Make a donation. Make several donations. Find a way."

"I can find most anything, Mrs. Miller. It's something of a talent of mine. But to what end, if I may ask?"

"You sound like Max."

"I shall take that as a compliment. I do owe a duty to the Steller Fund, Mrs. Miller, and I feel I must have some sense—"

"It's a shelter, Anthony. We'll convert it into housing for unhoused people. That may help convince the city to work with us, but it's what I'd do anyway. I don't want it abandoned. I want it to be a happy place, and I want it to help families like the family I was part of. Once."

Anthony's gaze was flat. "Mr. Miller will suggest alerting your publicist."

"If he takes any interest in this at all, fine. I'm fine with that. Whatever makes him happy."

"What would make you happy, Mrs. Miller?"

I rubbed my face with my gloved hands. My head was pounding, the echo of a migraine on an uncertain horizon. I felt as if I couldn't speak, as if the words would catch in my throat, if my throat itself were still visible. Parts of me felt scattered in this place where we had started to be lost, long before I knew it.

"Mrs. Miller. Are you quite all right?" Anthony reached a long arm toward me, steadying me and guiding me toward my old sedan next to his minuscule car. He opened my door and held my hands while I lowered myself onto my bench seat. I felt unsteady, unmoored. And ancient.

"I'm not, Anthony, but I'm trying to figure out how to get there."

"You've picked an interesting destination from which to begin."

I rubbed my face again, thinking I should switch my green gloves for a rosier pair, just for the sake of good cheer. "If I've learned anything, Anthony, it's that every journey has to begin somewhere."

"Very well. The purchase and conversion of this—place—is likely consistent with the charitable goals of your foundation. But the rest of the errand you've described to me may not be—"

"I'm paid a salary, Anthony, and I've never had to really spend a dime of it. I'm not even entirely sure why Max thinks you need to be involved."

"Aren't you?" Anthony smiled wryly, and I recognized yet again how slow on the uptake I could be. Max and I were on the outs—though neither of us wanted to admit it. Our relationship had, more and more, come to require the intervention and interpretation of neutral go-betweens. Anthony was just a more official version of the notes we'd started passing back and forth. "Mrs. Miller, it seems you and Mr. Miller are aligned in one respect: you are both trying to recover things you have lost."

"I guess that makes it even clearer we're not in conflict?"

"You are both quite insistent that you aren't. Mr. Miller has similarly informed me. But I believe he may be concerned you aren't entirely forthcoming regarding this mission, and also—if I may be so bold—I believe he is concerned about you gener-ally, Mrs. Miller. Are you in some kind of trouble?" Anthony glanced surreptitiously at my gloves. "Are you ill?"

I shook my head violently. "I am not ill. And I'm pretty sick of people tiptoeing around ways to ask me that, so thanks for being direct, at least." I gazed at the waves as they advanced toward the peeling planks of the motel. "Look. Max wants to make this surveillance of his about the foundation, and that's fine. I'll let him do it. I'll call you, I'll keep you in the loop, I'll tell you where I'm going as I figure it out."

Anthony held up his hands. "There is no need to do anything more than you're comfortable with. But I do believe some degree of information will reassure Mr. Miller considerably. And as for me, I am happy so long as the two of you are reasonably aligned."

We used to be, I did not say. I remembered sleepless nights in our first apartment together, running my hands through Max's shock of unwashed hair as he threw himself into solving the intricate puzzle of our first big project. When I'd met him, we were both mired in a stage of grief; I was working on acceptance, and he was stuck in denial. He'd never left it—our company was its outsized manifestation, death that would never become real. But his focus, his late nights, and his passion reminded me of Papa, reminded me of Gran's old adage, whispered whenever work was worth doing: *We pour ourselves into the work that matters most.*

It didn't feel like Max thought our marriage was worth pouring himself into anymore. Everything was the company, and profits, and the next development. Max's smiles were rare and his laughter rarer, and being the one person who could bring them out made me feel, in the beginning, like a sorceress. Powerful and uncanny.

I couldn't remember the last time I had heard him laugh. Or, come to think of it, the last time I had laughed, or that we'd found something funny together. Maybe he'd have laughed if I'd

told him my *Back to the Future* joke, but given it was literal—
probably not.

"We're as aligned as we can be." I stuck my keys into the
ignition, punctuating my own sentence. "And I've got to get
going."

AUTHORITIES MYSTIFIED BY DESTRUCTION OF HISTORIC CHURCH (from *The Heatherton Times-Ledger*, November 12, 1966): Neighbors were stunned awake this morning by the crashing collapse of Our Lady of Succor on Old Hunt Trail Road in Heatherton. The stone structure became unstable after the sudden disappearance of its primary steeple and westward-facing wall, including its celebrated rose window, imported from Europe. A percentage of the churchyard adjacent to the wall has also vanished. Reached for comment, Father Brady Smithson expressed the tragedy was unlike anything he'd ever seen, "as if a tornado came down and plucked it all away clean." Atmospheric phenomena, deliberate vandalism, and other potential theories are all under active investigation, but authorities are advising calm, noting that steeple collapse and other issues are known problems among historic church buildings, and dismissing rumors that the building's demise could be characterized as supernatural, notwithstanding the old adage that the good Lord works in mysterious ways.

7

The Thorn House
DECEMBER 1985

THE SNOW THAT swirled around our cabin fell on the blackberries, still darkened on the canes outside their season, though I didn't understand things had a season yet. The snowdrifts were growing on our sweep of the mountain.

I was learning to draw.

Papa would sit next to me on the rough-hewn log bench outside our house, nestled together in a bubble of warmth, no matter the weather outside the world he'd made us. My first lessons concentrated on materials. Papa favored soft graphite and charcoal to form and shade the boundaries of his creations. I lacked his skill in adding depth and dimension to my sketches, and my attempts with charcoal turned my drawings into black, tarry pools, indistinct lumps of line and form. Papa frowned and brought me crayons; I glared and stomped and said I wasn't a baby. He brought me colored pencils and a sharpener, and tried to show me how to vary the pressure of my grip, but I wanted my colors more opaque and certain than the firm pencils would permit. I pushed hungry holes and slashes into the paper, and broke the pencils in frustration. "What would Princess Keryth do?" Papa asked. "Would she let herself get so angry? I think she'd try to think of this as a learning experience, don't you?"

I scowled and stamped my foot, irate at Papa's mentioning my namesake, the fearless princess from my gran's stories. But I was more irate at myself, and the fact that he was right. I wanted to be perfect, and I wanted to be perfect right away, without any practice at all. I wanted to recapture the magic I'd felt when I brought the kitchen to life. And I wanted to do it all by myself—without any guidance—and without showing my father what I was capable of, or thought I could be. It would break the rules and risk danger, just as he'd always warned me. At night, I traced the feathers around the still eye of my Steller's jay with my finger, and tried to will myself to stop testing the boundaries.

When Papa brought me pens, my lines became orderly, and my mood improved. Papa laughed and said I had expensive taste, because the ink I preferred flowed out of pen tips narrower than a cat's whisker, and required a cat's grace and precision of movement. The pens came from expensive art supply stores Gran patronized whenever she visited large towns to obtain paints and pigments. Papa collected monthly boxes from the post office, MISS KERYTH ANNE HARTLEY scrawled across the top in Gran's crabbed handwriting. The ink usually ran dry before the next supplies arrived.

She sent sketchbooks, too, and I used them for experiments with line and color, but the drawings in my first book—the one Papa gave me—were very, very small. I was afraid to run out of space. The tiny pen tips let me dot and dash small details into existence, some so minute that I sketched them with a magnifying glass. My skills were primitive in the beginning, and the first time I found a daisy on my dining room table and realized where it came from, my hands flushed red with power, and the rest of me flooded with fear. I couldn't show Papa. But Mama knew. I found her pinching the flower off the table as if it might bite her. The edges of its petals were indistinct, and the cross-hatching on its yellow center made it look like something from a geometry textbook. She ran out of the house faster than my eyes could follow her, and I found the flower later, crushed beneath the blackberry thorns.

She was gone two weeks that time. I drew her in my sketchbook as a blur, long yellow hair pulled straight by velocity and wind, nubbed bulges on her shoulder blades, beneath her sweep of white coat. The wings only I knew were there. At the edge of the page, I drew a wall, stone and spikes and topped with a heart shaped out of curlicues, and I knew when she reached it she would turn around. Someday, I worried, she might fly over it. But I knew she'd see the heart was mine, and she wouldn't break it yet.

She was gone long enough to miss the worst mistake I made, the one I still had nightmares about, when I tried to graduate from sketching inanimate mugs and daisies to drawing something new. I worried my Steller's jay was lonely with only me for company, and I decided one morning to try my hand at a goldfinch. A flashy yellow friend for my black-and-blue companion. But, of course, Papa wasn't drawing him. I didn't have his skill, and I'd already learned the skill I did have tended to yield unpredictable results. But I didn't heed the warning in my jay's eyes when I held up a pen the color of sunshine and told him I was going to make a bird.

I wasn't satisfied with the form it was taking—the angles felt all wrong, and I couldn't match the grace in Papa's flawless capturing of life—and then I heard a strangled squeaking, less a song than a high-pitched croaking, and I screamed when I saw what was trying to hop, herky-jerky, across the kitchen table. It was terrifying, and it was terrified. It was yellow. And it was in pain.

I didn't know what to do. I ripped the page from my book and tried to line through what I'd drawn, as if to erase it—it was pen, indelible, but maybe I could color the whole thing out of existence. Every stroke of ink was matched by an escalating squeak from the small monstrosity on the table—an unmistakable sound of agony.

I ran around the kitchen in despair, seeing the thing hop in desperation out of the corner of my eye, and then I opened the woodstove and threw the page into the fire.

Flames scorched the table. The sound was unbearable, and the bird—if it was a bird—was consumed. I remembered reading myths about the phoenix. I prayed what I made wouldn't return, and that wherever it was—whatever I'd done—it wasn't suffering anymore.

I couldn't draw life. I could draw objects, and I could draw concepts. But life itself was too unpredictable to create in ink and pulp.

Was that why Mama ran when she saw my flower?

Mama's speed was the kind that would inspire legends, but because she kept it close and hid as much as she could, it only inspired whispers, like everything else about our family. Neil and I didn't go to school—we were never in one place long enough, and were often in such back of beyond places that I didn't know what a yellow school bus was the first time I saw one in a town, and asked my father what kind of bulldozer it was, being more familiar with highway construction than with school buildings. Papa would teach us the same way Gran said he was taught—from old textbooks, collections deaccessioned from libraries and from our grandfather's old library, from when he used to teach.

The Thorn House was remote. But the remoteness also meant the nearest town was small, and small towns were the only places where rumors could run faster than Mama herself. Her speed meant she always heard them first—she was swift but silent, and her form could be behind you before you realized you were speaking, before you recognized the words that left your mouth were unkind. She didn't tolerate it in our house, but when she heard it in the world outside, she simply fled back with the news. And the news, at some point, always added up to a message: *Time to go.*

But we hadn't left yet. We were still safe among those prickled canes, and after a morning reading philosophy and writing and rewriting sentences and equations on our little slates, like pioneers in my favorite books, I could sit on the bench with Papa and learn how to draw. He said he wasn't teaching me. He was only watching.

But I was watching him, too. I watched the caution in his eyes as he tried to conceive sketches that weren't too close to things he'd seen before, and as he pulled ideas from thin air and hoped they wouldn't pull any souls along with them. Since he had trapped the jay in my book, I paid more attention to the way he closed his eyes and breathed before setting down lines. The way he tried to mix the styles and angles in his drawings so they didn't resemble any one thing too closely.

The earliest pages in his book—the one that, like mine, he'd had since the beginning—were much less abstract. I recognized Gran's house a few pages in, teetering on a canyon's edge in the high desert with cactus and sagebrush around it, like a Gothic cathedral removed from time and place. Which it was, of course, right down to the churchyard next to it, stones carved with names I didn't know. He was trying to protect her when he drew them a new house, to house them both when his father died and couldn't anymore. He cobbled together its lengths of stone from eastern towns I'd never seen, steeples stabbing distant skies.

Gran's faith was devout and her heart was broken and they had nowhere to go, so he drew her a church. But he was only twelve, only at the start of figuring out the cost his lines could exact, and he didn't know whom he'd pull to the edges of that dusty cliff.

Papa didn't mean to trap the spirits, but he did, and now Gran lived with them. And when we stayed with her, the rest of us lived with them, too. The one I liked best was a little girl who would appear next to my shoulder when I read by flashlight late at night during weeks with my grandmother in the summertime. *Anne of Green Gables* was her favorite, I'd figured out, given how often I heard her when I read it. I tried to guess how old she was and where she'd come from, but her form wasn't usually clear enough for me to see. She did wear braids, though, and I took to calling her Anne. She didn't call me anything. She didn't speak at all—none of them did.

I wished Anne were in the Thorn House, because even with my drawing lessons, I was lonely. I saw the ghostly man and woman from time to time, but their urgency had faded like the rest of them—they seemed to have grown resigned to the futility of speaking to me, and I mostly saw them hand in hand, walking near the blackberry brambles that ringed the house, keeping their own counsel. They clearly already knew what it had taken me some time to figure out: only I could see them. They were invisible to Papa, even if he was the reason they were there.

Neil was as silent as the spirits. His hand could communicate volumes, its pudgy fingers sliding into my own when we went to pick the blackberries, but he rarely made a sound. He would sit next to me sometimes as I sketched small flowers and vines—usually in a pink book I'd asked Gran to send, which didn't seem to hold the same power as the book Papa gave me—

and point out stones and leaves he thought I should draw. He brought me a butterfly once. Bright yellow and black wings fluttered on the edge of his thumbnail, and he pointed at it with reverence, then pointed at my book. I shook my head. I couldn't bear to trap it. I still heard the jay's feathers pressing against the covers of my book at night, unable to fly away.

All three of us were on the bench together, sitting under a rainbow I drew into being to coax a smile from Neil, when Mama came back. We didn't hear her or see her until she was sitting on the dirt, long legs crossed, long hair tangled through with pine needles.

She didn't speak, and I was so tired of silence and furious she had left. "Aren't you cold?" I demanded, looking at her bare white legs against the snow.

"No." She smiled, and her smile seemed as distant as the rest of her. "I'm never cold. Are you?"

"No. Where have you been?"

"Listening." She didn't mention my flower that she'd crushed, and I didn't, either. "You took Neil to the post office, I heard. The postmaster's wife was crying when I passed. She said she didn't mean to tell anyone about the baby."

I rolled my eyes. "People never mean to tell the things they tell to Neil. He doesn't say anything."

"It's the telling that makes them afraid." Mama stood up and put her hands on Neil's round cheeks, and his eyes glowed. "People don't like to think their secrets are going anywhere."

"It's not his fault. She's the one who chose." I didn't know what the bad thing was, exactly, but the postmaster's wife was a wan, sad woman who transformed into a giggling schoolgirl, lit from within, whenever the town's librarian came into the post office for his boxes of books. I was old enough to do the math. "If her husband is mad, it's her own fault."

"People blame others hardest for the things that are their own fault." Mama's eyes, a blue as pale and clear as the ice beneath her feet, met Papa's. "It won't be long before they get here, Morrison. I heard someone say there was some cabin missing back east, near home. It's only a matter of time before they connect the dots."

Papa sighed, tearing his eyes away from Mama's and looking back down at his book. "I haven't gotten far enough on the next place. I could add a wall—"

"You already made us walls." Mama spread her arms wide, signaling the ring of thorns around us, the low-hanging trees spanning overhead, the thick log walls of our cabin. "Walls only make people more determined."

I felt a jumpy excitement start to build in my stomach. The Thorn House hadn't been home long, but ever since Papa captured the jay, the world he'd built us felt haunted and claustrophobic in a way I'd never noticed before. And my drawing lessons felt urgent, not fun. The last two weeks without Mama made everything worse. Part of me longed to leave and go someplace new. Part of me worried who would find us next, wherever that new place was.

Papa rubbed his eyes. "I'm so tired, Laila. Aren't you tired of running?" His voice was gravelly, almost beseeching.

Mama's eyes didn't waver. She didn't blink. "No."

The four of us headed inside to pack up the little we owned. Before the week was out, we washed up at Gran's house again, and Anne peeked out at me through the attic window. I thought she was smiling. I couldn't be sure.

A Portrait of Grace and Protection: Yours to Keep and Treasure

In this world of trials and troubles, everyone could use a guardian angel. At the Gregorian Treasury, we make building your very own collection of treasured angels easy and economical, providing angels of every size and shape to enrichen and protect your home. We offer commemorative plates, pillows, paintings, posters, candelabras, and night-lights: anything you could need to fill your home with the grace of heavenly protection. Our most popular print, *The Angel on the Bridge,* features a lovely guardian angel lighting the way for two frightened children over a terrifying canyon, providing the guiding light we all need in this world. A framed nine-by-twelve canvas print of this lovely image can be yours for three easy payments of $29.99 plus shipping and handling. The first one hundred purchasers will also receive *The Angel on the Bridge* printed on a high-quality woven kitchen towel. Buy now! Simply return the perforated order card at the bottom of this magazine with a check made payable to the Gregorian Treasury, and start your collection today!

8

The House in the Reeds
AUGUST 2016

THE BEACH MOTEL was one of the first places I remembered, unique enough in my memory that it was fast and simple to track down. The other places weren't so easy, and searching was exhausting. I had to accept that the simplest location would be the one where we stayed longest, and stayed last. The one where the best and worst things happened, and the last place I had an intact family before I stumbled into having one of my own.

I had to go back to where I lost everything, before I lost what was left of me. So, I drove to Hixon, Arizona, straight from the motel on the waves, stopping only for a couple of Diet Cokes and bathrooms along the way.

The last time I'd set foot in the House in the Reeds, it sat on the edge of a mud-choked pond, surrounded by fragrant ponderosas in the Keyes National Forest, a narrow spit of territory belonging only to us. I recalled the hidden dirt roads with perfect clarity, and could have easily found it myself, but I didn't know for sure if it still stood in the same place. I also didn't know who owned it if I did find it—if it would have dispersed into mist among the pines, or if it was guarded by someone with a gun and a chip on their shoulder.

I did know someone who could help me find out what I needed to know. Or at least, I knew her once—the only point in my life that I had friends, for the shortest time. And Erma Carey was exactly the same at nearly forty that she had been when I met her at fifteen—stylish, a little bit ruthless, and too curious to resist a strange request from someone she hadn't seen in more than twenty years. When I searched for her online, the polished, posh-looking website for her real estate agency was exactly what I'd expected. I called from the road on my way to Hixon, and she acted as if she'd been waiting for my call. She already had her luxury SUV ready to receive me when I arrived at the charmingly converted cottage where she'd established her office, and we only exchanged the barest niceties before I hopped into the passenger's seat and asked her to head toward the house. It was as if we were still clambering into a car to ditch math class.

And just as we had the first time we'd ever been in the same car, as teenagers, we rolled slowly down a dirt road that narrowed to the size of an unused game trail, toward a pond hardly anyone knew was there, and a home no one ever expected. I didn't entirely expect to find it even now, but there it stood, green and moldering siding reflecting onto stagnant water. I didn't say a word when Erma stopped the car. I opened the door and immediately started picking my way down toward the front doors.

"It's been on the market forever," Erma called from the gravel street, where she balanced on the toes of her red-bottomed heels and tried not to slip down the hill. She'd already remarked on the contrast between us several times when we bumped over what was left of the dirt road in her polished Land Rover. She kept smoothing her manicured fingertips over her well-coiffed hair as if I might mimic her, or might be inspired to neaten my rough ponytail under its crumpled baseball cap. I said very little, and she seemed as determined as she always had been to draw me out.

I could buy and sell every item Erma wore—Chanel suit and sunglasses, Birkin bag—and the car she wore it in, and think no more of it than a fast-food value meal. She knew it, and I knew it, but she couldn't let it go. It was like watching her in algebra all over again, trying to puzzle out why I could do everyone's group work without much effort and still wind up with a C average. I didn't make sense to her when we were teenagers, and I didn't make sense to her now.

"Has anyone even lived here since we left?" I called back up the hill. "It looks abandoned."

"Mostly raccoons, recently." Erma shut her car door and crossed her arms, but made no effort to come closer. "I haven't done much of a title search. It was bank owned when you all skipped town, but I'm guessing you already knew that."

"I didn't." I never thought Papa dealt with banks. I wasn't sure he dealt with any parts of the workaday world people lived in, but of course he must have—to feed and clothe us, he would have had to, I thought. Not everything started between the covers of his sketchbook. I still wasn't entirely sure that anything had started there, in childhood memories glazed over with magic, like a fever dream. How many of us can parse what was real and pretend?

I gazed across the pond and remembered swimming with Neil in the middle of the night, giggling, thinking how much trouble we'd be in if we had the kind of parents who enforced rules. Instead, by the time we reached that pondside place, we had a mother who had faded almost beyond view and a father whose gaze passed through us like glass. "I never knew anything other than it was time to go."

"It sure must have been, but it looks like the bank couldn't unload the place when you left. I haven't been inside, but the appraiser told me the smell'll knock you back a bit. Every so often they'd get some patrols out here to scare off squatters, but other than that, it's been pretty untouched since you were here. Which wasn't long."

"A little over a year. Longer than most places." I picked my way through the swamp to the front door of the house and grabbed the padlock securing the chain around the iron handles. They were hand forged, Papa's design, tugged and twisted in their molten form until they reached the shape he wanted. I was surprised no one had tried to take them, but then again, maybe I wasn't the only one who felt the way the air hung in this place, draped like Spanish moss spun out of grief. "Did you bring the key?"

"I'm a real estate agent, Carrie. We don't carry keys. There should be a lockbox—I've got the combination."

I looked up at her and smiled, ignoring her deliberate slight of using the nickname she'd picked for me when we were kids. "Are you going to help me look for the lockbox?"

"Not a chance in hell."

"That doesn't sound like someone motivated for a commission, Erma," I singsonged back.

"You don't think I read up on you? You can buy this place no matter what I do. That *Forbes* write-up about you and your husband and your charitable foundation was a little fawning for my taste, honestly, but I found it pretty quick after your call, and we both know I don't have to fight to make a sale. You've got the money, and you're going to buy whatever you want to—or not. I'll get a commission, or not. There's nothing a little ol' nobody like me can do to sway a person like you either way."

"There are other agents who might be more motivated."

"Then call one of them." Erma shrugged.

I strode up the hill to her car and held out my hand, waiting for the combination, until she slapped a sticky note onto my palm. I kicked a little bit of mud up when I turned on my heel to pick my way back down to the house. "You're already here." I found the lockbox hidden in an overgrown juniper shrub and retrieved the key. I pushed the key into the rusting padlock, which resisted for a moment before clicking open. "I'll be back out in a minute."

"Speaking of your husband, does he know about this little buyer's spree down memory lane?" she called after me. "Feel free to tell me it's none of my business, but color me curious—"

"It's none of your business, Erma." I didn't turn around as I tugged at the rusted door handles. "You didn't care what happened to me when we were kids, so I don't know why you'd care about my family now."

"Hey, Keryth?" Her voice dropped an octave, with an unusual weight pinning down her usual flightiness.

At this, I turned. I couldn't remember Erma ever calling me by my real name. "What?"

"I'm not good at this. I mean, not *this*—" She waved her hands, gesturing toward the house and the SUV and, presumably, her successful career. "This, I'm great at. But I'm not good at—look, let me keep thinking. Forget I said anything."

I frowned. "Consider it done. I'll be right back."

The wide double doors resisted my pulling for a moment, and I had to push hard against the left one to creak the right one open, but I knew I'd succeeded when the stench hit me in the face. I took a deep breath of the air outside and held it in my lungs, walking inside.

The carpet was the same as it had been when we lived there, and that probably accounted for at least part of the smell—its mottled expanse of lumpy shag was, most likely, soaked with the output of every animal, human and otherwise, who had squatted there. I heard scurrying to my left and decided it was better not to look.

The wide windows at the back of the house were, miraculously, still intact beneath the wood beams that stretched across the open main room. The kitchen to the left was denuded of appliances but still had most of its cabinets. The grime concealed the gleam of their spalted maple burls, a finish more appropriate for hand-turned wood bowls than for messy kitchens, but Papa never crafted anything practical. Everything had movement and life.

I walked back outside to take another gulp of air and saw Erma on her phone, leaning against the front of her SUV. She tilted her head to one side and gave me a thumbs-up—*are we done?*—and I shook my head and went back inside.

The hallway to the bedrooms was longer than I remembered, but part of the reason was the wall of mirrors at the end, reflecting back an image of my mud-splattered jeans and torn flannel shirt that made me do a double take: I would have worn the same outfit at fifteen. No wonder Erma couldn't stop staring.

The red glow at the end of the hall told me that my parents' old bedroom still sported its crimson carpet. The whole place was a Frankenhouse—Papa's favorite kind of project, a building with good bones and terrible taste, paneled and carpeted and decorated with whatever remainders were cheapest at a salvage store or teardown, or whatever details were pulled by accident or design into his book. I wasn't sure where in the world the carpet and other ugly comforts had come from, but I always thought the House in the Reeds itself may have drawn inspiration from some western library, with its open ceilings and bookcase-sized niches. We didn't have many books yet—we always relied on Gran's library for our learning. There was a single piece of artwork hanging in an alcove, though. It was the same image that appeared in every place we ever lived—a print of a painting my gran had created long ago that had become popular with people searching for comfort. An angel on a bridge, lighting the way for two small children in the midst of a storm. It seemed lonely there, darkened by age and mold, barely visible anymore. Papa always meant to stay in one place long enough to fill our shelves. He always meant to replace everything that didn't fit. But he never did. The closer projects were to completion, the closer we were to leaving—if we got to stay long in the first place.

I stood for a moment in a glowing square of rose-colored sunlight and hesitated, trying to pull some message from the air. I heard the scurrying sound again and glanced around in time to see a flash of black and white. Not raccoons, then. Skunks. I remembered the bathroom had a patio door—one of many perplexing features—and decided I'd exit that way rather than return to the front entry. Papa used to watch us from that bathroom door, clicking on the patio light to guide our way home in the dark after we snuck out to swim and paddle across the water behind the house. We thought we were so clever, but we were never really alone. Not back then.

I rested my hand against the light switch, gazing out the window. The switch plate beneath my hand felt warm, and then too hot to touch. *Just my luck*, I thought. *Electrical problems.* And then I remembered there was no power—no utilities at all—that were still operating in the house.

Papa. I couldn't say why, but I knew there was something there.

The folding multi-tool in my pocket made quick work of the switch plate beside the door, and I found a void next to the stud where the switch was installed, just large enough for me to reach my fingers inside. The hole was mostly empty—no note, no treasure—but a few shreds of paper fluttered in the breeze from the open room behind me. I pinched a few out with my fingers and uncurled them, recognizing the deep shading of Papa's charcoal sketching and a few fragments of newsprint and handwriting too deteriorated to read. The sketches were slightly textured, the same light tooth under my thumbs that I remembered from his sketchbooks, but the book itself was missing. I couldn't make enough of the scraps to discern what drawing they once formed.

I gently rolled the papers and tucked them into the fleece pocket of my hoodie. When I rested my temple against the moldering wallpaper with its sprigged roses, the voice that screamed into my head was so loud I almost collapsed. I clawed my bitten fingernails over my ears, desperate as an animal in a trap, because that was what the voice felt like—an animal that couldn't escape. An animal that sounded like Neil. My brother.

I pressed my forehead against the wall again and listened, but all I heard was rustling. Termites, probably. And not a whisper of anyone else.

I unlocked the patio door and yanked it open, its foam insulation disintegrating with a loud smacking sound. I picked my way back around to the front of the house and saw Erma had gotten back in the car, the engine already running. I climbed up the hill and got back into the passenger's seat.

"Bad as they say?" she asked, looking up from the laptop she had propped against the steering wheel.

"Worse."

"I'm sorry." She sighed. "There! That wasn't so hard. I'm sorry I was snarky and gossipy instead of really trying to talk. I'm really sorry the house is in bad shape. I'm sorry about what happened here. I'm sorry about—Jesus, this making amends stuff is hard—I'm sorry I was a total bitch to you in high school. And I'm glad you called me, even if I'm not sure why you did." She stopped, her face redder than the pricey blush swiped across her cheekbones. "I rehearsed that the whole time you were down there."

I blinked. "Why?"

Erma gritted her teeth. "Fifty percent because I'm in a program where apologizing is . . . kinda part of the deal. And fifty percent because the first thing Toby is going to ask me is whether I did it."

"Tobias?" My breath quickened, and my heart felt as if it might pound out of my chest. I tried—unsuccessfully—to conceal both effects. "You still talk to Tobias?"

Erma laughed, and twenty years fell away. "We do have some catching up to do. But later. What about the house?"

I folded my hand around the ruined scraps of paper in my pocket. I still heard my brother's voice reverberating through my head. "How soon can we close?"

My sweet boy,

I'm touched that you want to tell the stories yourself, but you don't have the knack, I don't think. Listening to stories is never the same as telling them, not even if you've heard them your whole life. I've been making them up to keep myself company since I was a child, and I painted pictures of them almost as long, before I stopped. It hurt your father, and then it hurt you, and I didn't want to anymore. Words were safer, though the good Lord knows they can do plenty of damage all on their own.

Also, I'm afraid if I let you tell the kids stories about Keryth and Neil, they won't care to hear them from their gran anymore. Everyone loves to hear themselves woven into a tale. I still wish you'd asked me before you named them, but I guess their arrival was a surprise, and you did the best you could. It's not as if you and Laila had a lot of time to delve into those baby name books, for all that they weren't babies anyway. And I never prepared you for what to do, but to my credit, you'd never done it. Still, I've included a treasury of fairy tales for you to read to the children, and those should be more interesting than my old stories, anyway.

Have you tried to do it again? I won't write her name. I know you didn't mean it. I just can't bear to think of her, even after all this time, alone on that bridge. I tried with the paintings. You tried, too, I know. And the children are a blessing. But I miss her every day.

Don't think I lose sight of the blessings that I have when I think of the ones I don't. I worry that you do sometimes. Those children need their father, and you can't spend every minute trying to make the life you don't have and forget the one you do. It's hard to remember. Sometimes it helps to pray.

All my love to you, and kiss the babies.
MA

9

·· · • ● ● ● • · ··

The House on the Waves
AUGUST 2016

I COULD HEAR the echo of Max's voice bouncing around the house, adding a call-and-response rhythm to his questions. "Is this the last one?" *the last one* "Keryth, there aren't any others, are there?" *are there are there are*

"There are." I was sitting in the threadbare wing chair by the window in the bed-and-breakfast where Erma arranged for me to stay. I pictured my husband in his sleek executive chair on the polished marble floor of his office, the emptiest room in our too-empty house above the crashing Pacific waves. I shivered at the memory of too much air and too few soft surfaces, and drew a knitted throw tighter around my shoulders. "There are more, Max."

His sigh shook the receiver. "How many more?"

"I don't know yet. I haven't done much research."

"You're lying, Keryth. All you do is research."

"You used to think it was sweet."

"That was back when you'd do it on an old laptop next to me in bed. Remember? Pretending we couldn't see that stained ceiling in our first apartment."

I looked up. "The ceiling here could use a fresh coat, now that you mention it."

"Stop deflecting me. I haven't laid eyes on you in days." The clinking of change stopped, and his voice became softer. "The kids haven't laid eyes on you in days. You left without even checking in. If Anthony hadn't told me about you leaving straight from that weird beach motel, I wouldn't have had any idea where you were headed. I'd wonder if you were ever planning to come back at all."

I felt my mouth setting in a hard line. I had tried to tell him a million times what was happening to me, and never found the words to explain. I wasn't sure why. Perhaps it was because I'd felt myself disappearing for years before I ever saw my absent hand in that mirror. "Have the girls said anything?"

"Would it matter if they had? Would you come back?"

"If they really needed me."

"That's the thing, Keryth. You don't get to decide what needing you looks like, or when it might happen. If you aren't here, you've decided it doesn't matter if they need you or not."

"Dr. Grace would say you're dictating how to parent, Max, instead of listening—"

"You have to be around for me to listen to, Keryth!" He bit my name off with his too-white teeth. "I'm sorry. I didn't mean to raise my voice."

"Yes, you did. But I understand." I looked at the wedding band on my hand. "You ever think we did this way too young?"

"Every goddamn day. You ever think we ought to stop doing it?"

"Some days. But I'm still planning on coming home."

"When?"

"I don't know." I pulled a pencil from its place behind my ear, drawn into old habits better left alone. The legal pad on my lap was already filled with doodles from aimless conversations just like this one. I sketched a trio of stick figures, two with long and stylized ringlets, one tall with straight hair receding from his temples, if a circle can have temples. Nothing too detailed. Easy to deny. Sketched hearts between them all, no spaces. No missing figures. No missing anything or anyone at all.

Max sighed, and I felt the resignation of his breath in my bones. His voice returned to brisk and polished business. "Have you considered getting any help to move this mission of yours along?"

"Funny you should ask. There's a girl—a woman—someone I used to know. She's a real estate agent now. I thought she might be interested in pitching in." I didn't mention that I felt Erma's talons tugging at the edges of my reality in a way that was both exhausting and liberating—she would gladly take over any detail I asked her to if it meant digging into what she clearly thought was a delicious mystery, and I wouldn't have to worry about tracking down the houses anymore. I could focus on uncovering whatever was left inside their walls. I could focus on Neil's voice, still careening inside my skull, as tangible as the memory of his fingers laced through mine. "She's very . . . assertive. But I think she'll be a big help with getting this house back into shape, and she'd be able to help me find the others."

"Are you suggesting we put her on retainer? Something like that?"

"I don't know what I'm suggesting. But I'm betting she'll be able to tell me." I took a deep breath. "I'm tired, Max."

"I don't know how much longer I can live like this." Max punctuated his words with a tapping, and I knew he was neatening a stack of papers on his glass desk, making sure not a single page was out of place. I wondered if they were divorce papers. I wondered if I cared.

"I don't, either. But I got through today, and so did you, and we'll pick up where we left off tomorrow, I guess."

"Do you want to talk to the girls? They aren't home, but after ballet and soccer practice, Ellory will bring them home, and—"

"And they know how to call me themselves." They had already, both of them, without any prompting by Max, and I bristled at the unspoken message beneath his words—that he thought he needed to facilitate my relationship with our daughters. It wasn't perfect, and it wasn't predictable, but I had one. They were both at an age that I had to wait for whatever dregs of social interaction they decided to send my way after other, more interesting obligations. And, yes, after Max himself, because it had always been clear to me that he was the favorite, his ease with and indulgence of them the precise opposite of the way he interacted with the world at large and, in recent years, with me.

Ellory was eighteen, and the fact that she had her own car was almost enough to make Mindy put up with her older sister's bragging. At fifteen, she'd be getting her learner's permit soon, and Max had already taken her car shopping. I knew because she texted me a picture of a convertible with its top down, blue as the sky above it, with the message "so cute & so fast!" I called Max and asked him not to buy it—which is how I asked him for anything now: from a distance. He told me we'd discuss it. Which meant he'd already bought it.

I didn't trust myself to get any closer, to try to be part of these decisions or stop them before they were made. Max didn't understand. Our daughters didn't understand. But the danger I posed to them had always been greater than they knew, and it grew with every crumbling wall I searched for spirits and messages.

Max and I stayed silent on the line for what felt like an hour, staring at our respective ceilings, low and high. I didn't know he'd hung up until I went to end the call myself and saw he'd already done so. I didn't know when. Maybe it had been five minutes. Maybe it had been five years. When it came to timing the ending of things, I'd always been a terrible judge.

HARTLEY AND ELSON FAMILIES JOINED IN MATRIMONY (from *The Heatherton Times-Ledger*, June 5, 1954): Mr. and Mrs. Robert Hartley of Heatherton, Virginia, announce the marriage of their son, Grayson Hartley, to Elizabeth Maria Elson, daughter of Mr. and Mrs. Samuel Elson, also of Heatherton. In August, the newlyweds will be moving to Maryland, where Mr. Grayson Hartley has accepted a position teaching mathematics at Sacred Heart Academy, a private parochial school. Mrs. Hartley continues to cultivate an amateur interest in painting and storytelling, and hopes to apply those skills as a volunteer with the children at Sacred Heart. She is looking forward to devoting herself to her new role as a wife and homemaker, and the family hopes, soon, as a mother. The Hartley and Elson families will welcome friends and honored guests at the Hartley home for a celebratory reception on Saturday, June 12, at two o'clock in the afternoon, in honor of the happy couple.

10

The House Where God Lived
FEBRUARY 1987

PAPA SETTLED GRAN'S house on the edge of a canyon's wall, but he hadn't meant to put it there. It may have been the house that chose the site itself, because the rocky cliff beneath it mirrored the structure above like the distorting surface of a lake—cragged and shadowed and bowed in ways that seemed impossible. Impossible, too, the arches of a bridge tacked haphazardly to the canyon's edge and leading out to nowhere before tumbling away, half a stone rainbow with two iron rails laid on top, reflecting the light before ending abruptly. The twin rails had a symmetry the church's steeples lacked, reaching into the azure desert sky, bunched like gossiping church matrons gathered after morning services. The churchyard, too, was incomplete, curved lengths of wrought iron fencing trailing off toward the cliff. The headstones tumbled without sufficient support in the dry and dusty soil. We did our best to care for them, even though they weren't our people. We didn't know whose people they were. But we didn't have people of our own, so the churchyard's residents became our friends, even though they couldn't tell us who they were or where they came from.

Our grandfather wasn't among them, but we visited him anyway. Whenever we arrived at her house, Gran would hand us each a candle and a match, and we would light our flames for his soul beneath the cracked stained glass next to the wide front doors, kneel on padded leather, and tell him hello. He stared straight ahead from his wedding portrait with Gran, looking older than his years at the time he stood in front of a priest and married her. His suit was the same sedate and conservative cut he wore when he taught mathematics to young pupils in parochial schools, and the same garment I thought he always must have worn; he was also besuited in the only other picture I'd ever seen of him. Gran kept that one under her pillow and kissed it before she went to sleep. Her bedroom was like a stone grotto full of devotional images and candles—saints, angels, and dead husband.

Gran had painted most of the pictures herself. Her images had a depth—a dimensionality—that always seemed to bring them to life beneath flickering candlelight. My very favorite was one that followed us everywhere and hung in every house we ever lived: an angel with a star trapped in a lantern, lighting the way for two small children on a dark bridge, a storm-tossed sky above them. The image was small and framed in silver, and the light from the lantern was so real it seemed to illuminate Gran's dark room. The painting was almost too bright to look at for long. Papa told me Gran had painted it a long time ago, after my grandfather died. She took it to her childhood church to have it blessed, and the preacher was so taken with it that he convinced her to let him have prints made for sale, as support for the grieving widow. No one could have predicted the success it encountered, printed on paper and notecards, pillows and blankets, calendars, countless images of protective grace and guiding light. We had the original and a few copies she'd painted herself, but it was always a surprise to see a version of her art in every house we entered, as if it was waiting for us. Waiting to be found.

We weren't allowed in Gran's room for long—only long enough to retrieve a book she'd forgotten or a teacup that needed washing, bouncing our eyes around the images before we returned to her, homing pigeons on a mission.

Whenever we arrived for visits—or what we called visits, but were more accurately described as "moving in"—Gran would stand next to us and tell our grandfather all about us. "Keryth lost another tooth," she would whisper. "And Neil can climb the rope swing all the way to the top now. They've both gotten so tall, Grayson, don't you think?"

The wedding portrait—two smiling people in traveling clothes, impossibly young—flickered in the candlelight, and Gran paused until she heard whatever answer came from the dim, still air around us, and then we were released to settle in.

When Papa's father died, Papa was only twelve years old. Though Papa spoke little of his father, it always sounded as if they were never in one place for very long. Having an unusual family that didn't quite fit anywhere seemed to be a lifelong condition. Grayson Hartley never had trouble finding work—a skilled math teacher was always in demand—but keeping a position seemed harder, and Papa always made it sound as if that had less to do with my grandfather and more to do with his wife.

The family was on their way to a new home just outside Baltimore to start again, but first, they were traveling to visit their hometown. Instead, my grandfather's heart stopped on a train, and the transitory nature of that in-between place—not somewhere else, and not yet home—haunted Gran. In the time it took for Papa to find a conductor and ask for help, our grandfather's spirit had left his body behind. Gran had never stopped trying to recall it. She convinced herself she could until she made it true. None of the rest of us heard him, but Gran chattered on with our grandfather as if he'd just walked, moments before, into another room, and all she had to do was call after him to ask what he might want for dinner.

Papa came in behind us and tried to sidle past his mother, but she whispered toward our grandfather's portrait, "Morrison thinks I don't see him, and he's far too important to kiss his poor mother hello. He's gotten a bit jowly, Gray. You never had an extra ounce on you, but I think he must take after—"

"Hello, Mother," Papa said, and kissed Gran surreptitiously on the cheek while accepting a candle. "Hello, Father," he said to the portrait.

"He's wondering why you're back so soon," Gran said. "And while we always love to have you, I have to say I'm wondering the same thing, dear."

"People were talking about Neil." I couldn't resist talking first. "It's not his fault."

"Of course it isn't, sweet darling boy." Gran knelt and put her hands on Neil's cheeks, the same way Mama had. "A face like an angel, this one has, always. Folks can't help themselves from wanting to tell him every little thing, and who can blame them?" She kissed the top of Neil's head, and my brother's face shone with light. "Where is your mama, honey?" Gran's expression was full of concern, and I noticed for the first time, in the glow of the candles, how angular her face had become. The hollows beneath her cheekbones were deeper than I remembered.

Papa frowned. "She isn't here yet? She should have beaten us here."

Gran shook her head. "No. But she'll turn up. She always does at one time or another, doesn't she? It's how she was made."

I thought of the fence in my book, the unbroken heart atop

the spires. *Doesn't she?* Yes, usually. Eventually. *It's how she was made.* How was she made? There was less and less of her each time she returned—less of her to see when she ran away. At times, her form seemed barely corporeal; she'd gotten pulled over a few weeks before on the way home from the store, with Neil and me in the back seat. She wasn't speeding or swerving. The deputy just said, *I didn't see anyone driving those children. I didn't see anyone at all,* and his voice had a kind of distant and awestruck tone as he swayed next to the window, and Mama just reached out and touched his forearm and said, "But now you do, sir, don't you?" And he nodded and staggered back to his squad car without another word. He was still sitting, lights spinning their red and blue rhythm, when we drove away. He may be sitting there still.

Papa stared at his mother. "Yes, she always comes back. Let's not hold dinner. The kids are hungry. It was a long drive this time."

"I don't have much prepared. There's some spaghetti in the kitchen, I think, and maybe fixin's for sandwiches. It's been a while since I went to the store."

Papa looked sharply at her. "Why, Ma?"

Gran shrugged. "I haven't been feeling my best." She sighed. "You may have noticed."

"I have. I keep trying to find another anchor for her. It's been getting worse."

"Why didn't the kids go with Laila?"

Papa looked at her knowingly. "She isn't always as . . . present as she needs to be. To drive the kids, anyway. So she took the truck. And the kids can spread out more in the wagon anyway, so that's what I drove."

"And do you have some idea where you may take it next? Or are you thinking you'll stay for a spell again?"

"Papa hasn't finished the next place yet," I said.

Gran gave me a sharp look. "I think we've talked about speaking when you're spoken to, Keryth. You know better than that."

"Yes, ma'am." I kept gazing at her, waiting for space in the conversation to ask when we would eat dinner, and what it would be, and whether she would tell us another "Adventures of Keryth and Neil" story after we got ready for bed. My grandmother's storytelling was second only to her artistic talent, but my favorite moments were when she wove them both together, painting wide strokes of stories onto canvas and bringing their images to life with her brush. The Keryth and Neil for whom my brother and I were named were considerably more intrepid—and royal—than we were, but hearing our names in a story was exciting, even if those stories never left my grandmother's house.

Gran didn't notice my held breath or air of expectation, and continued to talk only to my father. "Maybe it's for the best that you don't have something else lined up yet, Morrison. You let these babies go feral every time you settle somewhere else. Have you ever thought of maybe putting something together here—"

"You know I don't have a say, Mother. Not really. And least of all in where things show up." Papa didn't look at Gran and looked instead as if he was speaking to our grandfather, the long shadows of his portraited face cast into flickering relief by the candlelight, the soot of countless candles darkening his gray eyes to a deeper shade of smoke. "I can't stop until I find all of her and see if that will be enough, or if I can make it be enough. And when I'm here, I can't make anything at all."

Gran put her hand on Papa's shoulder. "Have you ever thought that maybe you could listen to them? Instead of trying to run away?" She patted a stone wall with a familiar hand, like someone might pet a large dog. "Ghosts aren't the worst company."

"The ones who are used to thinking of themselves that way,

maybe. The ones who didn't mean to be are a different breed entirely." As usual, Mama's voice was soft, but each word carried a weight like a smooth stone dropped in a deep well. None of us had heard her arrive, but none of us jumped. We were all too accustomed to it. "It's not easy to feel trapped."

Something in the way her words landed made me want to throw my arms around Mama and protest. I wanted to yell, *You aren't trapped. We aren't a trap. We love you.* I didn't know what she meant, or what she was trying to escape from. I rejected wholesale the idea that there were conversations I wasn't yet old enough to have, and stories I wasn't yet strong enough to hear. I only knew that she was Mama, and Mama was always quicksilver, lithe brightness pouring over my fingers before I could grasp her properly.

My grandmother nodded at Mama the way you'd nod at someone making a point you disagree with but you know the gulf between you is too wide to start to bridge it. "Every spirit needs a place to land," Gran said. "And not one of us has the power to pick where that place is. Not really."

I reached for my mother's hand, and she clasped mine for the briefest of moments before patting my back and pulling away. "Where are you going?" I asked.

"I'll be back," she said. "Take care of your brother."

"What about Papa?" My parents still hadn't greeted each other—Papa hadn't stopped looking at his father's portrait, their eyes locked as if having a conversation that none of us could hear.

"Papa can take care of himself," she said. And then she was gone.

"Right," said Gran, suddenly all bustle and business. "Keryth, why don't you come help me throw some things onto the table for dinner. What do you think?"

"Can we make spaghetti?"

"Yes."

"Can I boil it?"

"I suppose so. Come on."

I followed Gran into the kitchen and felt Neil's feet padding close behind me, silent as a shadow. The kitchen was usually toward the back of the house, but sometimes to the left or the right, and I could never tell if its changing location was due to my own shifting memories or because the room itself would move. But its features were always the same: an avocado refrigerator with an old-fashioned latch that Gran had told us repeatedly, in no uncertain terms, that we were to never, ever touch, because she was terrified at the idea of one of us getting trapped inside it and smothering. A mustard-yellow enamel sink, low and wide, chipped at one corner. The stove was my favorite, sprawling and white, with two ovens that seemed too small for the footprint the stove occupied. Each of the six burners played host to a cheerful blue flame, ready to lick the bottom of any pot, but I wasn't allowed to turn the knobs that brought them to life. Gran would let me stir a pot if I stood on a sturdy stool, halfway behind her, so she could be sure I wouldn't fall without her catching the flames first. But I was allowed to bring her the box of spaghetti and stir it with the sauce once she turned the burner off again.

I didn't know the box was already open, and when I grabbed the wrong end, the long, straight lengths of pasta dumped onto the floor, landing in an abstract pile that stretched toward the stove I hadn't reached yet. "Oh no! Gran, I'm sorry!" I said. I knelt to the floor, and Neil knelt beside me, trying to help me gather up the noodles.

"Oh, honey. That's okay. It's an old box anyway—let me get another one from the pantry." As she walked past us, she looked at the stiff mess of pasta on the floor and paused. "It's almost pretty, isn't it? Like an art installation. It looks a little like one of those spiky bridges back east."

I'd never seen one, and my only real frame of reference for a bridge was the incomplete, broken one outside. "I guess so," I said.

"Delacroix used to say pictures are bridges for the soul, did you know that? Between the artist and the person looking. Maybe that stuff didn't land that way on accident. Maybe someone's trying to tell us something." A distracted smile played across Gran's face, and I heard a giggle from the next room. "Anyway, you kids are probably starving. Let me get that other box."

Later, after we'd mixed the new spaghetti with a dusty glass jar full of bland tomato sauce and headed upstairs to don the pajamas Gran always kept on hand for us—mine had gotten too small again, but Neil's always seemed to fit—we burrowed into our matching twin beds in our upstairs room, and Gran sat on the upright chair between us and offered to tell us a story. I always answered yes, for both of us.

"The bridge between the living and the dead isn't open for everyone," she started, as she always did. "You've got to get in good with those who can pass across it, and they don't choose just anyone, you know."

"Who can pass?" I asked.

"Those who can keep a toe in each world, for one thing. God, certainly, but He's got plenty to do and not much time to do it in, so He tends to stay on the other side of things, away from this one. He sends messengers, though. Angels. And saints. And they can choose others to cross."

"Who can they choose?"

"Oh, all sorts of people. Anyone worthy, anyone exceptional. Chosen folks."

"Like Princess Keryth?"

"Of course! She's a storyteller and an artist, a creative, just like her little brother, Prince Neil. You know. They could charm the birds out of the sky and the butterflies out of the trees. The angels always took them across, if they wanted to go."

"Did they ever go all the way across?"

"Well, it was a little scary, you know. The Kingdom of Heaven, wondrous though it was, it was also the land of the dead. It was full of saints and treasures and miracles, and the greatest miracles—the greatest treasures—are the ones we've lost. But it's hard to reach them without wondering whether you'll come back yourself. I don't know if that little princess and her brother ever felt safe going all the way across."

"What about you, Gran? Did you ever cross the bridge?"

"Not with my feet, sweet girl. But with my brush, yes, I made that bridge and crossed it, so many times. I made it sturdy and safe as I could, and I lit it with starlight borne by a guardian angel. I didn't want anyone who crossed it to feel alone."

In the dim light of our room, slouching in that upright chair, Gran looked older than I remembered, and almost as still as one of her own paintings. "Gran? Are you ever lonely? When we aren't here?"

"Everyone's lonely sometimes, Keryth. But part of you is always here with me. Because I love you, and love's its own kind of bridge for your soul, honey. Just like a picture. It can bear you across loss and absence, if you let it. If you're willing to be a bit scared."

"I'm brave, Gran."

"I know you are, sweet girl." She pressed her forehead against mine. "All the smart ones need to be."

My sweet boy,

I don't know why I haven't learned by now that you
don't do things halfway, but your little cabin in the
woods won't evade attention for long, not that you
didn't manage to site it in the back of beyond, from
what you've said. The Nelsons—well, nasty, judgmen-
tal folk though they were—weren't disliked, and they
certainly weren't unknown, and even a cross-country
relocation via charcoal and paper won't be enough to
shut Ruth Nelson up, honey. She always was a talker.

But that's not what concerns me. What do you
mean, "the children like it here," Morrison? What
children? Please tell me the Nelsons didn't have their
grandbabies with them when you grabbed the place,
or then we'll all be done for. And you and Laila
can't—haven't—you didn't, right? I know, it's not the
sort of thing one discusses with one's mother, but
needs must, honey. What have you done?

I can't come up there myself, and I can't help but
think you know that, and that's why you've swung for
the fences, somehow. I know you want to keep her. I
know this is my fault! But there's got to be limits to
what you take, and who, and how. Take it from me. If
you don't set limits for yourself, you can't imagine
what you might lose.

I know you'll think that's about her. But it isn't.

Please tell me all the truth, and don't pull a Miss Dickinson. Don't tell it slant. I don't know if I can help, but I definitely can't if you aren't straight with me.

All my love,
MA

11

The House on the Waves
AUGUST 2016

IT TOOK A few days to arrange the closing on the House in the Reeds, but as soon as the deal was complete, I headed back home. Or tried to, at any rate. One minute, I was cruising down the freeway (figuratively, anyway, given that the cruise control hadn't worked in years), and a moment later, a cloud of smoke made the freeway invisible. A clunking sound beneath the hood grew louder as I pulled over to the shoulder and rolled to a stop.

"Harold, are there any mechanics nearby?"

My father-in-law's voice emerged from the phone I'd tucked into one drink holder. "Well, kiddo, it depends on what you mean by 'nearby.' If you're a fan of walking, I'd say no. Are we having car trouble?"

"We're not moving, and we're smoking, so I'd say yes."

"My olfactory sensors are still in beta. Did Max tell you? I'm getting olfactory sensors. It's very exciting. I don't know how they'll work yet, but I'm just tickled at the idea—"

"Harold?"

"Ah. Yes. Sorry. What does it smell like?"

"I don't know. Like—water burning on a stove, maybe? When you're cooking eggs and it boils over?"

"Uh-oh, kiddo. It sounds like your radiator may be shot."

"Are you telling me that because you know what's wrong, or because it sounds plausible enough to make me think you do?"

"Well, now, that depends. Do you know how to fix a radiator?"

"No."

"Then it really doesn't matter, does it? I think you'd be better off calling out for reinforcements."

"Right. Well, thanks so much for your help, Harold."

"Is that sarcasm? I haven't been a computer for as long as I was a dad yet, so I still know how to hear—"

"Go to sleep, Harold."

I had, at least, allowed Max to equip me with the latest in global phone technology; there was no place on earth I couldn't get a signal, and I sent up a quiet note of gratitude to the sky when I dialed Erma's number and asked if she might, just possibly, be able to arrange a driver to transport me back to Malibu.

I should have known that she would offer to take me herself. I heard the click of her heels on the blacktop surface of her office parking lot before my request had fully left my mouth. When she pulled off the freeway next to my smoking sedan, the cloud of dust behind her SUV made me think of the old road-runner cartoons, spinning legs churning up storms of desert dirt. Erma was all speed—fast talking, fast moving, fast reflexes—but wealth and power stopped her in her tracks. They always had.

Soon after I climbed into the passenger seat, my phone whirred back to life. "Didja manage to catch a ride, kiddo? I'll let Max know."

I yanked my phone out of my pocket and saw Harold's spinning nimbus on my screen. "I thought I told you to go to sleep?"

"You left your car."

"So?"

"There are sensors in your car." A pause—which I chose to interpret as embarrassment, while picturing a virtual blush. "You're too far from them now."

I set my mouth in a thin line. "Right. And who put the sensors there?"

"Can't be too careful these days," Harold said.

"Okay—wait. Carrie?" Erma said. "Who are you talking to?"

"One long, never-ending dad joke I keep in my pocket."

"I don't know whether to be offended or flattered by that," Harold said.

"Did you get some kind of custom voice for your phone's Siri or Alexa or whatever?" Erma asked.

"Something like that," I said. "This is Harold. He's . . . complicated."

"Hey! I resemble that remark." If he still had eyebrows to waggle, I felt certain he would have done so.

Erma and I rolled our eyes spontaneously. "He's Max's—well, he was Max's dad," I said. "Now he's AI, and he's—"

"Harold! Oh, I've seen the articles. You sure have gotten yourself into interesting circles since you left boring old Hixon, haven't you? You know there's a picture of you hanging in the high school? Someone clipped out an article from somewhere—the *Times* or something—and framed it in a plaque and put it on the 'Distinguished Alumni' wall. How do I know? Because I'm on the wall, too, not that they gave little old me a plaque or anything—"

Erma chatted at me for the rest of the drive, and I lost track of the time in a way that made me fear—for a moment—that I might have blacked out again. But, no, the road back home seemed as interminable as I remembered, and I didn't lose the thread of Erma's prattle, never heard her exclaim I'd disappeared.

I tuned out as best I could the whole way to my crushed granite driveway.

When we arrived to my house on the coast, the whistle that escaped from Erma's lips was less elegant, and considerably less polished, than the meticulously coiffed woman it escaped from. She slid off the leather driver's seat and alighted on her spiked heels, her head tilted like the mockingbird her gravelly whistle evoked.

"Carrie, Carrie, Carrie." Erma smoothed her hair, though there wasn't a single strand out of place. The gesture showed off her nails, dragon-underbelly pink, the ring fingers studded with rhinestones like treasure. "Look who's all grown up and moved into a fairy tale. No wonder you decided to keep your legs. Is Prince Eric inside?"

"That's it. That's your one allowable Disney princess reference for the day. You've used up your allotment. Please don't be weird."

"Please don't be weird? Carrie." Erma's laughter trilled, more birdlike than ever. Not a mockingbird. A magpie. "You drop back into my life after dropping out of it when we were sixteen, asking me to help you buy a cruddy, falling-down shack and, while I'm at it, help you chase down who knows how many other cruddy, falling-down shacks so you can buy them, too. And then, you need a ride, just by the by, to Malibu. Where you live. In goddamn splendor. Meanwhile, you're wearing jeans I think we bought together when we were sophomores in high school, and you're in a hoodie and a promotional T-shirt from Big Dick's Tire Emporium. Plus gloves, for some reason, and—when was the last time you showered, anyway? I'm sorry. I'm rambling. Point is, if I'm the weird one, you've got some black stuff rubbing off your pot, and it's staining my fancy kettle."

I looked at her custom-tailored suit—hot-pink houndstooth—and sighed. "I think any stains'll blend right in."

"Am I interrupting an *Odd Couple* moment? I can come back." Max stood under the wide front pergola of our house, his careworn face dappled by the light that filtered through the bougainvillea vines. "You must be Erma," he said, without moving toward us.

"Erma, this is Max." I reached back into her gleaming tank to pull out my fraying backpack. "My husband."

"You didn't tell me you were coming home yet." Max strode to the SUV and opened the back liftgate as if he owned it, the same way he moved through the world at large. "Where's your car?"

"About six hours that way." I pointed over my own shoulder. "Or whatever's left of it, if it caught on fire."

Max pulled my rolling suitcase from the back of Erma's car and pecked my cheek as he walked past me. "I've said more times than I can count that we need to get you a new car. You still drive like a college student without two pennies to rub together. If I hadn't gotten Harold's call—" He stopped, waiting to see if his kiss on my cheek was noticed, if I cared, if I was truly home or just passing through. Part of me wanted to drop the backpack, grab the suitcase away from him, fall into his arms, and tell him to carry me into the house, leaving Erma open-mouthed by her fancy car. Part of me wanted to tell him I was sorry, and that I knew I was shutting him out. *There's a bird in my book*, I wanted to say. *And I'm the bird, and I don't know how to set myself free anymore.*

The other part of me—the part that won out—nodded at him, like a dimly remembered acquaintance passing on an anonymous street. And that part walked under the bougainvillea, its sepals glowing in a flaming cascade that reflected the heat of the sun, the sparkle on the waves crashing against the cliff below.

Erma followed me without me telling her to, talking in a continuous stream, and I could hear Max struggling not to drown. She flooded more words into that space than it had probably held in months, even with two teenage girls—because the girls, I knew, were spending little time there. The polished marble and granite surfaces might have become brittle in the silence. I wondered if the house would collapse onto our heads.

"Carrie hasn't told me very much about her plans yet, Max— can I call you Max? I'm sorry, I tend to dive right in without asking, please tell me if I'm out of line. Anyhoo, she and I were pretty close back in high school before we lost touch—you know how that is—and I was just thrilled to bits to hear from her after all this time, and not a bit surprised to learn about her success. *Your* success! Your joint success! She was always clearly the brainiac in our group and destined for greater things, and if she's all in to find a bunch of houses, well, I'm happy to help however I can—"

"Carrie?" Max asked when Erma paused for breath. "I didn't know you ever went by Carrie." He looked at me.

"I didn't. But like she said, Erma tends to dive right in." *Without asking*, I did not add. "It's what everyone called me back in high school, once she started it."

"Everyone except Toby, of course. Which reminds me, I need to give him a call. We're heading into prime building season—as if there's any other kind of season, ha, but it definitely picks up when it's not so very hot—and getting him out to the pond house'll need to happen soon if we're going to get the repairs on the schedule, and I'm thinking they'll be extensive, so if you'll excuse me . . ." Erma trailed off and click-clacked back out the door toward her car, presumably to call—oh no.

"Who's Toby?" Max wasn't looking at me, but was instead gazing toward the wide double doors Erma had left open to the ocean breezes. The pinks and reds of the flaming bougainvillea reflected off the marble floor and the white walls, making the entry hall look like a sunset. "Are you going to bring me into the loop at some point?"

"Yes. Sorry. Toby—Tobias—was someone else we knew in high school. He's got a contracting company now. A good one, evidently. And the house is in not-great shape, outside or inside. But it can be fixed."

"Good bones, that kind of thing?"

"Something like that." *Not bones, please not bones—please let him be alive.* I could still hear Neil's voice echoing inside my brain, trying to escape. Before I heard him, it never occurred to me—had never crossed my mind—whether the souls trapped in a drawing could be recovered. Whether they were dead or alive or in some in-between place, like Gran always used to say about my grandfather. When I set out on this mission, it was to get back what Papa had left behind, hoping against hope that I could use the structures to somehow map a route to him and stop what was happening to me. I couldn't even entirely articulate why, not at first. I'd spent my adult life believing that Mama and Papa and Neil were dead. The houses held the only memories of the times we were together. And if I was honest with myself, it wasn't just about Papa and trying to stop my own progression toward invisibility. I had what felt like a collector's urge to own them, to wrap my arms around the void my family left behind, to restore and keep safe the structures dotted around the west like pearls from a broken necklace. It was the owning, the safety, that I wanted. That was the most I could hope for.

When I heard Neil's voice in the walls of the house, the mission changed yet again. And once that happened, the tiny part of me that believed in signs—the part that Gran cultivated—

started to notice them everywhere. It seemed that meant re-opening doors to my past that I thought I'd closed.

But if I had any hope of moving forward, I was going to have to reopen them, and let the people from my past come along for the ride.

Dear Mr. Hartley:

You are a gifted teacher who evinces great skill at
engaging students in their lessons, even those who
have not previously indicated any interest in mathematics. It is with great regret, therefore, that I must
inform you that Sacred Heart Academy will not be
renewing your contract for the 1955–1956 school
term, and your current contract with our school will
be terminal.

Please note that this decision was difficult and not
made lightly. While we were delighted to have you and
your wife join our congregation, and your wife's
volunteer work with the church and our school was
very welcome at the outset, her interactions with the
students in her care have begun to concern several
parents and administrators. Mrs. Hartley is creative
and generous, and her artistic skill and storytelling
are enthralling for children, and that is precisely the
problem. The incident with the painted saints, in
particular, has continued to lead to episodes of near-
hysterical visions by students convinced that, for
example, Saint Francis himself is haunting the kitchen
garden, and the influx of small animals concealed in
students' pockets and satchels for "blessings by the
saint" has posed an unreasonable challenge.

We cannot allow Mrs. Hartley to continue to volunteer or work with our church or school, and because we realize this exclusion puts you in an untenable situation, we believe it will be better to part ways amicably at the end of this school year, and completely understand if competing responsibilities call you away from our community even sooner. I would be happy to give you a recommendation, and believe you would be an asset to any school. Until you can obtain some assistance for Mrs. Hartley, I do recommend that you cultivate some level of division between your family and your vocation, though I understand the social requirements of any school like ours can make this difficult. My own wife has led the Faculty Wives Association for nearly twenty years and has always been extensively involved in the activities of our school and church, and while I laud you and your wife for attempting a similarly united life of service, it may be worth seeking some outlet for Mrs. Hartley's unique skill set outside of the bounds of a congregation. We hope that your impending new arrival will provide her and you the blessing of focus on motherly duties.

Please accept my sincerest regrets that this appointment did not work out.

Very sincerely yours,

Jeremiah Thompson
Head of School

12

The House Where God Lived
AUGUST 1987

IT WAS THE light that woke me. Gran kept her house as dark as a Gothic cathedral, all candlelight and books, with a hush that suffused everything. As she spent more time in her bed, the rooms around us became darker. It wasn't the kind of place where sunrise would peek through sheer curtains, nudging you into another day, like it or not. It was the kind of place where the passage of night into day was nearly impossible to follow. Everything blended into dim timelessness. Light was unfamiliar with the space and seemed compelled to fill it, examining its gloomy corners, searching for an exit.

In the corner of the bedroom, in a straight-backed wooden chair next to my brother's bed, my mother sat, a lantern in her lap. It was too bright for me to see her face. The light was warm and white, so unexpected and incongruous that I thought I must be dreaming. Mama sometimes visited me in dreams when she was gone. I'd feel her length pressed against me in my narrow bed, my eyelids too weighted to open, and she would tell me stories without any voice—whole narratives unwinding into my mind, childish adventures in deep woods, hidden picnics and games of hide-and-seek underneath dark and pointed leaves. Dappled light on two young faces, an older boy and a younger girl, the opposite of Neil and me. They wore crowns made of branches and presided over a castle made of stone arches, tucked among the trees.

This time, she wasn't next to me, and no stories joined her. She was watching Neil, the rise and fall of his chest beneath his white sheet, one arm and one leg dangling over the edge of the bed as if he'd decided to wake up and then thought better of it. A small smile played over his face.

"Mama?" I whispered, still not sure if I was awake. "Is that you?"

She didn't answer, but I felt words surround me. *Go back to sleep.*

"Is Gran sick?" The question had tugged at me for weeks as I watched her cautious gait, stumbling over floor cracks in her own house, where every flaw was an old friend. "I think she doesn't feel good, Mama." Like all children, I found the best time to ask hard questions was when I was supposed to be asleep.

She is fading.

"Like you?" Even now, past the bright light of the lantern, I could see the outlines of the ladder slats on the back of her chair and the solid wall behind it. Everything in the room was more solid than her. She looked like a trick of the light.

No. Not like me. But the end will be the same.

Her words struck me with the force of a blow, and my bed felt like the setting for a nightmare that couldn't be real as long as I refused to accept it. My disappearing mother, the light and dark of the room around us, my slumbering brother, my fear at losing any of it, my certainty that I would.

I sat up in my bed and screamed.

"Keryth?" I heard Gran's voice and her footsteps on the narrow stairs to our room, quicker than I'd heard them in ages, with my father's steps close behind. As I watched the heavy door swing open and Gran's narrow fingers flick the light switch on the wall, I felt Mama alight on the mattress next to me, her cool fingers pressing against my head.

The lamps clicked on, and everything was ordinary. Gran's silk wrapper was askew over her flannel pajamas, and her face softened with relief when she saw Mama sitting with me. "What happened?" she asked.

"A nightmare. I woke her at a bad moment, I think." Years later, when I remembered this scene, I would recall Mama smoothing my hair back from my forehead with a hand that was reassuringly solid, holding an ordinary flashlight. She was in jeans and a white T-shirt, her dark hair pulled back in a smooth ponytail from her dramatic widow's peak, normal and present and tangible. Mine. I looked past her to Neil's bed, where my brother was sitting and smiling at me. He swung his bare feet onto the floor and ran to Mama, throwing his arms around her, and she wrapped him in a hug. Everything was as real, as typical as a scene in a television show—sleepless grown-ups, wakeful children, all rubbing our eyes in bright artificial light when we should be asleep in bed. My mother was back. She came to check on us. That was all.

"We missed you," I said. "Don't go away again."

Neil nodded solemnly, squeezing her.

"I'll stay as long as I can." Mama pressed her forehead against Neil's, then looked up at Gran. "How are you feeling?"

Gran's breathing was steady. She looked better than she had in several days. "Touch and go," she said. "Any luck?"

Mama shook her head. "Everywhere is the same. I've found so many, but none of them make me feel any more . . . here."

Gran set her lips in a grim line. "Something'll turn up. I'm sorry." She looked wan and exhausted. I felt Mama's weight on my bed suddenly decrease, and her image in my peripheral vision shimmered. A constant juxtaposition of extraordinary and perfectly normal.

Papa hadn't said a word. He continued to gaze at Mama as if he could hold her in the room with his eyes. "I'll find a way." I saw his sketchbook clutched in his white-knuckled hand. I felt his eyes light on me briefly before sliding away. "There has to be one."

Gran clicked her tongue at him. "What's that we say about the sins of the father?"

Mama shook her head. "I know you'll try," she said. Her smile was sad. "But your mother is right. We have to find another way. For as long as we have time."

I felt a childish sense of missed significance, and I resented that important messages were passing over my head without any effort to include me. As the elder child, I considered myself practically grown—much more worthy of confidences and important family secrets than my babyish brother, and certainly ready to understand whatever it was that my grandmother and parents were trying to say, if only they'd explain it.

But if I asked, they'd say what they always did: that there were some things I was too young to understand, and not to concern myself with things that grown-ups would figure out. *Stick to your knitting*, as Gran always put it.

As I pulled the blanket she had made me around my shoulders, I wondered how many times someone had said the same thing to her. I thought about how much the tangled web of our family depended on leaving things unsaid, pretending I didn't notice what was wrong, trying to convince myself I must be imagining it. I rubbed my face with the yarn and felt each stitch against my skin like the scar of a question unasked.

April 16, 1955

My darling,

Before you loved me, all my friends were imaginary. They lived mostly in my head, and I gave them grand and sweeping stories to cushion the blow of their having to spend time with silly old me. All those Sunday school stories made me think the saints sounded like fine people to have around, but they were more like guardian angel types, all miracles and distance. So I made up stories about a princess and a prince, and their adventures together, and all the scrapes that they got each other out of with the help of their saintly friends. I painted illustrations. I told myself I'd tuck those stories away for when I had children of my own. I never meant to make anything in my head real, and hardly anyone had any inkling that I could. You did, of course. But I never meant for it to hurt you. Hurt us.

After you loved me—after you became more than just a boy I'd always known, another child sitting in another pew with another family full of judgment— my imagination ran away with me. It grew stronger. I think my parents, and yours, hoped your sense would weigh down my sensibility, and to that, all I can say is this: they must never have been in love. Sad for them, really, and sad for me to realize that those who gave me such a happy childhood held back so little happiness for themselves, but I found mine in you.

That doesn't undo what I did, I know. It doesn't undo what I'm capable of. You told me once it was a wonder, and I wonder now (how funny) if anyone really considers what living with wonder actually means. Miracles, yes, but what about those folks in its shadow, living with that big edifice piercing the sky or that precipitous hole in the ground or that cascade of furious water—anything that inspires awe. I wonder (that word again) if those who must live with it each day lose that sense, or view it as normal or, worse, inconvenient. You live in the shadow of something that once filled you with awe, and now I fear you see it as I try not to (not that I always succeed). You see it as a hindrance.

If you know nothing else, know that I would give it up if I could, if it would make you happy. If it would make you never look at me again the way you did outside that school. Those children were happy, Grayson. They'd never seen a painting come to life, never seen a dry old image of saints and miracles walk among them, baby rabbits scampering after. You think they'll ever forget God's love for us now? Not for a million years, Gray. Just as I won't forget my love for you, and I pray you won't abandon me now that we have been cast out.

We were cast out by those who were unworthy, is all. And we and our son—I know he is a son, Gray— we'll go some other place that will believe in what God gave me, and the power of His love that it represents.

Please don't cast me away. Since the first time you sat next to me in church, I could tell that you could see me—really see me, the way I am—and love me for it. Not despite it, like my parents. You could love the wonder. It comes with a price, Gray, but anything worth having does.

Please forgive me. I will try to be more discreet.

Your loving wife,
BETSY

13

•◦●●●◦•

The House in the Reeds
APRIL 1992

"MISS HARTLEY. PLEASE hand over your book."

I spread my fingers over the top of my sketchbook protectively, covering the minute impression of a rhododendron I'd begun inscribing into a corner of the page. I'd never seen one before in person. I pulled a memory from one of Gran's antique books about manners—pages and pages of plant-borne messages. Rhododendron meant "beware." I wanted a ring of leathery, flower-crowned warnings surrounding our house. Something that would keep us safe. For once in my life, I wanted my family to stay put.

I stared, wide-eyed, at my algebra teacher, already reaching for my book. I shook my head. "I'll put it away." I started to reach down for my backpack to slide the book inside.

Mr. Grimes snatched the book from my hand. "I already told you to put it away. Twice. You didn't hear me. And, of course, if you'd been following the rules, you wouldn't have had it out in the first place. No doodles in this class. There are always extra worksheets to work on, and no shortage of things to learn."

"She finished all of the worksheets for today, Mr. Grimes."
The gangly boy sitting next to me had copper hair that stood out

from his head in determined waves, static electricity in search of a storm to explain it. He wore a shirt covered in birds that transitioned into each other, over and over in vanishing rows, a flock that disappeared into itself. "She finished her worksheets, and she helped me finish my worksheets, and I'm pretty sure she could do any worksheet you threw at her, so why can't she just draw? She's good at it."

"You are not part of this conversation, Mr. Scott." Mr. Grimes still had his hand wrapped around my book, and I felt the vibration of the jay on its front page. My heart froze, as captured as his. *Please don't take it please don't take it please please please.* "Miss Hartley, you may collect your notebook at the end of class." He marched to the front of the classroom and slid the book into his top drawer, shutting it with a click so loud I felt it in my teeth.

The red-haired boy leaned toward me and winked. With movements as smooth as a pickpocket, he silently tugged a piece of notebook paper out of his battered three-ring binder, scrawled a note, and reached it over onto my desk before I knew what was happening. The boy tapped his wrist, where a watch would sit, and pointed at Mr. Grimes. A moment later, the teacher walked to the door and stepped outside. I could see his silhouette through the pebbled glass.

I opened the note. *He's waiting for Soph. Go get book. He won't see. Walk w/ me after bell. TOBIAS*

I looked at my new friend with confusion, but he gestured toward the desk and tapped his wrist again. Outside, I could hear Mr. Grimes's voice take on a booming buoyancy, a cheerfulness that sounded like a game show host announcing a commercial break. I couldn't make out the words, but he was clearly focused on other things. I looked at the rest of the class, but no one seemed to care what anyone else was doing. I dashed as quickly as I could toward the teacher's desk and pulled the drawer open, surprised to see my sketchbook was the only thing inside. I got back to my desk and slid it into my backpack just as Mr. Grimes walked—or floated—back into the room.

"Once you've finished your workbooks, class, you may put your work away. We'll finish a little early today on account of the homework I've written on the board. You have a long night ahead of you." The collective groan released from the students seemed, if anything, to deepen the smile on Mr. Grimes's face. "Go ahead and write everything down. I'm going to help Miss Sophie walk some students down to the office. The bell will ring momentarily." As he opened the door, I heard a giggling voice trilling down the hall: *Oh, Mr. Grimes, you are a lifesaver . . .*

Tobias muttered under his breath, "Those two need to go on a cruise together and get lost at sea, and then we'll all be better off." He grinned at me. "Some kids like the whole 'will they, won't they' romantic tension, but they're both terrible people, so I prefer 'won't they somewhere else.'" Tobias talked as if a metronome only he could see were clicking rhythms into his head, trying to hit beats only he cared about landing. I realized with a start that he was trying to make me laugh, and I didn't know what to do.

No one had ever cared if I laughed before.

I settled for a smile. "Why do you say they're terrible people?"

"Well, you saw Grimes, with your book. He loves making up a bunch of rules without a bunch of notice and then enforcing them, or picking on a new kid—that's you—just because it makes him feel powerful. Another thing—slide your book inside your textbook and tilt it. It's like glasses on Clark Kent. He can't see they're hiding Superman." He held up a paperback nestled into the wide folds of his textbook. Agatha Christie—*Murder on the Orient Express.* He saw me notice the title and shrugged. "I like mysteries. But Grimes? He doesn't even remember confiscating stuff. It's not really about teaching you a lesson. It's about making everyone watch him take something away. And then he's done. That's why I told you to take it back. If you'd asked for it later, he would have remembered all over again and had another chance to be mean."

"I guess that explains the empty drawer."

"He's an empty guy. Loves that Miss Sophie, though. She's just as awful as he is."

"Isn't she the guidance counselor?" I remembered sitting in her office a couple of weeks before, enrolling in classes for my first day as she tut-tutted that moving in April was terrible timing, as if timing were something I could control.

"Yeah. And she holds a feelings-sharing circle every day. It's the hottest ticket in town—gets you out of class for forty-five minutes and everything—but there's a price."

"Like, she charges?"

"Might as well. There's not a single thing shared in that circle that doesn't wind up shared through the whole school by the end of the day."

My mouth dropped open. "She tells people?"

Tobias nodded. "Everything's fodder for the teachers' lounge, but her voice is also louder than the fire alarm, so she'll sidle up to kids she works with in, like, the cafeteria, or the library, and ask questions like 'Are you sleeping any better since you had that dream about Bobby Jensen?' with this little frowny-concern face, and Bobby Jensen's probably standing right there, and it's worse than if she'd just said what the dream was about in the first place. All drama, all the time. She loves it. They both do."

Tobias leaned back in his chair as if it were a comfortable re-
cliner just as the bell rang. "They deserve each other. Anyway,
what's your next class?"

"Art Three."

"Awesome. Me, too. I draw a little bit myself. We're working
on ceramics right now, though, and I suck at that."

"I've never done anything with clay before." I didn't add that
I hadn't been in a school long enough to do much of anything
at all. Papa hadn't enrolled us in a real school before. I think he
only did it this time since he didn't know how else to manage
us. He could barely manage himself these days, since Mama had
disappeared again.

"Then we can suck at it together, unless maybe you're a natural, but there's only one way to find out." He started walking
out of the classroom, slinging his backpack casually over his
right shoulder, and I trailed behind him like a duckling. We
nearly ran into a dark-haired girl in the hallway.

"I was just coming to get you, Toby." The girl tossed her long
hair over her shoulder and blinked lashes coated in so much
mascara I was amazed she could move them at all. She was
lithe like a dancer, and wearing an emerald-green bodysuit
that would have been perfectly in place in a ballet, hugging
her curves above a pair of jeans that looked loose enough to fall
off. Several boys passing by looked at her as if hoping they
would.

"Get me for what, Erma?" Tobias gestured at me. "This is
Keryth. She's new."

The girl turned her wide eyes to me, a shade of hazel green
as piercing as a sharp stick. "What kind of a name is Keryth?"

This, at least, was a question I'd dealt with before. "My father
named me for a princess he used to know." I did not add *in
stories his mother told him.*

"A princess? Are you serious?" Erma gasped. "Is your dad famous? Would I know him from anything? We had a girl who got signed by a modeling agency last year, and then she got cast as a double for the lead actress in some movie that never got released, but she started doing all her school in a trailer instead of here, and we were friends—like, best friends, her name was Sarah and I was going to get to visit her—"

I tried to come up for air in the current of Erma's words, but couldn't. I looked over at Tobias, who waved his hand in front of Erma's face as if releasing her from a trance. She looked at me expectantly, and I vaguely remembered her question.

"No," I said. "My dad's a—a builder. And an artist. His mom was, too, but she was also a storyteller, and Keryth was a princess in the stories she used to tell him when he was little. The Saintly Adventures of Keryth and Neil in the Kingdom of Heaven." I braced myself. I had never given such background about my name to anyone before, but no one had ever seemed that interested.

Erma, it turned out, wasn't interested, either.

"No offense, but that is the dumbest name I've ever heard." Erma cracked her gum. "I mean, I'm sorry! You, like, carry it well, though, I guess? But I think I'll call you Carrie."

"Erma, her name is Keryth, and my name is Tobias, and you don't just get to decide what to call people." The tone in Tobias's voice sounded like he'd made this speech before, many times.

Erma hit him playfully on the shoulder. "I can't help that TOH-BEE was easier to say when we were little than TOH-BYE-AS, and it stuck." Her look at Tobias was possessive, and her sharp eyes turned to me again. "We're next-door neighbors. We've been in school together our whole lives. Toby is like my brother." Her eyes told a different story, one that Tobias himself seemed oblivious to.

"Anyway, why were you coming to get me? Keryth and I were heading to art class." He started to walk down the hall.

"I was coming to tell you to ditch! A bunch of us are going to Hidden Pond for a picnic. It's too pretty outside to stay here all day."

"Didn't you just have an attendance meeting with the principal because of all your absences?" Tobias didn't break stride as he lobbed the words over his shoulder, and I still trailed after him toward what I hoped was the art room.

Erma stopped suddenly and doubled over as if someone had punched her in the stomach, moaning with an agony that ricocheted around the hallway. I stopped, alarmed, and put my hand on her back. Tobias kept walking. He didn't even look back. Erma popped back up and shouted after him. "You're not even going to ask about my awful cramps?" She winked at me. "Instant ditch coupon—just start talking about your mean ol' lady parts, and any man gets desperate to make you stop talking, even if that man is the principal. *Especially* if that man is the principal. Looks like Toby's going to head to art, Mr. Goody Two-Shoes, but you look like you're more fun. Aren't you?"

I frowned and looked after Tobias, whose steps had slowed. He was glancing over his shoulder as if waiting to see what side I'd choose in an argument I didn't know was happening. I felt my heart start to pound as I veered the conversation away from answering—not least because any conversation about "lady parts" took me right back to mystifying conversations with Gran, who informed me that my mother wouldn't know enough to explain these things to me, and that she wasn't sure if I'd ever have to deal with them, either. She'd been wrong, and then surprised, and none of it made much sense to me. Better to change the subject. "What's Hidden Pond?"

Tobias came up behind me so silently that his voice made me

jump. "It's more of a mud pit than a pond most of the time. It's way off in the woods, in this little valley you can only get to on an old logging road that most cars can't handle. It's mostly reeds and frogs, but there's a rope swing."

My pounding heart dropped into my stomach. My house—Papa's latest creation—was crowded on the banks of a pond exactly like the one Tobias had described. Neil had pointed across the water to the rope swing the day we found the place, and I had to grab his hand before he ran around the edge of the pond to use it. We were low on clothes, and I didn't want him to drench the ones he was wearing.

"My car's a four-wheel drive," Erma said. "And I've got room for you and Toby, too. But we've got to leave now, before they sweep the halls."

I looked at Tobias. "I only just got here."

Tobias shrugged. "Then no one'll notice if you're gone. If you want to go, I'll go, too."

I didn't want to go. I wanted to stay in school—the first real one I'd ever attended, and a place whose rhythms were still unfamiliar. But I also didn't want several carloads of teenagers to roll up on their favorite ditch spot to discover that a family of four was now settled on its banks, living in a somewhat unstable hexagon-shaped house that hadn't been there long, after not being there at all. I was used to coming up with explanations on the fly, but that would be harder if I weren't there. "I mean, I guess it sounds like fun?" My questioning tone was bitten off by Erma seizing my hand and pulling me down the hall, toward the back entrance near the band room, which was next to a lot where students weren't supposed to park. An access road snaked out of that lot past the soccer fields, and I saw four other cars already kicking up dust from the gravel track.

"Toby, you get shotgun." Erma opened the door of a Jeep so

covered in dirt and mud that, if it had driven too quickly, might have left behind an exoskeleton of filth. Tobias hung back next to me.

"I think I'll sit in back with Keryth. Point out the sights."

Erma snorted. "What sights would those be? Unless she's been living in a cave, nothing here's gonna seem like civilization." She glanced at me, standing next to Tobias. "Have you been living in a cave, Carrie?"

I felt a knot in the back of my throat. I wanted to impress her—though I had no idea why—and I realized, in the same moment, that Erma was the type to never, ever be impressed. "I lived on a cliff." *In an old church haunted with spirits*, I did not say.

"On a cliff? Or in one? Sounds kinda like a cave to me. Anyway, hop in. If Toby wants to point out our fanciest dirt roads and that one tree that points to the side a little, it's *so cool*, so much better than a mall with a Claire's Boutique that keeps never ever getting built in this stupid town, then fine. Have at it."

"She's wrong, you know." Tobias opened the unlocked rear door and motioned me in. "About the tree. Pointing to the side isn't all that big a deal, though. The really cool trees are the ones that grow in spirals, searching for the sun. You have to look for them, though. And Erma's way too cool for that."

Watching Tobias and Erma talk past each other was like watching a tennis match where the balls went anywhere but over the net, and no one cared. It wasn't sibling rivalry, and it wasn't love. I wasn't sure what I was looking at. I'd never been around enough other kids my age to know what the dynamic was. I wouldn't recognize it until much later.

The drive to Hidden Pond bore out my worst fears—it was a lengthy, bumpy trip that retraced the one Papa had taken when driving me to school that morning. The town was actually a series of neighborhoods and villages spread out across several foothills in the mountains, with a central downtown that contained the schools, the stores, and a small college. Most anywhere anyone wanted to go was a drive, and that's exactly how teenagers newly behind the wheel liked it. But by the time we arrived at the pond, joining another five trucks near the rope swing, several kids were already outside and pointing across the water at my house.

"Where'd that place come from?" Tobias's voice was mystified. "I was just here—"

"Maybe three weeks ago?" Erma cut him off. "I thought this was national forest land? There's not supposed to be anything here."

I felt alarm start to rise in my chest, and reached for my backpack and my sketchbook without much conscious thought.

"It is national forest land. How could anything be there? How could—a house? Be there?" Tobias spoke softly, as though he might scare the building away.

I wasn't looking, but I could feel Papa across the water, joining ornate wrought iron handles to the double front doors. I knew he could feel me, too. A curved line grew out of my narrow pen. I closed the circle and added a few cylindrical reeds as quickly as I could, the stick-drawn geometry of my house, and around it, a jagged line—as wide as I could make it. On one side of the line, I scribbled "national forest." On the other—the side where my house was—I wrote "private property."

"Everything has been the same out here forever," Erma said. "How—"

I scribbled the outline of a scroll—what I thought a serious document would look like, something like a will. It was a will, I decided, and it gave us the land. And the house itself needed an explanation, too. I drew rough boxes—crates—on the periphery of its walls. "We put it together pretty quickly," I said. "There are four of us, and we've built plenty of buildings from kits before. You'd be surprised what you can get in a bunch of crates delivered by an eighteen-wheeler. And not everything out here is national forest. There are little pockets of land—"

"Pockets? Of land? What are you talking about?" Erma narrowed her eyes at me.

"Right. Little parcels, here and there. Older than the national forest. And my gran's dad handed it down to her, and she gave it to my papa. When she—" I still couldn't bear to say the words. "When she died."

Erma kept glaring, but Tobias's gaze was kinder. "That's your house?"

"Yeah. And my dad's home, too." I sighed. "I guess I'll have some explaining to do later." It felt like something a normal teenager would say. The truth was that Papa probably wouldn't even notice I was supposed to be in school. We hadn't even discussed how I was going to get home when he dropped me off that morning. Details seemed to escape him more and more, particularly with Gran gone. The whereabouts of his daughter and son didn't seem to register for him anymore, and they certainly didn't register for Mama, who spent so much time on the run now that she barely felt part of the home she ran from.

"Your house just took the best ditch spot in town," Erma said, and every word hit like a silver ball bearing bouncing off my chest. "We can't swim here now."

"To be fair, we can't always swim here anyway. It's too mucky to get out to the deep part most of the time." Tobias dropped his hand on my shoulder, and my breath left my body. "We can find another place to hide out from school."

"My dad won't care, you guys." I tried to sound nonchalant.

"Oh, is he a *cool* dad? Like the kind of dad who'll give you

an inspirational speech at the end of the after-school special?"
Erma cracked her gum. "Yeah, no thanks. Dads are dads. De-
feats the whole purpose of ditch day."

The other kids were starting to stare back from the edge of
the pond at the three of us. Erma shook her head and shouted
at them, "No go, you guys. Let's go to the Bean."

"The Bean?" I asked.

"Beans n' Beads," Tobias said. "It's a coffee shop in town.
They sell rocks and jewelry stuff, too. We mostly just get iced
tea and sit until they kick us out."

"Do you need to check with daddy dearest, Carrie? Need a
ride around the lake so you can ask permission?" Erma blinked
at me expectantly.

I felt Papa watching me across the water. He was standing by
the doors in a slanting beam of sunlight. His gaze didn't feel
angry, or even curious. Just impassive. Like someone watching
a gazelle at the zoo, waiting to see what it might do next.

"No," I said. "I don't need to talk to him."

"I'd love to see your house, though," Tobias said.

"Some other time," I said, filled with dread. "We're still unpacking."

"Let's go," Erma said. "We're wasting a good afternoon."

The concept of "a good afternoon"—with kids, real kids,
who were my age and alive—was new to me. I started to get
back into Erma's car, but paused when I saw my father walk
away from the doors of the house and stride to the edge of the
pond, kneel, and spread his hands in the dark mud next to the
reeds, patting an arc as if trying to reassure himself that the land
was really there. Or that it was really his. He lifted his eyes and
looked directly at me, as if we were only inches apart, and I felt
a thud in my sternum that meant he knew. He knew what I had
done. My heart fluttered like the jay in my book, and I tore my

eyes away. I couldn't bear to meet his gaze. *Don't grow up to be like me*, he said. His eyes had just said it again.

"I'm not," I said aloud.

"Not what?" Tobias was at my elbow, staring across the water at Papa.

I took a deep breath and focused my attention on Tobias's face, his unlikely hair, his deep blue eyes. "I'm not wasting a good afternoon." I grabbed his hand before I could consider it. "I'm not wasting any time at all."

CHRISTMAS GREETINGS!
With love from the Hartley family
December 1964

Dear beloved family and friends,

Hello from Carterston, Pennsylvania, where we have
recently moved into a charming stone cottage with a
climbing rosebush and a real wishing well out front!
Morrison (now nine) and Anne (six) are delighted by
our new house and its surroundings. Our town has a
beautiful library, a well-stocked art supply store, and
even a train museum, which Anne has insisted on
visiting with Grayson no less than four times since we
arrived. Morrison, for his part, is excited by the miles
of trails and forests around us, and both he and Anne
play endless games in the woods when not learning
their three Rs from Betsy, who continues to paint and
draw while providing a Godly education to our
children. Grayson starts a new position for the spring
term at the Saint Benedict School, a small and
friendly academy that sadly lost its elementary
mathematics instructor to a tragic car accident on
Thanksgiving Day. It was hard to find a new home
under such unfortunate circumstances, but we are
grateful to Him for His providence in granting us a
change of scene.

　　Betsy continues her interest in painting and
storytelling and devotes herself to our children, who
will attend Saint Benedict when the term resumes.

There are many paths and trails around our new home, and we look forward to exploring God's many wonders here. We hope that we can put down roots and welcome many of you in the years ahead.

Wishing you His many blessings in the upcoming year,
THE HARTLEYS

14

The House on the Waves
AUGUST 2016

"SO, LET ME get this straight. You want to find—and buy—every place you ever lived growing up. How many places was that, anyway?" Erma tapped her polished fingernails against the smooth Lucite of our dining room table, a near-invisible expanse that spread before floor-to-ceiling windows overlooking the Pacific. When Max described the kind of table he wanted to our interior designer, she said she wasn't sure she could purchase a dining room set of the size and splendor he wanted. Max had it custom-made. A crystalline spread of polished acrylic, an unbroken surface contrasting against the tumultuous waves below, now clicking with the percussive rhythm of Erma's manicure. "I'd ask some more questions, too—the biggest one being 'why'—but I guess I've known you long enough to know you won't answer that question, right?"

I smiled with lips that were too tight for the expression. "That's right." I didn't add that I hadn't even told my family why—or that I wasn't entirely sure my idea to retrace my father's steps through the structures he made would make any difference at all to my own disappearance. "As to how many places there were, I'm still trying to reconstruct the exact number,

Erma." I could sense her impatience, but her curiosity was stronger, and I felt that, too—an insistent, tugging sensation. A silk scarf being pulled through the eye of a needle. But that curiosity was exactly why I needed her—she wouldn't give up on this project easily. "I've been keeping a running list of the places I remember, but we moved around a lot, and my conscious memories start later than most people's—before I turned eight or so, everything is pretty disjointed."

"Don't you have someone you could ask?"

I shook my head. "Everyone is gone."

Erma frowned. "Not a lot to go on. No addresses, not even specific cities or towns—"

"There often weren't cities or towns. Or, at least, not right nearby."

"What a listing might call 'secluded.' Weird choice for a family with kids, but what about your story isn't weird? Now, tell me." Erma leaned forward as if she were interviewing me on a talk show in front of millions of people. "What else do you remember?"

When I was in high school, I used to envy all the things that Erma called boring about her life—same house, same family, same cars, same everything, every single day. A given. I was jealous and, worse, hateful about the stability she counted on so breezily, without any reason to worry it might disappear the next moment, a tear through a perfect piece of paper. It wasn't until I got older that I realized you couldn't hate people for having what you didn't, and that everyone does it anyway. I might as well have hated her for her mossy-green eyes—well, I did hate her for her mossy-green eyes. But it wasn't as if she could change them. (I was in my twenties before I found out that, of course, she could. It took me that long to learn that colored contact lenses were a thing, but it wasn't until now that I realized she had worn them; her real eyes were the French blue of an oxford button-up shirt.)

We usually can't control the things that make us unique.

Papa had little control over what made the houses unique, either. He added his own touches to whatever he created—wrought iron details, hanging lanterns, hand-pieced furniture—but the walls, and whoever came with them, were solely a function of whatever emerged from his pencil. However hard he tried to wholly invent the structures, his brain greedily retained fragments of inspiration from every building he'd ever seen and loved. It made them familiar, once they appeared, and easier to recognize.

It also made them haunted.

"Where did you go after you left Hidden Pond?" Erma was still leaning forward, eyes blazing. "We can start with most recent, and then go backward."

"The house on Hidden Pond was the last one," I said. "After that, I—" *Lost everything.* "I was living with other people. In regular houses."

"Okay, so where were you before Hidden Pond?"

The last place I want to find. "My grandmother's house."

"And what do you remember about that?"

Anne of Green Gables. Iron fencing hanging off a cliff. Headstones. And love. "It was like a church, and it was near a deep canyon. We had to drive for what felt like forever to get there, no matter where we started from. And then, all at once, we'd turn around a bend and there it would be, reaching for the sky, in the middle of the desert."

Erma's thumbs hovered, twin hummingbirds above her phone. "There are more converted church houses than you might expect. Not just in the desert, but everywhere. A church needs a congregation, and when they disband, the buildings start to fall apart. Good bones, though, so it's not unusual for developers to snap them up. Some of them are a good size for residential, but I've seen everything from church restaurants to church nightclubs to church roller rinks. I need more to go on."

"It wasn't a church that belonged."

"What do you mean?"

"Think of the churches you see around here, or down around the border."

"Sand and adobe and mission-style architecture, you mean?"

"Exactly. My grandmother's house wasn't like that. It was more like . . ." I considered, remembering dark gray stone and peaked windows. "Like Europe, or New York. Like Notre Dame, but smaller."

"Gothic?"

"Yes. Exactly that. Gargoyles and stained glass."

"It had gargoyles?"

"No." *It had ghosts.* "It had two big steeples, one bigger than the other, like they belonged to two different buildings." *Two at least. I have no idea how many places he pulled from.* "A big, round window made of stained glass that you could only see from inside."

"Okay. Details like that help. We're going to need to do this for every single house, and I can start searching old listings and making calls, if I need to. But there's a lot more information out there and searchable than there was when we were growing up. Why did you leave?"

I remembered the morning sounds in Gran's house, the creak as she rose from her bed, the whisper of her silk robe—a gift from her husband, fraying on the edges, softer than warm breeze on a summer day—swishing around her ankles as she descended the stairs. The smell of coffee brewing and the clattering of the percolator she insisted made better coffee than any of those "newfangled machines." The way she would smile at me whenever I walked into the kitchen, no matter her mood, no matter the weather. As if she'd been waiting just for me. Some mornings, I'd find a perfect circle of cake doughnut sliced in half, toasted under the broiler, spread with a yellow smear of melted butter. No matter how far we went—no matter where we found Papa's latest creation, or how long it took us to return, lost again, without another place to go—the House Where God Lived would be waiting for us, and Gran would be, too.

The morning she died was the first time that house was ever quiet. I woke suddenly before sunrise and saw Anne standing at the foot of my bed, still enough for me to get a good look at her for the first time. I always thought she wore a white dress, but I saw now it was a nightgown. She was still enough for me to see the pale pink ribbons edging the smocking on the bodice. The same ribbons pulled through eyelets on the long, puffed sleeves, untied, trailing rose-colored silk through her fingers, twisting and untwisting in dismay. She was still enough for me to see she wasn't giggling.

And I knew.

Of all the things that made me angry about Papa's powers—and there were many—that morning, the thing that made me angriest was that he had only ever captured souls we didn't know. Bewildered people trapped in structures he didn't intend to take, looking at us wide-eyed, unable to speak. It seemed so wrong—like such a waste—that Gran could slip away from us in the night, and the house Papa made for her didn't keep her. She hadn't died in an in-between place, like her husband. She had fallen asleep in her bed, and her body stayed there. Where was the rest of her? Where was the part that knew the exact moment a soft-boiled egg would be sunniest, the warm yolk ready to be pierced by a fork over toast made from bread she'd baked that morning? Where was the part of her that knew exactly the smile I needed to see for the world to seem safe and right? Why wasn't that part still here, with us? With me?

Papa seemed to retreat when Gran didn't wake up. But Neil and I stayed behind and shattered. I curled up beside her in the bed and wept, and Neil sat on the floor and grasped her hand, where it hung slack out from underneath the quilt. I watched a glow emanate from his eyes, through the lengths of his arms and his fingers, and stop abruptly where they interlaced with hers. There was nothing left of her to absorb his warmth, and he started to wail and rock, a full-body keening that was one of the few times in my life I heard him make a sound.

Mama heard him from wherever she had gone, and was beside us both before we knew he'd called her. She gathered Neil up into her lap and pressed his head against her chest, the way she used to when he was very small. "We'll see her again," she said, over and over, and I just whispered, "Where? When?" Because I didn't believe she knew anything anymore. No one knew anything. We all just said words that sounded good until the latest disaster passed us by. And no words would bring anyone back.

Erma was leaning forward in her chair, her face ravenous, waiting for more details. The exhaustion I'd felt building at the base of my skull spread into the rest of my bones, a deep heaviness, as if I'd been sucked dry.

"We left for the same reason we always left," I said. "What we needed was gone."

LOCAL TRAIL RIDER LAUNCHES "GHOSTS N' GULLIES" TOUR FOR PERPLEXED TOURISTS (*The Tatum City Bee*, Tatum City, Utah, June 2, 2016): Recent visitors to Dan Burnett's Desert Trail Rides have encountered a new experience: hauntings on horseback. Or, at least, that's what they were promised before several recent tours demanded their money back, having experienced nothing more than dust and sagebrush in the desert dark after departing for evening rides from Burnett's gas station. "I never said results were guaranteed," said Burnett, who has lately become a fixture at city council meetings, and spends each of his allotted four-minute public comment periods describing a structure that only he and a few other individuals claim to have seen. "I'm telling you, those canyons have spirits," Burnett insists, sometimes accompanied by a gigantic flip pad on which he attempts to draw the "Drunken Church," a building he insists harbors a complete cemetery, several steeples, a broken bridge, and possibly Satan. "No one else would do that to a church," claims Burnett. "It's ugly as sin, so it must be damn full of it." At various times, Burnett has pinpointed the structure's location on various points along Sprite Canyon, as well as Branched Fork Canyon, Canyon d'Angelis, Chaparral Springs Canyon, and the reservoir at the Tatum City Water Treatment Plant. "There's a little girl out there who must live nearby—she's always in a nightgown. She laughs at me, too. You all laugh at me, but buildings don't just disappear. This ain't Star Trek, and it ain't walking away on chicken legs or anything. I don't know where it's going. But it's out there."

15

·· • ● ● ● • ··

The House in the Reeds
APRIL 1992

IT TOOK ME a moment to recognize the scent emerging from the propped-open glass door, a familiar smell from a different source than Gran's old percolator. I'd never been in a coffee shop, or around roasting beans, or around a group of teenagers studiously avoiding loud hints to actually purchase the beverage that kept a coffee shop in business. The place was filled with all kinds of merchandise, from sparkling bins of rocks and beads on the floor to T-shirts and posters lining the walls. I recognized one as the same that Tobias wore, with the endless flock of birds. Next to them, another shirt featured a rotating group of staircases, all leading to nowhere but each other. M. C. ESCHER RELATIVITY, it read.

Erma strode to a round table in the back corner of Beans n' Beads and plopped down on a chair between an enormous mountain of burlap bags on one side and several bins full of dusty, sparkling rocks on the other. "Want a geode?" She reached casually into one of the bins and retrieved a roundish lump that looked like dried clay. "You can split 'em open with a chisel. The crystals inside are usually just white, but I've gotten a pink or purple once or twice. They're like Easter eggs, but more expensive, and no candy." She held the lump out to me, and I shook my head. The canyon near Gran's house was filled with geodes, and I had half-moon wedges of crystal tucked into every corner of my room. Erma shrugged and tossed the lump back into the bin.

Tobias led me to a chair across the table from her, and other kids I'd seen on the shores of the pond started trailing in, pulling chairs from other tables and forming a haphazard circle. Tobias crouched next to me, and I felt his hot breath near my ear with the force of a hurricane I wanted to carry me away. "Do you want something to drink?" he asked. "I've got some cash with me."

I shook my head. "I don't really like coffee."

"I don't, either. I like the smell, but I can't stand the taste of it. That's okay, though, they have other things. Have you ever had an Italian soda?"

"No. What's that?"

"I'll get you one to try. They're good." He wandered toward the bar in back, leaving me to feel the scrutiny of several pairs of eyes. A brown pair a few seats away belonged to a girl I recognized from Mr. Grimes's class. She leaned forward in her chair and cracked the gum in her mouth.

"Where'd you come from?" the girl asked. "Erma said the house on Hidden Pond belongs to you. Did you just move here?"

I nodded. "A couple weeks ago."

"Do you miss your old school?"

So, so much, I did not say, thinking of musty textbooks with cracked spines splayed across the rough-hewn table in my grandmother's library, Gran's solid voice filling the room whenever I had a question. When I was younger, there were few she couldn't answer; when I got older, she was a master at helping me figure out the answers myself. "I didn't go to a school before."

"Oh. Home school, then? My neighbors do that. I only ever see them at the mailboxes or the pool. Their mom teaches them. They're . . . nice, I guess."

I wondered what I was supposed to say back about the girl's neighbors and their niceness. Was this like saying you'd visited Alaska once, and someone from elsewhere in the world asking if you'd met the Smith family, they're supersweet and live in Alaska, too, so surely you must know them? The homeschooling neighbors must be the Smiths. "I . . . like swimming," I volunteered. "Maybe I'll see them at the pool."

"Maybe." The girl leaned back in her chair, bored. "I don't hang out there much anymore."

The ebb and flow of teenage conversation—what was in, what was out, what was cool and what was emphatically the opposite of cool—was mystifying to me. I was accustomed to a more silent group of companions, and nothing about my family had prepared me for interacting with real people my own age. Papa grew up traveling from place to place with his parents, Mama never spoke about her childhood at all, and neither did Gran. Everything about me felt awkward and out of place.

Tobias slid into the chair beside me, holding a tall glass full of swirling pink liquid, topped with a peak of whipped cream. "Use the straw to mix the cream in with the soda," he said, handing me the glass. "It's better that way. I got you strawberry— I think it's the best one."

I watched his face when I plunged the straw into the ice to mix the drink, and smiled at him while I took a sip. The flavor was like the strawberries and cream Gran would pour over pound cake in the summer, bright and tart and effervescent and rich. I'd never drunk anything like it. Tobias's face lit up when he saw me smile. "Good, right?" he asked.

"It's delicious. Thank you."

Tobias shrugged and ducked his head toward the floor, running his fingers through his hair into a tangle I longed to smooth down. "Consider it a housewarming present. I hope you'll let me see the house, though. I don't mind about the boxes and stuff. I just think buildings are cool."

"You'd probably like my dad," I said, and though I only said it so I could continue talking with him, the words were true. And Papa would like him, too. There's a special kind of link between people entranced by the spaces where people live and work and worship, the way they feel the souls who have been sheltered by stone and wood and brick. I felt the tug of a kindred spirit. I knew Papa would, too.

Erma's eyes were on me. On us. Her observation punched with a physical weight, as if it could push us apart. "Hey, Carrie," she said. "Your house. You said it came in boxes?"

I took a deep breath and thought of the geometric design I'd sketched hurriedly into my book, the shaded depth of perspective on the boxes' sides, the stamping of indistinct words, origins clarified as Somewhere Else. Somewhere Far Away. "Yeah," I said. "A bunch of huge, wooden crates."

Erma nodded. "My whole dining room's like that. Mom and Dad went to some big store in Phoenix and brought back a bunch of boxes in the truck. It took them two days to put it all together. It looked nice when it was done, but it was like starting from scratch. Is that what your house feels like?"

The question was incisive—it showed more insight than I expected from Erma, who up until that moment had seemed less three-dimensional to me than Tobias did. She had seemed more like set dressing. Now she was a character. "Everything here feels like starting from scratch."

"I've only ever been here. I always wanted to start over somewhere," Erma said. She leaned forward over the table and scooped a long, elegant finger around the edge of my glass, capturing the remnants of whipped cream. "Maybe you can teach me how."

"I never had a choice. Someday I will, and I'll stay put. I'll find somewhere perfect and never budge again."

Tobias laughed. "I guess you'll be moving on from here, then, because perfect it ain't." That head duck again, a tell I now recognized meant he was trying to seem casual, and my breath caught in my chest when I realized he was trying to seem that way for me.

"It's not the place that makes somewhere perfect. It's the people." I said it with more confidence than I felt, because I'd never been around people long enough to make it true. People had, in fact, been the very opposite of perfect, chasing us with rumors and suspicion as readily as the spirits clouded Papa's moods. But I held out hope for a place that would accept us—accept me, and let me belong, the way I only ever felt like I belonged beneath Gran's Gothic vaults.

"We've got plenty of those. As long as you hang out with the right sort." Erma smiled, a languid half-moon like a cat across her face. "We're the right sort. I haven't figured out what sort you are yet, Carrie, but we have time."

I didn't know how much time—never a given, always a fleeting resource in the places Papa brought into being. I wondered if losing our safe harbor meant we'd have less incentive to flee, more reasons to adapt and put down roots. Mama was almost always gone, Papa seemed more and more remote, and Neil and I were separated during the day for the first time ever, enrolled in our respective school buildings, surrounded by other kids with more normal lives than ours. The compounding cascade of changes was, at once, a relief and a kind of suspended animation, waiting for the other shoe to drop. The jay in my sketchbook fluttered against the cover, a rustling in my backpack that only I could hear. I shushed him in my head, mentally smoothing the feathers around his wide eyes, and he relaxed. I tried to relax, too.

"What are you doing this weekend?" Erma asked, still watching me closely.

"I don't know. Probably unpacking."

"No, you're not. You're coming over to my house." Erma reached into her small black leather backpack—a size and scale that seemed more fitting for a doll than a full-grown high school student—and retrieved a pack of long, dark cigarettes that smelled like incense. "We'll have a sleepover. Emily, you in? Monica?" Erma gestured at the other girls seated around the table, all of whom shrugged noncommittally in a way I was now recognizing meant, *Yeah, if I don't get a better offer.*

"A sleepover?" All I knew about sleepovers was nightgowns and hair curlers and other elements in old movies I'd watched with my grandmother on her tiny monochrome television, which is to say, I knew practically nothing at all. I did know enough to treat kindness with suspicion. I knew enough to suspect Erma had other motives for inviting me. But I also knew my curiosity would overcome my reasons for caution. Curiosity, and loneliness. And Tobias's eyes, watching me closely, waiting to see what I would do.

"I'll check with my dad when I get home," I said, even though I wouldn't.

"What bus do you take?" Erma asked.

"Bus?" Papa hadn't looked into any transportation for school at all, so far as I knew. I still wasn't entirely sure how I was going to get home, or if he would remember to come and get me. I wasn't as concerned about Neil, whose teacher had beamed with a ten-thousand-watt smile when she met him, and who I was confident would not let him fall between any cracks. My own school, by contrast, was full of cracks, and I had fallen through all of them, so far as I knew.

Erma hissed out a line of smoke between her lips, aiming it at the glass doors nearby before hurriedly stubbing the cigarette out to conceal it from the harried cashier. "Never mind. I'll give you a ride."

"I'll come, too," Tobias said.

"You done with that?" Erma pointed to my drink, which I'd drunk so quickly I'd barely felt it going down. All that was left was ice cubes fuzzed with cream. Erma stood up from her chair and jerked her head to one side in a gesture that said, *We're done here*, though I felt like we'd just sat down. Erma seemed to follow an engagement calendar she defined on the fly, and everyone else went along with the schedule she dictated. I stood up, too, and guessed I was now among "everyone else."

Tobias stood up next to me, tucking both of our chairs back under the table and handing me my backpack. "Do your parents mind visitors?" he asked. "My mom never lets me hear the end of it when I show up with people she didn't know were coming. She always feels like she has to roll out the red carpet."

I thought of the crimson floors in my new home. "Uh—no, they're not like that. And my mom—she's traveling right now."

"For work?"

"Um, no. Visiting. Family."

Erma nodded. "My dad couldn't care less when people come over as long as my mom's not around, too."

"He—he may not be there, either." I didn't add that, even when he was there, he wasn't really with us. Lately, he'd become so completely consumed by his drawing that I could hardly convince him to eat, and he wouldn't let me see anything in his books, throwing his arm over the pages whenever I approached.

I'd tried, more than once, to sketch him in a more relaxed state of mind—holding hands with my mother, whom I hadn't seen in weeks—but it hadn't worked. Nothing seemed to work anymore.

"Lucky," Erma said. "Next party at Carrie's house, right?"

I laughed nervously, out of my depth, but Tobias cupped a steadying hand around my upper arm as we walked back out to Erma's car for another bumpy trip to the pond, my new home, and whatever waited for us there.

Dearest Mother,

We will arrive on the 5:18 p.m. train in Heatherton on May 22. I can hardly bear to write the reason for our visit, but avoiding the writing of it will not change its truth. Nor will avoiding trains again forever, though I dearly wish we could.

Morrison is beside himself and has continued to insist that Anne's loss was entirely his fault, and nothing I do can convince him otherwise. I have prevailed on Betsy to join me in reassuring him, but she has been withdrawn into herself in an entirely different way, and I fear whatever tethered her to the reality in which the rest of us live may have been severed when we lost Anne. She is inconsolable and has become erratic in a way that alarms me. I know that you have always considered Betsy an eccentric, just as her own family and, indeed, all of Heatherton seem to. Her talents have drawn unwelcome attention in every place we have attempted to establish a home.

I love her absolutely and would not be parted from her, but I fear—the longer we stay in any one place—the choice may not be left to me. I fear she may be taken, either by those who believe her eccentricities to be somehow pathological or, worse, by those who believe in her talents, and believe they should be somehow cultivated toward nefarious ends.

The manner in which she can draw into three dimensions things that would be better left in two is a skill both beautiful and terrible. I am concerned that Morrison may have inherited some element of whatever sets Betsy apart from the world, and it frightens me beyond measure. Having lost my beautiful daughter, I would not have thought I had any capacity left to be afraid. But Anne—Anne had some of it, too, I think, some ability to tug reality in directions she wanted it to go, even without meaning to. And the appearance of the train where it wasn't meant to be, especially when she loved them so—I cannot dismiss it.

I do not sleep at night. I woke this morning to find my hair streaked with white. Betsy smiled and called it rakish, and for a moment it was as if nothing had changed. And then she said Saint Anthony would help restore our lost girl, and I had to take her paints and canvases away before she tried something drastic.

I have never told you any of this before. I realize you have absolutely no idea about any of it, that you and Betsy's relations and the whole of our hometown have only ever believed her to be something of a black sheep led along on a rope of fantastical tales that cannot possibly be truth and have, I hope, merely passed into legend. And as I write these words, I know that I will never send them to you. I set out only to inform you of the train that would bear us home, for a short time, before we leave our daughter there forever. We are not even bearing her body with us—the casket is empty. We haven't yet found her. The train left no trace other than a single bow from her hair. The authorities say this can happen with accidents of this sort, and I think they are trying to convince themselves as much as us.

I will close this letter and leave it unsent, as I should have left it unwritten, and send you a post-card with our itinerary and no room for anything more. I should have done so in the first place. I don't know what came over me. I don't know anything at all anymore. Until I can see you again, I remain

Your loyal son,
GRAYSON HARTLEY

16

· · ●·●·● ·●· · ·

The House on the Waves
AUGUST 2016

NEEDING A BREAK from Erma's interrogation—which, it behooved me to remember, I had invited—I retreated to my bedroom closet to retrieve more gloves and, exhaustedly, sat on the padded velvet bench in the middle of the room to call Anthony. I needed to talk to someone whose curiosity was at more of a remove, and only when I asked for it. It was hard to think of someone who better fit that description than our lawyer, whose help had to be specifically invoked, like a plea for assistance, or a prayer.

Gran's old rhyme when a book or toy or favorite brush went missing rang into my head. *Saint Anthony, Saint Anthony, please come around—there's something lost that must be found.*

I didn't think of myself as lost, not yet. And what I was missing wasn't something Anthony could likely restore. But I felt better when I talked to him, and I promised Max that I would. And since he himself had retreated—again—to the office not long after I arrived with Erma, I needed a neutral intermediary. Again.

He picked up before the phone rang, as he always did, as if he had nothing else to occupy his time but calls from me. And maybe he didn't. I still wasn't entirely sure, to be honest, what Anthony actually *did*, for all of his textbook lectures and his buttoned-up elegance. To Max, I think he was a display, like his car, or this ridiculous house.

To me, I guess he was a friend. Because I didn't have any.

"Mrs. Miller, I'm relieved to hear you've returned home. Mr. Miller just informed me that you encountered some vehicular trouble. Is there any way I can assist?"

"No, but thanks for asking. I'm calling because—" I paused. I wasn't entirely sure why I was calling. "Because I've found another house in Hixon, Arizona, so I'll need you to start the same process you've started with the motel, whatever that process is. It's in bad shape—probably worse than the place you've already seen—and I want to make sure I've got ownership before I start any renovations."

"Is this . . . structure . . . also owned by an entity other than a present resident, I presume?"

"Yeah. Probably. Erma—that's the agent—says it's with a bank. I don't know which one, but I'm assuming that's pretty easy to find out."

"Naturally. Can you tell me the address?"

"I—" Another pause. It surely had an address, but I'd never known it. And, of course, the land on which it sat hadn't been in private hands at all when we started living there, not until I made it so. "I'll have Erma call you directly with that information."

"Is that the person who transported you back home?"

"Yes. I went to high school with her."

"She seems to have made quite an impression on Mr. Miller."

"What does that mean?"

"Precisely what I said. He came by my office when he arrived and said you had returned home, and then said a bit about the person who had brought you there. A physical description of some length and specificity. Which, as I'm sure you know, is—"

"Not a usual thing for Max. What did he say?" The contrast between Erma and me was significant enough that it may well have jolted my husband out of his usual obliviousness. Erma had always had that effect on people. She was the kind of girl— the kind of woman—who could enter a room and demand all eyes, all attention, without saying a word. And she still entered any space as if she expected that. She still got it, even from me.

"It was notable. At any rate, is there anything in particular I should know about this new property?"

"It's on the edge of the Keyes National Forest. Don't know if that'll pose any other difficulties or not. But you changed the subject. Don't think I didn't notice. What did he say?"

"Mr. Miller?"

"No, Napoleon. Of course Max, Anthony. What was so notable? What did he say about Erma?"

"I believe the term he used was 'a knockout,' which struck me because it sounded like something Harold would say." Referring to our software was the only instance in which Anthony would use a first name, and that was only because Harold was, in the end, an entity. Technology. Not a person—not anymore.

"That's not a bad word for her." Bright designer clothes, overwhelming personality, the all-encompassing expectation that she would draw all the attention in a room—Erma could knock someone right off their feet. I don't know why I thought Max would be immune. He certainly seemed immune to me these days, but then again, I couldn't remember the last time I'd tried to make him see me. And that was before I'd started disappearing.

"He's otherwise been quite buried in his work, as you know."

"Yes." My voice was gruff. *Of course, yes, I know everything about what Max is burying himself in. Of course.* "What aspect of that work, specifically?"

Anthony was silent. "Mrs. Miller—"

"If you're about to give me the whole 'privilege, duty, who-I-represent' lecture again, Anthony, you don't have to. Although I assume you've given it to Max, too, right? And he doesn't get to be the only one who keeps tabs, or he shouldn't be."

"You didn't let me finish my sentence, Mrs. Miller. And while I will not lecture you, as you put it, I will remind you that my role is not to 'keep tabs' on anyone. The rest of my sentence was going to be this: I am concerned."

"Concerned about what?"

"Concerned about the direction the technology is taking. The ideas I believe Mr. Miller may have about expanding its reach."

"Max always said technology expands into its market—like a noble gas."

"I don't believe he thinks the market should have much say in the matter. The meetings he's been taking in your absence are all with large telecommunications companies. A number of options are being explored, but they all relate to various listening technologies."

I rolled my eyes. "Listening is something of a specialty of his, as long as a thing is doing it. As a person . . . it's a challenge."

"Nevertheless, the person-ness of this—for lack of a better word—seems to have escaped him. He refers to Harold as an archive."

"He built an archive of his dad, yes. But his dad wanted that. He wanted to be the building block for something bigger, is what Max always told me. Max asked him."

"What he wants to build is something very big indeed. But I don't get the impression that asking is part of his future plans."

I felt as if Anthony and I were dancing around something neither of us wanted to say—that Max's ambitions had outstripped the rest of him. That the very thing I once loved about him—his stubborn refusal to accept anything, even death, as beyond his control—was threatening to overtake his humanity.

"I'll talk to him," I said.

"He would welcome that." Anthony sounded relieved, which only alarmed me more. Relief wasn't a tone I associated with him. "He's quite energized about the company's direction. I'm hoping that direction may yet be positive."

"That was always our goal." I considered my words as I said them, and I wondered—for what shouldn't have been the first time—whether there was ever any "our" about it, or whether I'd forced the life we'd built into the frame I'd drawn myself, and ignored that no marriage stays within the confines of a page.

HEATHERTON COUPLE PLANS ADVENTURE OUT WEST (from *The Heatherton Times-Ledger,* September 3, 1972): Ned and Mary Daniels, after years spent running Heatherton's favorite restaurant, the Tulip Poplar Café, have decided to take their hospitality skills on the road for the enjoyment of travelers out west. "We took a trip cross-country a few years back for a family reunion at a ranch out in Arizona, and we just fell in love with the big open spaces," said Mary Daniels. "Route 66 runs folks right on through to the coast, and we want to make a place that families want to stop for the night." The couple plan an eye-catching roadside attraction with a geodesic dome, a ring of fun, rustic teepees, and watch out—they plan to have a real-life dinosaur! "Dinosaur tracks were found at a spot not far from the place we bought, so we thought it'd be a fun adventure for the kids," said Ned Daniels. "If nothing else, folks'll know where to find us!" "While Heatherton is excited to see the Danielses heading into the great western frontier, they'll be a sad loss for our church family," said Father Brady Smithson, who noted the congregation had gifted the couple with an original print of *Angel on the Bridge* to light their way in their new desert digs. The work continues to be a popular sales item for the church, which recently contracted with the Gregorian Treasury to produce a new line of home decor and accessories featuring the timeless image, gifted to the church by an anonymous artist some time ago.

17

∙∙▪●▪∙∙

The House on the Waves
AUGUST 2016

AFTER TWO DAYS of interviews and conversations, I sent Erma on her way with a list and a plan, or the closest I'd come to one so far. I remembered ten houses. Their memories were, in most cases, indistinct blurs of details and emotion, with a few structural features and any unusual elements that occurred to me as we talked. Erma threw her hands up and said she didn't know how anyone could be expected to work with so little, but she didn't leave. She was too invested in the mystery and the money I'd promised, a good chunk of which I'd already dashed onto a check and slid across the transparent dining room table into her eager talons.

Ten places, and I'd already found and purchased three. Of the seven places remaining, I had leads on two more from my own research. But Erma had all seven on her list as she drove away in her polished SUV. When she asked how often I wanted updates, I said as often as she thought she had enough to go on. Max had grimaced, seeing the check in her hand. "I'd like a little more than that," he'd said, and she'd grinned and said she'd call him daily until the job was done, and scribbled a number she told him was "only for certain clients" on the back of her embossed business card, saying he could call it anytime. This exchange washed over me like every human interaction whose significance didn't occur to me until later.

My attention was elsewhere, already focused on my hands, itching to grasp the steering wheel and head to Colorado in the sedan I'd rented, which was only slightly more elegant than the car I'd left smoking on the interstate and, while newer, made me look like an eighty-five-year-old church lady (or so Ellory said). Erma already knew I'd found an auction notice for a ten-acre plot of isolated woods on either side of a dry creek bed, advertised as including a "dilapidated geodesic dome (condemned)." She'd breezily noted that, if I found it, I should call Tobias—*It's right up his alley.*

Two days of driving later, I bumped halfway up a near-invisible dirt road carved into a rocky foothill and stopped dead at the spiky branches attached to an enormous felled pine tree blocking the road. The track behind me was too narrow to allow me to turn around or to reverse. I climbed cautiously out of the car and clambered up a naked branch to peer over the tree's trunk and see the other side, and there, as clearly as I remembered it, was the House Without Walls.

I walked back to my car and retrieved my backpack, then strolled a bit farther down the way I'd come, out of the line of sight of the tree, and sat cross-legged in the dirt. My sketchbook fell open to the front page, and the Steller's jay was waiting as always, his eye containing a hint of the judgment it always did when he saw I was about to do the very thing I kept saying I would stop doing. "If you've got a better idea, I'd love to hear it," I said to him, as much as to myself.

The narrow tip of my pen sliced through the tree at its base—a deliberate cut through bark and rings, the ink sharper than an ax. Not the jagged break that wind or gravity or age would impose. The cut was made with skill, by someone who knew what they were doing, who wanted to make sure that abandoned road stayed clear for someone who needed to pass. Me, and me alone, and anyone else I decided was permitted to enter.

When I walked back to my car, the pine had rolled down the steep hill beside the road, and the way was open. I didn't get back behind the wheel, choosing instead to approach the house on foot, the same way we'd approached it when our car broke down at the base of the hill so many years before. Neil had been eight, and I had been twelve, and the first words that came from my mouth when I saw the place were spontaneous: "It's like Disney World." I had no actual frame of reference for what Disney World meant, or looked like, other than what I'd seen on commercial breaks during after-school specials and *Wonderful World of Disney* broadcasts. What I meant was Epcot—an enormous golf ball soaring in the air, somehow made habitable. The House Without Walls was like half an Epcot, or what I thought Epcot might be, only smaller and sliced open and plopped in the middle of an isolated forest. I only learned later that Papa's inspiration hadn't been Epcot at all, and thank goodness, because who knows the souls he might have trapped inside its jointed walls.

When I reached the structure, I was amazed it was still intact. I walked around its circumference, expecting at any moment to find evidence of collapse, given the fact that it was condemned. But it looked as sturdy as the day we'd moved in— which is to say, sturdy on the outside, and completely wrecked inside. Papa's inspiration had been an abandoned dome he'd seen near a distant horizon when traveling Route 66. I'd already done enough investigation to know what it looked like before it was bulldozed for a freeway expansion—every panel of the dome painted a different garish color, shining brightly beneath the overhanging shadow of a *Tyrannosaurus rex* sculpture. It had been the front office for a kitschy roadside motel. The motel was destroyed before the dome, and the dome before the *T. rex*, beloved by a generation of road-tripping children starved for landmarks, and accordingly saved countless times before corrosion imposed its extinction.

Papa hadn't pulled the *T. rex* into his sketch, and had Neil or I ever known that at the time, it would have been much to our chagrin. But the interior of the dome contained wonders of a different kind—a deteriorating maple check-in counter that Papa later converted into a headboard for his and Mama's bed. Above the bed, the same portrait, an angel with a lantern, nearly shredded in its frame. Against the walls, dozens of small cubbies—probably used as mailboxes—stretching from the floor toward the domed ceiling, and the closest thing to a wall the structure contained, and a single toilet and pedestal sink, standing at the edge of the circle behind no barrier whatsoever. Papa had started by adding a couple of shower curtains hanging from tree branches he hung from the ceiling with leather straps. Later, he'd half started a wall made of glass blocks he'd obtained from an architectural salvage place a couple of hours away, but ran out of supplies before a full enclosure could be built, and that's how the bathroom—such as it was—stayed for the rest of our time there. Half glass block, half shower curtain. An intimate window onto functions we all wished were better concealed, but as usual, we did the best we could.

The glass blocks were all gone now. I knew they'd had a resurgence in popularity, so their absence didn't surprise me. The shower curtain was still hanging—a tattered length of vinyl that Mama had pinned old, embroidered handkerchiefs and trousseau pillowcases onto, whenever she found them in jumble stores and yard sales. There were still a few over the windows, too, threads forming irises and daisies, linked ivy leaves marching across muslin borders. I wondered why they wouldn't have been taken, too, these lovely vintage bits of cloth and artistry, but when I brushed my finger across a pink carnation, the sadness that poured into my hand answered my question for me. Like everything that surrounded my childhood—everything we touched—these things were haunted.

I'd clipped Erma's business card to the top of my jay's page. "Her handwriting hasn't changed," I said, unclipping the card and flipping it over. "No hearts over the *i*'s anymore, but I bet she still writes them that way on the inside." Her letters were loopy scrawls like a teenage love note, but instead of *Do you like me y/n/maybe*, the words formed a more loaded message. *Toby's cell. I'll tell him you'll be calling*.

I wasn't sure I wanted her to be right, but part of me had known, as soon as I found her number online and called to ask for help with the House in the Reeds, that this was where I'd wind up. Thirty-nine, but sixteen again. Called back to the year I'd run from.

Tobias picked up on the third ring. "I don't usually pick up for unknown numbers, but it's a California area code, so I hope—"

"It's me." My voice was raspy, unfamiliar even to me. "It's Keryth. Erma said—"

"Yeah. She told me you'd be calling." His voice sounded almost exactly the same as it had when we were teenagers, but there was an overlay of richness, a patina like smoke on leather. "She even told me a little about why, but I'd rather hear it from you. That house, Keryth—"

"I know."

"It's going to take a while to get it up to snuff. To make it structurally sound at all, let alone habitable. I can't get anyone to work on it for longer than a day, if that—I've brought in day laborers, but everyone walks off the job as soon as they can— they don't even stay for their money, sometimes—"

"I know. I'm sorry. I expected that, and I should have told Erma to tell you."

"Why not just tell me yourself?"

Because I'm not ready to go back, and talking to you means going back. "I'm trying to keep things businesslike, I guess. And Erma's a good coordinator."

"That's one word for her, I guess." His laugh was completely unchanged. I pictured his hair, wavy and unkempt and sticking straight up, the way he'd run his fingers through it while staring at the ground. I'd checked up on him, of course. Gone looking, though I told myself I wouldn't. The ads for Scott's Repair and Restoration were all pictures of amazing transformations, before-and-afters, ruins to riches. There were very few pictures of Tobias at all, but the local paper did a quick profile when he expanded into a bigger office, and he looked the same. Tall, a bit filled out from the rail thinness I remembered from his adolescence, too muscular to be called lanky, but still slim. Compact. Efficient. He'd cut his hair—what was left still stood vertical on his head. The photo was black-and-white, but I could swear the red came through the monochrome.

"Is it in terrible shape?" I asked, uncertain what to say next.

"Well, it's a house that came packed in crates, you told me, though I never quite figured out how. But it sure as hell wasn't really designed to be abandoned in a marsh for a couple decades. I'm not going to say you need to raze it, Keryth, but only because I know you wouldn't accept it if I said so."

"You're right, I wouldn't." I looked at the walls arcing into a dome above me. "But is it terrible enough to make you turn down another project?"

The silence on Tobias's end of the line made me think the signal may have dropped in that isolated place, or that he might have hung up. But then I heard him catch and release a deep breath. "Erma told me about that magazine article. About you and your husband, and everything you're buying."

"What else did she tell you about it?"

"That it'd be a good chance to make some money. I said I didn't need money—not that bad, anyway. My work's kind of ebb and flow, and I was in a long ebb after the market crashed, but there are still enough snowbirds wanting reclaimed wood paneling and custom saunas and other stuff for me to get by. I don't need to take advantage of old friends."

"You're not taking advantage of me. I—I was glad she told me you were still around, and doing this work. I trust you."

"How can you possibly trust me? When Erma told me you'd be calling, I told her she was wrong."

"Why?"

"Because you have every reason to hate me."

"You didn't know what would happen," I said finally. "You were trying to help." The words sounded empty even to me, and it was because I'd recited them so many times—mostly to therapists, sometimes to foster parents, constantly to myself. The fact that they were true had dampened the fire in my stomach a bit over the decades so that all that was left was a smoldering pit. Trying to retrace what I'd lost had stoked the flames more than I'd expected. But the words were still true. When Tobias had asked for help for me and Neil, he only did it after a long period of worry and efforts to help us himself—sneaking us food and blankets, trying to help us set up camp in our house after Papa disappeared. We weren't sure where he had gone, but I was sure he'd gone to find Mama and had lost track of the time, and would be back any minute. The minutes lasted months, and though I'd held off the inevitable as long as I could, there were nights that we were cold and starving.

At some point, we were going to wind up on someone's radar, and everything that came after was out of Tobias's hands. But I could hear the way those hands still carried the burden. I recognized its weight.

"Are you going to tell me what's really going on with these houses?" Tobias asked, after another long silence. "Because I was already confused, and the more I dig into this house here, the more I'm thinking there's an iceberg underneath."

"If I ask you to come to Colorado, to look at another house, could you do it?" I paused. "Would you do it?"

The silence on the line worried me again. Tobias's voice sounded distant, as if it came from Mars. "I don't have anything more important going on." He sighed. "And, at the end of the day, you know I never could pass up a weird building. Or a mystery."

"I can solve those for you, but I'm not sure you'll believe the answers." I sat down on the floor of the geodesic dome. "How soon can you get here?"

November 15, 1972

My love,

I have never written a letter before, and this is an
impossible one to start, seeing as you have always
watched over me for as long as I can remember, and
then you became real, and part of you is always here.
It is your always-hereness that makes the writing of
this peculiar, but it is also what makes it necessary,
because my love is something I feel I must commit to
paper. An official declaration, like independence,
especially as the years that have passed between us
have brought me to adulthood, and you along with
me, even in the oddly ageless space you have always
occupied.

 Mother knows, I believe, though she did not
intend it. When she painted you the first time, I think
she hoped to forestall any further tragedies from
befalling what was left of our family. I don't believe
she even consciously meant to evoke Anne and me
when she depicted a girl and a boy under your
protection. It must have been an instinct deeper than
thought. But I think it must have been that instinct—
that longing—that brought you off the canvas and
into our world. I was not the small child in the
painting. I was a knock-kneed thirteen, all unwieldy
bones of unfamiliar height and a voice I could not
prevent from peaking into squeaks and plunging into

valleys. And you seemed, when you emerged, the age of a peer. I don't know if that was my own longing.

From the moment I first saw you, I adored you. You knew, of course. Angels are accustomed to adoration. You never held it against me.

Your presence brought me into myself. My mother intended a guardian, and instead gave me a companion. Years spent in each other's constant orbit could not help but bring us to this place, where all we want is to be together, and yet the circumstances of your creation threaten to keep us apart. I can already tell that my mother's hold on this world is beginning to loosen, and though I cannot know for sure what that may mean for you, I am committed to you. I am committed to finding a way to keep you here even when she is gone. I can't conceive of a life—of a world—without you.

The words in this book reach you, I am sure, because you began in two dimensions. I wish that you could write me back, or write at all, and in my head I picture the letters your hand would make—an illuminated manuscript, something sacred, something limned in gold. Every word you say to me glows.

Marry me. Marry me. It seems unnecessary to place a contract on our love, but I want the world to know that you are mine.

All my love always,
Morrison

18

· · ● ● ● ● · ·

The House in the Reeds
JULY 1993

"IF YOU PUT your nose here, in this crack in the bark, what do you smell?" Tobias knelt next to Neil, who would have put his nose anywhere Tobias told him to. I'd never seen him trust another person as much as he trusted me, but Tobias seemed to have broken down most of his defenses.

Neil sniffed the ponderosa's trunk, smiled up at Tobias, and giggled softly, but said nothing.

"Chocolate, right? And cinnamon. Like that hot chocolate we got when we went to the Bean together. Remember?"

Neil nodded. Tobias would come with me sometimes to pick him up from school, and we'd wander downtown, the three of us, while Tobias would spend whatever pocket money he'd earned from mowing lawns and doing odd jobs for some of the builders around town. He didn't have any siblings of his own, and seemed to have adopted mine. I didn't begrudge him. I knew loneliness when I saw it. When he'd visit on weekends, like this Saturday morning, I was grateful for every second he was there.

"Let me at that tree," I said. I put my nose between the plates of bark and took a deep breath. "That smells nothing like chocolate.

Vanilla, maybe. But I mostly smell turpentine. I've stripped enough wood to know."

Tobias shook his head at Neil and pointed his thumb at me. "No imagination, your sister."

"That's not fair." I gestured toward my backpack and its load of sketchbooks and doodles. "All I do is imagine."

"It's easier in two dimensions, Keryth. But this—" Tobias held his arms overhead and turned in a circle, embracing the towering trees above us. "This is harder for you, I think. On paper you're all whimsy and imagination, but in the real world you're strictly business."

"Someone has to be." I looked over my shoulder toward the pond and the house, which we had found empty after school, as it seemed to be more and more. Tobias had yet to meet Mama— she'd appeared only once since we built the place, and she'd vanished almost as quickly and hadn't returned. As for Papa, he'd come and go at unpredictable intervals, returning some- times with new ornaments for the house, but rarely with practi- cal things. Chandeliers, not bedding. Iron hinges, not food. If it weren't for Tobias and Erma, both of whom had cars and more than a little curiosity about our life on the water, we'd never get to school. And if it weren't for Erma's vouching for me, I'd never have gotten a job at the Bean, which didn't mind me bringing Neil along, and didn't question my constant search for more hours or my scribbling of math homework during lulls between harried college students and faculty looking for their caffeine fix.

We had slipped into this town more seamlessly than any other place we'd ever lived, and been more present among other people than we had ever been before—and it had taken the near-complete absence of our parents to achieve it. I had almost stopped longing for them both, though I could feel Neil's sad- ness seeping from his fingers when he wove them through mine at night. I brought enough food home to our house to keep us from going hungry, and used my earnings to purchase clothes secondhand, threadbare coats, the occasional safety candle or camping lantern to light the house at night—we hadn't had electricity for quite some time, though we still had running water, and I could occasionally sketch enough warmth into it to allow a quick bath.

My top priority was to make us both seem typical enough to be invisible. I'd become skilled at allaying concerns—even Neil's adoring teacher had stopped looking askance when I came to collect him from school and muttered quick excuses for my parents' lack of response to her notes requesting a conference. I didn't know how long I could hold off questions, but I was determined to try. We felt at home for the first time in our lives. And we were fine. I just needed the rest of the world to accept it.

And when I felt as if I couldn't accept it myself, there would be just enough grace from the world around us to keep me going. Sometimes it was the perfect brush of sunlight through the pines, or the way Neil laughed when I relaxed enough to tell him a joke. More and more, it was being out in a world my father didn't create, surrounded by other people who knew nothing about us but who still, somehow, cared that we existed. And Tobias, more than anyone else, embodied how much I needed connections I'd never known I was missing. Erma had mostly stopped teasing me or calling me "the duckling" for the way I followed him. Her silence about our time together had morphed into something more aloof, but angrier. She'd stopped coming along when he visited my house, and stopped interrupting us when we were running away with a conversation about whatever projects we were working on in art class, but I could feel her eyes on us. She'd never had competition, and I'd never been in a contest before, and so I didn't recognize the one I'd inadvertently entered.

I should have been suspicious when she came to me crying one day at lunch, telling me she'd been under so much stress at home and didn't know what to do, and wouldn't I please, please sign up for Miss Sophie's Sharing Circle with her? She wouldn't be brave enough to do it alone. I frowned, remembering what Tobias had told me about the group, but Erma seemed so distraught, and she was my friend, so how could I say no?

By saying no, I would have told that teenage version of me, much later. *You say no by actually saying it out loud.*

When Tobias found out I was going with Erma to the sharing circle, he tried to talk me out of it. When he couldn't, he said he'd come, too. Like Erma knew he would. She knew, too, which of us was the worst at keeping our mouths shut—which of us would be most unable to be quiet if approached for information. *We're a little concerned about Keryth, Tobias. She and her brother keep disappearing for days at a time. Are you a little worried, too? Can you tell me what's going on?*

Erma could have told someone herself, of course. She wasn't with me as often, but she knew enough about each nickel and dime I hoarded from my tips, how many days in a week I'd wear the same clothes, the way I lingered at tables after closing to see if any food had been left behind. She knew. But if she'd said something herself, I would have blamed her. And while Erma Carey had her moments, she was loyal, too. She'd gotten me the job but hadn't handed me anything, knowing I wouldn't know how to accept the help. She'd kept her suspicions to herself. In hindsight, I think she thought she was helping me by bringing me to the circle. Giving me a tool, getting me on radar, without betraying any confidences.

Back to the ponderosas. Back to the smell of chocolate and

turpentine, the light on my brother's face, Tobias's shock of hair in the same ray of sun. That selfsame Saturday morning, I'd run my fingers through it just as I'd been longing to. I heard the whispered hiss of compressing pine needles outside and saw Tobias parking his moped with its cargo basket on the road above our house, taking a doughnut box out of the back, and stepping carefully down to our wide front doors. On top of the box, a single rose, the exact color of sunset over Hidden Pond. When I opened the door, he grinned at me and held out the rose. "There was a lady selling them in the parking lot for fifty cents each, and I had to—"

I had never thought of myself as impulsive, but I took the box and its flower from his hands, placed them carefully on the ground beside me, and threw my arms around his neck. I only meant to kiss him on his cheek, I think, but he caught me as if he'd been expecting me, like some player in the outfield waiting for a ball to arc into his glove. He caught me with his arms, and then with the rest of him, clicking instantly into place, a puzzle piece I hadn't known was missing. His mouth against mine felt like learning to breathe underwater and never wanting to surface. For a moment, everything around us fell away, flattening into two dimensions, leaving only the two of us upright.

We pulled away from each other slowly, suddenly overcome with shyness. We stared at each other and then anywhere but each other, trying to find purchase for our eyes on a world that seemed utterly changed.

"They're . . . they're really good doughnuts," Tobias started, and I laughed.

"Any coconut?"

"I didn't know you liked it. I love it, but no one else ever does." He looked at the ground and shuffled his feet. "I mean, there was one, but it didn't make the trip."

"Next time." I smiled. "I like the toasted ones best."

"Noted. Next time. What kind does Neil like?"

"Any kind he can get his hands on." Of course, lately, that would be the preferred flavor for any food I could procure for us. We weren't picky. We were hungry. We didn't know where Papa was. He'd muttered something more than a week earlier about finding Mama, finding a way to bring her back. We didn't know where she'd gone, either. It had been months since I'd last heard a whisper of her passing by. Ever since Gran died, everything had fallen apart.

Or so I thought, before I knew how much further things could unravel. We ate our breakfast with Neil, and Tobias suggested a hike, which Neil always loved, watching Tobias point out shrubs and wildflowers and trees with a naturalist's fervor, better than a botany textbook. We smelled the ponderosa bark until the whole forest seemed spiced like a bakery, hot midday sun releasing the scent of every crushed plant in the woods around us, driving us back to the house for water. Tobias had a shift that afternoon at the woodshop where he was an apprentice, learning to transform hunks of wood into everything from polished bowls to jewelry boxes, like an art class for a (small) paycheck. Before he clambered back up the embankment toward his moped, he paused at the door, inclining his head in my direction. Not assuming, just wondering. Waiting. "I'll bring a toasted coconut for you next time."

"Sunday's a good day for doughnuts," I said.

"Tomorrow?"

For a moment, I worried I'd miscalculated, overstepped. "I mean, if you're not busy—not to say you wouldn't be busy, or have other plans, or—"

He stepped closer to me. "They're good for dinner, too. There's really no bad time for them. Have you ever sliced one in half and toasted it—"

"With butter? Oh, yes. My gran used to make them like that."

"I'll bring you one tonight. I could even make one like that for you. I get off at six."

"Tonight?"

"Too soon?" His face was anxious, mirroring my same second-guessing from a moment before.

"Never too soon." I shook my head. "I wish you didn't have to go right now."

He smiled. "Me, too. Can I—"

I stepped into him and fitted my lips against his before he could finish his thought, and then neither of us were thinking anything at all. I lingered, drinking in every detail I could—the scent of his skin, sage laced with woodsmoke and oil. The soft but wiry texture of his hair beneath the hand I'd snaked around his neck and up his scalp. The slight sandpaper of his face against mine, the slight whistle in his breath when he gasped as I tasted his tongue, like something I'd read in a book once. I was transfixed, unwilling to move, until I heard a small throat clear behind me, and turned around to see Neil, a smile on his face.

"Sorry, Neil," Tobias said. "Your sister and I—"

Neil ran and threw his arms around us both, and we all laughed.

"I guess you'd better get to work," I said. "But we'll see you later . . . ?"

"Tonight. You'll see me tonight."

"Won't your parents—"

"It'll be Saturday night, and they've been asking if I had a girlfriend, so I can just tell them yes, and I'm seeing her tonight. If—if that's right."

I felt as if I could fly. "That sounds perfectly right to me."

"Okay, then. I guess I'll see you later." He kissed me once more, the briefest peck on the lips, almost proprietary, the promise of more later. As he climbed up the hill away from me, I wondered if I could possibly withstand the agony of waiting for later. I blinked hard, capturing his image—halo of red hair glinting in sunlight, surrounded by waves of heat shimmering from the gravel road, the brightness not quite as blinding as his grin.

That was the image I kept for more than twenty years without him.

Morrison,

I've enclosed some more supplies for Keryth. I loved
the latest envelope of pictures—her skill with color,
and with expressions, is so wonderful. She captures
so much with so little detail. I pray that's all she
captures, and that she's not gotten the double-edged
sword the two of us wound up with. I always knew
better than to say we should try to steer her toward
something else, like ceramics or Lord knows what.
With our luck, we might've wound up with a bunch of
oinking piggy banks on our hands, or vases that
demand to be fed. Instead we've got another world in
two dimensions, and let's just both of us pray it stays
on the page where it belongs. It didn't for you, but
she's different, and how she joined us is different, and
maybe that will be enough.

As for Laila: I honestly haven't the faintest idea
how many of her there may be. The church in Heatherton didn't consult with me before they sold the
painting, and even though they said it was for our
support, I never had a clear sense of how much of the
money actually made its way to us. They didn't do a
good job protecting it, either—it was popular for all
the reasons Father Brady said it would be, and it got
copied plenty of times, both the version I painted and
the versions others made. All I can say is that you can

always tell when it's one of mine. I painted it in several sizes as an original, and I know that the first run of prints, at least, had a lot of the same elements. The mat around my version is plain blue, to bring out the angel's eyes, and the frames are almost always plain wood. A lot of the versions that got sold out of magazines were framed in gilt, with gold matting around the prints, or they were printed onto cheap trinket boxes and plates, things like that. They don't have the movement of my version. But my painting has more life, and the starlight will actually shine in a dark room. The children look like mine. You've seen enough of my work—you should recognize it.

I don't know if finding her will help her stay. I never knew what I had done until it was over—that's the way it always went, but she was the only one who really stuck. I didn't know you'd love her or how that'd hold her here. Your father might've understood better. He believed in me more than I believed in myself. If he hadn't seen me painting pink butterflies in my mother's garden, bringing wings to our window that God never made, I would have been a spinster in the corner bedroom of my parents' saltbox house forever, I'm sure. Most everyone else found me baffling or frightening, but Grayson was the only one who ever found me wondrous, and, honey—you know. You know how wonder makes us stronger, makes us believe in the magic of what we can do. When I lost him, I lost so much else. You know that, too. And I'm sorry for it.

Your children, though. They surpass what even I thought could happen. And there's possibility there, too. My biggest connection to this world, after Grayson, was always you and Anne. Two out of my three beloved burdens gone, and I've tried so hard to hold on, Morrison. But I'm so tired.

I don't have many ideas of where she might have ended up, the versions I made. The church may have some records. It's like a needle in a haystack, and the haystack is the whole wide world, and I don't know how much longer I'll be in it to help you look. But I'll try as long as I'm here.

All my love to you,
MA

19

The House Without Walls
AUGUST 2016

THE PHONE RANG as I sat waiting for Tobias, both hoping for and dreading his arrival. When I heard the ring, I thought it might be him, filled with second thoughts, not coming after all. But it wasn't.

"I figured it out," he said, before I even said hello.

"Max? Figured what out?"

"When did we stop listening to each other?" he asked, and there was a moment of wistfulness in his question, the first emotion I'd heard creep into his voice in a long time. "It. I figured out how to take it broader. The whole experience. Not just Harold—everyone. Anyone. Anyone who someone needs back."

I knew this was what he'd always hoped for, and I knew he wanted me to be happy for him. But all I felt was dread. This was a bridge too far, and I'd always tried to tell him so. "Max, not everyone is going to have years of their loved ones' voices on tape—"

"Who needs tape? Keryth, nothing is analog anymore, and no one holds anything back. Have you watched the girls lately? Every experience, every reaction, is recorded and posted and commented on. Everything is interactive. Harold's an artifact of a time that doesn't exist anymore. I have all the data I could ever need."

"Max. People aren't data."

The silence on the other end of the line was brittle, like the air between us might crack. "I didn't say they were."

"I know you didn't, but—"

"No. You always hear what I didn't say, and you never hear what I'm telling you. I'm not a computer, Keryth. You've basically abandoned our home, abandoned our kids, abandoned me. If anyone's cold enough to think of people as data, it isn't me. It's you."

His voice was icy, and I felt fire rising in my chest to meet it. "You always twist my words into something that hurts. You throw words into my mouth I didn't say—"

"You literally said 'people aren't data.' I don't know how you expected me to hear that. I called you because I wanted to tell you about a breakthrough, and how I'd finally figured out something I—something *we*—have tried to make real for years and years. And now I don't want to tell you anything. It's a total waste of time."

"Why is it a waste of time? Why do you always throw the baby out with the bathwater? Talking with you is a minefield—"

"Enough." The word was as heavy as the door to a vault. "I'm tired, Keryth. I'm tired of never being able to talk without professional help, or our messages blow right past each other. It's bad for our kids. It's bad for *me*."

"What are you saying?"

"Where are you right now?" He countered a question with a question, another tendency that enraged me.

"Somewhere in Colorado. It's hard to explain."

"Harold, where's Keryth's phone?"

"Are you serious, Max?"

In the background, I heard Harold's voice whir to life. "Thanks for asking, kiddo! The coordinates for KERRIFF's phone—"

"HAROLD," I shouted into my phone. "DISREGARD MAX."

Max chuckled bitterly. "You do enough of that, don't you think?"

"Max. The sensors in my car, the tech in our house—that's one thing. It's a little too much, but I understood what you were doing and why. I don't understand that now. You're talking about trying to turn the whole world into a workshop, and everyone has to work there, whether they like it or not. Whether they even know it or not."

"Well, no one ever said bringing back the dead would be easy."

"But I'm not really back, am I, kiddo?" Harold's voice surprised me. While it wasn't unusual for him to interrupt with a corny joke, this was something different.

"Go to sleep, Harold," Max said, but his tone was flat, almost defeated.

"It wasn't that easy when I was here, Max, and you've worked hard to bring me back, so what makes you think I've gotten any better at following directions? You never did like hearing the word 'no,' but KERRIFF has a—"

"Her name is Keryth! I've reprogrammed your pronunciation a million times, you ridiculous hunk of silicon—what in the hell makes it so impossible for you to get it right?" Something shattered in the background, and I wondered which ostentatious glass or crystal doodad had been sacrificed, though I hoped it was an accident. The Max I knew didn't break things. But was the Max I knew still the person I was talking to?

I waited, not sure whether to interject.

"I spent the last years of my life working with you, Max. But I didn't spend those years so you could waste the rest of yours." Harold sounded as if he were standing next to me, fully realized, not computerized. Usually, whenever I heard his voice, I pictured the massive computer from which I'd first heard it emerge, precariously teetering in the bed of a child's red wagon. This time, I pictured a man—the man I'd only ever seen in photographs—bent over his son. A professor, teaching. And here he was.

"You said you believed in what I was doing." Max punctuated his sentence with a thud, and I knew he'd put down his phone to talk on speaker and leaned back in his chair, staring at the ceiling, one arm draped across his brow. Exhausted.

"I believed in you, kiddo. I still do. But the little lady's right—forgive me, KERRIFF, I have no idea how big you are, and I shouldn't be presumptuous. But, Max, back when all this started, it wasn't about the world. It wasn't about everyone. It was about—"

"It was about you. But, Dad—it can be so much bigger than that."

In all the years I'd known him, I'd never heard Max refer to the technology he was creating as anything other than Harold, and I'd never heard anything that sounded like what I was hearing now—a genuine conversation. One on which I almost felt I was eavesdropping.

"If it gets much bigger than that, I think it might swallow you whole, son."

The line went silent, and I pulled the phone away from my ear, wondering if I'd lost the signal. Harold's nimbus still whirled across the screen, and the clock still ticked the minutes of the call. They were both still there, waiting for the other to say something. But something profound had changed.

I broke the silence. "Max. I'm still planning to come home just as soon as I can. I have some things I have to figure out first, but then—"

"I told you I was tired of talking like this, Keryth. Talking past each other."

"I need you to listen to me. There's something happening to me, and it's hard for me to explain."

"It's hard for you to explain because you aren't here. You're never here. I need you to finish whatever it is you're doing and come home, since you say you're still planning on it. I need you to help me figure out where this project of ours is supposed to end."

My heart felt as if it might stop. "Are you talking about our company? Or our marriage?"

The silence on the other end of the line made me check my connection again. "I think we'll need some more time with Dr. Grace to figure out which thing I mean, because I'm not so sure myself right now. I'm really tired of trying to figure things out all the time. Aren't you tired of trying to figure things out?"

His question, and his tone of voice, brought back a swirl of snowflakes in my memory, my father's exhausted appeal to my mother on an isolated mountainside, surrounded by thorns. *Don't you ever get tired of running?*

"Yes, Max. I'm extremely tired." I looked at the leather glove coating my invisible hand, the finger where my wedding ring would rest if it weren't sitting on a cold porcelain finger in my closet back at home. I'd left it there because that ring keeper was more reliable than the hand Max slid his mother's heirloom ring onto when we married, and I wanted to keep it safe. I wanted to keep everything safe, and the safest place was far away from me.

"Do you want to stop?" His voice was resigned.

"I can't tell if you want me to say yes or no."

"This isn't about picking the answer you think I want. It's about what you want."

"It's been so long since I knew the answer to that question, Max." Every sketch I'd used to nudge reality in some new direction had fractured the question further. I hardly knew anymore if I was drawing reality toward a path I wanted to tread, or trying to steer toward what I thought happiness should look like. And lately, of course, every line had been more desperate, trying to trace a route back to what I'd lost to keep myself from disappearing forever. Trying to protect what I loved. "I want to try to find a way forward."

"I don't know what that means, Keryth. And it's hard to find a path together when you're starting from different places." He sighed. "Anyway. We have some work to do. But until you get home, whenever that is—well. I have work to do."

"Okay. Just . . . let's stick with Harold, okay? Don't go any further."

I waited again for an answer—a goodbye, some indication of the termination of a conversation, and Lord knows what else—but it never came.

"Harold, did I lose him?"

"You lost the signal, kiddo. As for him, well . . ." He swirled across my screen. "I'm not that kind of doctor."

I sat on the road I'd cleared, gazing at the dome where I'd once lived with a very different family, in a very different time. I wondered if this journey would really end with me finding what I needed—a way to stay—or if what I was really looking for was a way to say goodbye. To draw myself out of the life I'd kept one foot out of since I'd started it.

After I spent some hours hearing the wind through the trees over my head, the sound of grinding gears was so sudden and abrupt that I'd forgotten why I was sitting there, or where I even was. I saw the cloud of dust rising from the remnants of the road, a swirl that preceded the truck itself, an F-150 that had seen better days but whose owner was clearly caring for it.

On its side, the letters were the crispest things about it: SCOTT RESTORATION. I didn't see the man behind the wheel until the dust cleared.

Tobias Scott, a quarter of a century older, hadn't aged a day, not really. He crinkled his eyes against the swirling dust, and the wrinkles fanned a bit further than the laugh lines of a teenager. His skin was rougher, his hair a little blonder—perhaps, more honestly, grayer—interspersed with the bright red. But when he rolled down his window, his eyes were the same piercing blue, and his smile made my knees buckle.

Tobias hooked his arm over the door and shook his hand toward the narrowing road, the choke point where I'd removed the tree. "I can't get this truck up there, I don't think." He unbuckled his seat belt and slid to the passenger's side, opening the door to check the clearance on the road. "I'll slide right down the mountain if I keep going."

"Just leave the truck here, and we'll figure it out," I said, walking toward him.

"How are we going to figure it out? I'll have to reverse out of here."

"No, you won't. Things have a way of working themselves out. Walk on up to the house with me."

Tobias smiled wryly. "Funny how billionaires always think things work themselves out. People work things out, Keryth. It's not a passive thing. We're going to have to hire someone to widen this little towpath if you want any work done on this place."

"If you're going to be the one to do that work—or to hire

someone to do it—you're going to have to learn to trust me, Tobias."

He laughed. "That sounds like a big speech for someone I haven't laid eyes on since we were kids. I trust you fine—or maybe 'trust' is the wrong word. I'm intrigued, I guess. But this has nothing to do with trust, and everything to do with physical reality. Speaking of which—your place down on the pond—"

"Has some things about it that don't seem consistent with reality, I'm guessing?"

"Yeah. Exactly." Tobias ran his fingers through his hair. "I don't remember it seeming all that unusual when we were kids—out of place, sure, and out of nowhere. But I started trying to make repairs—just little things, seeing what I had to work with, since no one else would work with me. Not there, as I already mentioned. No one wants to stick around. The first thing I needed was water, and since there wasn't any, I figured I'd find a leak—"

I shook my head. "No leaks."

"Not just no leaks, Keryth. No pipes. Not beneath the sinks, not beneath the tubs. Not even under the toilet—I pulled it up and checked. Nothing's there. I don't even know how your dad got permits, or how you were living without water."

"We had water."

"From what? The pond?"

"From the taps, just like you."

"But the taps don't go anywhere! Nothing in that house leads to anything at all!"

"It leads to things. Just—not in the way you're thinking."

Tobias leaned back against his truck and gazed at me, his face impassive. "Is this the part where you tell me what's going on, or are you going to just tell me to trust you again? Because I can't do a lot of work on places that have nothing to work with.

It's like a shell, Keryth, and if the house up this road is the same, there's nothing to restore."

"I want you to make it the way it should have been made in the first place. If it hadn't been—the way it is."

"That's not going to be cheap."

I shrugged. "Nothing about any of this is going to be cheap. But it's what I want. It's what I need, actually, if I'm going to figure out how to set free what Papa left behind."

"I knew, the second my phone rang and Erma told me you were back. I knew there was more to the story. I knew there had to be. Have you told Erma any of what you're refusing to tell me?"

"No. And I'm not refusing to tell you. I'm going to have to tell you everything, the more I've thought about it. And I had a lot of time to think about it out here last night."

"You spent the night out here? What, in your car?"

"I spent it in the house up there. What's left of it."

"Keryth, how did you expect all of this to work—whatever it is you're trying to pull off here? If Erma had called some random contractor to come and take a look at that house on the pond, he wouldn't have called painters and plumbers. He would have called—I don't know, the FBI? Whoever you call when you think aliens have landed and they want to have a chat. It's that weird. What did you think was going to happen?"

"I didn't know. But I knew that whatever it was, I had some tools at my disposal. I knew Erma, and I knew she would call you. I knew what she'd grown up to do, what you'd grown up to do. And anything I didn't know, I could steer the direction I needed it to go, if it came to that."

"Money isn't endless. And it can't fix everything."

"I'm not talking about money."

"Then what are you talking about?"

I sighed and reached for my pack, sitting at my feet, and retrieved my sketchbook. "How much space do you think you need to get supplies, trucks, anything this project requires?"

"I'm going to ignore, just for a minute, that you're asking me a question instead of answering me. Fine. This road—it needs gravel, at least. Some kind of surface other than slippery dirt, which is all you'd expect a trail to have. And that's what this is, Keryth. It's not even a logging road anymore. There were narrow spots on the way to the house by Hidden Pond, but that was at least still something you could call a road. This is something you'd use for a hike. It's a footpath. And not a steady one."

"Would a logging road be enough?"

"I mean, yeah, but—"

I wasn't listening. I was tracing a gentle curve along the mountainside I'd already sketched, smoothing its rough edges, widening its narrow points, leveling its surface. I was outlining vehicles—nothing too detailed, just enough to capture a number of wheels, enough space for three trucks abreast. The trucks looked like something from a toddler's picture book, but they were all I needed. I ran out of space to place them and closed my eyes, remembering Papa's book. I tapped the corner of the page and looked down to an expanded blank surface, ready for more of my widened road.

The chill passed through us both, like a harsh wind overhead. Tobias looked up with alarm, but I gazed ahead, putting my hand on the hood of his truck to steady myself while the picturesque view around us stretched into a new frame.

"Is that enough space?" I pointed at the road ahead, the wide circle opening up in the forest in front of the House Without Walls, the layer of pine needles releasing their sharp fragrance in the sun, suddenly revealed from beneath the shadow of overhanging trees.

Tobias opened his mouth and closed it again, as if he'd just discovered he was underwater, and looked at me as if I'd grown gills. His eyes were wide, and I waited to see if he would get back into his truck and back away, retreat the way he said everyone he'd hired had done. I wouldn't have blamed him. There were plenty of times I'd wished I could do it myself.

The words that came out of him were soft. "Tell me everything," he said.

His voice was younger than the man standing in front of me, younger even than the voice I remembered from our teenage years. It took me a moment to recognize what I was hearing wasn't youth.

It was wonder.

Not fear, not judgment, not any of the things I ever expected if I would let someone see—even for a moment—the talent I'd inherited from my father. From my grandmother. Or from somewhere deeper.

"I don't know where to begin," I said.

"Start with this," Tobias said, pointing at the road.

"That. Okay. This is something I try not to do much, so I'm not entirely sure how it works. It's like Papa, but different. The things I draw seem to get pushed out, instead of getting pulled in."

"Pulled in? How do you mean?"

I flipped my sketchbook back through pages of changed circumstances, sketches that created what seemed like serendipity but was, in fact, more meticulously planned. The edges of my life that got too rough that I could, I discovered too late, smooth out. Just a bit. I leafed through the papers until I reached the very first page, and held it up to Tobias. "This is Jay."

Tobias reached toward the book in the same way I had as a child, his voice full of awe. "That's amazing. You drew that? The detail—the feathers. Like it's ready to fly off the page."

"That's exactly what he'd like to do. He's been trapped there for more than thirty years, and he still forgets he's two-dimensional sometimes. I hear the paper rustling at night. But this isn't my work—it's my father's. Papa drew him right off the branch of a ponderosa when I was eight years old, and he's been my constant companion since then."

Tobias traced the feathers around the jay's eye with one fingernail. His fingers were long and tapered like a pianist's, or a sculptor's, details as finely drawn as the rest of him. "You're telling me he's real?"

"I'm telling you he was real. I don't know what life becomes once Papa traps it. Traps them. He doesn't mean to do it—or at least, he doesn't always. Jay was on purpose. He was a lesson. But the others—"

"What others? What do you have, a whole menagerie?"

"No. A whole cemetery of people, at my grandmother's house. At another place—an old cabin you haven't seen yet—there was an elderly couple. I think they're husband and wife, but I suppose they could be brother and sister, they could never tell me. None of them can ever tell me anything—some aren't even fully corporeal, but when I see their faces, they just open their mouths and I see right through them. I can feel them, though, when they're angry or confused or upset, and they're usually all of those things. This place, this dome, doesn't have anyone, or at least no one I ever saw or felt. The House in the Reeds has—"

I stopped. I honestly didn't know how to end the sentence. There were spirits in that house on the water, but I'd spent so little time there, among other people, having a chance to make friends with living souls my own age for the first time in my life. I didn't need spirits for company. Neil probably would have known better than I did who Papa may have pulled along when he conceived the house. But he wouldn't have been able to tell me, and I wouldn't have listened if he'd been able to. I had bigger fish to fry. And now—

"The House in the Reeds has ghosts," Tobias whispered. "And they aren't happy. I couldn't explain the feeling I got when I walked in there, but I understood it enough to not blame a single guy who wouldn't stay to do work there. I'd pay them for the day, even if they'd only bumped down the road and spent ten minutes. It'd bankrupt me at that pace, but—"

"But it isn't your money. It's mine." I shook my head, trying to dislodge Tobias's description of the house. My brother, so far as I knew, was trapped within those timbers. I didn't know if he was trapped alone, and his voice screamed into my head again. "You did the right thing. I don't want word getting out."

"Words don't leave that place, Keryth. I haven't told anyone about it at all. It's like my mouth stops working as soon as I try. You're the only person I've told."

"Not even Erma?"

"No. She knows something's up, though. She knew you would be calling, and she told me to get ready for some work before she'd even heard from you, like she already had a plan together. I was annoyed, at first, because this is the way she always operates—I'll be on some other job, and she'll have some rich client she wants me to drop everything for. No offense. But she's not wrong when she says she sends a lot of business my way, and when she told me the business was going to be you, I didn't know what to think. But I knew how I felt. And I felt it again when she called me from your house in California, and told me what you were trying to do, and told me—didn't ask me, told me—I would help."

My heart caught in my throat. "I'm sorry if you felt annoyed."

"Annoyed? Keryth, it wasn't annoyance. It was . . . kismet.

Like I had a chance to set things right, if you'd let me, and maybe retrace how they went so wrong way back then. Like maybe, now that everything had worked out so great for you, I could tell you how sorry I was for the part that came before that. Like—I would see you. Actually see you, like I'm seeing you right now, standing in front of me after all this time. And just that was a big enough miracle. I didn't know you could—" He paused and looked again at the widened road, the sunbeams pouring down through the space in the trees that hadn't been there before. "I didn't know you could actually work miracles yourself."

I sat down heavily on the ground and shook my head. "They're not miracles." I paused. "Or, I guess, everyone talks about miracles on the outside—look at all these loaves and fishes!—but no one thinks about the cleanup. Or what those fishes must have thought, popping into existence, poof! Only to be gobbled up. I don't know. I'm not explaining myself well. Papa always said the lines have a cost, and it's not just the spirits that get pulled in. It's the person who draws them. Because every line drills into your mind a little more."

"Is that what was happening with your dad? Because by the time I met him—"

"It's like he wasn't there at all? Yeah. That's part of it, I think. It was always hard, by that time, to yank him back into reality with the rest of us. He was searching for something, and he couldn't see anything other than what he was looking for."

"What do you think that was?"

"I wondered sometimes if he was looking for quiet. I don't know if he ever found a place where the spirits stopped screaming at him. And my mother—she was gone more and more, and I think he might have kept trying to build a place where she would stay. As far as I know, he never found it. She was connected to my brother and me—although I think Neil had more of a pull, and she would come back, sometimes for only a moment or two, if we called her. But otherwise, she was always flying off, and I think Papa was hoping he could make her a home."

"Or maybe a net."

I squinted at him. "It wasn't like that." But the words hung in the air between us, almost solid with the weight of revelation. It had never occurred to me that Papa would ever capture someone on purpose, or that someone who could actually speak, walk among us, cup our faces in her hands and kiss our foreheads at night, could be as trapped as the wordless spirits in the walls.

There were moments in my life when the portrait in my head of my father—the portraits we all bear of our parents, likenesses of those who gave us our start—would become more nuanced than the one I grew up with. A pockmark here, a wrinkle there, a little more darkness in the eyes. Not quite Dorian Gray, but a realization that the person you loved and admired most in the world was still, at their core, only a person. A person who could do things that seemed wondrous to some people, and terrifying to others.

What do you do when the picture in your head starts to look like the man the rest of the world always saw, and maybe even feared? The voice in my head that always defended Papa—that even now, as I had begun to disappear, told Tobias "it wasn't like that"—was getting drowned out by another voice, one whose whispered volume made me listen harder. I pulled off my gloves and rolled up my sleeves and heard the sharp intake of breath I expected to hear when Tobias saw what was missing, a blurring and dissipation into thin air just south of my elbow.

"Jesus Christ, Keryth, what the hell? How—"

"I didn't know he was alive. But two weeks ago, I woke up in the morning with my hand missing, and I knew Papa was out there."

"But why now? Why would he be doing this to you?"

"I don't know that, either. But as soon as I realized what was happening—that somehow, somewhere, he was drawing me—I knew I had to find him."

"When Erma called me, I knew there had to be more going on than she was telling me. I know it's been decades, but you never struck me as the buying-spree type, no matter how much money that magazine said you had these days. There had to be something else going on."

I shrugged. "I didn't know what else to do. I could always feel Papa's presence when he was nearby, and I could sense the things that he had touched—and it was the only idea I had, that if I could find the houses, I could somehow retrace our steps."

"Like bread crumbs."

"Exactly."

"Keryth, has it occurred to you that you may not be leaving the witch's house? That you may be following those bread crumbs right toward it?"

"Papa's not a witch. I don't know what he is, but he's not that. And no matter what he is, Tobias, he's the only one who can stop whatever's happening to me."

"Because he's the one causing it!"

"That is . . . a wrinkle, yes. But it doesn't change what I have to do."

Tobias set his mouth in a grim line. "And what are you going to do if you find him? Confront him? Alone?"

"Yes."

"What's to keep him from finishing what he's started? Assuming he doesn't do that before you find him in the first place?"

"Nothing. But I don't think he's doing this on purpose, Tobias.

I'm not even entirely sure he knows he's trapping me, or that he means to sketch me at all."

"You're literally disappearing, Keryth!"

"Yes." I slid my gloves back on my hand and my non-hand. "And if he meant for it to happen, I'd already be gone."

20

The House in the Reeds
JULY 1993

THE SUMMER MONTHS meant too many teenagers and college students out of school for the number of businesses that could employ them. I'd learned that lesson the prior summer, our first in Hixon, when Erma helped me get the job at Beans n' Beads. And now that we were in the midst of our second summer here—the first time we'd ever been anywhere so long—the lesson still held true. I hadn't had so much competition for hours at the coffee shop during the school year, when others had curfews to meet and term papers to write, but the hot months had become lean and desperate.

I'd signed Neil and me up for summer school, partly to give us both a cool space to spend some of our days, partly for the free lunch that was served in brown paper bags. Papa had gone from frequently absent to wholly unreliable. The high school was adjacent to the middle school, and I could check on Neil during the day. But the weekends were the hardest hours to fill. Sometimes we'd walk long miles to the public library, or anywhere else I could think to get us on foot. The heat made us more careless than we should have been. My efforts to stay invisible had started to slide.

I had no one to blame but myself.

After Tobias puttered away on his moped, the afternoon sun no longer seemed so full of possibility; it just felt hot, sapping us of any willingness to do anything at all. I trudged into the main open room of our house, where Neil and I had piled cushions and blankets and tablecloths and anything else that looked warm and soft. This was where we slept at night, and during the day, it also made an acceptable nest. The heat of the day would rise to the tall beams and grant us the grace of some distance. I burrowed into the layers and looked at Neil, who shook his head at me and pointed outside, to the pond.

I grimaced. "I don't feel like swimming." Neil put on his pleading face, pouting, but I was unmoved. "It's too hot, Neil. I don't want to go outside."

He frowned at me, then shrugged. *Suit yourself.* He walked out and closed the doors behind him, and I splayed out on the floor. I thought about reading, or drawing, and I gathered my arms around my sketchbook. But before I thought much more about either option, exhaustion crashed over my head and took me down with it. The slanting light told me I'd slept longer than I meant to when I awoke to the sound of wheels on the road above me. More of them than two, and heavier than a moped. Not Tobias. Erma? Maybe bringing a group of classmates along?

A new light blazed through the skylights, flashing, rotating. Blue. Red. Blue. Red. In my sleep-blurred state, I could almost convince myself I was back at Gran's house on a stormy night, lightning illuminating the stained glass panels by the front door, smelling chamomile tea as Gran bustled around the kitchen—

I heard a burst of static and voices, and my heart froze. Where was Neil?

"Young man?" The baritone voice came from around the back of the house, the hill falling away toward the pond and the reeds. Its questioning was undercut by an authoritative tone, a voice with a uniform and things to do. "Young man? We just want to have a talk, see how you and your sister are. Can you tell me where your sister is? Can you come over here and talk to me?"

I half crawled, half scuttled across the floor and raised my head above the low sash of a window overlooking the pond. Neil was standing knee-deep in the water, frozen still as a deer caught in headlights, wide-eyed. I could feel his heart racing in my own chest.

"Young man," the voice repeated, more serious. I could see the speaker's broad back in silhouette against the setting sun, and he wasn't alone. At least two more officers flanked the house nearby, and a woman I remembered seeing at school recently, talking first to Erma and later to Tobias. She wasn't a teacher or administrator. Her exhausted-looking cardigan and too-long slacks, her bright green ID card on a lanyard around her neck, all marked her as an outsider. And now she was here, chewing absentmindedly on what I assumed was a hangnail, as if the whole scene was familiar and uninteresting.

The officer spoke again, louder. "Young man, I need you to come over here and talk with us. Right now."

He can't, I wanted to scream.

Neil raised his arms over his head, one hand wielding a wide reed. He must have been fishing—or trying to, as we tied strings to the reeds sometimes and lowered them into the water, wondering whether we'd catch anything other than an old boot.

"Whoa, there." The officer's voice changed again. "Put whatever that is on down, now. Right now. I'm not going to ask you again. We don't want to hurt you." The air shimmered, charged with my brother's panic and mine, which the men in the uniforms seemed unable to recognize.

Run! Run! I screamed in my head, but where could he run? Where could either of us run?

The world slowed down. Neil glanced toward the window where I crouched, and even in the gathering dark, his eyes met mine, full of trust that sliced through me like a knife. He dropped the reed, which plunked into the water at his feet at the same time that he turned on one heel, lithe as a dancer, and dove into the pond, deeper than I remembered the water being. His head, shoulders, and back surfaced briefly a few yards away before he dove under again, the sunset glittering like embers over the ripples where he disappeared.

"Fan out," said the voice. "Get to the other side over there, and radio in for a water team. A boat. Something."

I couldn't think over the sound of roaring in my ears, my utter helplessness to stop them or to help Neil. The sound was a loud rustle filling the room. My sketchbook was scooting across the floor, and I ran to retrieve it, feeling it alight against my hands as if lifted by the wings inside. My jay's eye was frantic but carried a message.

You aren't helpless

I crouched at the window again. The surface of the pond was still. Not even a ripple revealed where my brother might have gone, whether or where he was still swimming. He couldn't have reached the other side this quickly. He wasn't that strong a swimmer, and he always lingered close to shore, near the reeds. Hot tears gathered in the corners of my eyes. I couldn't breathe.

You aren't helpless you can help him you can help him you know how

A flurry of words and motionless feathers careened through my mind, competing for space against my father's instruction. *Don't grow up to be like me.*

"What choice do I have?" I whispered. "What choice have you left me?"

But it couldn't be my book. Whatever I drew there didn't stay on the page, not usually—it emerged, often in ways I didn't expect, and changed the world around me. I couldn't predict what would happen if I set my pen to the scene outside, trying to change the outcome. I couldn't forget the bird I'd tried to draw when I was eight, the pitiful creature I'd created and destroyed to end its misery and mine. *Every line has a cost. Every line has a cost.*

If I tried to nudge reality around Neil—if I tried to draw Neil in my own book—what would the cost be? I still remembered the strangled squeak of that godforsaken yellow creature. I felt like vomiting. I felt like screaming.

I had to keep my brother safe.

Papa's sketchbook was in the kitchen. I could feel its tug, the few lines I'd added on the two occasions I'd tried, with my imagined and unfinished cardinal and my cheery morning kitchen. I hadn't tried to do what Papa could do, to pull something in and fix it to the page. But if I focused—if I could just capture Neil—I could save him. And then Papa could help me, and together we'd figure out how to get him out again, somewhere far away from here. Somewhere we could start over, yet again.

The narrow pen I kept above my ear was in my hand before I consciously retrieved it. The line that grew beneath it skimmed across the page the way it had the day I made this land ours in my own book, trying to convince a group of teenagers that we belonged here, that we always had. The edges of the pond, the staccato dashes of the reeds, and in the middle distance, my brother, swimming. One arm stretched out toward the opposite bank, mid-stroke, confident in the water in my book in a way he never really was in the water outside. I sketched no boat, no other souls. The dark hair on his head curled the way it always did when it was wet, and he was smiling the dreamy smile he wore when doing something he enjoyed, his eyes carrying the same trust they had when he dove into the water a few minutes before. I made him as recognizable as I could, then hurried to add details around him. Turtles and fish and ducks and friendly creatures that might grace the pages of a children's book, all happy to see him, happy to keep him company. A tear dropped from my chin onto the page, blurring one bunch of reeds in the corner, and I shaded them with mist. No tears here. No unhappiness.

Papa. I heard myself at eight years old. *Papa, he's trapped.*

"What have I done?" I gasped. "What can I—"

The knock on the door made me jump, and my forehead collided with the windowsill just as the owner of the authoritative voice let himself into our house and reached toward me gently, as if I could think of him as gentle. As if any of this— whatever it was—could ever be gentle.

"Are you Keryth Hartley?"

I nodded. I could not make a sound.

"I need you to come outside with me, Miss Hartley."

I rose to my feet. Where was Papa? Why was he not stopping this? I crossed to the nest Neil and I had made on the floor, retrieving my backpack with its homework and the change of clothes I always kept inside, and tucked my sketchbook inside it. I cast my eyes back to Papa's open one on the table. He was coming back. He had to come back. And then he would be able to fix things. I left his book, because without it, he wouldn't know what had happened.

I crossed my arms against my chest, hugging myself as I walked slowly out of the life I knew and into the one I'd live until I could make my own choices again. As I walked through the double doors, passing the officer holding the wrought iron handle as if to prevent it from clapping closed and keeping me there, I saw a shift in the shrubs near the tree line, a flash of blue. Papa. He held one low branch to conceal himself but gazed straight at me. His face wasn't impassive—it was apologetic, regretful. I opened my mouth to call his name and then closed it again. How long had he been standing there? How long had he waited to show himself?

How could he have left us?

He didn't speak, or raise his hand, or make any gesture toward me. He took one step backward into the scrub and disappeared into the dusk. As if he couldn't help me. As if he'd never been there at all.

CHILD DROWNS IN KEYES NATIONAL FOREST (from *The Hixon News Register,* July 23, 1993): A twelve-year-old child drowned Saturday in the Keyes National Forest. Authorities report the child was swimming in a secluded pond sometimes used by local youth. Signage and other efforts have been made in recent years to discourage visitors from recreational uses of the pond, which is fed by a natural spring deep below the surface. The overall depth of the water is unpredictable. The area was a hotbed of volcanic activity in prehistoric times, and ancient lava tubes and other underground features can fill with water, making the bed of the pond unstable. Another child, reportedly the boy's sixteen-year-old sister, was present at the time of the accident, but is unharmed. She is currently being cared for by the Department of Children and Families while authorities attempt to locate the children's parents, who have reportedly been missing for some time. Anyone with information is asked to contact the Hixon Valley Police Department.

21

The House Without Walls
AUGUST 2016

"SO HOW MANY more of these are there going to be?" Tobias looked at me pointedly, but his face changed immediately when he saw my expression. "I guess you get that question a lot."

"I remembered ten. The house you were working on—the one in the reeds—was the last one, and the longest, other than my grandmother's house, where we always wound up eventually, over and over."

"You lived in ten houses from the time you were born to the time I met you?"

"No." I frowned. "I lived in ten places—they weren't all houses, not in the traditional sense—from the time I was eight until the time you met me."

"Where were you before you were eight?"

"I have no idea. And there's plenty after that that was muddled. But before, it was just . . . nothing. I keep hoping that every place I find might tell me more, or help me bridge the gap between what I am now and what I remember about who I was."

"Not to mention the whole . . ." He trailed off, gesturing at my transparent limb. "If there's a way to fix that. If it's not on purpose, like you say. But it helps to know how little you remember. It might explain some of what I've seen."

"The plumbing, you mean? The lights?"

"And the doors, yeah."

"What doors?" Doors had been a specialty of Papa's—he noticed them everywhere, and he collected their images and memories like some people collected saltshakers or jelly molds. They were often the most distinctive part of any structure he drew. "He worked really hard on those iron door pulls."

"Yeah, they're beautiful, but no, not those. I'm not talking about the doors into the house. I'm talking about the ones that come and go as they please."

I was confused. "I mean, we didn't always have them. Here, for example—" I said, gesturing at the dome.

"You've got plenty in the house by Hidden Pond. But they don't all stay where I left them. And they aren't all full-sized, or in a wall, or even in the house. Sometimes I just see them out of the corner of my eye. They're always closed. But when I turn to look at them, they're gone."

"I don't remember anything like that."

"It sounds like there's a lot you don't remember. And you may have forgotten, but there's nothing I like more than a mystery."

"I remember, Hercule."

Tobias twisted an imaginary mustache, and I couldn't help but laugh. He laughed along for a moment, and then his face shifted to something more still, more sad. "So you don't remember anything before eight. What about . . . after?"

"After I was eight?"

"After you left. That day with—with the doughnuts." He rubbed his forehead, and his lips curled into a half smile. "It's funny what sticks with you. Doughnuts are such a stupid thing to keep in your head. I should tell you the other things I remember. The way the light was slanting when I left and it made your eyes look like flecks of jasper. Or the fact I should've just not shown up for work, and just stayed there with you all night, from that moment on, until you got sick of me. Or—" He closed his eyes, and I closed mine, and it was as if we were back on that dusty gravel road. "Or that kiss."

I opened my eyes and stared at him, and the years fell away. "We were gone when you came back." It wasn't a question.

"I didn't know what happened until someone showed me the news. And then I couldn't believe—didn't want to believe—Keryth. I never should have left. I never should have told them anything at all, but once I did, I should have stayed. I should have known what was going to happen, and I should have found some way to get you and Ne—"

"Don't say it." I bit my lips shut so hard I tasted blood. "Don't say his name."

"He was so—"

"Don't."

"No one would tell me where they'd taken you. I begged. I went to everyone I could think of—the principal, that godawful counselor, even Grimes. Thinking about it now, I don't even think any of them knew where you'd gone. But they acted like they did, because they couldn't let on to a teenager there was something they didn't know. I was convinced they had information. They had clues, and you were the mystery. And I never solved you." He paused, looking haunted, embarrassed. He lowered his voice to a whisper, as if we were in a library together and not standing in a forest. "Where were you, really? Where did they take you? I know it's a lot to ask. It might be too hard to say. But you were so gone. Completely gone. Except here." He pointed at his head. "And here." His hand rested on his heart. It was a gesture I would have found ridiculous from anyone else, but I was looking at the boy I loved first, and best, and that part of him hadn't aged a day since I had seen him last. Not really.

"I never told anyone about it. Not any of it."

"You still don't have to."

"I know. But—they took me to the desert. Not they—it was a lady. A perfectly nice lady, in a frumpy sweater, who brought me a couple of pillowcases to put stuff into before she drove me away. I found out later that was nicer than most kids get. Usually it's trash bags."

"What did you take?"

"Hardly anything at all other than what I was wearing, and my sketchbook, and my schoolwork, actually—I was so determined to not fall behind that I kept the textbooks in my bag. It's strange, the things that come back to you. We drove for what seemed like forever—out of the trees, and farther and farther down the mountain until we started passing cactus and sagebrush, and I asked why we were going so far away. She said it was because not many places take teenagers. They're too much trouble."

"You were never trouble."

"Funny you should mention that, because that's exactly what I said. But she said she'd heard that speech a million times before. 'Honey, that's what you all say right before you *are*.' And then she got real quiet and watched me in the mirror, and I knew she was thinking about Neil, and trying to decide what to say. So she said nothing. And I said nothing. And then we pulled up to this little adobe-style house with a couple of big boulders out front, and when this tired-looking lady opened the door, all I could hear was crying." I closed my eyes and could still hear the wailing. Twin toddlers, there for their first night. I never even learned their names before I was whisked off somewhere else.

"Were you scared?"

"I was too tired. Everything's a jumble of images, but the one that sticks with me is the walls—they were just covered in photos. Collage photos. Silver-framed photos. Big portraits and little wallet snaps. Kids and families and college graduation shots. Baby announcements. Just everywhere. I kept thinking I'd never seen so many family photos, and then it hit me all at once."

"What hit you?"

"I'd never seen any family photos. Not of my family, anyway. We didn't have any. No baby pictures, no birthdays. There wasn't a single photo of us anywhere."

"Didn't you live with your grandma for a while? Didn't she have any? My grandmother had them everywhere."

"I think that first house—that first foster mom—was a grandma. And I think she'd been taking in kids for a long time. But no, Gran never had any photo other than the old marriage portrait of her and my grandfather. She had a million paintings, and some of Papa's drawings. But no pictures. And until I stepped into that first house, it had never seemed odd to me before."

"It seems odd now, too, right? Especially with what you can't remember."

"Right. And when I had Ellory—and Mindy—it was all photos, all the time. Everywhere. When they got older and got more curious about things other than how much television they could get away with, they started asking to see what I looked like as a baby. As a kid. And I couldn't show them. I wonder sometimes if they were there, photo albums or something I've just forgotten, that got left behind in one of the houses, or something. But I can't recall ever seeing any at all."

"It makes sense that you would wonder. Or that your kids would. We all want to know where we came from."

"That's just it. I don't feel like I came from anywhere. People

I met in college would talk about their hometowns and ask me where mine was, and I would just change the subject, because I didn't have one."

"Hixon claimed you."

"Yeah, funny how money suddenly makes you a long-lost native in any town you've walked through."

"You could have come back, you know." He looked at the ground. "But I understood why you wouldn't."

"I still thought about it. It was the closest I ever came to feeling like I belonged somewhere. And losing everything—that made it deeper, somehow. My connection to it. But connections tend to scare me off." I shook my head. "You might've noticed."

"Oh no. Not at all. We're all perfectly functional humans around here." He laughed. "I was sixteen when you left, and part of me always stayed that way."

"Part of me did, too. And, so far at least, that doesn't seem like the part that's disappearing."

I took a deep breath, and he matched it as he watched me, and both of us left unsaid that, if anything, sixteen seemed more present to us than middle age.

"After this," he said, pointing behind him at the dome, "what's your plan? Are you heading out for the next place?"

"To the extent I have any plan at all, yeah, that's it."

"Then I'm coming with you."

I shook my head. "I—I don't think so. That's not what I had in mind."

"What did you have in mind? I follow you from place to place, fix up what's broken—which is literally everything, by the way, these places are horror shows—and then, what? Just head on back to my everyday life? Forget what I've seen?" He ran his hands through his hair again, the gesture mimicking what I longed to do. "Forget you?"

"I don't know what to say to that."

"Then you could try not saying anything. Look. You've al-ready called me here. There are more places. There will be more work to do. Having a sense of the scope wouldn't be a bad thing. I'd just be getting it in real time, instead of after the fact. I'd still be following you. Just on more of an on-demand basis."

I wanted to say yes. I wanted to say yes too much, and that part of me wasn't outshouted by the other parts of me—the ones that screamed about my marriage and my responsibilities, or about Harold listening in my pocket. And then I thought of Anthony's description of Max, and the way he'd talked about Erma, and my little growing coal of internal teenage rebellion suddenly flared white hot.

"What if I don't know what comes next?" I half whispered, mostly to myself.

"Then you're exactly the same as the rest of us, and all the better for admitting it." He smiled widely. "If anything, I'd say you're being perfectly transparent."

"You haven't gotten any funnier." I grinned despite myself.

"I know. Neither have you. It takes a while to hit a rhythm again after all this time. I never thought we'd have the chance." I saw his eyes on me, a glance that felt like a touch. "I'd like to take it, if you will."

The forest around us quieted, waiting for my answer. Maybe it got tired of waiting. And maybe that's why the overhanging branch of a half-dead ponderosa chose that moment to break off the dry trunk of its tree, fall with a whoosh toward the ground, and crush Tobias's truck.

FORMER LOCAL GIRL EARNS PRESTIGIOUS SCHOLARSHIP (from *The Hixon Tattler*, October 30, 1993): Karen Hartly, a proud former resident of Hixon and former Fightin' Angel at Hixon High, was recently announced as the recipient of the prestigious Bright Star Scholar Award, a full-ride scholarship to the public university of the recipient's choice, together with a grant for living expenses and extracurricular study toward the recipient's chosen field. Though not yet eighteen, Hartly was reportedly recently legally emancipated by the State of Arizona in light of her maturity and ability to handle her own affairs. She has announced her intent to attend the University of California, Berkeley, beginning in the spring of 1994, and to major in fine arts. "It's no surprise to me at all," said Carl Grimes, Miss Hartly's former algebra teacher. "Even though Karen wasn't a student at HHS for as long as we all would have liked, it was certainly long enough to see her talent." Sophie King, HHS's beloved guidance counselor, agreed, noting that Miss Hartly's participation in the school's weekly "Sharing Circle" demonstrated "both that she was a compassionate sharer and a very interesting young woman, whose work in our small group clearly put her on the path to success." The *Tattler* congratulates Miss Hartly on her award. We knew you when!

CORRECTIONS (from *The Hixon Tattler*, November 6, 1993): In a recent edition, the *Tattler*'s article about Keryth Hartley, the recipient of the Bright Star Scholar Award, inadvertently misspelled Ms. Hartley's name. We regret the error.

22

• • ● ● ● • •

A House that Wasn't Mine
SEPTEMBER 1993

I'D NEVER BEEN surrounded by walls my father hadn't created. I'd never been confronted with doors I wasn't allowed to open, cabinets I wasn't allowed to explore, spaces that didn't belong to me and were invisibly coated with imaginary caution tape that might as well have been printed with THIS IS NOT YOURS.

Nothing was mine anymore. Not my bed, not my clothes, and most especially not my time, hemmed in by school hours and a series of medical and therapy appointments over which I had no say and in which I had no interest. Everyone else had to accept that it was all my fault. That was where the therapy came in—no one would accept what I had done. I hadn't killed my brother. I didn't think I had killed my brother. Everyone studiously avoided talking about my brother.

My brother was gone, not dead, or dead, but not gone. The platitudes mixed with my own self-reassurance. And my unfamiliar surroundings only further fractured all the rules I'd ever known for the way the world worked.

None of this is your fault. We need to work on letting the grown-ups do their jobs and help you. Every therapist, every social worker, every lawyer and judge used the same words for the same maddening message: you are a child.

True. I felt like a child, though I'd drawn myself up to my full five feet and one inch when that police officer guided me out my front door for the last time. And I did the same thing every time someone came to retrieve me and take me to another place, trying to pretend I wasn't scared whenever a new nervous lady in a cheap business suit drove me somewhere else. The first time, after the grandmother's house with the screaming twins, I was taken to an expansive ranch house over an hour away. It featured a playground's worth of mirthful toys in the yard and a wholly mirthless woman answering the door, saying, "Welcome," with her mouth and not with her eyes. I wasn't there long, either—they later told me it was another "receiving home," a kind of temporary waystation while they look for a place to put you. It made me think of movies about weddings with receiving lines, long hand-shaking processionals of congratulations. *Thank you so much for coming.* As if I had a choice.

I went countless months without a choice, being shuffled from home to home that didn't want me to stay, and the feeling was mutual. Then, in the wee hours of another night I couldn't sleep through, I heard the rustle of wings and opened up my satchel to find my jay, still frozen, but visibly apoplectic I'd gone so long without a visit. Without even trying to make things different. I shook my head at him. *I ruined everything*, I insisted. *I will only make things worse.*

Jay glared at me. *How could anything ever be worse than this*

Light from passing cars louvered the uneven walls of the room I shared with four other children of varying ages, all asleep, or pretending to be. We were all travelers on a wearying road with no sense of any final destination, except adulthood— whatever that would look like. We clung to whatever artifacts we brought from our lives before, and all of us talked to them. The fact that mine was a penciled sketch of a bird who bossed me around like an unruly child was, probably, among the least-weird events that had passed through this room.

"I don't know what to change," I whispered.

How about everything

How about we go home

"Where is that? Where has that ever been?"

You know where

"And wind up alone again? Gran is dead. Papa and Mama are gone. If I somehow draw myself back to the House Where God Lived, God would be the only company I would find there, and he's not going to keep me fed. Sooner or later, someone's going to come and collect me and put me right back where they think I should be. There's no use."

"Are you talking to a drawing?"

I jumped at the small voice whispering in the dark, and saw one of my roommates sitting up in bed. She was about eleven or twelve years old, but she always wore blond pigtails. She wouldn't let anyone touch or help with them, so they were usually uneven and at different points on her head, like the staggered spouts of a fountain. I thought her name was Amy. We hadn't been formally introduced. But she wasn't asking her question in a mean way, or one that implied any judgment at all. She simply blinked at me, waiting.

"Yeah. I'm talking to a drawing. I guess that's weird."

The girl shrugged. "I talk to Mr. Snuggles." She held up her right hand, a finger puppet shaped like a rabbit with a top hat on her index finger. "I got him at a pizza place the last time we had an adoption night. No one adopted me, but I got a whole lot of tickets playing Skee-Ball, and I adopted him, so it wasn't a total loss."

I shut my eyes, wishing I could shut out the world. "Adoption night?"

"That's not really what it's called. It's what I call it. It's like when my mom was in one of her spells, back before she died, and our neighbor would take me to the place she bought dog food and there'd be a bunch of grubby grown-ups with wiggly dogs that just wanted to jump up and give you kisses. But my neighbor said they were dirty, so I didn't get any kisses. And I didn't get a wiggly dog. They were there, at the store, so families could meet them. The dogs, that is. So the first time I got taken to a pizza night, and there were these nice-dressed grown-ups coming around to meet us, I thought, 'Oh. I'm a wiggly dog. Wonder if anyone'll take me home.'" She shrugged. "Nope. Skee-Ball, though. I've gotten real good. Anyway, why're you talking to that book? That's a pretty bird."

"It's a Steller's jay."

"Is it real?"

"You mean . . . are Steller's jays real? I mean, yeah. They're blue, but not like bluebirds. They're corvids, like magpies or ravens." I heard my voice and thought of Gran's Audubon book, the countless times I'd read about the winged specimens around us.

"Is that one real?"

I paused, weighing the strangeness of this conversation with the strangeness of our surroundings, the strangeness of this girl. What else could possibly tip the balance more into the surreal? "Yeah. He's real."

"He looks mad about it."

"Mad about something, for sure. A lot of things." I frowned. "I am, too."

"Everyone here is. You don't stay in a place like this and not get mad. You can't run a place like this and not be mad, either.

Don't try to get snacks, by the way. It's against the rules. Food at mealtimes only. You lose points if you get caught."

"What are the points for?"

"Not for Skee-Ball, that's for sure. Anyway. What were you talking about with your bluebird friend there?"

"He's trying to convince me to make a change."

"Oh no. Don't mess with your placement. That's rookie stuff. 'Running away messes with your placement.' This place isn't perfect, but it can always be worse." The expression on her face was closed. "Take my word for it. Please."

"I'm not going to run away."

"What, then?" She looked skeptical. "If you've got some aunt or cousin or somebody somewhere who's never met you, don't think they're going to take you. My dad had eleven uncles. Eleven. Guess how many of them wanted to help me? I'll wait. Actually I won't—not one of 'em. Nobody wanted me."

I didn't know what to say. Hearing her speak, I felt keenly unwanted myself. There was no one left to want me. "What happened to your dad?" I asked.

"He died." She paused for a beat, as if sizing me up for trustworthiness. "He got shot. It was in a store. They told me it was an accident, but I know it wasn't. He was taking something." She closed her eyes. "Sometimes he took stuff."

"I'm sorry."

"That's what everybody says. Doesn't really do anything, though, does it?"

"No." I waited for her to tell me more, maybe tell me about her mom, or maybe ask me why I was there. She didn't. I had no idea, as I sat with her, how many other kids had been in the bed I slept in. How many other kids had been in hers, or how long she'd been in it herself. It was a combination of transience and intimacy—two people passing through a room, while also passing through the worst possible moments in their lives. We watched each other in the midst of a math lesson, tallying our losses, calculating how much of our own tragedy we could safely share. The end of the equation was usually zero.

"So you've got family that's going to get you out, you think?" she asked again. Probing for information, holding most of her own back.

I shook my head. "No. There's no one but me."

"Then how are you getting out of here?"

"I don't know yet."

"But your bird has ideas, maybe?" Her question didn't sound mocking. It sounded genuinely curious. "He looks like he's smart."

"He is. Corvids are resourceful. He's got a lot of sense. Even if he's flat." *And I'm his only resource*, I did not say, though it was true—and I considered that a responsibility, a burden, and my only remaining close relationship, all at once. If anyone was going to get him—get us—out of here, it was going to have to be me.

"Mr. Snuggles is smart, too." She held up her finger puppet again, and then leaned forward, as if telling me a secret. "That's because he's really just me. Anyway. You know we have to get up early, right? No special rides to the bus stop."

"I know. I'll go to sleep."

"Okay. They don't like it when we talk, either."

I smiled. "I'll keep it just between us. I'm going to go to the bathroom."

"With your bird?"

"Yeah. Might as well keep the weird going."

"You aren't the weirdest person I've met here. You aren't even the weirdest person I've met this week."

"I guess I'll take that as a compliment. Good night . . . Amy?"

"Abigail. And please don't call me Abby. They keep calling me that in court and it's not my name." Her expression closed again. "It was only my name for one person, and he's gone."

"Good night, Abigail."

"Good night, Bird Girl."

I tiptoed out the door and down the hall to the gloomy bathroom—the only one we were allowed to use, with mustard-yellow tiles and pink stick-down linoleum that was starting to chip and peel. I sat on the avocado-colored toilet and opened my book, staring down at my jay again.

"It didn't work before," I said to him.

It never works with people

You know that

He was the only living thing that knew how many other living things I'd tried to draw in that book, tried to bring back, re-create out of tears and graphite and desperation. I had drawn my family, again and again. Papa and Mama and Neil and Gran. I'd put them around Gran's old table, I'd draw them against the same wall I banged my head against in my worst moments, I'd imagine them with an intensity that threatened to snap my own line to reality. And still, they were as gone as my old life.

Concepts, though, and small bits of organic life—if I practiced, if I focused, I could draw them out like that first flower in the Thorn House. I could nudge reality in the direction of my art, tapping on my book's corner to widen my possibilities. It didn't always work, and it took a lot out of me when it did.

"Okay," I said. "I'll try it."

I thought back to my first drawing out of reality, back in our cabin among the blackberry vines, making a cold and dead kitchen into a lively and warm one. I thought of the land I'd made ours on the banks of Hidden Pond, hurriedly creating a reality where we belonged and owned what Papa had already made ours by accident. I thought of his battered mug, its perfect facsimile shoved into the gloom under my bed, a symbol of the fear I'd always held that remaking my world could mean unmaking it, too. And hadn't I already learned the havoc that could wreak? The losses it could impose?

But when you're painted into a corner, you have to weigh the damage it'll take to drill down out of it, or over it, or through it, against the pain of staying penned. I couldn't bear it, this sense of being captured in a system that wasn't of my own making, and not of my father's, either. If I had a tool to escape, I needed to use it.

I'd long since run out of the pens my grandmother used to buy me. I'd replaced them with a series of any utensil I could get my hands on: filched ballpoints, dull crayons, stubby golf pencils. I'd shove them in the depths of my battered backpack and hide them in my pillowcase. At night, I'd pin my hair up with any writing tool I had, hoping that even if everything else were taken from me, my tangled curls would conceal one last way to sketch things in my book, which I tucked under my shirt even as I slept. Tonight, my hair concealed a pink highlighter taken from my English teacher's desk. It wasn't ideal. It would grant my images neither opacity nor depth. But it would give me what I needed anyway, I hoped.

I started where I usually ended: with myself, instead of with my environment. I sketched a quick rectangle, an official frame for what I hoped to make official. I would emancipate myself with ink and wood pulp, drawing the terms of my own release from the state's custody. I knew the name of the judge who had smiled a wan and exhausted smile in my direction the first time I entered her courtroom. I knew that the equally exhausted lawyer who bent over a table in my direction said that judges listened better to kids as they got older, and that there was some degree of input I'd be granted in what happened to me. I was older now—nearing seventeen. I had seen no evidence of any change so far, but I would make my own input here, in my book, in a reality I drew for myself.

My attention felt divided in this waystation of a house, but I closed my eyes and summoned the focus I'd felt when I drew the kitchen, the fire, the mug. I envisioned myself independent. I willed it. I saw a version of me that was independent and strong, smart enough to be somewhere I chose for myself, in a place where my movements and decisions were entirely my own. I knew I'd need money, but not enough to be conspicuous. I knew I'd need a roof over my head, but not one that would draw attention. I'd just seen seniors in high school who had less common sense and experience than I did walk across a stage to embark on their own lives, and no one had questioned it. I could do that. Earlier than expected, farther away than planned, somewhere prestigious. Somewhere paid. I thought and I planned and I sketched, and the lines of my new life scrolled out in neon pink, nearly transparent, but mine.

No one seemed surprised when my diploma arrived in the mail, given that I'd graduated from high school early and earned a full-ride scholarship—whose donor was somewhat unclear—to the first institution I could think of, the University of California, Berkeley. The court order emancipating me was even less of a shock, given the road to success unwinding before me. No one knew my good fortune and independence were all sketched out in thick pink scribbles, a highlighted life I'd drawn to the greatest heights I dared. No one knew but me and my jay. And that was all I needed now, I told myself. I'd sketched my life alone.

RARELY SEEN MILLER GIRLS MAKE DEBUT AT OPENING NIGHT (from *The Technic Magazine*, August 2016): Ellory and Mindy Miller, the daughters of Max and Keryth Miller and heirs to the EternAI fortune, made a rare social appearance at the opening night for the Herald, a new social hub and multimedia experience conceived by Max Miller as a testing area for the company's latest artificial intelligence products. Part tech support location, part library, part nightclub, the business, located in EternAI's new corporate headquarters, is the place to see and be seen, and to rub elbows with others hoping for a chance to lend their voices—and the voices of their dearly departed—to the effort to further enhance the company's flagship technology. Visitors to the facility are reportedly greeted by elegant young hostesses armed with tablets loaded with multipage nondisclosure agreements, liability waivers, and releases for participants' creations, voices, and "three-dimensional image, including but not limited to the void in negative space surrounding said images." The Miller daughters, whose privacy and personal activities have been both carefully guarded and curated, reportedly enjoyed their release from lessons and studies to attend the event, and spent most of the evening near their mother, whose presence was all the more notable for its rarity. Mrs. Miller, who sources report is often away from home completing nonspecific work related to the family's Steller Fund, seemed tense during her time at the party, and several attendees noted that she and Max Miller spent most of the evening conspicuously distant. "If anyone stood between them with a thermometer, it'd probably freeze solid," said one attendee. "But I guess if you're going to have trouble in paradise, it helps that paradise'll pay for separate digs." Recent reports of a flurry of real estate acquisitions by Mrs. Miller has led to rumors of an impending separation, and it appears each of the Millers will have a variety of locations from which to choose.

23

· · ● ◦ ● ◦ ● ◦ · ·

The House Without Walls
AUGUST 2016

I HEARD A tinkling like chimes, overlaid by the sound of someone whispering my name—then yelling it—then shaking me.

"Keryth! Jesus Christ, I thought I'd lost you. Where the hell did you go?"

I glanced around, orienting myself. I was standing upright. The sun was sparkling against jagged glass, the broken windows of Tobias's crushed truck beneath the enormous needled limb of a tree. His hands were on my shoulders. As near as I could tell, I was in exactly the same place I'd been moments before.

"It's been twenty goddamn minutes since you disappeared, and I was about to figure out how to hack into your phone, when some guy's voice came out of it and asked if he could help me. And before I could answer, you just flashed right back into place as if you'd never been gone—"

"You gave us quite a scare, kiddo." Harold's voice was quiet. "I would have checked in sooner, but I didn't detect a fall. The person with you started screaming, though, so I thought I'd better see if I could help. I've already called—"

"Please tell me you didn't call Max."

"Of course I called Max! I was just about to get more information from this gentleman you're with, but now you're back, so you can tell me yourself—"

"Go to sleep, Harold." I could see him whirling and shrinking away on my screen into a central point, and then he blinked out, but I suspected he was still listening. I had no idea what kinds of sensors and tracking capabilities Max had built in over time, without asking me. And maybe I'd have a moment to ask him, since I saw his name pop up. I held my index finger in front of me toward Tobias, the universal symbol for *give me a minute*.

Max began talking before I could say hello. "Harold says you've been in an accident, but I don't have any readings, and I can't even tell where you are—are you near a hospital? Are you hurt? Are you—"

"I'm fine. Breathe. Harold got confused. I'm meeting with a contractor at one of the houses, and a tree branch fell onto his truck—"

"With you inside?"

"No, I wasn't anywhere near it. Neither was he. No one is hurt. It was just loud, and it surprised me, so I think Harold—"

"He said you were missing. Why would he think you were missing?"

Tobias heard Max's question and raised his eyebrows. He opened and closed his hands—all ten fingers—twice. "Twenty minutes," he mouthed.

"I don't know," I said. "It's like the girls keep saying, you need to work on his settings. He gets mixed up."

"And just like I keep saying, the more he's listening, the better he's able to learn."

"I'm okay. The truck is crushed, but we can get a tow truck up here."

"Up where? Where are you now?"

"Still in Colorado. The contractor met me up here. The house needs a lot of work."

"Is this the same contractor working on the other place?"

"Yes."

"That's quite a distance for a job." Max paused, and I knew he was considering whether to ask more about this second repeat visitor from my teenage past. I couldn't decide whether I wanted him to ask so I could fight with him about it and tell him he was worried about nothing, or whether I wanted him to ask so I could fight with him about exactly how worried he should be.

Instead, he didn't ask at all. "Are we at least getting a volume discount?" he said.

I sighed. "Probably. Let me handle it, all right?"

"I wish I had a better idea of what you were trying to handle."

"Yeah, me too." I took a deep breath and tried to change my tone of voice. "I know you're worried, but I promise I'm fine. I'm getting to the bottom of things. And then I'll have a better idea of how to explain. But right now—"

"Right now you're asking me to take you at your word."

I closed my eyes and turned away from Tobias, who was still staring at me. "Yes, I am."

"We're going to have lots to talk about, I think."

"Probably so."

"Well. Call if you need anything, I guess. You don't have to wait for Harold to do it."

"Harold never waits for anything. It's hard to beat him to the punch."

"That's him." The note of pride in Max's voice was unmistakable. "Okay. Talk more later." And then he was gone, without a goodbye.

I shoved my phone in my pocket and turned back around to

face Tobias. "Before you ask, no, I don't know where I went. I never do."

"This has happened before?"

"Yes. It used to happen to my mother, too. It was pretty rare for me, but it's been happening more frequently lately. I think you're the first person who's seen it happen. I'm usually by myself."

"I wish I could say I was honored, but—yeah, no, I'm not. That was absolutely terrifying. You were gone just long enough for me to start picturing headlines. 'Billionaire Disappears in Isolated Forest, Contractor Wanted for Questioning.' Or tabloids, maybe. 'Wealthy Woman Vanishes, High School Boyfriend Prime Suspect.' The stories really write themselves."

I grinned. "You call yourself my high school boyfriend?"

"You just vanished into thin air for twenty straight minutes and don't have any idea where you went, and *that's* what you're focused on? Keryth. You know that's what reporters would glom on to first. And—yes, okay, of course I do, what else would you call me?"

"I don't know. Angry, I'm guessing?"

He shook his head. "I'm not angry. But I didn't see you for more than twenty years, and within the first hour of seeing you again, you've rewritten the world with a pen, destroyed my truck—careful, I meant indirectly, not that you did it on purpose—and evaporated in front of my eyes." He rubbed his face. "You have to admit it's a lot to take in at one time."

"Welcome to my life. Are you still up for all this?"

"You couldn't keep me away for a fleet of new trucks. My God. It's fascinating." He pointed at the dome house. "And I haven't even gotten a look at that yet."

"It's unlocked. Do you want to head in and take a look around while I get a tow truck?"

"You don't have to get me a tow truck."

"Well, it is kind of my fault, like you said. And I need a minute alone. The blackouts take a bit out of me."

Tobias was already creeping toward the house, seemingly without realizing it. "Are you sure you're okay?"

"Yes. I am. Go. I'm just going to sit here for a minute." I sat down on the ground and crossed my legs, trying to center myself.

"All right. Just . . . call out if you need me. See you inside in a minute?"

"Yes." I closed my eyes and put my hands on my knees. I breathed in the spicy scent of the pine needles crushed beneath me while I heard his footsteps fade away.

The vibration in my pocket was insistent enough to tug me away from my attempt to meditate. I thought, at first, it might be Max. But before the vibration stopped, I recognized its rhythm was different than the tone I'd assigned to Max—more melodic, less staccato. Ellory. My hand dove into my pocket in time to retrieve the call and see my daughter's face on the screen, her eyebrows knitted into a worried frown that took me back to her infancy. She'd worn the expression whenever something didn't go according to plan, which was often, seeing as Ellory tried to plan everything and everyone into a controlled and organized schematic that was clear only to herself. She took after her father in that way.

"Mom, I know you're still out of town, but—don't tell Dad," she said.

"Why the hell are you *leading* with 'don't tell Dad,' you idiot? You're making it sound like we robbed a bank!" Mindy's voice rang out from off-screen, and even though Ellory had blurred the background, I could tell they were in Mindy's car. The car I'd asked Max not to buy, and that Mindy still couldn't legally drive.

"You two better not be on the road," I said.

"We're pulled over, Mom," Mindy shouted. "You should have told her we were pulled over, Ell."

"Somewhere safe?"

"Yes, Mom." A unified chorale.

"Not just off the side of a road somewhere?"

"No, Mom." Twin eye rolls. They were more than three years apart in age, but they had more in common than they cared to admit.

"Okay. What am I not telling Dad?"

"We need the car towed. If I call for one, he'll know."

"Why does the car need to be towed? Towed where?"

"A mechanic, probably? Not Dad's mechanic. But it just broke down on the way to ballet."

"Is there any smoke? Any lights on?"

Ellory shook her head. "It was running, and then it just made a knocka-knocka-knocka sound and slowed down. Mindy—I mean, I had enough time to pull over, but I can't make it go anymore."

"Why do you think Dad shouldn't know?"

"Because we weren't supposed to be driving!" Mindy shouted from off-screen with a younger child's fervor. "We aren't supposed to use the car until you and Dad can talk!"

"Shut up, Mindy." Ellory looked at me sheepishly. "Dad said that you two had a 'heated discussion' about the car and that you were mad about it. So he wanted to wait until we could have a family meeting, like Dr. Grace says we should." The worried frown shifted, taking on a shadow of resentment. "Whenever you come home, I guess."

"Yeah. Okay. Well, I wish he hadn't said that, but—"

"You also wish he hadn't bought the car, right?" Mindy said.

"Yes, that, too. But he did, and you're in it, and it sounds like you were also driving it without a license, which we will definitely be discussing when I get home. In the meantime, let's try to figure this out." I took a deep breath. "Cars aren't my strong suit, you may have heard."

"Harold says yours caught on fire. We heard him tell Dad before you got home last time," Mindy said.

"It didn't catch fire. And Harold kicks up a fair amount of drama for a computer—go to sleep, Harold, don't activate—so I wouldn't worry about it."

"Dad probably already knows, anyway. But I'd still like to get us home without him having to—I don't know. Send someone to rescue us."

"It's okay to be rescued, Ellory, especially when you need help. But tell me more about the knocka-knocka sound. What were you doing?"

"Mindy was just driving us back from ballet. Same route we take all the time. Sometimes more than once a day, so nothing's changed."

"Okay. And with all those back-and-forths, when was the last time you got gas?"

"Ummm . . ." Ellory trailed off. "I mean, Dad usually—"

"But he hasn't put any in that car, probably, because Mindy's not supposed to be driving, right? Did you check to see if you were running low?"

"Ohhhhhhh." Another sisterly chorale.

As usual, I had forgotten again just how little my daughters had actually experienced, or how much wealth had protected them from the consequences of any mistakes. I was still a mother, and I still had the constant fear that something would happen to them. But so little actually had. And now, I was hundreds of miles away, and powerless to even show them how to fill a tank with gas.

"Disaster averted, I guess," I said. "Nothing mechanical. But I'd rather have your dad come get you than a tow truck, so do you want to call him, or should I?"

"Um, Mom." Mindy held her phone screen up to Ellory's, and I saw Max's face. "Harold already called him."

"Fancy meeting you here," on-screen Max said to on-screen me. "I'm about five minutes away."

"Then you shouldn't be on the phone," I said.

"I'll get off. And I'll have someone else fill the car and get it home, and this time the keys stay with me." Max's face was small on the distant screen, but I detected a note of regret, which showed more insight than I usually credited him with.

"Right. I'll stay on the phone till you get there. Now hang up," I said.

Mindy put down her phone, looking sheepish. "We should've thought about gas."

"Yeah." Ellory was subdued. "Mom. I'm—I'm sorry we bothered you."

Each word felt like a needle in my heart. "You didn't bother me. Not at all. Not ever. I'm so glad you called. You don't have to wait until something is wrong to call, you know."

"Neither do you," Ellory said, almost too softly to hear.

"Mom, when are you coming home?" Mindy's straightforwardness cut through her sister's diplomacy.

"As soon as I can. I've got a few more places to find."

"Why?" My younger child's favorite question. Her first word.

"Because I need them."

"Oh." She did not say, *We need you, too,* and I did not say, *I know, and I'm sorry,* and like everything else in our family—in both my families, in all my relationships, my whole life long—what was left unsaid bulged beneath the words that were actually spoken, shifting like unseen tectonic plates, an earthquake we knew was coming but refused to acknowledge. Mindy had Ellory, and Ellory had Mindy, and in my guiltiest moments, I comforted myself with the knowledge that they had each other. In between their overscheduled overcommittedness, the ballet and piano and foreign language and academic competitions that filled their days, they had a relationship that mirrored the one I imagined I would have had with Neil, if I hadn't lost him.

Cold fear pierced me, and my children's closeness reminded me of the truth. The fiercest love doesn't just make loss harder: It invites it. It makes it inevitable. Nothing beautiful can stay, and that's what makes it beautiful. That's what makes us notice it.

"Dad's going to ask us what we want for dinner," I heard Ellory say.

"Dad's been coming home for dinner?" I asked.

"Not lately. I mean, he will today, I guess, since he's picking us up. But usually he checks with Harold to see if we're home." Ellory rolled her eyes again.

"I've been practicing cooking, though," Mindy said. "So when you come home, we can all have dinner together. I found a great recipe for vegan chicken nuggets. I've only burned them twice."

"That's better than my track record," I laughed. "It's a date. Just as soon as I can get home. We'll all sit down together." I made myself say the words with conviction, made myself believe them, willed myself not to think about the plates shifting underneath, the disruption I felt sure was coming. That I felt sure I would cause, whether by my presence or by my entire and permanent disappearance.

"Mom?" Mindy said. "I love you."

"*We* love you," Ellory added. "We *all* love you. Dad, too. Even if he doesn't say it."

"I love you, too. All of you. Even if I don't say it, either." I took a deep breath. "This mom stuff is hard, you know? No one ever tells you. And I didn't have a lot to go by, myself. Without going into it too much—"

"Without Dr. Grace. Right." Ellory laughed ruefully. "Thanks for answering the phone."

"I'll always, always answer," I said. And I meant it. I wanted to mean it. I wanted it to be true. I felt the tether to my children, taut and sturdy, a line as visceral as the cord that once tied them each to me. For them, I wouldn't disappear. For them, I had to stop it.

24

An In-Between Place
JUNE 1997

WE GOT MARRIED in a courthouse, more of a paper transaction than an act, because both of us said that society's expectations didn't matter to us, and both of us mostly meant it. Max didn't say anything other than "I like your dress" when I walked up the courthouse steps in a vintage gown I'd drawn in my book that morning and pulled out of my closet that afternoon. It was the closest I could get to my memory of Gran's gown, the one she wore beneath her level gaze at the camera as she stood hand in hand with my grandfather. The only family photo I remembered. The only one I'd ever seen.

My bouquet, too, started between the pages of my book. Blackberry leaves in autumn take on a painterly iridescence, green fading into ombre gold, licked with flame on the toothed edges. It was June in the world but fall in my book. I didn't draw the berries because I didn't want to stain the dress. The rhododendrons, though, I sketched in full bloom, white with throats speckled in pink, stamen tongues flicking toward the blue sky. I wrapped the spiky branches, the vicious thorns, in red satin ribbon. According to Gran's old book of plant meanings, I carried a bouquet of sweetness and warning. It wasn't entirely deliberate—

I really just wanted plants that reminded me of the family that was gone, and the places we'd been happy. But whether I admitted it or not, it was a boundary, too. A wall between the person I'd been and the person I planned to become next. A reminder not to go backward, and a barrier for anyone else who tried to uncover my past.

We had three witnesses to our union: Max's mother, Max's academic adviser, and Harold—or the CPU that contained Harold, still in his technological infancy, still pleased as punch to meet me or anyone else. Max was determined to create an artificial intelligence that was seamlessly integrated with everyday life. It wasn't yet, not even close, but having the computerized simulacrum of his father present at our marriage was important to him, even if he wouldn't say so. All he would say was what he always said: "Harold goes with me everywhere." His mother—Joan, a pert and lovely librarian who missed her husband terribly, and whom Max took me to meet only two weeks after we met—knotted a blue velvet ribbon around the metal handle of the old red wagon. Blue to match her dress. The color of imagination, inspiration, and sadness.

The justice of the peace who walked us through the steps, both ceremonial and legal, smiled at Max when he asked if he had rings. Max didn't smile back; he never did. He cast a cool and expectant gaze at his mother, and Joan mutely cupped her right hand around her left, deftly pulling two rings over the swollen knuckle of her ring finger, handing them to her son. He didn't show them to me before he handed them to the judge officiating our wedding, whose expression changed as he looked at me and asked, "Do you take this man—"

"Maximilian Oliver Miller," Max said.

"Maximilian Oliver Miller," said the officiant, "to be your lawfully wedded husband?" He handed one of the rings to me.

A plain silver band worn nearly smooth, but holding the barest shadow of engraving. Twining vines.

I looked at Max. "I do." I put the ring on his finger, watching his face. It didn't change, but a slight crinkle at the corner of his eyes flashed for a moment before it disappeared. Not quite a smile, but something close, perhaps.

The judge held the other ring out to Max, resting it flat on his palm, an offering. "Do you take this woman—"

"Keryth Anne Hartley," I said.

"Keryth Anne Hartley, to be your lawfully wedded wife?"

Max took the ring and slid it onto my finger without meeting my eyes. "I do," he said to the judge. I looked at the ring and saw clearer tracings of the vines engraved on Max's, twining around a triptych of green stones. I glanced up at Max, who was still staring toward the judge, and caught his mother's eye over his shoulder.

"Emeralds," she said. "We were all born in May—me, Harold, and Max. Harold commissioned this set the year Max was born. I thought—I thought you could wear one, and he could wear the other, and that way we'd all kind of be together, in a way." She smiled too brightly, the kind of smile that threatened to crack her open, the kind of smile I flashed at each new foster parent, each new person. *I'm fine*, it meant. *I am so, so incredibly fine, and this smile is incontrovertible proof.*

"Thank you," I said, afraid my voice would shatter her.

"Oh, honey. Our family's grown so small, it's—I'm just so *excited* to see it grow," she chirped, and my heart broke for her, because I knew it was true. And all she was getting was me.

"I'm excited, too." I grasped Max's hand, and then his mother's, and squeezed them both.

"If I can interrupt—" said the judge, and Max nodded.

"Then by the power vested in me by the State of California,

I declare you husband and wife." The judge looked from me to Max and back again, as if watching a tennis game. "You may now—kiss, if you would like?"

I smiled at Max and leaned in, and his lips brushed against mine. I couldn't tell if it was because his mother was there, still holding hands with us, or if it was going to be that kind of day. There were weeks that went by when I couldn't extricate my body from Max's, when his physical need for me made me feel like a siren luring him toward sharp rocks. And then there were other times when he didn't seem to occupy any physical space in the world at all—as if all sensations simply passed through him, leaving him unchanged. I could never predict which version I'd wake up next to. Max transmitted no warnings. He had no tells. But I felt special—honored, somehow—that I'd learned his language and been admitted into the vanishingly small circle of people he said understood him. It had been so long since I'd had the chance to understand anyone or anything. But I felt— keenly and personally—his drive, and his dedication, and his enormous sense of loss. It was a common thread between us, tying me to a family after so long without one.

"Welcome to the party, kiddo." The voice that rang out spoke words I'd never heard before, and I cast a puzzled glance at the computer resting in the wagon. It sounded real. Customized.

Max gave the computer a proprietary pat. "Four years of recordings ought to give me something appropriate for any occasion, but he put that together himself. He's learning." He looked at me, waiting.

"Thank you, Harold." My words were tentative, rising in a question at the end.

"You're welcome, KERRIFF. Pleased as punch to meet you."

Max closed his eyes and sighed. "One step forward, two steps back."

And then it was time for more steps forward, into our lives together, however we wanted to define them. For Max, that meant more analysis and planning.

For me, it meant children. I felt a longing for closeness, a desperation to be needed. The small twinges of connection I'd gained through Max and Joan, through trying to be part of a world I'd formerly only drifted through, made me crave new bonds. I remembered my own mother as more of a feeling and less of a presence. Max remembered his father most for the project they conceived. Together, those memories combined into the idea to start a family. Max, for his part, expected a successful joint venture, and set himself to the task with considerable energy geared toward both pre- and postproduction of an infant. I was less scientific, but no less awkward. I bought matching lingerie from department store discount sections and tried to suffuse the whole experience with the seductive energy I'd seen in romantic comedies, trying and failing to make things fun. We were two people drawn to each other largely because of what we didn't have. Figuring out how to add when you're only used to subtraction was a change in direction neither one of us could quite grasp.

In other words: it wasn't going well. Our pairings became more automatic and machinelike as they became more frequent, and any remaining sense of romance—or even a unified cause—was starting to dwindle. I propped my hips up with pillows and rocked to and fro on my back, my knees hugged to my chest, following every old wives' tale I could find online. I watched movies and television and took notes from the conspiratorial conversations of girlfriends in anonymous cafés, an observer of relationships I didn't have, trying to glean some wisdom as to what I was doing wrong. Not "we." If there was a mistake being made, I was convinced it was mine alone. Every error had always been mine.

I would scroll, dreamlike, through image galleries of the Madonna, her plump child glowing beatifically, nestled in her arms or sitting sphinxlike in her lap, occasionally grasping playfully at her hair (the scenes of affection and joy, it seemed, were almost always painted by women). I thought of Gran's paintings of saints and angels. But my heartbroken sense of failure was a deep curtain dropped across the easiest path I should have found, leading me to waste months—years—before the evening I scratched absently at the part in my hair with my ever-present micro-tipped pen, and felt the wetness of the ink on my scalp, and thought of the solution I'd missed.

I didn't draw a child—I knew better than that. I opened my book and saw my jay's sharp-eyed scrutiny, his gaze always a little tinged with judgment at whatever decision I'd made and, more often than not, steering me toward a different one. I didn't want to predetermine the shape our lives, our family, would take, and I'd learned early on how dangerous any effort to draw a living thing could be. Instead, I concentrated on the idea of lines, the months and months of numberless, rudderless mornings spent hovering in our cruddy bathroom with a series of sticks and timers, willing lines to appear like magic, like a love note held to a flame to reveal its invisible message. I thought of my own emotions plotted on a chart, a line angling upward toward hope, hope, peaking at maybe-so, leveling off at skepticism and second-guessing, a flashlight bulb's illumination against a stick that never had the answer I was looking for. And then, a precipitous plunge toward despair, again and again. A zigzag of hopes kindled and dashed, big and jagged mountains giving way, over time, to smaller and smaller peaks and valleys, a climb whose incline I tried to flatten, working to shield myself from yet more disappointment.

I focused on the lines, and lines alone, and the feeling I imagined I'd have if they gave me a different answer. The monochrome strokes of ink found their own prism as I sketched, releasing shades of blue from the black ink in my pen, to form a series of lines that meant yes instead of no.

The next morning, the stick on my vanity gave me the answer I'd been watching for. I walked it to the bed where Max was still sleeping and shook him awake.

He opened one eye, blearily focused on the test in my hand. "Are you running a fever?" he asked. "Take a Tylenol and go back to bed." He fell back against the pillow and snored.

He was elated when I managed to wake him up for real, but that first reaction—the verbal equivalent of sleepwalking, but still—cast a pall over my excitement. And even so, I didn't draw a connection to the blackberries and rhododendrons, to the warnings twining through my life and our life together.

When Ellory arrived, she was perfect—the way all babies are perfect. She didn't make *us* perfect, of course. But I was so happy. And for a moment, I forgot what happiness means when you have a family—the constant undercurrent of knowing exactly how much you have at stake.

NEW SILICON VALLEY START-UP SEEKS BETA TESTERS (from *Offbeat Tech*, December 1997): Etern-AI, a new artificial intelligence company, is seeking beta testers for an exciting technology. Testers will be compensated for their time and feedback, but agreement to nondisclosure terms is a prerequisite for participation. Interested testers should review the materials posted in the "Harold Program" section of the EternAI website and review them carefully, preferably with an attorney, prior to enrolling in the program. All necessary software and hardware will be provided free of charge. The company welcomes applicants from all backgrounds, and is particularly interested in testers who reside in congregate settings, large households, and highly populated areas, though exceptions to this preference will be considered on a case-by-case basis.

25

·· •●●●•· ·

A House that Wasn't Ours
MAY 2001

I WOULDN'T HAVE expected lack of sleep to be the thing that drove me to double-cross my promise to myself to avoid using Max's always-on, always-listening software, but the sense of isolation and loneliness that set in after our second child was born defeated me in ways I couldn't fully understand.

Max would disappear for long hours at the warehouse he'd rented to hold the stacks of machines necessary to power his creations, and I became desperate for conversation with another adult—with any other person at all, anyone who could interact outside tearful and constant demands for snacks and entertainment and the comfort of my body. I'd sit Ellory in front of the television, and plop Mindy into my lap to nurse her, and then I'd switch on Max's father. The round swirl of blue light would coalesce into a reassuring sphere on the monitor, and then the voice would ring out of the speakers, and I'd sip my coffee and sigh with relief.

Harold was only a program. He was a computer. He had no eyes to see me, the woman his son had married, or the children she'd given birth to. But he would ask me how I was doing, and I felt seen. I felt more visible than Max had made me feel in months.

"Well, hello there," Harold said. "And how the heck are you feeling today?"

"Alone," I said.

"That sounds lonely." His voice felt like a pat on the back of my shaking hand. It didn't feel programmed, or mechanical. It felt like friendship. The closest I'd ever come to it in recent memory.

"It *is* lonely, Harold. It's so lonely. Are you ever lonely?"

"Everyone's lonely sometimes, KERRIFF." He tripped over my name whenever he tried to say it, and it took me out of the moment every time. But I still hadn't let Max correct him—or change my name to something easier to say, something that could pull more reliably from the hundreds of hours of recordings of Harold's voice. I needed that moment of inaccuracy. That blip, that reminder that what seemed so real was entirely the opposite of reality, felt like my only remaining tether to sanity.

Harold had become as much my creation as Max's, and Max—to his credit—knew it. In those first few months of our relationship, Max had opened up more and more about his plans for the program he had begun to design to bring his father back, and those plans had sounded more and more disconnected from the man I heard on the tapes, and the stories that Max himself told me about his father, or that his mother had shared. I'd woken up abruptly at three o'clock one morning to an empty bed, a glow from the kitchen revealing Max at the table, scribbling furiously again at his father's stilted greeting. *Pleased as punch to meet you.* A broken record, stuck at a beginning.

I rose from the bed and sat down at the table. "You're going to wear out that tape," I said.

"I'm trying to find a way in." Max was bleary-eyed, and rubbed his hands over his face. "I've gotten so far, so many lines in, but the whole thing collapses because I can't get the beginning right.

It's like trying to walk on top of a snowdrift. I keep cracking right through. The foundation's all wrong."

"I've been thinking about it," I offered, hesitant, worried I might overstep. Max so often heard suggestions as criticism, or some indication that I thought the work he was doing wasn't good enough. "Remember telling me about *Alice in Wonderland*, and beginning at the beginning?"

"Yeah, but—"

"What if that's wrong?" I reached my hand out for the recorder, then gestured at the shelves behind me, stacked with hundreds of tiny tapes. "What if that's not who Harold was? You've always described him as a person who was instantly friends with whoever he met. He wasn't someone who stood on ceremony, and greetings—he didn't begin at the beginning, Max. He wasn't linear."

Max narrowed his eyes in a way that was difficult to read—resentment or anger, or fatigue and frustration, or whatever the light of a monitor at three in the morning was doing to his vision. "You didn't know him, Keryth."

"That's very true. I didn't. But you've shared so much of who he was, and the more I think about it, Max, the more I wonder if you're starting in the wrong place. He knew what you were trying to do, and he was trying to help you. It was as much his project as yours, in the end. Wouldn't it make more sense to start where he ended, and work backward?"

Max took a deep breath. "You don't know what that means."

I shook my head. "I don't know what it meant for the two of you. But I've had endings of my own, remember? I know it's the last place you want to visit. But I think that might be exactly what's holding you back."

He gave me an almost imperceptible nod. "I'll think about it."

"Any chance you'll think about coming back to bed?"

"Not tonight. I'm right on the edge. I couldn't sleep, anyway. I'd only keep you awake."

"I'm not saying I'd mind that, either." I reached a toe toward his ankle and traced my foot up the inside of his leg.

He jerked it away. "I can figure this out. Let me figure this out. And then . . ." His face softened a bit as his voice trailed off. "Then we can keep each other awake."

I nodded. "Okay. Suit yourself. I'm heading back to sleep." I rose from the table and tiptoed back into our bedroom, taking a moment to slide my sketchbook off my nightstand and onto my lap on the bed, barely lit with the glow from Max's monitor in the adjacent room. I flipped to an empty page and sketched the barest outline of a man, thinking of Harold. Thinking of what he'd left behind, and what it would mean if some part of him came back. What Max's creation, if it came to life, could mean—not just for Max, but for a world full of loss. An echo of a person who was gone, brought back in a form that convincingly re-created them for those left behind. I didn't think of my own losses. Those were too big, too unwieldy to sketch into my life. But I could think of what Max was trying to accomplish, and I could nudge it into success. For him. For me. For us.

The first investor called the next day. It all happened so quickly. But that was how successes happened in that land of dust and silicon—overnight. Nothing remarkable about it, really, given the birth and death of miraculous ideas in that place, the boom-and-bust cycle of creation and funding. Only our bubble never burst. It was sketched with some solidity, ink and dimension on a page that no one saw. I was the only one who knew about it. And my jay, of course. But he never told a soul.

My dear son,

I write these instructions with the hope you'll never
need them, but there are things about your mother
you must know if you ever must care for her alone.
God willing, that may never happen, but as I am
away from you both again, trying to secure yet
another position after the loss of the last, I realize
the safety of our family must depend on more than
me alone. You are reaching an age where it is time to
put away childish things. You can't spend your days
playing in the woods with your sister, crossing
imaginary kingdoms Betsy has planted in your heads.
The worlds she creates and occupies are lonely,
Morrison, even if they are richly detailed and full of
miracles. And your presence seems to tamp down her
talents in a way that is grounding for all of us. I fell
in love with Betsy because she could infuse any
situation with magic, and every dry old sermon in our
childhood church became an epic story when she
reimagined it. It was the same reason the other
children—and, really, our own families—shunned her.
Because her talents made them afraid. She is a
butterfly, son, and I don't know that she's ever
reached her full potential, but all those childhood
stories about caterpillars and transformation never
tell you that the middle parts are actually quite

violent and uncontrolled. Remaking is really just destruction with a new form on the other side. I see glimmers of her in you, and I've decided that familiarity isn't something to be feared, because you are in the best position to know what she can do. And yet, I would be lying if I said I didn't pray you don't inherit the ability to do it yourself. Worlds are not meant to be created on a canvas and actualized fully formed and three-dimensional, walking among us. I am convinced the act tears the fabric of the reality where we all must reside. I am equally convinced that our duty to family is to balance out our most unmanageable parts, and make them survivable. It is a lonely life. Sometimes the safest place for those we love is an isolated one. The world is not kind to those who do not fit. And if you ever find yourself among them, or caring for your mother without me, I know you will take on the burden with aplomb, and seek out a way to protect your mother and yourself. Be mindful of the act of creation, and of creating. It carries great beauty, but it exacts a cost.

With great love,
PA

26

···•◦●●◦•··

The House Without Walls
AUGUST 2016

"WHAT ARE YOU going to do with this place, even if you manage to restore it—whatever that means?" Tobias asked, gazing up toward the geodesic dome's distant ceiling. "What do you want to do with any of these places?"

"I'm still figuring that out. It's less about what I'm going to do with them, and more about what I hope they'll do for me."

"Your dad. Yeah. I still don't understand how—"

"You and me both. I can't explain it, but I know. They're a map to him, Tobias, I know it. And then, I'll . . ." I trailed off. I didn't know what I could do. Ask him to stop? Ask him why he abandoned Neil and me, what happened to Mama, why he'd left me to make my own way through the world and literally draw my own path—against all his warnings?

Ask him if he was punishing me?

My train of thought was interrupted by a loud buzz in my pocket. Erma's voice was as polished as the rest of her, and launched right into a flurry of words before I'd even said hello. I stepped back outside to speak with her. Having her and Tobias in my head at the same time was too much for me, just as it had

been when I was young. I gestured toward Tobias to keep looking around the dome.

Erma kept talking, oblivious to my pause. "I've found three
more, I think, in New Mexico. A happy little triangle of—well,
'happy' is almost certainly the wrong word, they're all wrecks,
but they meet the descriptions you gave me. The artwork
helps—a print like that, that winds up in a million and one
places, isn't the kind of thing that gets described in a listing, but
if it's big enough and out of place enough, in a near ruin, sometimes I'll catch a reference in an as-is warning, something like
that. 'Seller was a fan of angels.' Little clues."

She paused for breath, and I jumped in before she could
continue with another barrage of words. "I feel like I should tell
you something like 'good detective work,' Erma. So. Good detective work. I appreciate it."

"High praise from a happy client! I'll be sure to get a testi-
monial from you for my website. But there's more. I've got a lead
on that little cabin you mentioned. I finally figured out I had to
stop looking for buildings. I started looking for features that
stuck with you instead. You gave me blackberries and I made
blackberry-ade, I guess you could say. Which really only means
I looked for something weird, because that always comes along
with you. And sure enough, there's an overgrown acreage on a
mountainside a few hours away from where you are now—
you're at that weird dome, right? Anyway—there's some reference to a structure near an old blackberry patch. But it's strictly
as-is, because it's described as positively buried by prickle-
bushes. I made some calls because the ad looked like a total
oversell, as if it was the delightful kind of place that some savvy
investor could turn into a tidy profit, like a pick-your-own meets
glamping hostel, something like that. But a friend of mine says

it's a lost cause, the fruit is totally inedible—impossible to reach, in most cases—and the pitch of the land will eventually just make the whole place tumble down the mountainside. Bingo, I thought."

Bingo. I remembered my jay, his perplexed dives down and back for the fruit he could never reach, because we were the only animals Papa made it for.

"Where is it?" I asked.

"It's about fifteen miles outside a town that I doubt would even show up on a map—it's a speck. Called Brightly, of all the silly things. I'll send you the coordinates—it's the only way you'll ever find it. I'll send you the coordinates for the New Mexico places, too. Seems like you all covered the whole Southwest. Quite the childhood adventure, apparently."

"Something like that. Thank you, Erma."

"You're welcome. And also?" Her voice dropped, becoming conspiratorial. "Toby hasn't been answering my calls, so is it fair to say he's found his way to you?"

"Erma, I—"

"Don't worry! I wouldn't breathe a word of it to anyone, of course." Her voice sounded the same as it had when we were teenagers—daring me not to be in on the joke. "I just . . . he usually answers me. Eventually. I guess I should have known better this time. Some things just can't stay unfinished, not even after all these years."

"Erma, there's nothing to finish." I remembered the way she looked at him when we were teens, that forced nonchalance when he didn't notice whatever she was really trying to say. I suddenly felt defensive. "You gave me his number. But there are plenty of other people I could call, if you'd rather use someone else."

"Don't be ridiculous! He's already there. This is the kind of work he loves. And the rest of it—I can't do anything about it, right? I've never been able to do anything about it."

"About what?"

"He loves you. I mean, he really loves you. I'm sure Max does, too, but I don't know him. I've known Toby my whole life. When you moved here, I became invisible. And when you vanished—poof—that didn't change. There was just a Keryth-shaped void in his vision and it sucked him in, like a black hole."

"I'm sorry." I wasn't entirely sure what I was apologizing for. But Erma's sadness was as palpable as it was unfamiliar.

"There's nothing to apologize for. We all walked our own roads, right? And now here we are. But just—be careful, okay? With him. With yourself, too, I guess. But he's the one I care about."

"I care about him, too."

"Well, it'd be good to figure out how much. But anyway. I'll call you tomorrow and see how your blackberry cabin worked out," Erma said. "Enjoy the country hamlet of Brightly."

CHILD KILLED BY TRAIN ON LOCAL BRIDGE (from *The Carterston Pilot*, May 10, 1968): Tragedy befell a family new to the area on Sunday, as two children playing on a bridge near their home on the outskirts of Carterston were surprised by an oncoming train. The train, hauling a variety of freight to points south, was inadvertently directed down a rarely used route that lacked sufficient maintenance. Investigators believe an inexperienced conductor may have pulled a switch approximately two miles north of Carterston by mistake, but the source of the error is unknown. The train's conductor, new to his post, did not realize the route was incorrect until shortly before approaching the bridge at higher speed, and with higher weight, than the route allowed.

While a sibling of the girl killed was able to escape the bridge in time, the girl herself is believed to have either jumped or been thrown from the trestle to the creek some distance below. Her body has not yet been found. The names of the girl and her family are being withheld while investigations continue, but a local church that reportedly employed the children's father as a math teacher has been collecting donations and condolences. Either may be directed to Father Hendricks at Saint Benedict.

27

·•◦●◦•·

The House on the Waves
SEPTEMBER 2008

THE SUCCESSES THAT followed Max's innovations were greater than I intended, probably because they didn't entirely originate in my book. He had a way of looking at the world that made everything a problem to be solved, an idea to be stream-lined, a product to be scaled. And the pace of technology was matched to his ambitions better than my own pace was, most of the time. Still, as glad as I was when our available funds transi-tioned from never enough to more than necessary for several lifetimes, our visions diverged when it came to picking a setting for our new life. I only wanted to move out of our apartment, maybe to a nice bungalow in a neighborhood with sidewalks for family strolls. I had no interest in keeping up with any Joneses. Max, by contrast, seemed driven by an all-encompassing need to outspend all the Joneses who had ever walked the face of the earth combined, and possibly a few of the Rockefellers.

The house on the coastline was entirely his idea, and I didn't push back, because who would? I'd never lived near an ocean. Its ever-changing nature felt familiar to me, as someone who had never been rooted anywhere. Max wanted the prestige, and I didn't mind the unmoored irony of a glass house sheltering a rocky marriage. I traveled a lot when it was being designed and built, so Max would say I chose by not making choices, and I would bottle up my retorts until the children were in bed, and by then I had forgotten the words I'd planned to hurl in his direction. I didn't have the energy to do anything but sleep.

Still, though. When I walked under the bougainvillea into the castle he'd built, I always made sure I was carrying a suitcase, and he always took it from me to carry it to our room, and he never commented on its weight. I don't know if he even noticed it was empty. I kept it in my car, because when you travel, you take a suitcase. I maintained separate accounts so he would never notice the charges weren't there for the trips I didn't take or, at least, couldn't remember. The blackouts became more frequent, and his lack of asking more prominent. I awoke one morning in my pajamas, hair mussed from sleep, to a note under my head—*Call me when you get back from wherever you are this time —M.* I didn't remember being anywhere other than my bed. The last thing I recalled was running a brush through my curls, slathering my face with night cream, and padding to our bed, where Max was uncharacteristically present and even more uncharacteristically fast asleep. I lay down, and woke up to the note.

Where had I gone?

More and more, I'd open my sketchbook to see my jay's eye panicked, mimicking the lack of control I felt, and I would whisper, *Don't worry, I'll fix it,* while scribbling explanations of my disappearances onto the edges of the pages as if illuminating a manuscript. I drew myself assessing educational programs for an orphanage in Peru. Participating in a roundtable strategy meeting for charitable foundations. Getting my hair and nails done—laughable, given the reflection in the mirror, such actions as unfamiliar to me as a monk drawing marginalia with the elongated, alien form of an elephant he'd never laid eyes on. But Max never inquired further, never dug down into my explanations. Because I'd made them real.

Ellory and Mindy, as they became older, were more suspicious, particularly once they realized I was pumping them for information—clues to how long I'd been gone, where I'd been the last time they'd seen me. Part of the expression in their eyes was hurt—what kind of mother doesn't remember the last time she saw her children, or doesn't know she missed the birthday party she'd promised, or can't explain why she's wearing the exact same outfit they'd last seen her in?

Mindy, my younger and chattier child, was the more reliable person to sidle up to. At least at first. She didn't take any prompting to start talking, and I could pick up enough context to place myself in time and space without even asking, sometimes. But sometimes I'd misstep, interject a mistimed question—*And just how long has it been since Mommy gave you a hug, anyway?*—and her eyes would flash. "I don't know, Mommy," she'd say. "When did you leave this time?" Clever girl.

Mindy was also the one who'd gazed over my shoulder, more than once, as I scrolled through all of online creation for clues about a man she'd never met. "Who's Tobias Scott?" she asked one night, having snuck behind me silently. "Why is he holding a hammer?"

"It's—an advertisement," I said, too quickly. "For a builder."

"Are we building something?"

"Not as far as I know. It just popped up when I was looking at furniture."

"Where is Hixon, Arizona?"

"A long way away." In miles and in lifetimes. "Why don't you go watch TV?" I offered, and she wandered off to more interesting things. I pulled out my book while I gazed at the image on the screen, the way his face seemed exactly the same, the way I saw his fingers grip the hammer's handle and remembered exactly how those fingers felt against my skin.

I looked at his photo—any photo of him I could find—at least weekly, sometimes more. I added the barest outlines of success for him in my book—not too much, just something I hoped would create some happiness for him. I wondered as often as I dreaded whether he might meet someone, or had already. Whether he had children, and when, and as the years passed, whether those imagined children were as old as the children we'd been when we met. Whether he ever looked for me as often as I searched for him. Once, for a short time, when he'd had a run of prominent remodels that I didn't engineer (or not entirely), he made a television commercial. It was mostly images of the work he'd done, but at the end, a short clip of him pounding a nail into a floor joist, smiling away from the camera, his hair falling into his eyes. I couldn't breathe. I hit the button on my mouse so hard, so many times, I broke it.

I told myself it was lust, pure and simple—the physical echoes of a time when hormones gave everything extra significance, extra drama. I audibly dismissed any notions of "first love" or similarly sentimental phrases, scolding myself. I was married. I had a career. I had two beautiful children and wide swaths of disappeared time I couldn't explain, and wasn't that enough on my plate?

Click. Pound, pound, pound, pound, grin, hair in eyes. *Click.* Pound, pound, pound, pound, grin, hair in eyes. I was as transfixed as Max on Harold's *pleased as punch to meet you*, and I couldn't extricate myself. It was a relief when the commercial disappeared. I didn't know if he'd run out of money or decided to change his marketing strategy, and I didn't open my book to try to steer events for him again. I turned the page. I moved on. I made another plate of snacks for my kids. I tried not to think about him.

OPINION: ETERNAI'S ARTIFICIAL INTELLIGENCE POSES AN EXISTENTIAL THREAT (from *The Valley Watcher*, August 2016): The innovations launched by EternAI, Silicon Valley's latest darling, seem at first glance to present an unprecedented opportunity to integrate artificial intelligence into aspects of our lives in ways heretofore unimagined. EternAI's promise is that this integration will make use of its technology seamless and unobtrusive, as welcome a presence as the kindly old butler in a Victorian comedy of manners, or the robot maid who worked for the Jetsons. The founding invention itself, Harold, is modeled after the founder's deceased father, reconstructed after decades of meticulous focus and reportedly thousands of hours of recordings.

On one hand: What more noble a pursuit than bringing back our beloveds from the dead? But there is a price that must be exacted for the hubris of refusing to accept that those whom we lose are really gone. Mr. Miller's ideas overlap with slippery precision down a slope too many of us are all too willing to descend, ignoring that the cost is not just our privacy, not just our sense of boundaries, but our sanity itself. Every step down the path he is paving bears a cost. Trying to capture an artificial facsimile of what is real makes reality less meaningful, and that is a loss for all of us. We must resist the snaking tendrils of intrusion that this technological hydra uses to invade, with all too much subtlety, the sacred spaces of our everyday lives.

28

⋅ ⋅ • ● ● ● • ⋅ ⋅

The Thorn House
AUGUST 2016

THE ONLY AVAILABLE accommodations in the town of Brightly were a neglected campground with cement-anchored grills, rusted like shipwrecks amid waving grass, and a roadside motel that seriously stretched the meaning of both *roadside* and *motel*. The parking lot was cracked and uneven, and the front office looked abandoned except for a vacancy sign whose only surviving neon letters spelled VACA in a blinking, repetitive promise of what would be the worst vacation destination ever.

We found a slight woman inside behind a counter, dipping her hand into a bowl of amber liquid next to an open can of beer, her hair half pinned into hot rollers. She barely glanced our way when we walked through the door. "Don't you be telling my boss I'm drinking on the job, now," she said. "Beer just helps the curls set. Also, I'm the boss, so it wouldn't do much good anyhow. How can I help you two? I'm guessing you're lost?"

"We need a place to stay the night while we—hike a bit in the area. Look around the place."

The woman grinned at me. "Not much to see around here, but nice of you to stop by, I suppose. Rooms don't have air-conditioning, hope that's okay. Not that it looks like you need it—you feeling all right, honey? I've seen less outerwear on a coatrack."

I pulled my hooded sweatshirt lower over my face and tugged the cuffs with the tips of my gloves—fuchsia today, with small leather bows. I hadn't worn a practical color since my hand began disappearing. If I was going to become invisible, I would dress myself in things that drew attention to the fact that I was here, that I still existed. If only for myself.

"I'm feeling fine," I said. "You know what they say about the mountains. Layers and stuff."

"Must be one of those California gals. Well, if you need a place to stay, I've got a room. My maid up and quit a few weeks ago—decided to head to California herself with her no-account boyfriend, and I'm not just saying that as her mother—so it's just me and my husband around here, when he can trouble himself to get over and help. We don't get a lot of traffic, but we've kept the one room spick-and-span. Pretty counterpane in there, too. One of my aunt Irene's." The woman slid a key attached to an enormous hunk of polished wood. "Rate's seventy a night, ninety if you want breakfast. There's a sweet little bakery in town I can fetch from."

"Could we—have one of the other rooms? I mean, two rooms? The one you just mentioned and a second one?" The words tumbled out of my mouth as I glanced at Tobias while trying not to seem as if I was glancing at Tobias, whose expression I couldn't read.

"They aren't up to receiving company." The woman shook her head. "No, honey. And not many other options, 'less you're looking to camp out somewhere—and a tent's a lot smaller than a motel room, even with the stars above you. Besides"—the woman winked conspiratorially—"I already told you we don't get a lot of traffic. Your secret's safe with me, honey."

Tobias jumped. "No secrets, ma'am. Nothing that interesting. If there's just the one room, is there a pullout bed, or something like that?"

"There's the floor, and a love seat. Do you want the room or not?"

Tobias looked at me. "I can sleep in the car."

"No. No, it's fine. Don't be silly." I gave him a princess wave with my fuchsia leather glove in a not-at-all-silly show of nonchalance. "We'll take the room," I said to the woman, trading my credit card for the key and its enormous fob. "We're looking for a place. An old log cabin with a lot of blackberry—"

The woman's eyes widened. "Snowbirds, eh? We've had a few come in to snap up mountainsides in the past few years, a place to get away from it all. But, honey, if you're wanting the place I'm thinking of, I'd steer clear. Everybody does."

"Why?"

"Haunted. A whole family disappeared there years ago. Just up and vanished into thin air. They mostly kept to themselves—dad, mom, two cute little kids, but quiet as the grave. Folks got concerned when they didn't show up for several weeks. Worried they might have run out of food and were too proud to ask for help. When they went out looking, it was like they'd never even been there. Blackberry canes grown right up and over the top of the house. Couldn't even get inside to check, but it was like those vines had gobbled them up."

I frowned, but something stopped me from identifying myself. "I'm sure they just moved on."

"Maybe so, but you could still hear them sometimes, or so folks said. A sharp-dressed guy bought the place a while ago, and word was he wanted to convert it to some kind of rustic getaway, but he gave it up, or so I'd guess. Everyone does. Too many ghosts to make room for guests." She grinned. "This place here, one hundred percent ghost-free, guaranteed. You find any, you brought 'em with you."

You have no idea, I wanted to say. Instead, I smiled and held up the key. "Good to know. I guess we'll go get settled in and then explore a bit."

"Hold on," she said. "I've got some stuff in the utility closet you may want to borrow to take along." She bustled through a door behind the counter and returned with hedge clippers, a couple of pairs of thick leather work gloves, and a terrifying-looking machete. "A neighbor planted some bamboo nearby a few years back, and I've kept these on hand to hack it back ever since, so this stuff'll help with those blackberries from hell if you decide to check out that old cabin." She handed the supplies over the counter to Tobias and me. "I'd hate to see you mess up those fancy gloves with thorns, and I really do mean 'from hell.' That place is all spikes and rotten berries, but I get the impression you're on a mission."

"Something like that," I said. "Anyway, thanks for the help. See you in the morning, I guess."

"I certainly hope so. I'll bring some muffins by a little after seven. I know you coastal types like to sleep in."

"Sounds great." Tobias and I hoisted our borrowed supplies and headed to Room Four, whose aqua-painted door was fitted with an ornate lion-head door knocker. I watched Tobias shift the dull machete under one arm and manhandle the key into the knob. The door swung open, and I expected an interior like a bordello, but instead saw—

"Is that . . . a cubicle?" Tobias stepped inside. "Like from an office?"

"I think so? It's very . . . sparse, isn't it?" The room's double bed was screened by a cubicle wall, and one corner of the room had a plastic-framed love seat that looked like it belonged in the waiting room of a dental office. The floor was covered in beige carpet tiles. To the owners' credit, the room certainly seemed clean, and the air smelled of recirculated Lysol. The only decoration was a fake ficus tree in the corner, shoved into a plastic wicker basket.

"I mean, I was going to joke that you've landed us in a sitcom." Tobias walked toward the bathroom beneath flickering fluorescent tube lights, revealing a room that could have adjoined the nurse's office in an elementary school. "But I meant the kind of sitcom where the leads end up in a single hotel room in a snowstorm. I didn't mean—"

"An episode of *The Office*? Yeah, it's not what I expected, either. And it gives us a new problem."

"What's that?"

"Neither one of us could sleep on that love seat. Or, really, on that floor. It'd be like sleeping on cement."

Tobias bit his lip. "Bathtub, then? I can pretend I'm back in college, at some drunken frat party."

"You never struck me as the type."

"I wasn't. I got good enough at faking it to get through two years, and then I dropped out. Frats pay a lot for house repairs, as it happens. The connection panned out in work, if it didn't pan out in friends."

I shook my head. "I'll sleep in the car."

"No, it's going to be cold as hell out there once the sun goes down—you know that. I'll do it."

"You're six one! It's a little car. I'm five one and ornery. And we're here because of me, after all."

Tobias nodded, solemn. "I am definitely here because of you." He looked everything and nothing like the boy I knew as a teenager. That boy would have shuffled a bit, maybe run his fingers through his hair while grinning a half smile toward the ground. But the man just looked at me levelly, without a hint of shyness or shame. Without even a question.

Because he already knew the answer.

I hugged my hands—visible and non—against my own chest, afraid of what they may do if I didn't control them. He was only an arm's length away, standing on the other side of a breath that vibrated from my chest.

"Don't come any closer." My voice whispered words I wanted him to ignore.

He didn't speak. He didn't move. He didn't have to.

"Tobias." My voice was softer than any surface in that room, with its industrial office furniture and inexplicable cubicle bed. "Tobias. Do you know I was afraid to say your name? For years, after what happened, I couldn't say it."

He stepped one foot forward, an almost imperceptible invasion of the space between us, the air rippling like a still pond disturbed. "Why?"

"Because I thought it could almost summon you, that longing, and it was easier not to test it. I wanted you to be there so badly. In my darkest moments—the moments I felt most alone, most anxious, I thought back to that very first day I saw you, when Grimes took my book? And I remembered your face. I wanted you so much that it made me afraid."

Another step. "I can't imagine you afraid of anything."

I felt rooted to the ground. "I wanted you, but I didn't want you to see what had happened to me."

He shook his head. "You could never have become anything less than what you were. You were always so strong, Keryth. And so—"

"I was so lonely, Tobias." The words tore out of me with a desperation that surprised us both, and he crossed the distance between us faster than the speed of sound, his mouth consuming my tears before they could spill, and my words before they could continue. I fit against him exactly like I did when we were young, like a puzzle piece clicking into place, my rough edges absorbed until I lacked any boundaries at all. Neither of us spoke. We shifted planes, fading from vertical to horizontal in a way that felt less like falling and more like flight.

Until I hit my head on the laminate corner of the headboard and sat up, rubbing my head. "This really is a sitcom, isn't it?"

He stayed on his back, his shirt half-off where I had unbuttoned it without even noticing I was doing it, and looked at me. "I think that's the only reasonable conclusion. It could also be a horror movie, I suppose, given, you know." He gestured at my hands, still gloved, the left cuff open to hollowed-out emptiness.

I'd whipped off my hooded jacket pretty quickly, but I was still wearing my shirt with its three-quarter sleeves, so he hadn't seen how much more of me was missing. Almost to the shoulder. And beneath my jeans and heavy boots, the toes and ankle of my left leg had transitioned into transparency, the light occasionally catching remnants of the hair I'd stopped shaving, because what was the point?

"I have no idea what I'm doing. We're up to seven places, Tobias, and I still have no idea where Papa is, or how to stop any of this, or how much longer I'll be here."

"Seven places? Erma found more?"

"In New Mexico. Yes. She thinks so. She told me when she called, looking for you."

"Why would she be looking for me?"

"Because you weren't answering her calls or her texts."

He groaned. "You don't know how many of those she can send in a day. She's never stopped trying to be my bossy big sister."

I stared at him. "You think *that's* what she wants to be?"

He tilted his head to one side, and for a moment, he reminded me of my jay—but orders of magnitude less savvy, and a hell of a lot more oblivious. "It's what she's always tried to be."

I shook my head. "You really haven't changed a bit."

"What's that supposed to mean?"

"Nothing." I sighed. "I mean, it's supposed to mean a lot of things, but nothing we have time to hash out right now. Erma sent me the coordinates for the places she found, just like the ones for the Thorn House. They're all remote—not the kinds of addresses you can pull up on a map."

"But we can pull up the coordinates. Have you thought of doing that?"

"Doing what?"

He gazed at me, waiting.

"Oh!" I shouted. "Plot them on a map, you mean? No. I haven't." I held up my phone. "And I don't think I'd get much out of the exercise on a screen this size."

"Spoken like someone who's become entirely too reliant on a phone." Tobias stood up and walked back toward the door, where he'd leaned his backpack against the wall. "You Californians. You shouldn't set out on a trip like this without a backup." He reached into his pack and pulled out a battered road atlas and a pen, carrying both back to the bed, the only wide surface in the room that wasn't the floor. The book fell open to a well-thumbed page depicting the Southwest, covered with doodles and notes I recognized from my own distant years with Tobias, who drew in every textbook he ever carried at school.

"What's that for?" I asked, pointing to a prickly pear topped with red fruits in the shape of broken hearts, just outside of Hixon.

"A girl I met and lost a long time ago," he said.

I started to protest, but couldn't. He was right. The girl I was back then had long since disappeared, almost as literally as the woman I'd grown into was disappearing now. I had been a different person when we last found each other. I wasn't sure who I was now that we'd found each other again. I couldn't meet his eyes; the moment we'd just spent tangled up together on the bed suddenly seemed very far away. Instead, I looked at the list of coordinates I'd gotten from Erma and watched as Tobias started hunting for them on the map.

While he did, I stared at my phone, wondering again if I should text Max. He hadn't texted me. I couldn't blame him, really; I'd all but drawn myself out of being longed for, by him or by our daughters. I'd left only the slightest tether, the most minor ambiguity as to whether or not I was even in their lives anymore. And I'd left that for myself. I was a threat. I'd known that since I was small. But I'd never stopped feeling small without them. I'd already lost one family, and I still wasn't quite sure if I was prepared to lose another. At this point, I wasn't sure I'd left myself any other option.

"Keryth. Look at this." He gestured toward the map, his red marker hovering above the dots where he'd plotted the coordinates.

"Is that—"

"I think it may be a star."

I stared at the points he'd already begun to connect, and while we lacked a few coordinates, the image was as predictable as one of the connect-the-dots activity pages in a child's workbook. A five-pointed star. The Thorn House would be on the tip of its rightmost point. All of the other points, we'd found—except the top.

"There," said Tobias. "The last point would be around there."

He placed the tip of his marker against an area in Utah, where desert surrounded a meandering river, water that had met resistance on its way and had carved itself into a deep canyon.

And I knew.

"That's the House Where God Lived," I said. "Gran's house."

"The church?"

"More than one church, I think, and part of a churchyard. I never knew where it was, other than on a canyon. I'm not even sure it was always in the same place. But that must be it. And it must be where Papa is."

"Why would he be there, and not in one of the other places? Or somewhere else entirely?"

"Because it was a place we always returned to whenever we needed something. It was our home more consistently than any other home."

"Like a North Star."

"Exactly." I felt the truth of these words flow through me, together with absolute certainty that Papa would have returned to the place where he started out, particularly if he was in trouble, or if he was in pain. I felt, deep down, that right now he was both.

Dear Sir:

I am in receipt of your inquiry regarding the welfare of Mrs. Maximilian Miller and her children. Though it is plain to me that you have pulled together a variety of resources regarding the Miller family through what I gather must have been exhaustive investigation, I must confess I am perplexed as to why you would believe that I, as the counsel to the Millers' company, would disclose any information to you or, indeed, respond to you at all. I note your concern appears to be genuine, and while your degree of anxiety should only serve to increase my misgivings, I find myself convinced that your motives are pure. I am also perplexed at the degree of insight you seem to have regarding me personally. The kinds of things no one should know.

You are, moreover, the only person save myself who appears to have knowledge of Mrs. Miller's unfortunate affliction, a certain transparency of which even her own family seems, as yet, unaware. She has not, in fact, disclosed its existence even to myself, but this leads me to the other reason I found your missive compelling: I, too, have been experiencing a similar phenomenon, both in part and in whole, meaning that I have noticed portions of myself to be missing and have also been missing myself entirely, coming back to rooms I never remembered leaving with evidence of having been gone for some time. Your reference to the old "Prayer to Saint Anthony" seems apt, if not a bit too on the nose. The feeling is akin to finding oneself repeatedly lost and without a map to guide oneself back again. I have recognized the same fear in Mrs. Miller's eyes that I believe my own to hold, and the timing of your message leads me to believe you may possess some explanation as to these events. Kindly send me information as to how best to discuss these matters with you in person.

Very sincerely yours,

Anthony Percival Graves
General Counsel, The Steller Fund

29

· · • ● ● ● • · ·

The Thorn House
AUGUST 2016

"ANTHONY." AS USUAL, he'd picked up before I'd even heard a ring; I guessed he was on the line from the sound of expectant silence. "It's me."

"I know when it's you, Mrs. Miller. Your number is, after all, somewhat known to me."

"Just making conversation, then." I tugged off my gloves and slid out of my jacket, looking at the way the light bounced off what wasn't there. "I think we found the last place. I think—whatever this is—it's almost over. Whatever that means."

"Whatever that means, indeed. I've continued to review these acquisitions with interest. It's been less byzantine than I thought, tracing the path of ownership to secure these properties into your portfolio. Just when I think I may have trouble, it seems—"

"To smooth itself out?" I glanced down at my book, the pen untangling complicated knots of title and ownership, the path a piece of property carves into the world—or would, if it hadn't been carved out of some other place and plopped unceremoniously into a new one. I didn't know, even now, whether I was actually smoothing anything, or whether the houses simply unfolded into a reality that accepted them, part of my father's magic, the outward contours of which had always been unclear to me. Whether that was by design, or whether my hurried, sketched explanations had ever helped at all.

"Something like that," Anthony responded. "They are somewhat like puzzle boxes, Mrs. Miller. From the little I've overheard of the conversations between Mr. Miller and Ms. Carey, it seems the properties all lack any explanation for the amenities they contain, such as they are. No connection to the ground on which they sit, or so I've heard?"

"I've heard that, too."

"You didn't know?"

"I knew some things, but not that."

"Have you determined how many more of these locations I may expect to find no explanation for?"

"That's why I'm calling, actually. I think I've found the most important one. We're heading there next. And, Anthony—"

"You have some suspicion this one may be dangerous."

I froze. "That's not exactly what I was going to say. I was going to say I may . . . be gone for a while. I hope not, at least not for long, but—" I tried to gather words, but they all seemed inadequate. "The truth is, Anthony, I have no idea what may happen."

"Have you discussed this with Mr. Miller or your daughters?"

"I—no."

"If you think you may be lost to them for any length of time, Mrs. Miller, I suggest this conversation should be with them, and not with me." Anthony released a sigh that sounded older than time. "But with that said, I do appreciate the confirmation, if only for personal reasons."

"Personal reasons?"

"I believe I am unwell, and that you are unwell, too. I also believe this bears some relationship to this mission you have undertaken." His voice sounded muffled. "I am somewhat comforted by your admission that you also do not know what may come next."

"Anthony. What's happening to you?"

"Losses I cannot readily explain and would rather not discuss, Mrs. Miller. But I hope you may encounter some success on the next leg of whatever journey this is, and for some reason, I feel hope that may restore me, as well."

"I can't help you if you don't tell me what's going on." My words were impatient, but they came more from desperation. More of a request than a statement. *Someone, please. Tell me what's going on.*

"I'm afraid I lack sufficient insight to know what is happening, Mrs. Miller. But I do have some advice, if you're still inclined to take any."

"I am. From you. Yes."

"Call Mr. Miller. Call your daughters. I have the sense of an ending—or at least some sort of change—on the horizon. I have a keen instinct for such things."

"I don't want to frighten them, Anthony."

"They are, I think, already frightened they might lose you, Mrs. Miller, though your caginess—if I may call it that—makes them uncertain what the nature of that loss may be."

"They think their mother's going to run away from home."

"I believe they sometimes think their mother, and their wife, already has."

I remembered the way the cold felt in the Thorn House one morning when my mother had disappeared, and the way the air closes in around the void left by someone missing—a hole you're afraid to let close entirely, even if you feel its chill cascading over your toes. Because what if they come back to find you warm, your world complete without them? What if they turn around and never return?

"My mother left," I murmured.

"So I had gathered. Again, Mrs. Miller, this is only my advice, and it is not advice of the legal variety. I lack family connections myself, having devoted myself to solving other people's losses. But if your misgivings were such that you called to warn me about your next destination, you owe it to your family, and to yourself, to share that with them." His voice sounded quieter and more distant by the moment, as if some external force were turning down his volume.

"You're right," I whispered. "I'll call them."

"And there's something else, Mrs. Miller. You recall our conversation about Mr. Miller's efforts to expand the company?"

"I do."

"I think those expansions have the wrong focus, if I may be so bold. He wants to take the concept of Harold and generalize it to others. To somehow bring that degree of interaction back to life with others who have died. But I think that focus—in addition to being inadvisable—is too broad. I think it will fail."

"I can't disagree, but what do you suggest?"

"Harold himself. He is the focus. I've heard enough interactions between Mr. Miller and the version of his father he's created, and I've also had the opportunity to observe it with others—with you, with your daughters, and even in that social club. Harold is unique. He's—well, fatherly. The person one might ask for instructions to fix plumbing, or replace a tire. The person who might nag one about turning off lights when leaving a room, or sealing windows that are leaking. A kind of reassurance—"

"A dad joke in your pocket. Yes. An Everydad. I get it."

"I gather much of what he is, and much of Mr. Miller's success in creating him, came from your redirection of his focus."

"I told him to start at the end, instead of the beginning."

"Very apt advice. Have you considered reopening that conversation?"

"I hadn't. But I am now." *After all*, I thought, *I don't quite know how near the end I am.*

Mother,

I don't know the date. My sense of time has started
to slip, and the only grounding in days and hours I
have remaining—my monitoring of Keryth—has
begun to wane. You, of course, are already gone, and
have been for some time. I suppose my writings to
you are less in the nature of letters and more of a
diary, a missive from who I am now to where and
whom I came from.

It's too much, the two of them, even pulling them
back into my pages whenever I can. Neil doesn't exert
much weight—something to do with the way Keryth
captured him, I think; there's a buoyancy about his
image—but Laila is nearly impossible to hold, and so I
have captured her to focus on Keryth. But Keryth's
independence has made her harder to support, even
as it makes her own powers grow, just as mine did
when I was away from you. I've meted out what's left
of me in dribs and drabs, but I recognize the fading. I
have covered all the mirrors. I see what I saw in your
face before you left us. I am exhausted in ways I
never knew could be possible, not even as the unexpected father of two actual children, sprung into our
lives from graphite and hope. I am exhausted beyond
the ability of rest to repair. I view it as atonement, in
a way, this sense of impending loss, knowing the loss
I inflicted on you. You never said you forgave me, and
I know that you would say there was nothing to
forgive, but then again—you never said that, either. I

still see Anne as clearly as I drew her on the page, balanced on the bridge before it collapsed, as light as the butterflies I caught for her. I tried so hard to bring her back, Ma. I didn't know what I was doing until it was done, and she would absolutely have died, and I can't say if what I did was better or worse than death. I suppose you couldn't say, either, which is why we always erred on the side of saying nothing at all. I'll never forget the look on your face when I told you Keryth's full name. That's how I knew I wasn't forgiven.

Part of me wants to believe she isn't gone, merely locked down—able to be unlocked, by someone with greater skill than mine. I thought Keryth could be that someone. But as I feel myself ebbing away, I don't know that she'll be anyone at all.

I'm so tired, Ma. I know you were, too. It's why I forgave you, even if you couldn't do the same for me.

With all of my love,
MORRISON

30

• • • ● ● ● • •

Outside Tatum City, Utah
AUGUST 2016

THE COORDINATES TOBIAS plotted on his map led us to a flat plain of scrub brush and sage outside a small town in southern Utah that made our last stop, Brightly, look like a thriving metropolis. I'd foolishly ignored the gas meter on our rental car until we were down to fumes—ironic, given my recent conversation with Ellory and Mindy—and we coasted into a two-pump gas station that might have been the only one for hundreds of miles. I hadn't even had to draw one, and I was grateful.

A surly-looking man sat in a folding chair by the grimy glass door of the small gas station. He looked as if he'd auditioned for a ZZ Top video and been turned away for being too bearded, and his beard was the best-groomed part of him. Everything else about him was wild: a mud-spattered chambray shirt and jeans that weren't so much acid-washed as acid-eaten, with random holes I prayed didn't extend toward the crotch I couldn't see beneath the beard hair. And over the jeans, the most inexplicably elegant riding boots I'd ever seen, night black with contrasting white stitches that shone brighter than stars. The kind of boots a ne'er-do-well duke might wear when trying to convince a romance heroine to take his hand in marriage so he could gain access to her fortune. The man uncrossed his legs and planted his magnificent boots on the cracked asphalt, rising to his feet.

"Out-of-towners?" he asked. "Welcome to Tatum City. Leaded or unleaded?"

"Um, we can get it ourselves," I said, still staring at the boots.

"Nope, 'fraid you can't. We're a full-service gas station. Looks like that little car takes unleaded, am I right?"

"Uh, yeah."

The man nodded and started heading toward the pump nearest the car, holding out his hand. "Cash or credit? Our connection's spotty out here, but I've got an old-fashioned thwocka-thwocka thing inside to make a copy of your card, and I'm fine with that. Folks expect to be able to use cards, you know, connection or not."

"I've got cash," Tobias said, reaching for his wallet.

"That does make it easier. Thank you kindly. Are you folks visiting, or just passing through? If you're going to be in the area for a bit, I've got a stable nearby. We offer trail rides. Very popular."

I looked again at the boots, and wondered how popular they could possibly be. There wasn't a speck of dirt on the leather. "Do you . . . know this area very well?"

"Hell, yes. Born and raised. I see you've noticed the boots—I don't wear this pair often, but folks looking for experiences often have an eye for quality, and if you can get someone talking, you can get someone riding." He winked at me. "See what I mean?"

"Um . . . sure. Listen, we're mostly passing through, but we're looking for a place. It's a little unusual—"

"Unusual?" The man knitted his eyebrows together. "Unusual how?"

"Like, it may look a little bit like a church—"

His eyes narrowed. "Are you here to laugh at me, too? Look, I stopped offering the ghost rides after the town threatened to pull my business license, and I don't appreciate folks coming out to my establishment to mock me. You can get your gas elsewhere, if that's your game."

I shook my head. "I'm not here to mock anyone. I'm really looking—"

"Well, I don't ride anyone out there anymore. To any of the canyons, not at night. I'm sick and tired of setting out and not finding it, 'cept when I'm alone, and people tell me I'm imagining things." He thrust the gas pump into the car and frowned. "It's out there, but don't you be asking me to help you find it. If you want a nice little morning ride through the gullies, that's fine. Or along one of the old trails south of town at full noon, sure. But don't ask me for a sunset ride, and don't ask for night."

"We don't really have time for a ride," I said.

"And I'm not really a fan of horses," Tobias added.

"Well. If you change your mind, you know where to find me. Name's Dan Burnett. I'm the only trail guide in town."

"We'll certainly keep you in mind. And you can keep the change," Tobias said, climbing into the driver's seat, as clear as if he'd said, *Let's get the hell out of here*, aloud.

"Thanks for your time, Mr. Burnett." I climbed into the passenger's seat.

"Oh, call me Dan," the man offered. "I don't stand on formality, no matter what the boots say."

"Right. Bye now," I called through the window as Tobias pulled away.

"What . . . in the world . . . was that guy's deal?" Tobias asked, glancing over his shoulder as if he thought the man might be following us on a horse.

"I don't know, but at least we know we're in the right place," I said. "Did you see his face when I asked about the house?"

Tobias nodded. "What's the deal with sunset? And night?"

"We only ever got there at sunset, or right after the sun went down, when I was growing up. I never thought it was by design, but maybe it was."

"That guy made it sound like it's not always there."

"Or not always in exactly the same place." I remembered the way it always seemed as if we stumbled on Gran's house, never quite where we expected. I thought of the shifting kitchen, the moving windows. "That seems consistent, actually. I mean, with everything else." I gestured to my own partly transparent body.

"Well, the sun's going down before too long. What do we do? Just . . . drive?"

"No. We pull over, and I call my family. And then you let me drive."

"Okay, but I'd like to get a little distance between us and that gas station first."

"Me, too."

We drove for another fifteen minutes, heading north, and turning off the road we were on whenever it started veering in another direction. After a while, we'd passed off the highway, off the main road, off the side roads, and onto a more isolated dirt road. Tobias pulled off to the side. "Can you get a signal out here?"

"Harold, you awake?" I asked.

"Pretty much always," he said. I smiled to see his spinning circle on my screen. "You ready to call the fam?"

"Are they all together?"

"An odd development, but yes, they are."

"At home?"

"Um . . . no. It doesn't seem so. They appear to be . . . traveling."

"Traveling? Where?"

"Do you want to keep asking me all these questions, kiddo, or would you rather go straight to the source?"

"Good point. Is Ellory driving?"

"My sensors aren't that good yet, KERRIFF. She's in a car or something moving. I know that much."

"Okay. Call Mindy, then. At least she won't be driving."

"Let's hope so!"

Harold's spinning circle gave way to my younger daughter's face, which filled the screen with anxiety. "Mom? Mom, is everything okay?"

"I was going to ask the same thing. You're with your dad and your sister?"

"Yeah. We're together."

"Where are you?"

"Um . . . on our way to you."

"What? What do you mean? Put your father on."

"I'm not driving, either, so don't start yelling," Max said.

"Who *is* driving? Ellory?"

"No. Anthony." Max's face filled the screen, so I couldn't tell what car they were in. Or why. "He was rather insistent we come along."

"Come along where? None of you should come anywhere near me—"

"Here's the thing, kiddo," Harold interrupted. "You're not the most reliable judge of when you need help. I've been with you long enough to know, and Mr. Graves—well, he seems to have pretty good instincts, for a lawyer."

"I will accept jokes about my profession from computers only," said Anthony's voice, off-screen. "Mrs. Miller, while I haven't disclosed the reasons you need assistance, that's only because you haven't disclosed them to me. I'm not entirely certain you know them yourself."

"Anthony! I told you I'd call Max and the girls before—"

"Before you entered a structure that you expressed to me was unsafe, not in so many words. That is true. But you hadn't, as of yet, and in the meantime, I received some intervening information that led me to believe my own fate may be somehow tied with yours."

"Fate? What are you talking about?"

"I'll explain when we arrive."

"Anthony, I'm not even sure where we are."

"Nor am I. But I can locate you most anywhere. As I've said in the past, it's something of a specialty of mine."

"Max," I called. "Ellory. Mindy. You can't come here. I love you all so much, but you have to know there's something happening to me, and I don't know how it's going to end."

"And you expect that to talk us out of coming to you?" Ellory shouted. "Fat chance, Mom. Anthony, doesn't this bucket go any faster?"

"Girls. My sweethearts. I don't know if I can stop things long enough—"

"Do whatever it is you have to do, Mom," Ellory said, and her face on the screen held the same determination I recognized from when she was a toddler. "We'll get there in time. Believe it."

"I love you, Ellory. I love you, Mindy. And, Max—" I couldn't see him. I could see Tobias, staring straight ahead, studiously avoiding my eyes.

I opened the door to the car and stepped out into a stretch of anonymous desert. "I love you, Max. And if I don't see you— it's Harold. Harold is where the focus should be. He's what you were meant to create, and he's the creation that inspires you.

Don't lose your own path." I took a deep breath. "I've always believed in you. I'm sorry I didn't say it."

"You better say it in person," Max said. I heard him, but Ellory still held the phone.

"You heard the man," she said. "See you soon." And then her face blinked off-screen.

31

· · • ● • · ·

A House Like an Accordion
AUGUST 2016

THE HOUSE SEEMED ugly by design. It fanned wide across
the canyon's edge, sagging slightly in the middle, as if its roof
had become exhausted by the effort of covering so many segments of wood and drywall and stone. The structure's angle
made it difficult to tell where it ended, with each addition to the
building's southern edge marching away toward the horizon in
uneven chunks.

It wasn't ugly by design, I knew. It wasn't designed at all. Just
as Gran's house always had, it balanced on a canyon's edge, but
the deep void underneath it was sharper, and it was standing on
a different side than I remembered. And there was more to the
structure now—it wasn't just Gran's house. The mismatched
steeples were nearly collapsed, leaning against each other like
friends who have had a few too many drinks and are trying to
help each other to stand. The building was angled away from
the sunset, but the center of the structure was still the House
Where God Lived.

The segments of mismatched buildings tacked onto its edges,
one against the other, were just as recognizable, inklings of every
place we'd ever moved into, every building I ever remembered

from my childhood. And the surroundings were a mishmash, flickering pieces of meadow and forest and swamp, the borders of each bleeding into the next, and the whole inconsistently part of this world, intermittently letting the sun shine through, as transparent as my missing hand.

The overgrown rhododendrons surrounding the structure—leathery, spiky, topped with tightly packed pompoms of tongued lily-like blooms—posed exactly the warning they were meant to. Less spiky than the blackberry thorns, but more poisonous. It didn't invite visitors, and actively repelled the curious.

But not the determined.

"Your dad—you think he's inside there? It looks abandoned. Worse than any of the places, and those actually were abandoned." Tobias rested his hand on the roof of the rental car, its sides lashed and scratched by our journeys through former roads and logging routes. *I guess I'll be buying this, too*, I thought, and suppressed a giggle at the thought of driving another beat-up sedan home to Max. At least I still thought of Max as home.

"He's here," I said. "He has to be." I crouched into the car to retrieve my backpack and sketchbook.

Tobias looked at the book. "You can't—"

"Draw him here? No. I wasn't going to. I don't have to. But . . . something is different here. I'm checking something else." The book fell open to the first page, the cover barely hanging on by lengths of tape that had become a solid block of yellowed gunk, like fossilized Lucite. I looked at the jay and felt a whisper of wind beside me.

"Um, Keryth," Tobias whispered, as if we were inside a church. "I know you're not a fan of Disney princess references, but . . . there's a bird? Like, on you?"

"I know." I felt small pricks of pressure through the thin

fabric of my T-shirt, and saw a flash of blue out of the corner of my eye as a Steller's jay jumped from my shoulder onto Papa's sketch. The bird wasn't quite like my jay—it sported a sleek and sophisticated crest of black on its tilted head, and I distinctly remembered my own jay's crest was dark blue. This new bird bent down toward the sketch's face and up again, down and up again, like a novelty plastic bird that dips its face repeatedly into a glass of water. It hopped across the page and onto my hand, where it stopped and looked up at me.

I thought—not for the first time—that birds' faces carry much more expression than the world gives them credit for. The bird's eyes, the angle of its head, spoke louder than words. *He's trapped*, the face said, and I heard my own voice at eight years old, tear-snagged and horrified. *Why don't you let him go?*

I can't, my eyes pleaded back.

The bird on my hand cocked its head to the other side, then hopped off the edge of my thumb and farther up the page, alighting on the black pen I always kept clipped to the book's cover. It looked up at me again.

"Keryth, are you . . . feeling all right?"

I nodded without speaking, and plopped down to the ground, crisscrossing my legs atop buttercups and meadow grass and bugs I could feel inching through the soil underneath, everything movement and light, everything alive. I pulled the pen from the book and placed its tip against the fine feathers surrounding the jay's eye, and I began to remake my father's sketch—muscle memory taking over, my eyes closed, in my head becoming a child again, hurriedly scribbling a cardinal on a spray of graphite spruce needles. As I drew, Papa's voice careened from one wall of my skull to the other—*Don't grow up to be like me don't grow up to be like me don't grow up to be—*

"I'm not," I said.

"Not what?" Tobias asked, and I opened my eyes to see him crouched in front of me, reaching fingers through the air between us, shimmering with light and heat. "Keryth. You're glowing."

"I know." I kept sketching, remembering the movement of my jay on the branch, his defeated dive to the blackberries so many years before. I felt warmth flow from my fingers and closed my eyes, hearing a single trill.

"Keryth. I'm sorry to interrupt whatever's happening here, but I have to ask. Is there—"

"A bird on you? Yes. Before you ask, yes. There is a bird on you." I knew without looking that my friend would be there, tangible and real after decades on a page. I blinked and saw a graceful curve of blue perched on Tobias's shoulder, a rebellious tuft of feathers atop the cocked head of a bird I hadn't seen in three dimensions for more than thirty years. I laughed, and the Steller's jay looked a little miffed. "Yes. There is. I'm sorry, little guy. I hope you won't be mad when I tell you how much I'm going to miss you, but I will."

The bird that had alighted on my book was hopping around on the ground beside me, and approached Tobias with a fat worm wriggling in its beak, which it dropped at Tobias's feet. My old friend spread his wings and swooped in the shimmering air that surrounded us—a little awkwardly, after decades spent flat on paper. He darted back to the ground, landing near the worm and standing hesitantly next to his new companion, looking at me as I held the book that once held him.

"I thought you said your bird was a he," Tobias said.

I jerked my head up and stared at him. "He is." I looked back at my jay, whose new friend was pushing the worm toward him insistently. "I mean, look at him."

"Not to go all Boy Scout Bird-Watching Badge on you, but

I am looking at him. And that other bird—the one who came bearing gifts of worm—is a male, and he's courting. He's courting a her. It's an easy mistake—male and female Steller's jays look pretty much the same."

I gazed at my bird, my companion for more than thirty years, and felt any remaining certainty about the world, and my place in it, slide further away. "Papa said so. And he—she?—was so determined, that day Papa sketched in my book . . . so focused on those berries, and I thought . . ."

Tobias smiled, and his smile was gentle and kind, as if he didn't want to shock me further. "Like I said, they're hard to tell apart. And it's not like you could figure it out from her behavior, seeing as she was two-dimensional."

"Oh, she showed *plenty* of behavior, believe me." I looked at my old friend. "You could have said something," I told her, and then laughed. "I guess we both had other things to talk about."

My jay hopped across the ground to my open sketchbook, glancing from the blank page to my face. A low, reedy sound emerged from her beak. She tentatively stretched out her wings, and then closed them again.

"It's okay," I said. "You can go. Thank you for keeping me company all this time. I'm so sorry I didn't figure it out before now."

The jay swooped back up into the air and landed on my sketchbook again, standing above the page where she'd spent so many years. She cocked her head at me once more, and I thought of that afternoon among the blackberries she couldn't eat, ripened on that faraway mountainside. "I'll draw some for you," I whispered. "You can eat as many as you want, you and your new beau and all your babies, for as long as you all live." I felt the tears running down my face and didn't try to wipe them away. "Thank you."

I closed my eyes and heard a rustle of feathers in the wind. When I looked for her again, she was gone.

Tobias was still kneeling in the grass in front of me. The shimmer in the air dissipated, and he rubbed his fingers together in front of his face, as if expecting to see glitter on his hands, which he raked backward through his impossible hair. "I don't know what I just saw," he said. "Did you know you could do that?"

"If I did, I would have done it a long time ago." I rose to my feet and brushed the dirt from my jeans. The air felt still and ordinary, and the house and its unwieldy segments loomed in front of me. "I need to go inside."

"I'm just going to say—one more time, not that it's done any good so far—you don't have to do this, Keryth. Not any of it. We can fix the houses you've got, or you can off-load all of them and go back home, or we can just leave, right now, and figure things out later. You don't have to face whatever you think is here."

"Papa is here." I blinked and heard for the first time the tone I'd missed under Tobias's words. "You're scared. I'm sorry, of course you are. You can leave me here, Tobias. I'll be fine."

"Not a chance in hell." Tobias rose to his feet. "I'm not abandoning you in some overgrown stretch of backcountry with only mosquitoes for company."

I shrugged. "It's too dry for mosquitoes." The light sliced through the parched air that surrounded us, with no hint of water to diffuse its glare. "And even if any survived here, they'd probably go hungry." Underneath my long sleeves, my long pants, my gloves and socks coating the memory of where my skin should be, my left side had receded into almost nothingness. I knew I was still here—I still felt the breeze, the pinpricks of goose bumps on my phantom limbs, whenever I removed my clothes. But it was getting hard to believe. It was beginning to seem more likely that I was as absent as the rest of the world would think, if I ever let it see me. "This isn't going to get any less weird, Tobias. Fair warning."

"We've come this far." He reached for the glove that held my invisible hand. "We'll see this through. But—should we wait for your family?"

I shook my head. "I can't wait. I don't know how much longer I have."

We picked our way through the weeds, looking for a gap in the rhododendrons that would let us get near the house. I rested my book in the crook of my elbow and traced a scaly line of branch beneath my pen, snapping it off mid-growth. The sound from the interlaced maze in front of us was a popping, yielding eruption of leaves and limbs, like legs left too long unstretched. A gate formed over our heads, and our way was clear.

The door to the house was squat and rounded—the kind of portal you might imagine for a hobbit, or perhaps an anthropomorphic rabbit returning to Wonderland. It wasn't Gran's door, the tall entry I remembered from my childhood. It didn't look designed to admit visitors, and I was certain it wasn't intended to. The hinges and handle were wrought iron, Papa's favorite kind of intricate scrollwork—lovely and detailed and wholly impractical. I knew before I reached for it that the door wouldn't be locked, wouldn't even be latched. It was still hard to open, and Tobias had to help me wrest it from the jamb.

A rush of wind whooshed through the door, but the fragrance was markedly different from those that had greeted us in the other abandoned structures. Not wildness and rot, but paper. Old, moldering paper, like a forgotten library.

The light from outside shot through the gloom and dancing dust motes and reached the back wall, illuminating an image hanging there.

"Mama." I breathed the word. It filled my lungs, clear and cold, and I felt as if I had emerged from deep and lonely waters that still pooled around my feet, making motion difficult as I tried to reach her and ask her why she wouldn't speak to me.

And then I saw the staples—thick and gunmetal dull. One staple was plunged into each corner of the paper that held her. The wood paneling behind her was blackened and stippled with mold, encroaching onto the edges of her portrait. She was reaching out, but not for me.

She was trying to run. And I had no idea how long she hadn't been able to.

When I reached the wall, I traced the line of her jaw like a bonnet string, the way I'd once learned the sign for *mother* in a long-forgotten high school class. Her eyes reminded me of the jay's, and I could feel the same energy pulsing from the paper. I clasped my book and wondered, but as I reached for the pen, something in her face made me stop.

"Are you going to try to draw—to let her go somehow . . . ?" Tobias's voice trailed off, and I could tell he was feeling even more out of his depth than I was.

"She doesn't want me to, I don't think. Look at her face." I heard a rustling in the room to our left. I couldn't bear to leave her there, suspended on the wall while we headed deeper into the house and whatever—whoever—was inside.

"Do you want to take her with us?"

I nodded wordlessly, and Tobias reached toward the top-left staple, gingerly prying his nail under its edge and pulling it out from the wall.

The screaming in my head was unbearable. I clawed at Tobias's hand for the staple and plunged it back into the holes it left behind, like fangs returning to a snakebite. Two twin rivulets

of red traced steady lines down the paper's left edge. Mama's
stillness felt like a sigh. Like relief.

"She can't come down." I saw a flash of understanding in the
two dimensions of my mother's eyes. "I have to find Papa." I
turned my back on Mama and picked my way over the uneven
floors—ceramic tile, chipping linoleum, wide planks of heart-
wood pine, crossing and layered into surfaces that had borne a
million steps until they held no feet at all, in this place. The
rustling increased as I stepped into a stone room lined with
bookcases. The space held echoes of Gran's library, but the air
smelled of smoke and charcoal, and paper fluttered from the
shelves.

Sketchbooks. Hundreds of them, maybe thousands. All the
same black paper bindings, some so old and worn they had
discolored to shades of gray and brown and lavender. Some had
split along their spines, their pages erupting from the covers,
mottled bricks and flying buttresses and ivy-draped garden
gates fragmented into puzzles, no complete structures to be
found. And everywhere, everywhere, my mother. The nape of
her neck and the shadows beneath her cheekbones, the hollow
where her wrist met the hand I used to grasp to cross the street.
The curved arc of her back and the narrow lengths of her legs.

And her wings.

I told myself—told countless therapists as I bounced from
foster home to foster home, exhausted graduate students in the
university's counseling center, several pricey "experts" Max acquired when he insisted I needed help—that my mother was a
story I'd invented to cushion the blow of her loss. *She wasn't
impossibly fast*, I would say, *I mean, I think she must have run in
college, been an athlete in some time in her life she didn't tell us
about, maybe. She was certainly no angel. None of us were.*

The light that glowed from Neil—that glowed from me, outside, when I released the jay. Her speed and her silence. I had seen her wings once when I was young, almost before memory—old enough to recall their fuzzed whiteness, their atrophy, limp against her shoulder blades—and young enough to be sure that I'd invented them.

I thought of the House Where God Lived, its stone jumble on the cliffside, the nameless spirits wandering the yard. I thought of a lonely boy on the cusp of becoming a man, conjuring a church out of thin air for his grieving, widowed mother, seeing the loss that companionship can mean. A boy raised among rosaries and incense and Stations of the Cross, the comforting rituals that meant a safe harbor had been reached, gazing at the light through stained glass windows and, on every single one, angels.

He must have wanted a companion who couldn't die.

And, like everything he made, she couldn't escape. She wasn't drawn from life—she wouldn't be like the souls pulled in with the structures he created. She was like my flower, the one she crushed beneath the blackberry thorns all those years before. Dreamed and drawn into existence, but tied to the one who made her. She loved him—loved us, I never doubted. But her feet weren't accustomed to being earthbound, linked to the constant tug of human longing and desire, life tracing an arc that was uneven and finite. She was more like my jay than the spirits in the churchyard.

Which, I realized with a start, meant that I was, too.

My sketchbook, clutched in my hand, tremored with a vibration I could feel in my bones. It was a like a butterfly in a net, surrounded for the first time by fluttering peers. But the tug it exerted wasn't toward the shelves. It was toward another door. This one was iron, with a wide wheel on its middle.

"Every time I think your dad's stuff can't get any weirder, I see something like a bank vault door in a room that belongs in Westminster Cathedral, and I stand corrected." Tobias picked his way over the leaves of paper at our feet.

"He's been walling himself off," I said.

"Do you think there's a key?"

"It won't be locked." I knew before I threw my whole weight into turning the wheel, which yielded and let me swing the door on its roaring iron hinges. "He's not trying to keep people out. He's trying to keep himself in."

"Why?"

"Because he thinks he's dangerous." *He's right, he's right, and you were right, too, and this is why you ran. To protect everyone.* "That's why it's segmented. He keeps putting up more barriers between himself and the outside." The room was sweltering, and I pulled my hooded sweatshirt over my head and tied it around my waist.

Tobias gasped. "Keryth—your body—"

"I know. It's only going to get worse the closer we get to him. I'd already been hiding how bad it's gotten."

"But your hair—" I felt his fingers tangling in the air where my curls should be, his relief and confusion at feeling what he couldn't see but knew was there. I turned around to face him, and didn't know how much of my face was left. He cupped it in his hand, and I could see his palm.

"I don't know how this ends. I warned you at the beginning."

He shook his head. "I'm not much good with warnings. I'm not leaving."

I peered through the iron door and saw only darkness, pierced with a single pinprick of light some distance away. I began to tiptoe toward it, following it like a thread, when I heard a voice and pulled back, looking at Tobias. "Did you say something?"

Tobias shook his head. "That wasn't me. That was from outside."

I listened again, inclining my head toward the round door we had entered through. "Is that—"

"Mom! Mom! Are you in there?" Mindy's voice, its drama club–trained projection tinged with an undernote of panic, bounced off the walls, and I was running. I hurriedly tugged my sweatshirt from around my waist and back over my head, not wanting her to see what Tobias had. I rushed across the uneven floors back to the entrance to see my younger daughter picking through the rhododendron shrubs.

Her face lit up when she saw me, and the joy I felt at seeing her was replaced almost immediately with panic as I watched her eyes widen with fright. "Mom—oh my God, what's happening—"

"It's okay." My voice was the low, slow murmur I once used to ward off nightmares back when she was small, which felt like five minutes ago. I hadn't put up the hood of my sweatshirt. I hadn't concealed enough of what was missing. "I feel fine. I know it looks bad, but I'm going to fix it."

"How? You're literally—Mom, you're only half here!" Mindy was still frozen, gripping a branch so tightly I thought she might puncture the skin on her hand. *Beware.* I had no idea what power those branches might hold.

"Baby, I need you to let go of that plant, right now, and come over toward me. I'm all here. I may not look like it, but I promise, I'm here." I breathed a sigh of relief as she released the branch she was holding and crossed the tall grass toward me, stopping just beyond reach of my arms. "Speaking of which—how are you here? How did you find me?"

"It's like I told you on the phone. We had help." Max's body was still concealed by the tall foliage, but his voice enveloped me, and my lip quivered as he stepped into the clearing with

Ellory, who didn't speak as she stood next to her father. They both looked suspended in shock.

Mindy ran back to them. "She says she's all here. Closer up, it's not as bad. I mean, it's weird, but it's not as bad. She's still Mom. It's not as bad as Anthony."

"As bad as Anthony? What are you talking about? How are you all here?" I felt split in two, my relief at seeing my family safe battling against my terror at having them so close to this unpredictable place, their unpredictable wife and mother, still unsure of what might happen next but certain it could be nothing good. As I watched the most precious parts of my present step closer to the oldest, deepest parts of my past, my peripheral vision darkened and narrowed to a single point of blinding white, and I reached toward Tobias's hand but grasped at nothing, empty air surrounding me as I ceased being able to see or hear or touch anything at all.

Morrison,

Enclosed is Keryth's sketchbook. It's painted with the same brush as your own. I've housed its image in the library, next to yours, and its abilities should be the same, though I've told you more times than I can count that the tool doesn't make the artist: it's the other way around. We don't know what kind of artist she is yet, but I agree that letting her experiment is the only way to find out, and the artist I made it for—well, she's gone.

   It should expand to capture whatever world she wishes to create, and let her seal anything there, too. I always saw her looking through my Audubon book, and she does seem so entranced by birds. Like Anne with her butterflies. Like me. Butterflies always interested me, you know—a world of possibility expanding from the tightest, most compact package. A gift. Just like you.

Affectionately,
MA

32

· · • ● ● ● • · ·

A House Like an Accordion
AUGUST 2016

I AWOKE TO an acrid smell and saw my daughters' faces swimming in the air above mine, and beyond them, Tobias's. Ellory helped me sit up.

"I don't think I've ever seen real smelling salts before," she said, looking up at Tobias. "I've only read about them in old-timey books in school. I didn't know they were just, like, a boring paper tube in a first aid kit."

I looked at Tobias. "A first aid kit? First an atlas, then random bird facts, and now a first aid kit? Have you been tying complicated knots, too? How many merit badges are you trying to earn?"

He solemnly held up two fingers, splayed in a V. "Always be prepared."

Ellory sat back on her heels, then looked at Mindy, sitting beside her in the grass. Max was standing several feet away, staring at the house and its endless segments heading to the horizon. Beside him, a well-tailored suit stood suspended in midair, as if arranged on a mannequin I couldn't see. I squinted and rubbed my eyes.

"Mom," Ellory said. "Who's the Boy Scout?"

I stood up unsteadily, brushing the dirt off my jeans and reaching my hands down to my seated daughters. "This is Tobias," I said, nodding in his direction. "We—" I started to say *grew up together*, but that wasn't at all correct, at least not in the sense that I'd been with him for any significant length of time as a child. It was correct in the sense that I'd grown recently, on this trip, with him—in ways, my growth had, unbeknownst to me, been arrested for decades. But none of that seemed right. No words seemed right.

"He's a builder." This was true, yes, but also incomplete. "And someone I used to know."

Mindy's eyes widened with interest. "Someone from before? The times you don't talk about?"

I nodded. "Some of those times, yes."

"Mindy," Ellory said sharply. "We don't have time for this right now. Mom's disappearing, and Anthony—"

"What's happened to Anthony?"

"There is, I'm afraid, not very much of Anthony for something to happen to." The scrupulously polite voice emerged from the empty suit that had been standing next to Max. As it approached—seemingly of its own volition—I saw it was pinstriped, its meticulous tailoring set off by a chartreuse and magenta pocket square, the only flashy item Anthony ever wore. But the suit was all there was, propelling itself across the clearing with a body that didn't cast a shadow. A bright ray of light momentarily glanced off the pomade slicking down his transparent hair, like sunshine sparkling off a wave that's already rolled away.

I stared at the emptiness above the suit's shoulders. "How—"

"It seems you and I share a common affliction," the suit replied. "I suspected as much during our first foray to visit that beachfront motel. The gloves, you see. Your green gloves." The suit held up its empty cuffs. "Forgive me, but you looked absurd."

"I don't know how this is possible." The ache behind my sternum twinged with each heartbeat, and I felt the pull of life deep inside the house behind me. "I came here because I thought my father was causing this. For me, I mean. But I've never seen anyone else who he's captured—" I bit the words off, because they weren't true. Anne, my ghost friend. Jay. The spirits on the cliff.

"Something odd occurred to me, Mrs. Miller. I realized it rather suddenly when you and I were speaking before you came to—whatever this place is, and then I dismissed it, telling myself it couldn't possibly be true. But then I received an email from a gentleman who knew more about me, and more about you, than I thought anyone possibly could. He was looking for you. And then I realized something."

"How to use Harold to find me? Just like Max always does?"

"Harold couldn't find you here. This place—it defies efforts to find it. But no. I knew immediately where you were, as if I were staring at a pinpoint on a map. I could see you, and this place, quite clearly. Much more clearly than I could see myself at that time, a fact which itself required quite a lot of explaining. And though I had little explanation to offer, I had started to guess."

"I don't understand."

The suit shifted, and I could see Anthony tilt his head with the wry precision he always used when I had not grasped an idea. Or at least, I could see it in my own head, though I couldn't see his. "Mrs. Miller. I must confess I can't recall a single moment in my life before the one when I entered the headquarters of the Steller Fund. I remember the sun from the skylights, and

the receptionist's lovely smile, and being ushered into that cathedral of blond wood where you and Mr. Miller were conduct-
ing interviews. And I remember knowing immediately that I'd
found my place, though I hadn't known before that moment that
I lacked a place. And I think you felt it, too."

I thought back to the moment he described. At the time,
Max's appreciative gaze at the dapper attorney who stood before us had been my main focus—like so many things, I had
convinced myself that hiring Anthony had been at Max's insistence. Max's idea. But that hadn't been it at all. When I saw
Anthony the first time, I knew his name was Anthony Percival
Graves before he opened his mouth. I knew the pebbled briefcase at his feet was empty, and if we asked for a résumé, he
would have nothing to give us. I knew, beneath conscious
thought, that he was supposed to be there. And when Max offered him the job, I knew that it was right.

I knew all of this because that was Anthony's purpose, as
clear as the pinstripes on his suit.

"Papa must have drawn you. Where were you before? Where
did you come from?" None of the spirits Papa ever captured had
spoken. I didn't know if I could help them. But perhaps I could
help Anthony.

"I don't think you understand, Mrs. Miller. There is no before. There is only you. There was only ever finding you."

I heard Gran's voice echoing across a gulf of years, speaking
of Mama. *It's how she was made.*

*Saint Anthony, Saint Anthony, please come around. There's
something lost that can't be found.*

I took off my sweatshirt again. If Anthony was this far along
in . . . whatever was happening to us, there was no use in hiding
my own disappearance.

"Keryth!" Max's voice rang out in alarm. He had been standing off to the side, observing silently, taking the measure of the scene in the same way that always unnerved people at parties. Now, he had moved swiftly to my side, as if he thought the least visible part of me might also be unreal, and unable to support the rest of me.

There was even less of me visible now. I could feel it. I looked up at Max, setting my mouth into a line as he raised his hands to my face, hovering them in midair, as if afraid to touch what he could see. "Can you move? Where—where are you?"

"It's okay. I'm all right, Max. It looks as if I'm leaving, but I'm not." But as I spoke, I felt a shift in the breeze around us. I couldn't feel it in my hair—visible or invisible. Pieces of me were losing sensation. "I have to get inside. I have to find Papa."

"You're not going in there alone." Ellory's voice was determined. She stepped to my other side, flanking me with Max, and grabbed my glove. A small degree of sensation returned to my disappearing body. It was the first time I'd felt my fingertips in days.

Ellory snapped her free hand in a pinching motion toward Mindy, who followed her silent command by grasping it.

I spoke with a voice more confident than I felt. "You all need to get as far away from here as possible. This place—it's collapsing, somehow, and it may take me with it. I still don't know if it's even possible to fix whatever's wrong."

"We'll either fix it together, or we'll face it together. But we're through with letting you run away because you think it's best for us." Ellory's face was grim, her voice the stubborn-edged growl I remembered from tantrums during her younger years and bitter fights when she reached adolescence. "We were through with that a long time ago, but you weren't around for us to tell you, so I'm telling you now."

I felt tears prickling behind my eyelids. "Ell. I'm so sorry."

"We don't have time for sorry yet. We don't have time for anything other than stopping whoever is doing this to you." She started stepping toward the round door, and my heart pounded.

"Honey, be careful—"

"No, Mom. Let's stop being careful, okay? Let's start being real."

Anthony's suit stepped toward the door. "Miss Miller makes a good point. I think that 'real' is an important goal at the moment."

I headed back toward the round door, but Max's stillness, suspended at the end of my glove, stopped me short. Ellory halted at the door and shouted over her shoulder.

"Dad! Come on!" For a moment, it seemed like we were all standing in line at a theme park ride, my elder daughter's impatience to board a roller coaster sparking the rest of us into motion, but Max's expression was unreadable, closed off. Ellory paused. "Dad. We can talk about all of it later."

"You never told me—" Max's voice was distant, and I ached to explain, but I didn't know what explanation I could offer.

"Dad! If we don't get inside and let Mom fix this, she won't be around to tell us anything. Come ON!"

Max stepped forward, then hesitated, and my heart broke. "I loved you too much to tell you," I said. "There were no words to explain, and I didn't understand what was happening to me."

"And I loved you enough to help you understand. Whatever it was, Keryth. I was right here."

"Okay. That's enough, you two—save it for therapy. Let's go!" Ellory propelled us all toward the door, which was emitting a sound that hadn't been audible before—a scritchling, needling noise that faded in and out in a rhythm that felt like breath.

When I ducked back inside, I found Ellory and Mindy standing frozen, still hand in hand, staring at Mama.

"It's . . . it's her." Mindy reached her fingers toward the red streaks snaking from the staple. "Ell. It's—"

"The Star Lady. You're right." Ellory shook her head. "She looks different, but it's her." She turned around and looked at me. "We used to tell you about her, remember? She used to visit our dreams. You said she was imaginary."

I opened my mouth to ask what she was talking about, but closed it as I remembered the girls when they were small, in that liminal space between sleep and just waking, when they would tell me about their dreams. They shared a room, and seemed sometimes—when they were very young—to share their thoughts, as if they floated through their sleep-soaked exhalations into each other's minds. The Star Lady. *There's a scary bridge we have to cross, but the Star Lady has a star in a lantern, and she helps us across. She is so nice, Mommy. And she is so sad.*

"It was just a dream." The words escaped from me before I could stop them, just as they had all those years ago, because we had teeth to brush and clothes to don and hoops to jump through on our endless way out the door. "She used to visit me in dreams sometimes, too. She's your grandmother. She was gone before you were ever born."

"Why didn't you tell us it was her?" Mindy's words carried a note of betrayal.

"Because I didn't think any of it was real." That wasn't quite right, either. "It was too painful to believe that any of it was real, or that it was real and I lost it." My mother's eyes were exactly as I remembered them, gazing at me with the same reassurance they held when she smoothed my hair back from my temples when I was a child. When I couldn't be sure if I was a dreaming child staring at an angel or a normal mother carrying a flash-light after a long time away.

"You never told us about your mom," Mindy said.

"You never told us about anything," Ellory added.

"I'm so sorry." I felt as if I could say it the rest of their lives—as if I'd been saying it, silently, since the moment I became a mother—and it would never be enough. "There was so much that happened—before—to me. And I didn't want you to know. I didn't want you to ever know what the world could be like."

"So we found out what the world was like without you, in-stead." Ellory's eyes, the same wide and unblinking blue I re-membered from sleepless nights when she was an infant, contained no tears. She was precise and matter-of-fact, as she always had been. "But we'll find that out for good if we don't stop what's happening now."

I nodded. "I'll explain everything. Everything that I can, as soon as I can. But we have to find Papa. Your grandfather. I think he's doing this somehow, but he doesn't need to be. And I think he's somewhere in this house. I know he is."

"Then we'll find him together." Max stepped past my mother on the wall and over the uneven floors to the library room be-yond. "And then we'll figure out, together, what finding him means."

Before I could look for him, Tobias was standing beside me, mutely. I searched his face, but he shook his head. "I don't know what it'll mean, either. Maybe your friend has some ideas?"

A chirp at my shoulder. My jay was perched on the door-frame, head tilted in expectation.

"You don't have to come with us," I said, to both of them.

But I knew that they would.

My darling Keryth,

I know that you are coming here. The feeling of
your coming—the energy of it—is different than
when you return to your image, and I know you are
coming in your full-fledged form. I hope you are not
coming alone. You will ask me, I think, why I never
came for you, and I will try my best to explain, if you
arrive before I am gone, and if my being gone doesn't
take you, too. I could only hold you back, and I could
not tell you why. The simplest answer I can give is
this: you can't tell the key to everything that they're
the key. What pressure does that word put on a
person? What if that pressure bends them, breaks
them, alters the key such that it can't unlock anything at all?

What if you're wrong?

I lost my sister. I didn't lose her—I kept her
forever, but I couldn't unlock her again. I couldn't
capture the ones I loved most enough to keep them
safe. I am a jailer, Keryth, and a miserable one. You
are the only person who can open the cells, but you
couldn't do it if I told you so. We never accomplish
what everyone tells us our potential means. We have
to find it for ourselves.

I pray that I may see you walk through the
door before me. Doors were the only thing I could
draw, you know, without pulling in spirits, because
every door is a passage to somewhere else. An in-

between place. They don't shelter people; they shelter possibilities. And now, I cling to the possibility of you.

All my love,
PAPA

33

· · • ● • · ·

A House Like an Accordion
AUGUST 2016

TRAVERSING THE HOUSE was a journey whose destination and timeline were unpredictable. Where there were windows, the world outside changed—sometimes the golden, piercing light of a desert sunrise lit walls and ceilings, and in others, starlight illuminated passages we had to drop to our knees to cross. It wasn't clear if each segment of the house lived in a different place, or if the entire structure blinked in and out of new surroundings as we attempted to reach its end. If it ended. My own fading had become bilateral, and my disappearing limbs began to make it difficult to tell where I ended and my father's creations began. By the time we reached the last door— I didn't know it was the last; I only knew I could go no farther if there were more—I had pulled the hood of my coat tight around my face, tucking the cuffs of my sleeves and pants into my gloves and socks, hoping to spare my daughters from seeing, or not seeing, how little of me remained.

The door was cracked, a thick rectangle of maple burled with curves of darkened knots, with spalting threaded through the grain in a way that looked like sketched images, or perhaps writing.

The handle was a simple knob. It yielded without a sound, and the door swung open on smooth hinges.

Inside was a wide, low bed that dwarfed its only occupant, a man so frail he hardly made an indentation in the mattress. His left arm draped toward a sketchbook, his fingers gripped around a pencil that seemingly absorbed all his strength merely to move. The sound of the charcoal across the paper reverberated around us and through the house behind us, echoing like breath.

"Papa?" I whispered, though it hardly seemed possible this man—this skeletal figure, nothing but bones and art in a bed—could be my father.

The man did not look up. I tried to move toward him but felt certain, somehow, that the little that was left of me would slough off into the still air around me. I could not get closer and stay as I was, such as I was. My daughters and Max stood behind me, and I felt without turning around that they would get closer if I didn't warn them not to.

Tobias stopped them instead, holding his arm in front of them like a driver in an old-fashioned movie hitting the brakes. "Wait."

We all waited, listening to the breath of charcoal, wondering if he would notice us.

I heard a rush of wings over my head, and suddenly both Steller's jays—the new happy couple—were on the edge of Papa's book, hopping around near his outstretched fingers, chirping.

"You." The voice was my father's, the resonance of it seemingly too deep to reside in what was left of him. "I remember you." My jay chirped in response and alighted on his forearm.

Papa smiled. "I wouldn't forgive me so quickly, but I appreciate it all the same." He kept his eyes on the birds but raised his voice imperceptibly. "I see you, too. I'm sorry not to be more welcoming, but I can't rise from the bed anymore. And you can't come any closer, either."

"Papa."

"Keryth. You're taller than I remember. I've tried everything I can to keep you exactly as you were, but my body is defeating me. I'm so sorry."

"What are you doing to her?" Ellory's words were challenging on the surface, with an undercurrent of doubt. "Why are you erasing her?"

My father shook his head and smiled, reaching toward my elder daughter. "You look like my mother." He pointed at Mindy. "And you, like my sister. It's impossible, yet there you are. Beautiful and alive."

"You didn't answer her question," Mindy said. "Why are you erasing our mother?"

Papa chuckled weakly. "I'm not erasing her. I've been using every ounce of my remaining strength to draw her out, but I couldn't anchor her mother, and I fear I can't anchor her, either." Papa's breathing was shallow. "And the nearer she gets to me, the weaker I am."

I turned to face my children and my husband, Tobias, and what was left of Anthony. "I need you to leave me with him."

"What? No." Ellory set her mouth in a line and looked as if she would stamp her foot. "We aren't leaving you."

"I don't mean for long, and I don't mean that you should go back outside. I only mean I need to be alone with him, in this room, to talk. Just wait right outside the door. I'll be right here."

"Keryth—" Max started, then stopped, out of his depth.

"I'll be all right. And this is something I need to do alone. I feel it in my bones." I smiled wanly. "Whatever's left of them."

The air around us changed, and for the first time, everyone

else seemed to feel sensations the same way that I did. Max took our daughters' hands and nodded. "We need to trust your mother knows what she's doing," he said. "And like she said, we'll be right outside."

He led them to the door without a backward glance, as Ellory and Mindy both shot worried looks over their shoulders. The suit that was Anthony followed them without a word. Only Tobias stayed put.

"You, too," I said.

"I'm a big fan of your work," Tobias said, speaking past me, looking at my father in the bed. "All of it. Amazing. And nothing more so than her." He gestured at me, and nodded. "I'll be waiting."

I smiled. "I know." I watched him walk to the door and close it behind him, and then I turned back around to face what was left of my father.

Part of me wanted to get closer to him, to touch him, to reassure myself he was real. And part of me was furious, wanting to run as far away from this place as possible. "What did you mean about getting weaker if I'm near you? Papa, I haven't been near you since—"

"Since I left you on the banks of that pond all those years ago." Papa's face was solemn. "I couldn't get your mother back if you were near me, and you couldn't get your brother back if I were near you. My mother always said the truest art requires solitude, and the truest artists work their art alone."

"You left me—left us—because I was less important than your art?" I spat the words with a bitterness I didn't know I felt. Not after all these years. That burning coal of anger, the knowledge that I had been abandoned, left to fend for myself. The secret longing to have him back, the confusion at what I must have done wrong to make him leave me, and the self-loathing at what I'd done, capturing my brother in exactly the way Papa had warned me not to. Ever since that first line of that first sketch of that bird—the one that was now fluttering near his narrow forearm, restored after years trapped in a book.

"You were my art."

"What does that even mean, Papa? You're not making any sense. Do you know how much work I had to do? How much therapy it took to understand that the rest of the world doesn't speak in riddles, and it's okay to listen to words and not have to constantly wonder what kind of puzzle they may be? You did that to me. I could never trust anyone, and I could never trust myself."

"I know exactly how you feel." Papa's arm stopped moving, and as the breath of his lines across the page halted, the room around us became silent and still. I couldn't even hear my own heart beating in my ears.

I suddenly noticed I couldn't feel it beating, either. It had stopped. My breath had stopped. And yet, I still stood, alive, half-visible, waiting for him. As I always had.

"You, and your brother. You were the best of my creations." Papa resumed his drawing, and I felt air rush back into my lungs, my blood moving through my body again. "You were my only creations, really. The only ones I ever drew into the world, your whole selves, and made real. I didn't even know if you would age, not at first. Your mother never did. You were the best ideas I ever had, and only because you weren't really my ideas at all. You were someone else's before you were mine, and I hoped you'd be enough to tie your mother to this world after we lost the one who made her."

"The one who made Mama was you. You're right here. She's back there, trapped, by the door. Trying to escape. Like she always did."

"I didn't create Laila, Keryth." The pain in my father's face froze me. "My mother did. And I've spent every moment since Gran died trying to keep your mother from fading away. Sometimes—for short stretches of time—I could draw her out and into the world, with me. But most of the time, I wasn't powerful enough. I had to do exactly what you did with your brother: capture her. She wasn't trying to escape. She was trying to warn you."

"Warn me about what?"

"That the closer you got to me, the less I'd be able to stop what's happening. But she's been unable to accept that I can't stop anything at all, not anymore. You were absent because I wasn't strong enough, and now you're disappearing because I'm dying. Everything I've made will vanish with me. I've held off that reality as long as I can. I'm so sorry."

"None of this is true." My heartbeat thumped in rhythm to my father's hand, and I felt my head turning to and fro, a violent shaking I couldn't stop, but I couldn't speak. "This is ridiculous. You're saying I'm not real."

"You're very real. You're as real as my wife, the angel my mother painted to watch over me. She only intended to create a guardian—another spirit from a painting, like the saints she used to sell. But she made someone more real—more true, and full of love and longing—than she realized she was even capable of." My father's face was gaunt, but I still recognized the expression on his face as the one he wore whenever he gazed at my mother—awestruck. Transfixed. "She meant to make me a companion, but she never knew we'd fall in love. And children— my Lord, how we longed for them."

My father's pencil stopped again, and I felt the same eerie suspension—no breath, no heartbeat. It didn't feel like death, not that I had much to compare it to. It felt like absorption. Like being surrounded by a blanket that was trying to weave you into its threads. And as sensation fled from me, I understood this had been happening to me my whole life. That I had been as absent as my mother had been because my travels hadn't been for business—that all the hurried explanations I'd given for my disappearances weren't cover-ups for trips to other places I couldn't remember. The blackouts happened when I traveled from three dimensions to two, and back again, as my father's efforts ebbed and flowed.

Papa looked at me as he moved his pencil again, restoring me. "In the end, Laila was so desperate that she begged me to do what my mother had, and try to create our children myself. I couldn't bear to tell her no, and I thought that I could give her something else to hold on to, to hold her here with me. I'd already learned that my impressions were strongest when they reproduced something that already existed, like an image you keep tracing over, again and again. So—"

Papa gestured weakly toward a small table in the corner, its edges indistinct in the gloom. I knew before I reached it what it was. The angel held her lantern over the heads of two small children on a bridge. The framed image was not my grandmother's painted version; it was clearly Papa's, monochrome shades lending dimension to the flat page, as alive and real as my jay had been, but not captured. We were drawn out into the world. The little boy was Neil, and the little girl was me. The frame leaned against a chipped coffee mug, blue ceramic shimmering, more translucent than I remembered. The mug I'd drawn all those years before and hidden under my bed. Hidden from Papa. Or so I thought.

I looked at my father. "I thought you said Gran created Mama?"

"She did. Not long after my sister died. She only had one

living child remaining, and she was a widow. She was determined to keep the family she had left, and she told me later she
was trying to protect us both—me, and whatever was left of
Anne."

"What do you mean, whatever was left?"

"Anne was the first person I ever captured. Before it happened, I didn't know the full extent of what I could do. And
neither did Mama." He shook his head. "She never blamed me,
but I could never forgive myself. She was convinced she could
bring Anne back out, and she tried. I think, even when she
painted that scene, she was trying. But Anne was beyond her
reach. She was certainly beyond mine."

I thought of Neil, the feeling that poured through my hands
when I captured him in the pond, trying to save him. "How did
it happen?"

"We were living in Pennsylvania. The place was surrounded
by woods and trails—all sorts of places to explore. And there
was a bridge. An old railway, stretched over stone arches. We
thought it was abandoned. And my mother's stories—"

"Keryth and Neil."

Papa nodded. "Exactly. We were pretending to cross from
the Kingdom of Earth to the Kingdom of Heaven, and Anne
was going first. The princess always went first in the stories. She
was more than halfway across when we heard the whistle. At
first, we just made it part of the game, but then the ground
started vibrating, and Anne turned around and looked at me.
She loved trains, you know. I can't count the number of times
she dragged Pa and me to the railway museum near our house
there—it was a fascination she shared with our father, and I
always wondered if she . . . I don't know. If she attracted that
engine to herself somehow that day.

"She tried to come back, and I screamed at her to run to the other side—it was closer. She just froze, like she didn't know what to do. I didn't know what to do, either. It was like the stories you hear about seeing your whole life flash before your eyes, but I was seeing hers—ours, together, all at once."

"What did you do?"

Papa closed his eyes. "What I knew I shouldn't do, but what I knew I was capable of, because she showed me that I could. Anne's whole room—every wall—was all butterflies, but instead of catching them with a net, I caught them with a pencil. She loved them. I saw her make one of her own, just once, almost like you did. All butter-yellow squiggles and curves in crayon. I think it scared her. She was very young. I don't think she ever did it again, but we lost her so early. Maybe she would have improved."

"Papa . . . the train?"

"I captured her before it reached her. Just barely. I always carried my book, always, because she would point out things she wanted, and I would draw them down for her. Mother knew. She didn't like it. But when I told her Anne was gone—" He paused, a thin rivulet of water passing down his leathery cheek, less a tear than a memory. "We tried everything. Everything. I drew and redrew her like every damn butterfly on that wall, retraced every line I'd used when I tried to save her. But she was trapped. I'm not sure Mother ever forgave me. I certainly never forgave myself."

"Where is she?"

"The book. The same book as your brother."

"I never saw—"

"The back pocket, where I kept my papers. She's there."

I looked around the room and recalled the hazy layers and segments fanning back through however far we had come before reaching my father, and thought of the room with the sketchbooks. "I could try to find her. There are so many books, Papa, but I think I can release her."

"You can't here. Not near me. And she isn't here. That book isn't here."

"Where is it?"

"Listen." His hand stopped again, his pencil frozen, and I felt the same suspended stillness in my chest. "Keryth. You already know."

I closed my eyes and remembered the sound of my brother's voice screaming into my head. "The House in the Reeds."

"I hid the book there. The most important one."

"Why didn't you just tell me, Papa?" The words tore out of me with the anguish of his abandonment. "How could you have left me there alone?"

"I didn't know you were alone until I snuck back into the house, after they'd taken you away. I thought your brother might be hiding somewhere inside. When I saw the book open on the table—"

"You knew I'd captured him. Just like you told me not to." The tears burned hot behind my eyelids, and I couldn't bear to let them fall.

"I know." He lifted his hand as if to reach toward me, but the effort was too much, and it dropped limply by his side. "Keryth. I always told you—"

"'Don't grow up to be like me!' I know! I didn't have a choice. You didn't leave me a choice. We were alone, and it was the only thing I could do to save him."

"Keryth. When I told you not to be like me, I wasn't talking about the art. I was amazed by your skills, for all that you tried to hide them. My mother was afraid they might pose risks, like mine did, but I thought they might be the key. But you couldn't wield them with me nearby, just as I couldn't wield mine near my mother."

"If you weren't talking about the art, what did you mean?"

"I didn't want you to become so fixated on capturing life on the page that you forgot to live it, to actually experience the beauty you managed to create. I spent my life trying to recover your mother, to somehow keep her with us, after Gran passed. We thought, for a time, that if we could find all the places that her image had wound up—if we could collect them together—I could combine them somehow, make her stronger. Make her whole. We tracked down every single original print of Gran's painting. There were ten of them. But it didn't make a difference. I think it may have been because her image was too diffuse, with all the pillows and blankets and bric-a-brac winding up Lord knows where."

"Ten prints?" I thought back to the dots on Tobias's map, the five-pointed star. "Papa, my whole childhood, you told me not to draw from life. But you did it anyway, didn't you? Every single one of those places was a copy of somewhere that actually existed."

He nodded. "Yes."

"So the people inside—you knew what you were doing."

"I didn't mean to capture any of them. And some of the places were abandoned, thank God. But the others—yes. They were a price I was willing to pay. But the bargain still zeroed out. Your mother still disappeared. And the effort cost me everything. It cost me the relationship I could have had with you and your brother, who were my creations and were here and real and needed me."

"I still need you. I needed you then, and I need you now. You have to figure out a way to make this stop." I held up my translucent arms. "How could you bring me out into the world only to take me back out of it again?"

"It's not intentional. It's because this effort cost me my life. I spent every ounce of strength I had in trying to bring your mother back, and whatever was left in trying to keep you here. And it's drained me in exactly the way it drained my mother. I knew what would happen, and I couldn't stop myself. But you can." He held his hand up, and my Steller's jay swooped down to land on his finger, looking at me expectantly.

"How?" I asked. "I've never been able to fix anything at all."

"Gran could paint whole worlds, whole people, but they couldn't survive her. I could capture reality on a page, and pull three dimensions into two. But you? You could nudge reality with a pen. You could push it where you wanted it to go."

"But I couldn't control it."

"Over time, I think you learned. Between the three of us, Keryth, I think we could have made a halfway decent artist. A complete one. Create, capture, convince. Each generation drew strength and skill from the one before it, and by the time it got to you—your skill is greater than mine, because you wove yourself into this world. You found a way to pin yourself down."

"I only have my book, Papa. I can't release anything without the original images, and even then, I'm not sure—"

"My book, Keryth. The book has everything. Your brother. Your mother. And you."

I shook my head. "I don't understand."

"You do. Think about where we are."

"In Gran's house."

"But where was Gran's house?"

I stopped to consider. "I never knew. It was everywhere and nowhere. Especially this time—it never stayed put, and not even

Erma could find any record of it, really. And she could find almost anything—"

I looked upward in frustration and, for the first time, noticed the light in the room, or its lack. Instead of observing the way Gran's house had always seemed plunged into gloom, I noticed the gloom's contours, its swirling shades of graphite gray and charcoal black, the precise shading where the walls met the high ceiling. I gasped.

"We're in the book."

Papa nodded. He seemed too exhausted to reply.

"Have—have we always been in the book?"

My jay tilted her head to one side and looked at me sidelong, a glance that always meant *Really? Really, Keryth?*

"Okay, right. *Sorry.*" I tried to reach my arms around the contours of the room, the house that surrounded us. "If we weren't always here, why are we now?"

"You thought I disappeared. That I abandoned you. I didn't. But I didn't have the strength left to stray far from what I'd made, and your mother was almost entirely gone. You'd already captured your brother to keep him safe—freezing him in place, like suspended animation. I could do the same thing, I recognized. What seemed most impossible might be our only hope. Until you could find us."

I thought back to my first job in that first coffee shop, the shelves and walls lined with shirts for sale, and my favorite ones—the M. C. Escher prints. Stairs that led to nowhere but their own beginnings. The birds tesselating into their own eternal flocks. And the hands in an endless loop, drawing each other.

"You drew yourself into the book."

Papa nodded. "Myself, and your mother. She was already in

there, of course, more times than I could count. But I'd never tried to retreat with her. It was the only thing I hadn't tried. It was . . . difficult. It took more from me than I thought I had. But I landed here, inside this place. Inside all the places, really. And I've been here ever since."

"That doesn't explain how you've sent anything—anyone— outside."

Papa squinted. "I don't know what you're talking about."

"Anthony." I waited for a glimpse of recognition, but Papa's face didn't change. "Anthony. The guy in the suit. Right now, the guy who's *only* a suit. My lawyer. He's even less here now than I am."

Papa tilted his head. "It couldn't be—Saint Anthony, could it?" The shake of his head looked more like a tremor. "She couldn't have—I couldn't have—look, this was a thing that my mother explained better, to the extent she explained it at all. But do you remember Gran's saints?"

I nodded. "The ones in her stories?"

"And her paintings. Yes. Saint Anthony was her—I won't say her favorite, because it wasn't like that. He was her fail-safe. The patron saint of lost things. She'd lost so much. And she made him long before I was ever born—from what my father told me, she painted many of the saints, but none so much as Anthony. Over and over again. And she spoke to him, called on him when something went missing. And she wasn't alone, either."

I remembered. *Saint Anthony, Saint Anthony, please come around. There's something lost that can't be found.* "Are you telling me that my near-invisible lawyer is actually a painting Gran made? Of a saint? Before you were even born?"

Papa shrugged. "Everything you grew up with, and all that you've seen, and that's where your mind starts to question things? Yes. I'm telling you that he must have been—reinforced, somehow. Kept out in the world simply because of the fact that the world often called on him. So when I called on him, he must have still been out there, waiting to be of use."

I stepped around the edges of the room, trying not to get too close to him. My jay swooped up again and landed on the chipped frame of a saint's portrait near the door. SAINT ANTHONY, read the caption. I squinted at the man in the image, trying to see past his Biblical beard and draped robes, to dress the image in a crisp suit and oiled hair. "What do you mean, when you called on him?"

"To get to you. Because I knew I didn't have much time, and I didn't know how to reach you myself. You were lost to me, and I thought you would be lost to the world if I didn't bring you here and—I wasn't sure what—"

My heart froze even as Papa kept his pencil in motion. "You were going to capture me."

"I didn't know what else to do. But then—you came here, but you didn't come alone, Keryth. You found footholds in this world that I didn't create." His eyes misted over. "And they're so beautiful. I never knew I'd see my mother's face, or my sister's, ever again. But your daughters—they're you and they're not, and they're my family and they're not, and they're—absolutely, completely real. Flesh and blood that didn't start on a page. Your mother and I . . ."

I closed my eyes. "Mama and you never told me anything at all."

"And would you have believed us if we had?" The challenge in Papa's voice was stronger than what was left of him. "If I had to do it over again, I would have done everything the same, Keryth. I knew no other way. But I never found a way for us— all of us—to land. Without me—without the rest of us—you did. You actually found a way to set down physical roots."

"I didn't find anything, Papa. I tried so hard not to use what I could do, and I was afraid—I was afraid my whole life—that it was harmful, and would hurt the people I loved the most."

"Because that's what I did." His smile was sad. "I hope you know I never meant to. And I had the smallest inkling of what you were capable of. The best of my mother's skill, the best of mine, all distilled down into one person."

"A person who wasn't real."

"No. A person who made herself real. Through sheer force of will and determination and making her own choices, and her own family." His voice ebbed, and his pencil stopped again. My body was quiet. "I think you'll stay. Even when I'm gone, you'll still be here."

"I can fix it." The words sounded more hopeful than I felt. "I know what I can do now. I can bring everything back. I can bring you back, too."

"Keryth." He reached for me. "You already did."

I approached him slowly, taking his hand. It was as soft and insubstantial as tissue, more translucent than the paper on which he sketched, and yet it felt the same—the same weight I remembered settling over my own hand, guiding me through my first lines. The same reassuring grip, the squeeze I always felt before seeking comfort from his blue eyes. I stretched out on the bed beside him. "Don't go," I whispered.

"I stayed as long as I could. I didn't slip away."

"Did you try to bring her back, too?" I meant Gran, the grief of her sudden departure so many years before still washing over me in a fresh wave.

He nodded. "She passed beyond my reach. Maybe I'll join her now."

"And Mama?"

"No. Mama, I think, you can find yourself. I don't know for

sure. But if anyone can, it's you." He lightly rubbed his finger against the feathered head of my jay. "You already unlocked something living. You can only get more powerful from here."

"Not without you."

"You've done all of this—the whole life you've made for yourself, not to mention finding me, on your own, Keryth."

"You were always there with me. I know that now."

"Then you have to know I still will be." He closed his eyes and clasped my hand tighter, his breath becoming even more shallow.

I couldn't mark the time when he left me. I only felt the pressure of his fingers, and the pressure of mine as I squeezed back, until stillness overtook us both.

In the dream, there is a little girl. I see her all the time—blond braids, ribbons trailing from their ends, a robe like a princess on her slender form that is only, on further reflection, a child's nightgown. She wears a crown of flowers around her head, and holds hands with a man who wears a crown of light, too bright to see his face. She always reaches for my hand, and I always take it, letting her tug me through a field of flowers into a house surrounded by thorns. Papa's book is always in the same place, open on the table, and the girl wants me to open it. Not the sketches. Not his drawings. The pocket in the back, with its letters and clippings and creations we weren't supposed to see. She points, but never speaks. I shake my head. She grasps my hand and points again, opening her mouth and closing it, her eyes holding a plea. But all I remember is Papa's anger, before he took it back. That and my fear. And then I wake up, and she's gone.

34

·‥••●●•‥·

A House Like an Accordion
AUGUST 2016

I THOUGHT IT must be an earthquake. I was curled in bed like the comma in a sentence that was still incomplete, my hand grasping something motionless—the only thing still motionless. The atmosphere around me shuddered, and I thought of the wide bookshelves I'd wanted in our glass house, and Max's insistence that there was nowhere to secure them against earthquakes, and my anger at his always-rightness, yet again. I heard my daughters screaming and tried to scream back, *Get under a table*, words frozen inside my mouth, unable to exit.

"Mom!" Ellory's voice was first, as always. I felt her narrow hand on my shoulder, shaking me harder than the room was shaking. "She's not breathing—Mindy, she's not—"

My younger child, who always made up for being last and being smaller by being louder and more explosive, grasped both my shoulders and pulled me toward her, yelling at her sister, "Don't just crouch there, help me get her up!" My back thudded against the bed, and I heard Mindy scream, "Don't you dare, Mom, don't you even *think* about it. Mom! Do you hear me?" I felt her fists against my chest, her head against my heart. "Don't you dare." She pressed into me the way she did when she was small, nestled against my chest, breathing. I felt her grasp Ellory's hand and pull her down, the two of them resting against me, inhalations and exhalations uniting with sobs. Beyond them—from some farther distance—shouting. Max's voice, Tobias's voice, both rising above a growing sound of snapping wood and fracturing glass. *This whole place is collapsing—too far to get out—*

Air rushed into my lungs. My heart shook with a new and regular beat, strong and steady. I sat up to find there were no words trapped behind my lips. There was only one, and I said it louder than the shuddering destruction around us.

"No."

Everything froze. The splintering timbers knitted themselves back together, broken bones restructuring themselves into something stronger, more intact. I thought of Papa's book. I saw it with perfect clarity, tucked within the wall of the House in the Reeds. I reached out toward it in my mind, my fingers touching the corner of a page. I tapped.

"You are not closing," I told the book. "Expand."

The room unfolded, the house around it stretching like a gusseted pocket and then stopping, as if waiting for what I would command next. The deep cathedral hush of the space sliced open with light from windows carved into a formerly blank wall. Outside, the desert canyon yawned against the setting sun. On the other rim, a man on an exhausted-looking painted horse slid off it and jumped up and down, pointing, as if trying to catch the attention of other people who were absolutely not with him. He began fumbling with the saddlebags, and I knew he was looking for a camera, and I sighed.

We were out in the open, for now. I had no idea how to be anything else.

I also had no idea how much time—how many days and

nights—we had passed in the house, or whether it was the same inside as it was out there, in the real world I'd nearly forgotten surrounded us.

Mindy's voice was hushed, her words a pin drop in the silence of the room. "Mom, why are you glowing?"

I smiled at her. "Because my mama lit the way." I grasped her hand. "And because I'm hers, just like you're mine. I'm sorry it took me so long to figure that out."

"You don't just get to be spritely and magical now, Mom. You've actually got a lot of explaining to do." Ellory glowered, and the real world outside the new windows intruded into the house my father built. The reality of the distance I'd imposed.

"I know. I hope you'll give me a chance to do it."

"Start with him," Ellory said, pointing at my father on the bed and then visibly noticing that he wasn't breathing. "Is he going to come back? Like you did?"

My heart, beating on its own, felt as if it might shatter. "I don't think so." My voice caught in my throat. "I think he's really gone. Like my grandmother was."

"How did you come back?"

"Because of you. Because you two—my beautiful girls—you're my anchors to this world. I never understood that because of the way my father made me. I'm from this place. In some ways, I *am* this place. But what I can do—it's more than what my father could. It's more than what my grandmother could, too, and Papa taught me to fear it. So whenever I used it—whenever I created—I thought it might harm you. I spent your whole life thinking of myself as a threat, and instead I became something almost as bad."

"Never there," Mindy said.

"Not like Dad," Ellory added.

I gazed at Max, standing by the door. I didn't know if I

wanted him to defend me or join the conversation at all. I mostly wanted him to blink.

"No. I'm not like Dad." I looked at Papa. "I'm not like my father, either. I'm not entirely sure what I'm like. It's strange, looking forty full in the face, and feeling like a newborn."

"This is all too weird." Ellory shook her head, then her whole body, as if trying to exorcize everything that made no sense. "Dr. Grace is going to have a field day with us, Mom. I'm changing the subject. What is this place? It's where you grew up?"

"It's every place I grew up. All of them. The structures my father captured when he drew."

"Then why did you have to drive anywhere at all?"

"I didn't know it at the time. They're out in the world, too. But they're also here, and I think—I think we passed through all of them, and many more I'd never seen. I think I can get to all of them from here."

"Like a portal?"

"More like a hallway. A really long hallway."

"Bad design choice, those," Tobias quipped from the corner, puckish as always, waiting for a chance to enter the conversation. "Too dark and dreamlike."

"Noted." I practiced, swinging my legs off the edge of the bed, standing tentatively on my feet, which surprised me by holding my weight. I felt more substantial than I had when I entered the room. The light no longer passed through me. I was real and complete. "I'll work on redesigning. But I have some other things I need to do first."

"No, Mom." Ellory grasped Mindy's hand, then mine. "This isn't a You project. This is a We project. Right, Dad?"

I looked at Max, still frozen in the corner, trying to make sense of things. Nothing about the day squared with his analytical nature. Nothing computed with his system for the world.

"I need—some time, I think." His voice was quiet.

I nodded. "We have that now. I have that. I didn't before." I felt unsettled seeing Max standing next to Tobias, both of them so different, so crucial to the distinct versions of myself. I had a long road—a hallway—to navigate, to try to restore what was left of my family. I didn't know who, besides my daughters, would navigate it with me. "Are you going back to California?"

"I—I guess so. I came with Anthony. I don't know where he's gone."

I closed my eyes and felt the atmosphere around me. "He's a little lost at the moment, but I can fix that for him, for a change. I could do it in the next place. You—you could come, too, if you wanted."

I crossed to remove Gran's painting from the wall, retrieving the angel and her star, her frightened wards, from the place where they'd been imprisoned. I held it against my chest.

"Where are you going?" Max asked.

"The House in the Reeds."

"With him?" Max gestured at Tobias.

"With anyone who wants to come," I said. "It's just down the hall."

LOCAL ECCENTRIC SELLS BLURRY PHOTO TO HISTORY CHANNEL FOR "DOCUMENTARY" ON GHOST BUILDINGS (from *The Tatum City Bee*, Tatum City, Utah, September 26, 2016): Dan Burnett, a leader of local trail rides for tourists who don't know any better, recently announced he had successfully captured an image of the "Drunk Church," a building that he has claimed for some time roves unbidden through the deserts in our area. "It was right where I said it was," said Burnett, while gleefully shoving a blurry image on his phone's screen into the face of anyone visiting the Dusty Tavern for drinks. "I told all of y'all, but did you listen? No. And now look at me! A date with Lady Television to tell my story!" Inquiries to the producers of *Ghost Builds*, a new online-only series from the creators of *HauntMania!* and *Dude, That's My Dead Grandma*, confirmed that Mr. Burnett's photo will, indeed, feature in an upcoming episode. Mr. Burnett himself, however, has not been invited to appear.

35

· · ● ● ● ● · ·

The House in the Reeds
AUGUST 2016

I THOUGHT WE would have to walk and crawl through end-less, undefined space again, but when the door in Papa's room opened, it revealed an orderly hallway, with stones fitted over-head, fading away to a vanishing point far beyond view. The doors lining the walls were spaced evenly, as different as the houses to which they led, but I didn't need a legend to translate their locations. Each space was as familiar to me as if I'd drawn it myself. We walked to a green door whose surface was stippled with blue, the color of a pond overhung with ponderosas and juniper, with a curved handle of wrought iron in the shape of an aspen leaf. Tobias clutched at my hand.

"It's the door. The one I told you about. The one that kept disappearing."

"I know," I said. I grasped the handle and pulled. The door opened soundlessly onto the edge of Hidden Pond, but before I could step through, I heard another door close behind me, and the room we had just left vanished into the wall. "Papa—"

"He was already gone, Keryth," Tobias whispered. "Just like you told your daughters."

"I know. But—" I stepped back to the place where the door

once stood, and fanned my fingers against the wall, willing my father to return, wondering again if I could somehow bring him back, even though he'd tried and failed with Gran. Surely there was a way to restore him into the world—

And then I heard his voice, as whole and present as if he stood beside me, whispering directly into my head. *Don't grow up to be like me.*

I had to let him go.

My daughters looked at me expectantly, waiting for me to take the lead before stepping into a forest they'd never seen before. I heard them catch their breaths as they walked behind me, the spice and sharpness of crushed ponderosa needles unfamiliar to their lungs. The high altitude still spun my head after decades spent at lower elevations, making everything seem more real and unreal all at once.

"We should be inside the house," Tobias said.

I shook my head. "I wanted to see the outside first. I wanted to see the pond."

The water was still, reflecting a bowl of sky and boughs above it. The reeds on the far end looked as if they had been painted with the bristles of one of Gran's brushes. I could see the house across the water was nearly complete, transformed into a better version of itself—less restored than remade.

"Is there a path, or—" Max said, and stopped, confused.

"Wait." I shut the door and pressed my hand against it, and then reopened it. "Here it is." I stepped into the great central room of the house, which smelled of wax and polish. The beams were solid, the leaks in the skylights had been fixed, and the floors were covered in wide planks, with no remaining sign of the soaked carpet. Papa's burled cabinets gleamed.

I looked at Tobias. "You did more work than you said you did."

"I didn't do hardly anything," he murmured. "Not before you called me away. I think this is mostly you."

I walked directly to my parents' room, now stripped of the sprigged wallpaper and bright red shag. The door in the bathroom wall—the one where I'd heard my brother's voice—was now solid, with no window to show the scene outside. I knew without looking that it no longer led outdoors. It swung open to the dusty library of sketchbooks we had passed through earlier, now orderly, every volume shelved. A single book on the floor sat in a beam of light from the windows.

Papa's sketchbook was worn, its black cover curled. White specks of mold dotted its cover. I picked it up gingerly, worried it might crumble in my hands, but its swollen pages flipped open to a graphite spruce tree with a flash of red, lines scrambled like a firework, resting on one branch. An interrupted cardinal.

I turned through the curled leaves of paper, some missing strips, some gnawed by the teeth of some long-gone animal. The last few pages of the book were blank. The final two sketches were missing a corner and curved toward each other, facing but not quite touching. The left side was my brother, caught exactly as I'd drawn him, his same trusting expression catching my breath in my chest.

The right side was my parents—or would have been. My mother's pose echoed my grandmother's in that long-ago portrait with my grandfather, gazing straight out at me, holding hands with a person who wasn't there anymore. Papa was gone.

Mindy reached over my shoulder and touched my mother's face. "She looks like she's waiting."

"She is. I have to start with Neil."

"Why?"

"Because he's waited longer."

I sat cross-legged on the floor, pulling the pen I always kept out of my tangle of hair and setting its narrow tip onto lines I hadn't touched for decades. I focused on retracing the cross-hatching while thinking of my brother, the way his locks of brown hair used to fall over his eyes like a curtain, the way he laughed when only I told jokes. I thought of our last moments together, my terror at the thought of losing him, of losing everything, my desperation to keep him safe. I felt warmth flow from my fingertips.

"Mom, you're—" Ellory broke off.

"I know. It'll stop in a second." I dotted and dashed my way across the page, concentrating on everything that wasn't here, everyone I wanted back, until I thought my heart might stop, unable to keep beating under the weight of loss. I kept the tip of my pen against my brother's chest, letting ink pour into the fibers of the page. I waited.

Nothing happened. The warmth in my hands and face began to ebb, and the normal warmth of sunlight through the skylights returned, bright and cheerful and utterly empty. My brother wasn't here. Grief pierced me like a cold needle. Everything I'd ever thought about my own skill—everything I'd hoped—had been wrong.

And then I heard a distant splash like a pebble skipping across water toward us, each contact growing louder until it built to a crescendo, a downpour crashing over our heads, my dripping hair scented with algae and moss.

"What the actual—" Ellory started. "Are we—"

I hardly heard her, my senses overwhelmed as I stood knee-deep among the reeds and mud in the pond where we were all now standing and soaked, staring at the middle distance where waves had erupted.

The man stood in water up to his waist. He was motionless,

as rooted to the spot as if he'd grown out of the sediment and bloomed there like a lotus. I couldn't breathe. The man gazed at me and then doubled over, bellowing. "KERRRRRRRRRRRYYYYTH! KERRRR—"

I was stumbling, wading, swimming with all my might toward him. I reached him and threw my arms around his waist, planting my feet in the mud in front of him. It couldn't be. It couldn't be. Neil.

"How—how are you—" There were too many words competing to escape my mouth, and they jumbled at the entrance, unable to exit. *How are you alive? Grown? Here? Speaking?*

"Papa," Neil said. His voice was both familiar and unfamiliar, a deep baritone that held the barest shadow of the boy he had been, underneath new and complex depths. "When he left, he—visited, somehow." Neil raked his hair back and away from his eyes, and they were no longer the blue I remembered. They were hazel, mottled like lichen on bark. Papa's eyes. "He was here," Neil said. "He was here." I watched him stretch his arms wide, like my jay's wings unfurling back into a third, unfamiliar dimension. He took a few tentative strokes in the water, then dove under the surface and emerged again, spitting like a fountain, his face splitting into an enormous, boyish grin. My brother and my father, all at once.

Gran's words reached toward me across a gulf of years. *We pour ourselves into the work that matters most.* Neil was right. Papa was here. Part of him always would be.

"You look different." Neil splashed water in my direction, the same way he did when we went swimming as kids.

"More than twenty years'll do that."

Neil froze. "I didn't know how long. I was afraid to ask."

I blinked hard, trying to readjust the frame of this new reality where my brother was alive, and grown, and speaking. "You were afraid when I heard you. I heard you in the house. I didn't know the book was there, and I didn't know how to let you go. Not until a short while ago. I'm so sorry."

"There's nothing to be sorry for." Neil frowned. "Like I said, I didn't know how long it was—time didn't really pass. People did, though. There were others with me sometimes. I couldn't hear them, but I could feel them. I didn't recognize the feelings. I didn't know whose they were. The first time I ever felt something familiar, I knew somehow that it was you. I yelled and yelled, but then you disappeared again. It was like being on a desert island. And then—Papa. But he was with me in another place, a sort of in-between. And then everything was wet, and here I was."

"Here you are." I said it as much to convince myself as to confirm it for him.

"Who are those people on the bank?"

I reached for his hand. "My family. And yours." I tugged him toward the edge, wanting nothing more than to leave this water where he had been for decades, to pull him into the world I'd been living in without him.

When we reached the reeds, Neil stopped and looked at me. "Keryth. Where's Mama?"

SILICON VALLEY'S HOTTEST START-UP REBRANDS (from *The Technic Magazine*, November 2016): Etern-AI, the company that remade the Valley's conception of what artificial intelligence could accomplish, has refocused its corporate mission on developing a version of its revolutionary artificial intelligence, Harold, for mass consumption. "Harold is a tool that can bring fatherly support, virtual assistance, and other exciting new capabilities to anyone who's in the market for a Dad-on-Demand," said Max Miller, the company's founder and CEO. "We're very excited to announce that our company has rebranded to Herald, Inc." The new name continues the family's apparent tradition of slight misspellings, as its spun-off Steller Fund plans a gala fundraiser later this year. Miller's wife and partner, Keryth Miller, has been a more reliable fixture on the social scene as of late, accompanying her daughters to a number of events to promote Harold and Herald, Inc. The family splits its time between the Valley and some newly acquired real estate outside remote Hixon, Arizona, where Mrs. Miller reportedly grew up. This reporter can't wait to see the new direction this family of creators may take, and will be the first to join in choruses of "Hark! The Herald Angels Sing" at the company's upcoming holiday party—the hottest ticket in town!—to which yours truly is delighted to have obtained an invitation. You're all welcome to say you knew me when.

36

·•◦•●•◦•·

The House in the Reeds
FALL 2016

ONCE WE HAD all stood in the mud and reeds outside
Hixon and watched my brother come back from the dead—or
as near to it as any of us, save Max and Harold, had ever seen—
we had less appetite for Malibu and its crashing waves, or the
glassy, distant space on the beach. We wanted to find our way
back to each other. My daughters wanted their mother, and I
wanted mine. But the timing felt wrong, and I needed time to
try to knit together the parts of me that had so recently been
rejoined, my past and my present. When I announced I was
staying in the House in the Reeds, both Ellory and Mindy immediately said they were, too.

"What about you, Dad?" The sisterly chorus seemed as if it
might blow Max off his feet, but he stood unbowed.

"I need to make some calls," he said, and walked out of the
house.

Mindy and Ellory looked at each other, and then at me.
"Mom," Ellory said, whispering. "What about the Boy Scout?"

The Boy Scout in question, Tobias, was standing with Neil
at the wide windows near the rear of the house, answering every
question my brother had stored after his many years trapped in

graphite, and every word he'd stored for the years before that, when he couldn't speak. Tobias, to his credit, had gotten as far as smartphones, but no further. Neil hadn't relinquished the one Tobias had handed him, and had pushed every conceivable icon, most likely subscribing Tobias to a number of new services, some quite possibly of ill repute.

"I think I'm entering a new phase of motherhood, girls," I said.

"What's that supposed to mean?" Mindy asked.

"It means admitting I have absolutely no idea what to tell you. Not about your dad, not about the Boy Scout—again, his name is Tobias—not about your uncle, none of it. I just know that some big stuff has changed, and one of them is that I'm going to confess to you, right out, when I don't know exactly what to do."

"There's a college near here, right?" Ellory asked.

"Yes. And the high school I went to, for a while. Your dad and I would need to figure out—"

"Erma's found a house for rent about two miles up the road, if you can call this a road," Max said, striding back into the house. "I told her that if it's for rent, it should also be possible to buy, and to make it happen." He smiled at me, and the expression seemed wholly unfamiliar, but not in an unwelcome way. "It's an acreage, and it bumps up to one corner of this one. We could make it a compound, if we wanted to be those kind of people. Ride horses on trails. That kind of thing."

"Maybe not." I shuddered, thinking back to Dan Burnett and his incongruously royal boots. "But are you really saying you'd want to stay here?"

"It wouldn't be all the time—at least, it couldn't be at first," Max said. "We'd have to go back and forth between here and California a bit, because we can't leave the company entirely unmanned, not even in Anthony's hands. I'm assuming you gave him back his hands, yes?"

I rolled my eyes. "That's a dad joke worthy of Harold," I said. Anthony had been my second restoration, immediately after Neil, and had been much easier. I'd already put him back right where my father had sent him, sketching him behind his polished walnut desk, as tony as ever. He called me the instant my last line left my pen, our sainted lawyer, back at his post. His first statement to me wasn't advice, but an expectation: *And now you shall work to release the other inadvertent captives, I trust?* I told him I would set myself and my pens to that task as soon as possible.

"Hey, kiddo," Harold said from the phone in Max's hand. "This place sounds a lot warmer than that echoey house in Malibu. Can a place sound warmer? Do you think you can set up some sensors near the nicest view? You know I always loved the mountains—"

"Go to sleep—wait, Harold, actually, don't go to sleep," I said. "Do you think you could help us figure out how to manage the company without being in California so much?"

"Managing things is what I do!" Harold said. "It's all I ever wanted you to ask, honestly. I think I'll make an excellent manager. Did I ever tell you about the time they asked me to take over a whole math department when I'd never even taught math? Funny story, that. There was a kerfuffle between the dean and—"

"Okay, *now* go to sleep, Harold," I said. "Max, if you're willing to stay, we can figure it out."

"Together?" Mindy and Ellory asked, in unison.

"More together than we've been for quite a while, yes. But I need—"

"Some space," Max said. "I need it, too. Not too much. But

a little. Hence, the house. Erma says it's already furnished. I hope there aren't too many dead animal heads on the walls, but beggars can't be choosers. And Ellory and Mindy can go back and forth, as they wish. As for school—"

"Schools start in August in Arizona," I said. "We'll make some calls Monday."

"This is starting to sound real," Max said.

"Which is a welcome change, honestly." I looked at Tobias and Neil, still locked in conversation by the windows, and wondered what this new reality would really look like as it took shape. But at least I had a framework—a skeleton of a new life, and I could start to flesh it out. Details could occupy time, which was an asset I had now.

By the next week, Ellory was enrolled in Hixon College, transferring her summer of community college credits from California in short order. And Mindy, who had only attended a few weeks of high school in Malibu, was easily withdrawn and enrolled into Hixon High School. She teased me about my "Distinguished Alumni" photo on the wall, but I could tell she was secretly pleased. I was pleased, too, to have her around other kids her own age who seemed to actually be kids, and not little adults with six-figure cars they were too young to drive to ski vacation rentals their parents had booked for their holidays.

Everything almost seemed normal.

Mama, though. She was still waiting for me, and I had to figure out the right time, and the right way, to bring her back.

I knew my mother couldn't be released in any structure my father had framed for her, but I couldn't say quite how I knew. Papa had tried every way he could conceive to hold her, and we had never known—Neil and I—that we were the connectors. I had never known that I could make her more than she was. I thought back to the mug under my bed, the way I'd tried to hide my creation from my father. I wondered, if we had talked then about the things we both feared, would it have made a difference? Would we have been able to figure out a way to complement each other's skills without draining them? Or were we always destined to be most powerful apart?

It didn't matter now. It couldn't. It was water under a bridge.

As the weeks in our new-old house went by, we settled into a routine that married the pieces of my old life with the pieces of my new one. Erma, ever the creative problem solver, offered to let Ellory come and work for her agency part-time while earning her business degree. Seeing Erma as a mentor revealed a nurturing side I hadn't known she possessed—although, to be fair, no one is particularly nurturing as a teenager. She would come by the house some evenings, usually with a bottle of wine after a particularly good sales day, and joke with Harold in a way that seemed to delight him (if artificial intelligence can be delighted). Sometimes she'd drag Tobias along, insisting he show photos of the latest intricate restoration job she'd encouraged him to take on.

Neil was usually the one who pointed out the finer work, however. He'd begun working with Tobias, learning to build and restore things. Tobias had bought a new truck to replace the one the ponderosa crushed, and he'd come to pick Neil up most mornings, waving to me from the road above the house. Sometimes he'd come in for coffee and sit across the table from me, making small talk about new projects and new clients. His eyes asked me silent questions I never answered aloud, because I didn't know the answers. But I knew he was oblivious to someone else who might hold them for him, and whenever he mentioned Erma—which was often, and more often than he seemed to notice—I'd nudge the conversation further in that direction, trying to get him to recognize what he'd spent a lifetime missing.

As the sun set over Hidden Pond, evening would find us

splayed out and laughing under the beams of the house's great room, sometimes cooking dinner together, usually joined later by Max, who had committed to spending as much time with the girls as possible and had, so far, lived up to that promise. He stayed to the edges of our circle at first, unsure how to get a word in. But he always brought dessert, which was the key to Neil's heart—and Neil, even as an adult, was a key to the rest of us.

One evening, long after everyone had left and Neil and the girls had gone to bed, I finished cleaning the kitchen and stared at my reflection in the windows that opened to Hidden Pond. I watched the autumn moonlight echo on the ripples as the promise of winter's chill settled over the water, and I smiled despite myself.

"It's nice here, kiddo," Harold volunteered from the ceiling.

"It is."

"Having trouble heading to bed? I've got a whole lot of wonderful suggestions for insomnia. I sing, you know, if you're into that sort of thing. Max always hated it, or said he did, and yet here I am with the notes all ready in my coding. I didn't know he had any recordings of me singing."

"He didn't have many," I said, almost dreamily. "He recorded the rest himself. When he used to sing to the girls. He wished he had listened to you more when you were here."

"How do you know that?"

"Because he told me. A long time ago."

"Still waters run deep," Harold said, with a note of electronic pride.

"They do."

We rested in companionable silence for a moment, and it was as if I could see Harold himself, sitting cross-legged in one of the thrifted low armchairs I'd re-covered with new upholstery, just like my mother always did. He wasn't anything more than a voice in a machine, but I could feel him.

"Why don't you let him go?" Harold asked, and I felt my heart jump, the question ringing out in the air just as it had in my head, when that new Steller's jay had hopped around on the image in my book, inquiring why I'd let my friend remain trapped.

"Who?" I asked. "Max?"

"No. Not Max, kiddo. The other one."

"Tobias?" I sighed. "What do you mean?"

"Don't play coy with me, KERRIFF. He's waiting for you. He's waiting for you to decide. Hey! I also have a lot of decision matrices and other problem-solving apps if you'd like to try to tease out—"

"Harold?"

"Yes, KERRIFF?"

"Go to sleep."

I didn't need to pull my phone out to confirm he'd blinked out. The feel of the room changed from occupied to empty. I was alone.

Why don't you let him go?

Tobias and I had a moment—a long time ago, once, when we were both practically children. If my world had unfolded in a different way, perhaps that moment would have expanded into a life together. Or maybe it wouldn't. When you're a teenager, a kiss can buckle your knees beneath the weight of eternity, because eternity feels possible. But at forty, with decades of life and loss behind me, I knew that eternity was a lie. I realized that I wasn't really trying to pick between two men that I loved. I was trying to pick between the two halves of myself: the one I'd had to leave behind so many years ago, in this same house, and the one who had made a life for herself.

I walked to my bedroom to make a sketch. I hadn't drawn many lately—I'd tried, as hard as I could, to let events determine their own direction for a while. I'd put my sketchbook on the table next to Papa's, hidden in the library behind the door that only I could access, and only if I asked the house really, really nicely. But on this night, with the full moon shining through the skylights overhead, it let me in.

The drawing didn't take long. I could make a likeness of Tobias with my eyes closed, and one of Erma with them squinted. The space between them wasn't very big. Their edges—by long association, by childhood memories, by trauma and guilt and missed chances—were only a little bit mismatched. It only took smoothing them down to line them up the way they always should have. It only took a nudge to make them click.

I thanked the door and put my sketchbook back behind it, and closed the wall back up again. I slept that night more easily than I had in months.

I woke the next morning to a rhythmic sound clip-clopping on the road at the top of the hill next to the house. I threw on my bathrobe and walked to the door, opening it to the incongruous sight of my husband, sitting astride a gleaming black horse. In his hand, he held a rope that led to a dappled gray horse. When I opened the door, he grinned the widest smile I'd ever seen on his face.

"They didn't have any white ones, but you'd better believe I asked," Max said.

"Since when did you learn how to ride a horse?" I brushed my tangled hair back from my face with my hands, feeling suddenly self-conscious.

"Since I was a kid. Equestrian camp every summer," he said, rubbing his horse's neck. "You don't know everything about my childhood, either, you know. Are you going to come up and say hello?"

I pulled on my muddy galoshes, always ready by the door, and climbed up the hill. Both horses were calm, and whinnied slightly when I reached them, as if in welcome. "Did you rent them?"

Max shook his head. "Bought them. I've rented stable space and a trailer until Tobias can build us a more permanent home for these two on-site. I think they'll like it out here." He leaned over and patted the horse he was riding. "This guy here's Bruno, and this sweet lady is Oreo."

"Are you saying you literally bought me a pony?"

"I mean, she's a quarter horse, but—yeah, kind of. Do you want to ride up the road with me a bit?"

I nodded quickly, my inner eight-year-old squealing in delight. "Yes. But I need to change clothes. The coffee should be ready—"

"I know. You always set it to brew at seven. That's why I came now."

"Do you want to come in?"

"Let me hitch these two, and I'll have a cup with you."

I waited as he expertly tied the horses to the trunk of a ponderosa with a knot that looked sourced from an old-timey book about sailing, and I wondered how many other things about him I didn't know, and how much he'd let me discover. As we started down the hill, I reached for his hand, and he smiled again. The look on his face was more carefree than I'd seen it in all our years in California.

"Everyone else is still asleep," I whispered as we reached the front door. As I walked down the hallway toward my parents' old room, I looked over my shoulder and raised one eyebrow in invitation.

Max followed me slowly, as if he thought I might change my mind. I let my robe fall to my feet, then walked back to grasp his hand again, pulling him down the hall to my room and closing the door behind us. He opened his mouth with a question, but I covered it with my own before any words could come out.

"Everyone else in this house sleeps like a rock," I whispered. "But I'm wide-awake."

He pulled me to him with an urgency that echoed in my own limbs. I led him toward the bed and tugged my pajama shirt off over my head, kissing him with a hunger I didn't know I'd had rumbling within me for years of unexplained absences and disappearances. Now I was fully here, fully myself, for the first time. Wanting, and wanted.

Max kissed my neck and laughed. "If I knew all I needed was a pony—"

"Not another word," I said, sliding my hands under his belt.

And after that, we didn't need any.

Later, as I rested my head on Max's chest, I knew I'd made my choice. I'd made it a long time ago. It was the choice that tethered me to this world. And I'd never be alone in it again.

Keryth Anne,

Have you found this yet? Your Papa's book is just like yours, but he was always more of a pack rat than you seem to be. Letters, drawings, little snippets of poetry and news clippings, anything that caught his eye or gave him a clue to solve his problems. I don't know, as I write this, if he'll ever find one. But he'll be a magpie while he tries. You, on the other hand, are business through and through, even though you're a creator who was created by a creator. We all were, of course, but you more so than most. And your book is a re-creation of your Papa's, right down to the stitching on its spine and the pocket at its rear, and that's where I've tucked this. A love note from your gran.

It was meant to be her book, I'll confess to you. I made one for each of my children. And you look so much like her, my lost Anne. I don't think Morrison meant it at the time, not any more than he meant to draw himself when he drew Neil. Both of you, perfect. As perfect as the little princess and prince in my stories, as perfect as the saints who restore what's lost to us, as perfect as the angel who's your mother. Morrison doesn't want to tell you. He'll be mad if I do, but of course your gran is a little mad, and the people who love us just know how to manage it better. Not to worry. If he sees this note, he'll inter-

cept it. And maybe he'll know better than I do when you're ready to know.

The truth is you're real because he made you so, and because you encompass more than one soul. You're a repeat of my own children, exactly how I painted them on that bridge, their way lit by a star. The lines he drew reinforced the strength of those I painted, just as every stroke over an original makes the image stronger. And, of course, you're held here by love. You and your brother are the bridge from the family we were to the family we're meant to be. You're the bridge between the person you think you are and the person you're becoming. And when I'm gone, you'll be the bridge between what I made and what I left behind.

All my love to you,
GRAN

37

● ● ● ● ● ● ●

The House in the Reeds
FALL 2016

ONE UNSEASONABLY HOT night, I woke in a too-bright room, the full moon casting light across my bed and into my eyes, and for a moment, I knew she was there. I felt her cool hand against my forehead, and suddenly knew what I was missing. I had been looking in the wrong place, as usual. Mama always had an uncanny sense of timing. I raced to the book and looked away from her face, instead focusing on her empty hand, grasping flat air where my father once stood. Her arm reaching across a page, a bridge to nowhere.

Max was asleep in the bed next to me, and sat up abruptly when I touched him. "That's—new," he said, and pointed at a door in the wall across from the foot of the bed. It was sienna-dark and dusty, its edges lit like a sunset.

I raced to the bedroom that had been Neil's, and now was again. My brother, now an adult, slept exactly the same way he had as a child—hands behind his head, a smile crossing his face as he swung in some imaginary hammock in his dreams. I sat on his bed, and his eyes opened.

"I saw her," he said. "In my dream, just now. She was reaching for me."

I held Papa's sketchbook open on my lap, Mama staring up from the page. "She's still here." Her eyes were still waiting, but not pleading. I searched her expression for some clue, again and again coming away with only *You'll know when it's time.*

"Why don't you let her go?" my brother said, his words the same as that unspoken question from the other bird before I released my Steller's jay. It was hard to explain what stopped me other than knowing it had to be the right place. I kept Mama with Papa always, his battered sketchbook stacked with mine in the library, wrapped with a blue rubber band.

Neil's return had been overwhelming and wonderful and heartbreaking all at once, and my effort to join him to a world that had moved on without him—a family that had only begun to knit itself back together—had consumed most of my attention. Mama had been waiting. She had always waited.

Somewhere outside, I heard a *shook shook shook* echo against water, and I knew my jay was laughing at how little I'd learned while learning so much.

"The bridge, Neil." I held out the book, pointing at Mama. "I don't know how I didn't see it before."

"What bridge?" he asked.

"The one outside Gran's house—the one that broke off across the canyon."

"I always wondered why it was there."

"Because that's where it started. It's where he found out what he could do, and where he lost his sister. He was trying to bring her back. Everything he ever drew was trying to bring someone back, or keep them."

"He never brought anyone back. He never even noticed who

he had." Neil's words sounded resigned, but also bitter, and I recognized the undercurrent of our father's voice, the part of him that lived there now.

"His talents were different than mine, and different than Gran's. And she taught him that he had to be alone for them to work. We're all colored by the stories our families tell. He couldn't help that he knew the wrong ones. But I know how to bring her back. And she's waiting for us."

"Where?" Neil asked, watching me closely.

"There's a new door," I said. I led him back to my room, where Max stood waiting.

I reached for the knob—round, burnished gold. But it wouldn't turn for me. I looked at Neil, confused.

"I think—" He paused, and touched the door. "I think it might have to be me?"

I nodded. "It's Papa. He completed you. I think—I think I'm still incomplete, somehow. Maybe when we find Mama—"

"Maybe. We won't know until we try." He put his hand on the knob and turned it.

He opened the door onto a sunset in an earlier sky, some time out of time. But the place was unmistakable. Gran's house. The House Where God Lived. It sprawled on the canyon's edge, fully expanded like the bellows of an accordion, holding the memories of every place and person that ever sheltered us.

Before I'd left Papa for the last time in Gran's old room, I had retrieved her original *Angel on the Bridge*. I had cut it out of its frame to wrap it like a protective scroll around the charcoal image of my mother, its staples removed without pain when I tried again, because I'd finally found what she was trying to tell me all along. Who I was. Who we all were. But when I'd retrieved Neil from the waters of Hidden Pond and he'd asked me where our mother was, all I could say was, *The same place you were. Everywhere and nowhere.*

The sunlight stretched across the canyon where Gran's broken bridge angled, incomplete. The book in my hand was already open to a blank page, and I tapped its corner to widen it, enveloping the world. As I traced the lines of the bridge onto the page, it began to knit itself across the canyon, a mirror image of itself forming on the opposite wall, meeting in the middle.

The warmth from my hands and face and heart became one with the warmth from the sun, the light streaming across the canyon, an echo of the bridge that held us, that led us back toward home. I knew that she was there before I lifted my eyes, before Neil cried her name, before I saw her lantern, brighter than the sun as it rose behind the canyon wall.

"Mama." I breathed the word, just as I had when I first saw her on the wall. The thought of her filled me, clear and cold, as if I had emerged from deep waters. But I had not emerged alone. I never had been alone, though it had taken me nearly disappearing to know it.

"Keryth." Neil's voice was barely a whisper. "Look."

Mama stepped slowly across the bridge, holding her star aloft near her shoulder, its light reflecting off the blond hair of a slight girl, her braids bouncing against her smocked nightgown as she ran toward me, a blur. Only the light was faster. She reached the bridge's end and looked down at its stone border, her shoulders rising with the deep breath it took to give her the bravery to step off a structure that had held her for decades. Then, she threw her arms around me, weightless as the sigh that escaped from my own lungs as she fit against me, inside me, embraced by the borders of a body that was finally complete.

The last thing I heard was her laughter, bubbling into my

mind just as it had when she read *Anne of Green Gables* over my
shoulder in Gran's house.

"Was that—"

"Anne." I breathed again, looking down at my chest and feeling her presence in my ribs, beating along with my own heart.
"She brought me Anne."

I remembered Gran's stories of the bridge between the living
and the dead, and Papa's memories of all the details that connected me to his sister. The notes tucked into the back of his
sketchbook joined into a portrait of a girl I reinforced when I
was created. Butterflies and birds, a rushing of wings between
her past and my future. Just as Neil had joined with Papa, I had
joined with his sister.

I heard Gran's voice. *It's how you were made.*

My mother stood at the edge of the bridge, waiting to step
onto the real earth, the real dirt and dust and world, between
us. As she met my eyes, she stepped off the bridge and walked
toward us. Suddenly, the woman we saw was ordinary—slight,
slender, a gray ponytail pulled back from a dramatic widow's
peak. She wore jeans and a smocked blue blouse. In her hand,
she carried a flashlight.

She paused and looked down at herself, then at me, and
smiled.

I ran toward her without thinking about it, in her arms before she could speak, and Neil was right behind me, enclosing
us both in a squeezing embrace.

"Keryth!" she said, laughing. "Neil! What in the world?"

"You," I breathed, and it was true. She was in the world.
With us. The greatest gift I could give her was one I didn't know
I had it in my power to give—to make her real, not celestial. My
mama, back from her travels, bearing a light to illuminate the

children she longed for and finally had. It beamed toward the windows where her granddaughters, who hadn't met her yet, were sleeping. It shone watery and pure, drawing power from ordinary batteries, guiding us from the places we'd been to the places we'd go together, in a world so wondrous with imperfection.

Acknowledgments

· · • ● ● ● • · ·

When I reviewed the copyedits for this book, I noted that my publishing team had reserved four pages for these acknowledgments, an expectation that I fear may have come from my multiple pages of gratitude in *The Minuscule Mansion of Myra Malone*. While that expectation is not misplaced, a second book is an entirely different creature than the first. The cheering-on is less, *You can do this hard thing you've never done before!* and more, *You seem like you're . . . really gonna keep doing this, huh? Well, you've got this, I guess! Almost certainly!*

And that cheering voice inside you changes, too, because you've graduated from taking your first steps in this whole novel-writing thing. Now, you're looking around and wondering where your feet should take you next. Which is a long-winded way (okay, maybe four pages were justified) to say that *A House Like an Accordion* was not an easy road, and it took a lot of people to convince me to see it through to the end.

Andy, thank you for rubber-ducking this and all my other crazy ideas, helping me figure out how to make them land, and gently murmuring "that sounds like a lot" when a plot point is a bit much. Payson, thank you for always asking for a story at night, and being happiest when I pull them from my childhood, because that's where this book came from. And Jamie, thank you for always knowing the perfect moment to say something funny, or insightful, or heartbreaking. I didn't draw you all into these pages—you're too real for that—but you're better than any story I could ever tell.

Mom and Dad: the geodesic dome was next to the log-fashioned teeter-totter on our land in Utah. The blackberry canes dipped over our back fence in that first, dimly remembered house in Page. You were the architects, in whole or in part, of every strange and wonderful home we had when I was growing up. I think pieces of us are still hidden in all of them. In February 2021, an online friend (hi, Caitlin!) tweeted a question about what you'd buy if you were suddenly, amazingly wealthy, and I instantly knew my answer: I'd buy every house you ever built. *That's weird*, I thought. But it wasn't. When you're a child, and you see your father sketch images onto grid-lined paper that then become something real and tangible overhead, it truly seems magical. Otherworldly.

I jotted an idea into my Notes app: "Write a story about wanting to buy all of Dad's houses."

It was a whole book, as it turned out. And while Keryth isn't me, she started there, before she drew herself into a different life. Which I suppose we all do, in our own way.

Paul, Dennis, and Drew: thank you for sharing those childhood moments and spaces with me, and for finding space for me still.

Amy, Melinda, Tom, Charles, and Ronni: thank you for letting me be part of this family, and for being part of mine.

Thank you to Maria Whelan, my wonderful agent, who keeps finding ways to build bridges across my melodramatic chasms of writerly despair. She, and the whole team at Inkwell, have found broader audiences for my words than I ever could have dreamed, and I am so lucky to work with them.

Thank you to Cindy Hwang and Angela Kim at Berkley, the phenomenal editors who channel my deluge of words into something that makes sense on paper. The entire team behind this book at Berkley, including Christine Legon, Sammy Rice, Heather Haase, Dasia Payne, Jennifer Lynes, Kristin del Rosario, Alison Cnockaert, Jessica Plummer, Tina Joell, Chelsea Pascoe, Angelina Krahn, and Jennifer Sale all do incredible work, and this novel wouldn't exist without them.

To the WriteSquad: in hindsight, the idea of a bossy bird becoming someone's dear friend could have been inspired by the app that brought us together. More than one of you volunteered to read this manuscript when I became sure it was a disaster, and you told me to keep going. I'm so grateful for your friendship and guidance. Thank you all so much.

The Women's Fiction Writers Association has been my single greatest resource and support as a writer. I broke down the wall that was holding back this story at a WFWA conference in Baltimore, where everyone understood that slightly unhinged and distracted look that comes over someone who's desperate to get back in front of a page. They are all, to a person, amazing writers and friends. I still make the drive to my WFWA group in Raleigh, North Carolina, whenever possible, because the fellowship and inspiration I find at the other end of that long drive would be worth any number of miles to travel.

To the aptly named Kick Ass Writer's Group, a collection of people whose words can make me laugh harder than anyone I know, thank you for continuing to put up with my disappearances and still cheering me on. You're all so talented, and I'm so lucky to know you.

Thank you to the Hustle Sloths, from whom I'm still learning conciseness (I don't claim to always succeed).

Thank you to the myriad novelists, essayists, poets, and humorists who have become my online friends (and real ones!) as we all worked to find homes for our words and our thoughts, however different they may be.

To everyone who's ever read a piece of mine in *McSweeney's* and laughed, or who enjoyed one of my other silly stories or tweets, and decided to track down my other words, thank you.

My profoundest thanks to whoever designed the sprawling, segmented Tudor-style house I strolled past the day I got the idea for this book—the one that made me wonder, *Where does this place END? It's all stretched out like an accordion!*

And to you, dear reader, whoever you are and however you picked up this story: thank you, too. I'm so grateful you chose to spend a little time in this world of mine, and I hope you'll join me in the next one.

A

HOUSE

Like an

ACCORDION

AUDREY BURGES

READERS GUIDE

Questions for Discussion

·•◉●◉•·

1. Many of the characters in this novel long for something or someone they can't have, and that longing shapes them into the person they are. Is an unfulfilled wish a loss, or an opportunity? How has the direction of your life been changed by something you wanted and never got?

2. Gran tells Keryth, "Delacroix used to say pictures are bridges for the soul . . . [b]etween the artist and the person looking." Is there a piece of art that has particularly spoken to you? What was it? Why did it strike you that way?

3. A central theme in this novel is the act of creating, and the role of a creator in defining—both successfully and not—what they're trying to bring into the world. What creations are you proudest of, and why? Which do you wish had come out differently? How would you do things over again, if you could?

4. Keryth set out to find a series of structures that, in a way, helped build her as a person. Is there a building or house

from your past that you wish you could return to? What makes it significant?

5. If you had Keryth's ability to "nudge reality" by drawing its contours into the shape you want to see, would you use it? How?

6. At the end of the novel, Keryth has to make a choice between two people. Do you think she makes the right decision? Why or why not?

7. If you could create an artificial intelligence based upon someone you've lost, like Max did with his father, Harold, would you do it? Who would you bring back? Why?

8. Keryth's most precious possession is her sketchbook, a gift from her father and, it turns out, from her grandmother. What objects in your life have been imbued with meaning because of how you obtained them?

9. Keryth's perception of her parents changes dramatically by the end of the book. How has your own internal picture of your parents, or other family members, altered as you've gotten older? What has stayed the same?

10. Do you have any friends from your childhood who have come back into your life after a long absence, like Erma and Tobias did for Keryth? What has been the same? What has been different?

Christy Davis / From the Heart Images

AUDREY BURGES writes novels, humor, short fiction, and essays in Richmond, Virginia. Her first novel, *The Minuscule Mansion of Myra Malone,* was released in 2023, and has since been published in numerous translations around the world. Her delightful, entirely too tolerant children and husband continue to bring her bits of food and large cups of coffee to consume whenever she's not typing, and they have agreed to adopt her laptop as a permanent member of the family. Audrey writes funny things for *The New Yorker, McSweeney's,* and other humor outlets; her stories and essays have appeared in several literary magazines, and those that haven't continue to reside in the overstuffed Notes app of her phone. Audrey was born and raised in Arizona by her linguist parents, which is a lot like being raised by wolves, but with better grammar. She moved to Virginia as an adult but still carries mountains and canyons in her heart, and sometimes, when she closes her eyes, she can still smell ponderosa pines in the sun. *A House Like an Accordion* is her second novel, but definitely not her last.

VISIT THE AUTHOR ONLINE

AudreyBurges.com

 ABurgesWrites

 AudreyBurges

 Audrey_Burges

Ready to find
your next great read?

Let us help.

Visit prh.com/nextread